Where Have All the Pop Stars Gone?

Volume 3

Marti Smiley Childs
and Jeff March

EditPros LLC, Davis, California, USA • www.editpros.com

Published by EditPros LLC
423 F Street, suite 206
Davis, CA 95616
www.editpros.com

ISBN-13: 978-1-937317-25-6

Library of Congress Control Number: 2011932632
Printed in the United States of America

CATALOGING INFORMATION:
Childs, Marti Smiley, and March, Jeff
        Where Have All the Pop Stars Gone? – Volume 3
    Filing categories:
        Biography
        Biography, musicians
        Biography, pop music
        Biography, rock music
        History, musical
        History, pop culture
        Music, popular
        Pop culture

Cover photo (1951 Seeburg Model 100C Select-O-Matic jukebox) and design by
Amanda Domingues (http://amandadphoto.com)

"Baby Boomers" know this, but for those who may not, the chapter ending
symbol (at left) seen throughout this book represents a 45 rpm adaptor, used
to convert the large center hole of 45 rpm singles for play on turntables with
small-diameter spindles designed for 33 1/3 rpm.

Table of Contents

Acknowledgments

We would not have been able to create this book without the enthusiastic cooperation of the performers about whom we wrote, as well as their family members, producers, managers and musical colleagues with whom we spoke. We offer our gratitude to all of them listed here.

Atlanta Rhythm Section

Barry Bailey
Perry "Buddy" Buie
Gloria Buie
James "J.R." Cobb
Dean Daughtry
Nan Goddard Jacobs
Paul Goddard
Rodney Justo
Cyrus "Buddy" Kalb
Michael McCarty

Love

Paul Diamond
Johnny Echols
John Fleckenstein
Diane Lee
Ronnie Haran Mellen
Georgiana Steele-
  Waller
Michael Stuart-Ware

Anne Murray

Marcie Meekins
Anne Murray

Billy Joe Royal

Billy Joe Royal
Savannah Royal

Standells

John Fleckenstein
Larry Tamblyn

B.J. Thomas

B. Darrell Moore
B.J. Thomas

Three Dog Night

Ami Albea
Michael Childress,
  MAC Creative
  Management
Janice Hermsen,
  LeRue Press
Leslie Hinton,
  MAC Creative
  Management
Chuck Negron
Floyd Sneed
Victor Warren,
  MAC Creative
  Management

Photography

Jude Bradley
Michael Childress,
  MAC Creative
  Management
Daniel Coston[1]
Katy Ann Davidson
Amanda Domingues[2]
Gloria Fletcher
M.F. Gaul Photography
Sherman Hines
Bill Langstroth
Gord Marci
Bryan MacLean
Courtni Meadows[3]
RHM
Photofest stock photo
  archive
Doug Potoksky[4]

Music chart data

Joel Whitburn's Record Research Inc. (www. recordresearch.com), Menomonee Falls, Wisconsin

[1] www.danielcostonphotography.com
[2] http://amandadphoto.com
[3] www.facebook.com/Courtni-Meadows-Special-Rhythm-
  Photography-424702690943588/)
[4] www.facebook.com/douglas.potoksky

Preface

One day in April 1997, we were driving west on Interstate 80 across California's Yolo Causeway following a business meeting in Sacramento. The radio was on, and a favorite tune from the '60s was playing. Both of us wondered aloud, "Whatever happened to that band? That was such a good group." We were curious if the band was still together, but no longer recording. Or if the band had broken up, when and why? And if so, what had become of the members of the band? Did they remain in the music industry, or did they change careers? Did they come off the road, settle down, and start families? Do they cherish their days as hit-making, trend-setting musicians and singers, or did they feel caught up in a frenzied blur of turbulent pop stardom that they were powerless to control?

We found those questions fascinating to contemplate, and we realized that other fans would be equally intrigued. By the time we returned to our office in Davis, our conversation had germinated the idea for a book about the lives of popular recording artists who created hits of the 1960s – the era of our youth.

We were most interested in what drew the performers into music. We wanted to learn about where they were raised, what their household environment was like, and which experiences and influences inspired them to pursue careers in music. We also wanted to know how they evolved, personally and professionally, during the years following their initial success on the pop music charts. We were especially interested in their insights as they reflect on their fame and the sacrifices they had made to achieve it.

A few months after we began work on that first book, *Echoes of the Sixties,* we contacted two of the most important figures in the pop music industry. We asked them to assess the manuscripts of our first three chapters to determine if we needed to make any course corrections. Here's what the late Dick Clark wrote in a letter to us in 1997 after reading those drafts: "The depth of detail is extraordinary. Anyone who is into the inner-workings of music should find it fascinating." Nationally syndicated disc jockey Casey Kasem told us: "Both of you are fine writers, and the stories are really terrific. I know that you're going to do very well with the book."

Readers responded enthusiastically to publication of *Echoes of the Sixties,* but as we began to think about writing a sequel, we decided to make a couple of adjustments in the content. We wanted to create biographical segments in greater detail than those in *Echoes,* and to sharpen the focus on the artists themselves, we decided against the "world events" timelines that we had incorporated in *Echoes.* That shift in emphasis warranted a new title. That next book contained a chapter about the Kingston Trio, whose hits included the poignant song "Where Have All the Flowers Gone?" That served as the inspiration for our title *Where Have All the Pop Stars Gone?*

The word "gone" in the title of this series of books is an intentional play on words, referring on one hand to performers who may have stepped away from the spotlight for a time before returning to appreciative audiences and productive resumption of recording careers. But it also refers to our principal focus on the lives of the performers, where their career paths eventually took them, and what they have done for personal growth and enjoyment – marrying, raising families, and pursuing personal interests outside the realm of music. Our books are about where performers have gone with their lives, professionally as well as personally. The content has everything to do with musical artists' attainment of success, some of which may have not been apparent to their fans.

Authenticated, authorized biographies

All of our books are the product of five guiding principles:
1. We obtained information about all artists we profiled from conversations we had with the performers themselves (and with family members of some of the deceased performers);
2. We collaborated with the performers, who reviewed and authenticated our manuscripts;
3. All performers profiled were soloists or members of vocal groups or bands whose recordings scored on the national pop music singles and/ or album charts starting in the late 1950s, and continuing through the '60s, '70s and beyond;
4. We have placed an emphasis on achievement, celebrating the personal and professional triumphs of performers within and outside the music industry;
5. We intentionally selected artists who are representative of the widely divergent musical styles of the era of AM "top 40" radio dominance – musical diversity encompassing and influenced by rockabilly, rhythm and blues, surf music, jazz, folk standards, calypso, pop ballads, the British invasion, novelty tunes, folk-rock, art rock, psychedelia, and country music.

This book does not dwell on the sordid or the sad. Although the text does acknowledge significant hardships, including financial and personal problems, our focus is on successful resolution of conflicts and discovery of what individuals learned about life as a result of confronting difficulty. Even though its content is entertaining and it has a nostalgia component, *Where Have All the Pop Stars Gone? – Volume 3* also seeks to teach and inspire by example.

Each chapter encompasses three segments:

- A historical overview of the highlights of each artist's recording career;
- A discography list of prominent hit recordings of each artist; and
- Biographical epilogues chronicling the life experiences of soloists and band members.

Our foursome is complete

You are holding the last volume in our series of books about pop music recording artists. Since beginning work 19 years ago on our series of four books (*Echoes of the Sixties* and the three-volume *Where Have All the Pop Stars Gone?* set), we have profiled the lives of 105 hit-making singers and musicians, encompassing nine soloists and members of 23 bands and vocal groups. We gathered information through extensive conversations with them and 25 of their family members, and we were in contact with more than 100 other people involved in the music industry, including talent agents, personal managers, record producers, label owners, concert promoters, nightclub personnel, music historians and curators, and songwriters. We accomplished what we set out to do: celebrate the lives of praiseworthy recording artists whose achievements were not as widely and consistently recognized as they should have been, and who deserved greater acclaim and more coverage than they received. All of them are artists whose music should be preserved and acknowledged in perpetuity.

We were saddened to learn of the deaths of 19 of the people with whom we had talked – guitarist, banjo player and singer Larry Ramos and manager Pat Colecchio of the Association; drummer John Petersen of the Beau Brummels; singer and guitarist Chuck Tharp of the Fireballs; bass player and lead singer Rob Grill and drummer Rick Coonce of the Grass Roots; guitarist Erik Braunn and bass player Lee Dorman of Iron Butterfly; singer, guitarist, and banjo player Nick Reynolds, singer, songwriter, and guitarist John Stewart, and manager Frank Werber of the Kingston Trio; singer Gordon Waller of the duo Peter and Gordon; keyboard player Harvey Kaye of the Spiral Starecase; singer Hank Medress of the Tokens; and guitarist Paul Atkinson of the Zombies. We were glad, though, that they had the opportunity to hold in their hands the finished book containing their chapter.

We were especially stunned, though, by the deaths of four people with whom we conversed but who died before their chapter was published. We fondly remember and honor them: the late singer Donnie Brooks (about whom *Where Have All the Pop Stars Gone? – Volume 2* includes a chapter); and producer Buddy Buie and bass player Paul Goddard of the Atlanta Rhythm Section, and singer Billy Joe Royal, all of whom are portrayed in this book.

We also thank the family members who helped us develop profiles of recording artists who died before we began chapters about their bands: bass guitarist Brian Cole of the Association; singer, guitarist, and banjo player Dave Guard of the Kingston Trio; lead singer Arthur Lee of the band Love; bass player David Martin of Sam the Sham and the Pharaohs; drummer John Poulos of the Buckinghams; and singer Dave Prater of Sam and Dave.

The seven groups and soloists portrayed in this book collectively amassed a total of 104 singles on the *Billboard* Hot 100, including 38 that reached the top 20 and six that hit No. 1. Their recordings also encompassed 84 singles on the country music chart, including 44 that peaked in the top 20, and 12 that hit No. 1.

We are grateful to all of these performers and their family members for their willingness to share their stories, and we are honored to participate in giving them a fitting tribute.

With appreciation,
Marti Smiley Childs and Jeff March
Davis, California, USA

September 9, 1997

dick clark **productions, inc.** 3003 WEST OLIVE AVE. BURBANK, CA 91505-4590 (818) 841-3003 FAX: (818) 954-8609

Thank you so much for sending along your sample of "Echoes of the '60s", Jeff and Marti. The depth of detail is extraordinary. Anyone who is into the inner-workings of music should find it fascinating.

I wish you much good luck with it. Thanks for sending it along.

Sincerely,

Dick Clark

Dick Clark

DC/as

Jeff March
Marti Childs
EDITPROS
P.O. Box 1981
Davis, CA 95617-1981

As we began writing manuscripts in 1997 for our first book, *Echoes of the Sixties*, we received encouragement from Dick Clark (Note: EditPros P.O. Box is no longer in use; our mailing address is 423 F Street, Suite 206, Davis, CA, 95616).

The Atlanta Rhythm Section laying down a track in the recording studio in 1971. Clockwise from left foreground, that's Robert Nix on drums, singer Rodney Justo, rhythm guitarist J.R. Cobb, lead guitarist Barry Bailey, piano player Dean Daughtry and bass guitarist Paul Goddard (photo courtesy of Nan Goddard).

CHAPTER

1

Champagne Jam

Atlanta Rhythm Section

The songs that we've grown to love became memorable not only because of riveting lyrics and catchy melodies, but also because they were recorded flawlessly. In concerts, performers may strive but struggle to replicate the impeccable phrasing and musical arrangements imprinted on their hit recordings. Studio recording is a discipline that demands prowess, patience, and perfection. Solo singers, of course, have long depended on studio backing bands for their recording sessions, but so have many bands that had inadequate experience in the exacting studio environment. As the big-band era of the 1940s yielded to the pop music era beginning in the '50s, cadres of polished session musicians began to emerge in musically important cities, and within individual recording studios or record labels within those cities.

At Motown Records in Detroit, the label's tight in-house band, the "Funk Brothers," played on dozens and dozens of hit records. Los Angeles had the legendary "Wrecking Crew." Nashville had the "A-Team," while the "Memphis Boys" held forth in Blues City. The "Swampers" performed on innumerable recordings produced in Muscle Shoals, Alabama. In a few cases, studio bands evolved from the cocoon of anonymity and established recognition with hit recordings of their own. In Memphis, the Stax Records in-house group of musicians emerged as Booker T. & the MGs. Toto, the Alan Parsons Project and Supertramp likewise had begun as groups of session musicians. And so did one of the most seasoned, talented bands of the 1970s: the Atlanta Rhythm Section.

An amalgamation of members of the highly successful group the Classics IV and Roy Orbison's backup band, the Candymen, the Atlanta Rhythm Section – known as ARS among its devoted fans – cut their teeth as a band with two underappreciated albums before making their mark in 1974 with their third album in which they laid bare their aspirations with a self-effacingly honest title: *Third Annual Pipe Dream.* The tracks of that album yielded their first singles chart entry: "Doraville," a rhythmic tribute to the country atmosphere of the small town in which their home base, Studio One recording studio, was located. Rhythm, after all, was what the Atlanta Rhythm Section was about. Commonly mislabeled a "Southern rock" band, ARS had little in common with Lynyrd Skynyrd, ZZ Top, Molly Hatchet, or the Marshall Tucker Band. Unlike 38 Special, which ballyhooed "Wild-Eyed Southern Boys" in song, ARS was a band of mainstream pop virtuoso musicians who just happened to hail from the South. Over the course of the band's seven most productive years, the Recording Industry Association of America (RIAA) awarded gold records for three ARS albums, one of which went on to earn platinum status.

The creative force behind ARS was the band's architect and producer, Perry Carlton "Buddy" Buie, who with the financial backing of three investors designed and built Studio One with recording engineer Rodney Mills. As the house band for Studio One recording sessions beginning in January 1971, the Atlanta Rhythm Section initially consisted of guitarists Barry Bailey and James B. Cobb Jr. (known as "J.R."), keyboard player Dean Daughtry, bass player Paul Goddard, drummer and percussionist Robert Nix, and singer Rodney Justo.

In high school and then as a student at Auburn University in Alabama, Buie (pronounced BOO-ee) was the manager and promoter of a band called the Webs, the members of which included Bobby Goldsboro, a childhood friend of his. As a teenager, Buddy found his voice by writing songs, and he entered the realm of headlining act concert promotion in 1961, when for $500 he booked Roy Orbison for a concert in Dothan, Alabama, and promised to supply a backing band – the Webs. Orbison was so impressed, he hired the Webs to become his touring band, which he dubbed the Candymen (inspired by his hit "Candy Man"), with Buie as his road manager to coordinate logistics. But that was a steppingstone gig for Buddy, who had his sights set on songwriting, music production, talent management, and music publishing. While working as a $75-per-week songwriter for United Artists Records, Buie found a kindred soul in Paul Cochran, a promoter he met at a Roy Orbison concert in Clearwater, Florida. Deciding to join forces in 1964, Buddy and Paul established the Buie-Cochran Management Company and drove to Daytona Beach, because they'd heard good things about a band performing in a nightclub there. They quickly became managers of that band – the Classics IV.

Although Buddy could strum a little guitar, he never became proficient as a musician. His songwriting ambitions, therefore, depended on finding a collaborator who could write music and play guitar, to work out the music that Buddy was hearing in his head. His first such collaborator was guitarist John Rainey Adkins of Roy Orbison's Candymen, and then Buddy began composing hits with Classics IV guitarist J.R. Cobb. Among the first Buie-Cobb collaborations was "I Take It Back," which became a hit for country music singer Sandy Posey in the summer of '67. As Buie and Cobb began writing collaboratively with the intention of cranking out material for more hit singles, they signed with Atlanta music publisher Bill Lowery, who co-owned a recording studio, Master Sound. As the Classics IV signed with Imperial Records in 1967, Lowery gave the nod to Buie to produce their recordings at Master Sound. Buie put together a top-notch backing group, consisting of two Candymen alumni – drummer Robert Nix and keyboard player Dean Daughtry; session bass and keyboard player Emory Gordy Jr. (who later played in Elvis Presley's band, became a producer, and married country music singer Patty Loveless); rhythm guitarist J.R. Cobb (who had been a high school classmate of Nix's in Jacksonville); and lead guitarist Barry Bailey (a locally active session musician who had been with Gordy in an Atlanta band called the Wayne Logiudice and the Kommotions). With those players in the studio and Buddy Buie in the control booth, they cranked out a succession of Classics IV hits.

As producer, Buie improvised with three-track recording equipment to achieve the signature sound of the Classics IV. "We'd record J.R. playing his tuned guitar on track 1, then he'd play it again with an out-of-tune guitar, *desafinado* style, and we'd combine those guitars on track 2, and then he'd play it again and we'd ping pong it that way. The trick was all in the tuning," Buie explained. "If those stacked guitars were in tune, you wouldn't be able to tell if there were two or just one. J.R. was the only member of the Classics IV who played on the records. The Classics IV touring band sang on the records, but they didn't play the instruments on the records."

Their success began with "Spooky" and "Stormy," followed by "Traces" and "Every Day With You, Girl" – with Buie and Cobb sharing writing credits on all of them. Gordy by then was the most in-demand session bassist in Atlanta, and as his schedule limited his availability, he recommended Paul Goddard (who together with Gordy and Barry Bailey had been a guitarist and bass player in a popular Atlanta bar band called

St. John and the Cardinals). With the addition of Goddard, the elements of the nascent Atlanta Rhythm Section were in place. Meanwhile, Cochran and Buie went into partnership with Lowery, reactivating a dormant publishing company of his, Low-Sal Music. That set the groundwork for publication of songs that would be written for ARS.

Buie's yet-unnamed studio group was increasingly booked for music recording sessions and soundtracks for radio and TV commercials – until Buie clashed with Bob Richardson, Bill Lowery's partner in Master Sound. Buie struck a deal with LeFevre Sound Studios in Atlanta, owned by the prominent LeFevres gospel group, and took his crew of musicians there. Buie quickly became impressed with the LeFevres' innovative recording engineer, Rodney Mills, who understood the needs of musicians because he also was a bass guitarist. During the few evenings when no recording sessions were scheduled, Cobb, Bailey, Daughtry, Goddard, and Nix would gather at the LeFevres' studio to jam, while Mills and Buie recorded their improvisational playing. The session musicians found the prospect of forming a band intriguing, but they lacked a lead singer. Paul Cochran was good friends with Rodney Justo, who had been the lead singer for the Candymen and also for a band called Rodney and the Mystics that he had hired a few years earlier. Justo agreed to join the new band, which needed a name. The guys initially thought of calling the group Terminus, because that was the name of the tiny burg that in 1837 marked the southern end of the Western and Atlantic Railroad, in present-day Atlanta.

"We were sitting in Bill's office talking about what we would call the band," Buddy recalled. "At the time there was the Memphis Rhythm Section with Chips Moman, and there was the Nashville Rhythm Section." The name Atlanta Rhythm Section was a logical extension of that archetype. In May 1970 Buie chose New York-based manager Jeff Franklin of ATI Public Relations to represent his production and writing interests, and to promote the Atlanta Rhythm Section. Franklin sent a tape of some of those tracks to Decca subsidiary MCA Records, which expressed interest and signed the band.

Intent on achieving perfection in their recordings, the musicians realized they needed their own studio to enable unlimited access to recording facilities. Buie, Lowery, Cochran, and Cobb agreed to invest $25,000 apiece, and hired Rodney Mills to be their head engineer. After scouting for affordable locations in the spring of 1970, Mills found a vacant unfinished building at 3864 Oakcliff Industrial Court in Doraville, 15 miles northeast of downtown Atlanta. "It was an industrial building with nothing but dirt on the floor," Buie said. "We leased the space and built the studio from the ground up, soundproofed it, and brought in state-of-the-art equipment. It was like a building within a building." The band members all pitched in building the acoustically superb facility. "We laid tile, installed glass, put up insulation, hammered wood. It was a great time," Rodney Justo said. The studio included three echo chambers, a drum booth, a custom Luellen and Martin console with Spectra Sonics mixing controls, a 16-track Scully tape recorder, and a V-shaped studio into which the control room protruded to enable excellent visual interaction with the musicians. The setup enabled musicians to play their instruments in the control room, if they wished, with their amplifiers in the studio.

Word quickly spread about the completion of Studio One in January 1971, but Buie declined requests from advertising agencies to record commercials there to avoid detracting time from sessions to record songs for albums and singles. The select few singers, bands, and producers that he allowed to book time there included songwriter, guitarist, producer, and Blood, Sweat & Tears founder Al Kooper, who had been friends with members of the Candymen and looked them up at Studio One. Kooper was so impressed with the sound quality of Studio One that he booked a month of time there to record his own band, with ARS backing them. And when Kooper launched his Sounds of the South record label, he signed Lynyrd Skynyrd and brought the band to Studio One to record during the daylight hours. Skynyrd had begun recording their anthemic "Sweet Home Alabama" in Muscle Shoals, Alabama, but did most of their work on the track at Studio One in Georgia. Billy Joe Royal, B.J. Thomas, and Joe South also recorded at Studio One.

Meanwhile, Buie, Nix, Cobb, Daughtry, Bailey, Goddard, and Justo set about writing songs. During intervals when the ARS members weren't doing session work for other performers, they intermittently gathered in the studio to lay down instrumental tracks for an album of their own. They often began rehearsing and recording late at night and continued into the predawn hours. "Let's say we were doing a B.J. Thomas session over 10 days to two weeks. Then there might be a gap for a couple of days until we had to work on a session for someone else or until the studio was rented. So we'd go in there and work on one of our own songs for a day or two, and then we might not touch it again for another three weeks," Justo recalled. Finally, in late 1971, Rodney recorded the vocals, singing along with the completed instrumental tracks. "I finished the vocals within three days," Justo said. In his bluesy singing style, Justo cruised his way through song after song with the cool confidence of a Gran Prix driver behind the wheel of a responsive Italian roadster on a gently winding country road.

In January 1972, Decca released the 10-track album, titled simply *Atlanta Rhythm Section,* encompassing ballads, rockers, and an instrumental track, "Ernestine." The album gave top billing on the cover to Rodney Justo and Barry Bailey. Decca immediately pressed two of the album's tracks as the band's leadoff single, "It's All In Your Mind," backed with "Can't Stand It No More." In March, the label released another single, "Another Man's

BUILDING ATLANTA

STUDIO ONE

Atlanta's newest and most advanced recording facility

PRESIDENT — BUDDY BUIE	STUDIO ONE
VICE PRES. — BILL LOWERY	3864 OAKCLIFF INDUSTRIAL COURT
VICE PRES. — J.R. COBB	DORAVILLE, GEORGIA
SEC.-TREAS. — PAUL COCHRAN	(404) 451-5129

Full-page advertisement in Billboard magazine for the newly completed Studio One (courtesy of Gloria Buie).

Woman (It's So Hard)," with "Earnestine" on the flip side. The album captured the attention of FM rock stations in some markets – notably, WGLD in Chicago, which was playing "Can't Stand It No More," "40 Days and 40 Nights" and "Days of Our Lives," according to the February 12, 1972, issue of *Billboard* magazine. ARS went on tour with Deep Purple and Buddy Miles, but their album was unable to make a dent in the charts, nor were two singles culled from it – the Buie-Cobb composition "All In Your Mind," and the Nix-Daughtry-Buie song "Another Man's Woman (It's So Hard)," which would later become a fixture in the band's live performances.

Dismayed by the lack of radio airplay or chart activity, and driven by the need to earn more income to support his young family, Justo decided to expand his horizons by seeking session work in New York, where he got steady work singing jingles for Coca-Cola, Mazda, Hardees restaurants, and other advertisers. His replacement was right at hand in the control booth, assisting Rodney Mills in engineering. "Ronnie Hammond was a kid who hung around the studio and cut demos. He sang pretty good, and I told him, 'Ronnie, you're our new lead singer,'" Buie said. Dean Daughtry added, "We heard some stuff that Ronnie had done on his own with multi-part harmony, and we realized 'this guy knows his stuff.' What a beautiful voice he had. He also played drums, guitar, and piano. Buddy knew how to work with singers. He developed Ronnie and made him a real incredible singer."

With new material that the band members composed, ARS recorded their second album, *Back Up Against The Wall,* which Decca released in February 1973. It was the first of a half-dozen albums for which artist Mike McCarty was commissioned to create wondrous cover art illustrations. *Billboard* magazine reported a few radio stations, including WRNO New Orleans, KRLD-FM Dallas and KNAC in Long Beach, California, that gave the album airplay, but chart activity was disappointing. Neither of two singles, "Back Up Against The Wall" and "Conversation," culled from the album generated any chart activity. Decca dropped ARS from its roster. "We wanted so much to be successful at it," J.R. Cobb told us. "We used to go to the studio, and sometimes I'd stay there for four days. The studio became as much a place to hang out and write songs as it was to record songs." Paul Goddard believed the label was at fault. "We were getting no support from Decca. They were supporting Wishbone Ash," Goddard said. Buie paid each of the band members $100 a week to tide them over during that disheartening period.

Undaunted, Jeff Franklin approached PolyGram subsidiary Polydor Records, with which Buie signed a contract for ARS in the late 1973. The

9

band went to work recording their next album, *Third Annual Pipe Dream* – which would prove to be the album to fulfill their dreams after it premiered on *Billboard's* "Top LPs & Tape" chart on September 7, 1974. The album's 10 tracks included some rocking tunes, a couple of blues-tinged tracks, an instrumental, and the song that became their first chart single, "Doraville," which Buie, Nix, and Bailey wrote about their home base. Beginning as a regional hit, "Doraville" premiered on the *Billboard* Hot 100 chart on October 5, 1974, peaked respectably at No. 35, and remained on the chart for eight weeks. "Everyone in the band was really excited about that. It gave us a psychological boost, but it still didn't bring in any money," Buie said. "I was amazed," Paul Goddard said. "Nobody outside of Atlanta ever heard of Doraville, and it was the last song I ever thought would break." Polydor released another of the album's tracks, "Angel (What In The World's Come Over Us)" as a single, but after making its debut on the *Billboard* pop chart on February 22, 1975, it hung on for five weeks but stalled at No. 79. "Get Your Head Out Of Your Heart," the third song from the album released as a single, missed the chart.

Meanwhile, the band had to develop as a stage act to go on the road to promote its recordings, and was booked for a six-night stand at a hot Atlanta nightclub beginning July 22, 1974. "Alex Cooley, a big promoter in Atlanta, hired the band to appear in his successful Cooley's Electric Ballroom. But when they got on stage, they didn't do any theatrics, because they were session musicians, they weren't road guys," Buie explained. "They just stood there and played great music. They had to learn how to become performers with stage presence. That didn't come easy for them." Barry Bailey acknowledged that was true. "We were aware of the need for stage presence, but we never got into choreography. I'm probably the least animated guitar player you'll ever see," he laughed. "It was mostly the front man, the lead singer – either Rodney or Ronnie – who needed to connect. They worked at it and they got it, of course." A *Billboard* article about the ARS engagement promoting *Third Annual Pipe Dream* at Cooley's said, "The LP, an excellent bright boogie work with just the right soft touches, was selling furiously in Atlanta and getting heavy AM [radio] airplay the week of the ballroom engagement. A tour of the South is ongoing, and the band will be on the West Coast in early fall." At the time, the dominant top-40 music radio stations in most markets were on the AM band, and persistent AM airplay resulted in vigorous sales of singles.

The band members did not embrace touring as Buddy had hoped they would, however. "Touring was a challenge because we were not a concert band at all. We had all played live before, but we were not an act. We were just a studio band, and it took some work," Barry Bailey acknowledged. Buie believed the band's unease about concert performances was regrettable. "If ARS had been like other bands and loved the road, they would have been huge. But they had no interest in the touring because it took them away from home, so they were never into it," Buie observed. "Achieving success as a rock and roll band is tough. If you don't have the radio playing your stuff, you're going to have to build an audience another way. Even the Allman Brothers had only two top-30 hit singles. The Allman Brothers was the model I built on for ARS. I loved the Allman Brothers, and I thought that's what we should be doing – performing on the road as a band. They were a very big influence on us all."

After reaching No. 74 on the *Billboard* "Top LPs" chart on November 16, 1974, *Third Annual Pipe Dream* began a slow descent. Back in the studio, ARS hunkered down and went to work on what eventually would become one of their most highly acclaimed albums, titled *Dog Days,* which Polydor released in the summer of 1975. Polydor issued the album's leadoff track, "Crazy" as a single – not the same song as the Patsy Cline favorite, but rather an original Buie-Nix-Daughtry composition that the band set to a rocking beat. Bolstered by *Crawdaddy Magazine's* declaration of Atlanta Rhythm Section as "the best band in the South," ARS set out on an August concert tour that put them on stage at the Gator Bowl in Jacksonville, Florida, with the Rolling Stones; at the Auditorium in West Palm Beach, Florida, with Uriah Heep and Blue Oyster Cult; at the Schaefer Music Festival in New York City's Central Park with B.B. King; at the Coliseum in Asheville, North Carolina, with Rod Stewart; and a series of other dates with Uriah Heep in Fort Wayne, Chicago, Milwaukee, St. Louis, and Indianapolis.

The year 1976 brought another ARS album, the harder-edged *Red Tape,* leading off with the band's next single release, "Jukin." That rocking country-flavored song, a Buie and Nix composition, gave an appreciative nod to the musical legacy of Texas, ranging from Bob Wills and his Texas Playboys (including a few bars of "San Antonio Rose") to ZZ Top. Promotional pressings of the single were released to radio stations in monaural on one side (for AM radio) and stereo on the flip side (for FM stations). "Jukin" made an appearance on the *Billboard* chart beginning June 5, 1976, but went no higher than No. 82, and was on the chart for only four weeks. "Free Spirit," a rocking Buie-Nix-Hammond song from the album that was released as a single should have been a hit, but after premiering on the chart on August 21, 1976, it went no higher than No. 85. All the while, ARS continued touring, performing gigs in clubs, auditoriums, and stadiums. Polydor was growing impatient, though, for a best-selling album that would spawn hit singles. Under pressure to produce, Buie and the band came through.

ARS reached cruising altitude with its sixth album, *A Rock And Roll Alternative,* which Polydor released December 15, 1976. The album, which premiered on the *Billboard* "Top LPs & Tape" chart on January 6, 1977, reflected the confidence of the band members in the stylish way they flavored their pop and rock songs by seasoning them with an infusion of blues traditions. From that album, the easy-rockin' Buie-Nix-Daughtry song "So In To You," released as a single, jumped onto the *Billboard* Hot 100 chart on January 29, 1977. "Dean, Robert, and I went into the studio with the Rhythm Section, and Dean played the keyboard while J.R. started playing the guitar sound," Buie told us. "Even though he wasn't a writer on 'So In To You,' he made that song come alive. The rhythm in it was all J.R. We hadn't finished that session by the time the band was scheduled to go on the road, but we finished it when we got back."

Dean Daughtry's realization that ARS had achieved success came when he heard WLS radio in Chicago playing "So In To You" in heavy rotation.

ARS in 1973: from left, Dean Daughtry, J.R. Cobb (crouching), Robert Nix, Barry Bailey, Paul Goddard, and Ronnie Hammond (photo courtesy of Gloria Buie).

"WLS didn't play anything unless it was a hit," Daughtry said. "That was the single that put us over the top," Goddard added. By March 12, "So In To You" was No. 21 with a star on *Billboard's* LP chart, indicating rapid upward movement, and it also turned up on the magazine's "Easy Listening" chart, indicating airplay on adult pop as well as "top 40" radio stations. ARS at last had that elusive hit single that they had sought for seven years. "So In To You" cracked the top 10 on the Hot 100 chart on April 9, and on April 30, peaked at No. 7. By then, *A Rock And Roll Alternative* ranked No. 13 on *Billboard's* "Top LPs" chart. "So In To You" remained on the Hot 100 for 19 weeks, into mid-June. Meanwhile, on April 12, RIAA awarded a gold record (recognizing sales of 500,000 copies) for the band's *A Rock And Roll Alternative* album. With its popularity accelerating, ARS took to the stage with the Eagles, Foreigner, Heart, and the Steve Miller Band at the Day on the Green festival May 28 at the Oakland-Alameda County Coliseum in Oakland, California. "The promoter was Bill Graham, bless his heart. It was a great show," Daughtry recalled. Even Paul Goddard, who described himself as "very shy," came to embrace touring. "We worked probably 110 jobs a year at fairly decent money," he said.

Trying to capitalize on the success of ARS, the MCA label had released "All In Your Mind," a track from the band's first album, as a single in the spring of 1977. But it was trumped by Polydor's single release of "Neon Nites," a Buie-Nix composition from *A Rock And Roll Alternative*. The jazzy "Neon Nites" made its debut on the *Billboard* Hot 100 chart on June 4, 1977, rose to No. 42, and remained on the chart much of the summer, for seven weeks. Then Polydor reached back to release the overlooked title track of the 1975 *Dog Days* album as a single. "Dog Days," which Buddy Buie, Robert Nix, and Dean Daughtry wrote about living through sultry, sweat-soaked summers in the South, hit the *Billboard* chart at the end of summer, on September 3, 1977. After a five-week run, though, the song managed to go no higher than No. 64. The single release coincided with ARS headlining on September 4 at the Dog Day Festival, a rock music festival staged on Grant Field at Georgia Tech that attracted 50,000 enthusiastic fans. Bob Seger shared top billing with ARS, and the lineup included Heart and Foreigner. ARS' next single, also from *A Rock And Roll Alternative,* was "Georgia Rhythm," a terrific finger-snapping Buie-Cobb-Nix tune that laid bare the rigors of the road and discomforts that a touring band endures, all for the love and thrill of playing music for audiences. After premiering on the *Billboard* Hot 100 on October 15, 1977, "Georgia Rhythm" stalled at No. 68 during its six weeks on the chart.

A phrase that kept recurring to Buie led to the title song for what many regard as the Atlanta Rhythm Section's finest album. "I had 'champagne jam' stuck in my head, and I thought it would be so cool for a title. Once we decided on that as the title for an album, we decided to title a song for it, too," Buie said. The *Champagne Jam* album, which Polydor released in early 1978, consisted of 33 minutes of highly polished, Southern-accented ballads and rock. It captured attention in the music and radio industries almost immediately.

The "Album Picks" section of *Billboard's* March 18, 1978, issue gave "Spotlight" review treatment to two newly released albums: Carole King's *Her Greatest Hits* and Atlanta Rhythm Section's *Champagne Jam*. The laudatory *Billboard* review of *Champagne Jam* said: "Group's first album since its breakthrough *A Rock And Roll Alternative* swings, from beginning to end. Most tunes are upbeat rockers laced with punchy guitar work by Barry Bailey and J.R. Cobb. Poll Goddard's thumping bass is evident throughout, and the flexible vocals of Ronnie Hammond covey the excitement the band generates within its instrumental jams. Group appears to have now fully matured, as its last LP, which produced "So In To You," hinted it might. The subtle Southern licks, mixed with an R&B flair, and delivered in a cohesive unifying blend, are among the finest rock 'n' roll being played."

Champagne Jam opened with "Large Time," a tribute to the Lynyrd Skynrd band, three members of which had died in a plane crash in October 1977. It contained the track that would become the band's second top-10 single, the hauntingly mysterious "Imaginary Lover." From a dark recess, Ronnie Hammond's vocal glides across a dreamy musical landscape and probes the mind of a man desperate for companionship. "Dean Daughtry had this melody and I remember saying, 'Dean, we've got to come up with something for that song.' When we started talking, the word 'imaginary' sang well with it, so started digging in and coming up with the whole concept that imagination is unreal. We talked about the fact that you don't have to have an actual lover – you can have a lover mentally in your mind, and you can imagine it," explained Buie, who composed the song with Nix and Daughtry. "We delved into it from that point of view. I really like that song, even now." Released as a single, "Imaginary Lover" premiered on the *Billboard* Hot 100 on March 4, 1978. It started climbing steadily, peaked at No. 7 (just as "So In To You" had), and remained on the chart for 17 weeks.

Buie's work habits inspired another track on the album that became Atlanta Rhythm Section's follow-up hit. "Anybody who knew me knew I was always having some kind of crisis about 5 in the afternoon, and then

I'd say, 'To hell with it. I'm not gonna let it bother me tonight, I'll worry about it tomorrow.' That became sort of my motto," Buie said. It also became the title of the ARS single that hit the *Billboard* pop chart on June 10, 1978. "I'm Not Gonna Let It Bother Me Tonight," another Buie-Nix-Daughtry composition, rose to No. 14 and remained on the chart for 13 weeks. "That song was one of my favorites," Buie said. The band "worked" the *Champagne Jam* album, living out of suitcases as they performed on tour night after night. On August 26, ARS was on stage with the Doobie Brothers, Kansas, the Commodores, Dave Mason, and the Village People in front of more than 80,000 fans at the first Canada Jam festival in Ontario.

Then a call came from the White House. ARS had been invited to perform on the south lawn of the White House on April 12, 1978, at a barbecue party celebrating the 28th birthday of President Jimmy Carter's son, James Earl (Chip) Carter III. The president had become acquainted with the band members at a social event back when he was governor of Georgia, and Chip was an ARS fan.

In 1974, the Atlanta Rhythm Section visited then-Georgia Governor Jimmy Carter. From left, Buddy Buie, Paul Goddard, J.R. Cobb, Dean Daughtry, Jimmy Carter, Ronnie Hammond, Barry Bailey, and Robert Nix, holding a copy of the band's *Third Annual Pipe Dream* album (photo courtesy of Barry Bailey).

"One of our roadies had been a longtime friend of Chip's," Barry Bailey explained. "I know it's common with politicians to learn the names of people, but the president actually said to me, 'Nice guitar playing, Barry,' which was pretty flattering at the time. We gave him an ARS jacket." Buddy Buie recalls, "The band played and Jimmy Carter came on stage with them, and then we all went with the Carter boy inside the White House and went up on the roof where all the guards were. I remember standing up there on top of the White House while everyone passed around a number. All those sharpshooters and guards just looked the other way, acting like we didn't exist."

Meanwhile, the *Champagne Jam* album title gave Buie an idea about another music festival. He approached promoter Alex Cooley, who enthusiastically organized the first "Champagne Jam" rock festival on September 9, 1978. With the Atlanta Rhythm Section triumphantly headlining on home turf at Georgia Tech's Grant Field, the festival also brought Santana, the Doobie Brothers, Eddie Money, Mose Jones, and Mother's Finest to the stage in front of 60,000 whooping, cheering fans. It was among many large-scale venues at which ARS performed. "At the time our ARS guys were extraordinary in the sense that they were a great studio group but they also played on the road. When we did Champagne Jam, that was the defining moment for the band," Buie said.

Polydor then released the album's title track, "Champagne Jam," as a single. That Buie-Nix-Cobb composition, a hand-clapping celebration of music itself, made its chart debut on September 16. During its nine-week stay on the Hot 100 it pegged at No. 43, but it should have been a bigger hit than that. By the time it dropped off the chart the last weekend in November, ARS had been on the singles charts for 37 consecutive weeks. The *Champagne Jam* album, for which RIAA had awarded a gold record on April 11, took a platinum award (signifying 1 million copies sold) on September 26.

ARS began recording its next album, Underdog, which Polydor released in June 1979. Its opening track, "Do It Or Die," was an introspective exploration of tenacity, an ode to perseverance against the odds, a lullaby to resilience despite disappointment. Composed by Buie, Cobb, and Hammond, it distilled the drive of ARS into a beautiful three-and-a-half minute ballad. Released as a single a few weeks before the album debut, "Do It Or Die" premiered on the *Billboard* Hot 100 on May 26, 1979, rose to No. 19, and impressively remained on the chart for 14 weeks – as did the band's follow-up single, a cover version of the Classics IV tune "Spooky" (for which Buie and Cobb added lyrics to the original instrumental version composed by Mike Sharpe and Harry Middlebrooks Jr.). The ARS version of "Spooky" hit the Hot 100 chart on August 11, and peaked at No. 17. Underdog by then had earned a gold record, which the RIAA awarded on June 12.

The band's high-energy touring and recording pace began to take its toll, however. Drummer Robert Nix had become stressed out. He told one interviewer that he was able to spend time with his family only two or three times during 1978, when collaborative songwriting, recording, and performing 262 dates on the road occupied most of his time. Underlying that, though, were differences of opinion that created strong friction between Nix and longtime songwriting collaborator Buie regarding the direction of the band. "Robert wanted to go a bit more Lynyrd Skynyrd style, but Buddy was going a little more towards ballads. After writing so much together, they no longer saw eye-to-eye," Bailey explained. Buie asked Nix to leave ARS, and replaced him in 1979 with Roy Yeager, a Nashville session drummer who had accompanied Joe South and the band Lobo.

ARS was part of Alex Cooley's second "Champagne Jam" festival on Saturday, July 7, 1979, at Georgia Tech. The lineup at that show also included Aerosmith, the Cars, the Dixie Dregs, and Whiteface – with general admission tickets priced at $13.50. After recording eight studio albums, ARS delivered what many of their fans had been demanding: a live double album that captured the electric atmosphere of their stage performances. The album took its title from the words of an announcer introducing the band: "Are you ready?" With a cover photo of the band onstage at Georgia Tech's stadium packed with an overflow crowd, *Are You Ready* is a tour de force of the band's signature songs, including "Champagne Jam," "I'm Not Gonna Let It Bother Me Tonight," "Georgia Rhythm," and a 14-minute version of "Another Man's Woman," spotlighting Paul Goddard's extraordinary lightning-fast picking in a three-minute high-register bass solo that *Rolling Stone* declared to be the best recorded bass solo in history. The conventional role of a bass guitarist is to lay down the rhythmic and harmonic foundations of a piece of music – but Paul Goddard was anything but conventional in his approach to music. He treated the bass lines as part of the melody. Goddard's distinctive bass playing style is attributable in part to his use of a pick rather than his fingers to pluck the strings. "That could be because I was a lead guitar player first," Goddard told us.

Are You Ready also contained live versions of "Doraville," "Back Up Against The Wall," "Angel (What In The World's Come Over Us)" and "Imaginary Lover." It also contained a 7:47 version of "So Into You" (which had been listed as "So In To You" on single pressings and on *A Rock And Roll Alternative*). The album aptly illustrated the breadth of the ARS repertoire over the course of their six years with Polydor, but the band's tenure with the label was coming to an end. In November, Polydor went to the band's catalog and squeezed out one more single, "Back Up Against The Wall," which ARS first recorded in 1973. It failed to make a noticeable dent on the charts.

By 1980, musical moods were shifting as radio programmers favored Blondie, Queen, Air Supply, the Captain and Tennille, Christopher Cross, and Kool & the Gang. *The Boys From Doraville,* released in 1980, was the last ARS album on the Polydor label. The album began by putting a lid on the '70s with the opening track, "Cocaine Charlie," a condemnation of the hard toll exacted by drug use excesses. Polydor released a couple of tracks as singles, "I Ain't Much" and "Silver Eagle," but neither received sufficient airplay to register on the charts. At that time, Buie bought out the interests of his partners and became the sole owner of Studio One.

Amid a dispute with Polydor over finances, Buie initiated a bidding competition in the spring of 1981 for the Atlanta Rhythm Section among several labels. "Polydor wanted to keep ARS, but Columbia came up with the best deal. Bruce Lundvall had become the president of Columbia, and we had no idea that he had a pedigree in jazz music," Buie told us in January 2014. "When I played him some tracks we had recorded for our next album, he said, 'You've got a deal.' So we made a very good deal with Columbia. The boys were able to put some money in their pockets, and I was able to put money in my pocket."

In 1982 Columbia released an ARS album titled *Quinella,* exquisitely showcasing the songwriting maturity and superb musicianship of the band, with messages about life, joy, and beauty. The album failed to capture the attention of radio programmers, to the detriment of their audiences and to ARS fans. Those who didn't hear this album missed out on a gem that encompassed country-influenced ballads, artfully crafted mainstream pop, and rollicking rock licks. The album yielded the band's final chart single, "Alien," which premiered on August 29, 1981, on the *Billboard* Hot 100. It punched its way up to No. 29 and remained on the chart for 15 weeks.

ARS began recording another album for Columbia, but before it was complete, label executives said they wanted to exclude a couple of the tracks from the album. Buddy disagreed, and the stalemate resulted in suspension of the project. The tapes were shelved, and Columbia cut the Atlanta Rhythm Section loose. "So there's this unreleased album with some pretty good songs on it," Rodney Justo said. That disappointment prompted lead singer Ronnie Hammond and drummer Roy Yeager to leave the band. Buddy Buie stepped away from ARS in favor of other pursuits: fishing, playing golf, traveling, and writing music, collaborating frequently with J.R. Cobb. "I still love the business, but I didn't like the business controlling my life. So I told the band, 'Ya'll go with it,' and gave them control," Buie said. After recruiting drummer Danny Biget, the band in 1983 persuaded original lead singer Rodney Justo to temporarily fill in for Hammond. Justo by then was entrenched in a career in the wine and beer wholesaling industry, but performed in gigs with the band on weekends. ARS was ready for another crack at recording – this time with producer Chips Moman in Nashville. "Paul Cochran, who is a wonderful guy and a wonderful friend, had become friends with Chips Moman, and he worked out a deal for Chips to produce the band. Buddy was very loyal to Chips," said Justo. Moman had produced Sandy Posey's 1966 hit version of the Buie-Cobb composition "I Take It Back," which was an important early career break for Buddy. "But I did not like Chips or his records, and Chips didn't like me. So when Chips suggested he would record the band but without me, I was doing OK in my life."

Moman wanted the new recording to have a country music flair, which made bassist Paul Goddard uneasy. After learning in that Justo had been cut from ARS, Goddard angrily split from the band. "Paul knew I had almost put my job on the line to bail them out when they had dates and they needed some work. But I hold no grudges," Justo said. Paul Goddard left music behind, and wound up working in customer service for a school supplies company. Biget ended his short tenure with the band, and in 1987 J.R. Cobb also departed and began working with producer Chips Moman in Nashville. (See the B.J. Thomas chapter for more about Moman.) The band hired Andy Anderson as lead singer and Tommy Stribling on bass, but the album tracks that Moman produced remained in the can. The Atlanta Rhythm Section continued touring on a limited basis with additional personnel changes and only Dean Daughtry and Barry Bailey as original remaining members, but it ceased recording as a band for much of the remainder of the 1980s. ARS wasn't done, however; it was only resting, and the band continued booking performance dates.

Buddy Buie shared the spotlight with Little Richard on September 22, 1984, when both were inducted into the Georgia Music Hall of Fame. In 1986, after Buie decided to focus on writing songs with Ronnie Hammond, he sold Studio One to Georgia Tech University, which began using it as a classroom "laboratory" to train sound engineers, but closed the facility three years later.

"There was a period between the mid and late eighties that the band was kind of adrift at sea, with different singers and different players," Bailey recalled. "Dean and I were just trying to keep the band together for a while, and we managed to do that, but some of those versions of the band were not among my favorites." In 1988, singer Ronnie Hammond, guitarist Barry Bailey, and keyboardist Dean Daughtry decided to rev up the ARS recording engine again. Buie and Hammond set to work writing new songs and ARS began recording at Southern Tracks, a studio that Bill Lowery co-owned with session drummer Mike Clark. In 1989 CBS/Imagine Records released the resulting album, *Truth In A Structured Form*. Reflecting the contemporary music scene of the late '80s, the album made rich use of crisp, synthesized instrumentation in mostly fast-paced tunes. Resumption of touring prompted Polydor to release the band's first compilation album, *The Best Of The Atlanta Rhythm Section,* in 1991. During the ensuing decade several other "greatest hits" collections would follow, including *The Best Of The Atlanta Rhythm Section – The Millennium Collection,* part of the Universal Records label's "20th Century Masters" series.

No longer intent on turning out a new album every year, Hammond, Bailey, Daughtry, and Buie held off until 1996 before committing another album to tape. With the addition of guitarist Steve Stone, bass player Justin Senker, and drummer Sean Burke, ARS recorded *Atlanta Rhythm Section '96*. Released on the CMC International label, the album was conceived as a live-in-studio capture of the band's new interpretations of its own classic hits. Included among the 12 tracks were new versions of "So Into You," "Champagne Jam," "Imaginary Lover," "Do It Or Die," and "Dog Days." That recording coincided with the 1996 induction of the Atlanta Rhythm Section into the Georgia Music Hall of Fame, established by the state of Georgia to recognize musical contributions of Georgians. "The electricity went out during the induction ceremony in Atlanta," Daughtry recalled. "During the outage, our new drummer, R.J. Vealey, played drums for six and a half minutes without stopping, because he was the only one of us who could play without electrical power. When the electricity came back on, then we all started playing." The band's 1997 album *Partly Plugged* brought Ronnie Hammond, Barry Bailey, and Dean Daughtry together with Justin Senker, rhythm guitarist Steve Stone, and R.J. Vealey for refreshing acoustic interpretations of a half dozen of their classic hits, plus four new songs performed with their guitars plugged into their amplifiers. Buddy Buie had a hand in writing all 10 songs on the album.

When writing songs, Buie was at his creative best in his fishing cabin – a trailer in the woods at the shore of the Walter F. George Reservoir, a dammed section of the Chattahoochee River forming the boundary between southern Georgia and Alabama. Most folks in Alabama refer to it as Lake Eufaula (pronounced YOO-fall-uh), in honor of the nearby town with antebellum roots. Lake Eufaula has large populations of bass, crappie, and catfish, but alligators as large as 700 pounds also have been caught in its waters. That cabin at the lake was the inspiration for the title of the band's 15th album, the musically artistic *Eufaula,* recorded in 1998 for the Platinum Entertainment label. The band could not have anticipated the label's financial difficulties that prevented it from promoting the new release. As a result, record sales languished.

The band continued touring, but following a performance in Orlando, Florida, in November 1999, drummer R.J. Vealey collapsed and died of cardiac arrest. He was only 37 years old. The shocked band recruited drummer Jim Keeling to take his place. And when Ronnie Hammond decided once again to leave ARS in 2001, Andy Anderson ably stepped back into the lead singer role. Another change occurred in 2006, after Barry Bailey was diagnosed with multiple sclerosis and he realized that with advancing mobility limitations he no longer was able to tour. "Until that time, I had never left the band," Bailey said. "Dean and I somehow kept the band together for 35 years. There was always some work out there – we could always get a gig on the strength of the name Atlanta Rhythm Section."

On March 25, 2010, Buddy Buie was inducted into the Alabama Music Hall of Fame, along with the Blind Boys of Alabama and Eddie Levert, lead singer of the O'Jays. Steve Stone shifted from rhythm guitar to replace Bailey on lead, as Allen Accardi came on board temporarily until David Anderson stepped into the rhythm guitarist role. And to the delight of fans, Dean Daughtry and Buddy Buie persuaded Rodney Justo and Paul Goddard to resume performing with the Atlanta Rhythm Section in May 2011. Nearly 30 years had passed since Goddard had left music behind.

Casualty revisited ARS on March 14, 2011, when Ronnie Hammond, who lived in Forsyth, Georgia, died of a heart attack at age 60. Tragedy struck again 14 months later when drummer Robert Nix, who had been living in Batesville, Mississippi, died at age 67 on May 20, 2012, following surgery. He had diabetes and had experienced intestinal failure. "Ronnie was sort of a brother to me, "Bailey said. "We had fun together in addition to performing together. Robert was influential for me in a musical sense, particularly in the world of composition and songwriting. I loved them both." Then, only two months after speaking with us, bass player Paul Goddard died of cancer at age 68 on April 29, 2014, and 15 months later, on July 18, 2015, Buddy Buie died after suffering a heart attack.

The band's legacy consists of 14 *Billboard* Hot 100 hits, three RIAA gold-certified albums and one platinum award – and the memories of hundreds of thousands of fans who were fortunate enough to see ARS perform live.

The Atlanta Rhythm Section plays on, with two original members – singer Rodney Justo and keyboard player Dean Daughtry (who never left ARS) – along with guitarists David Anderson and Steve Stone, bass player Justin Senker, and drummer Rodger Stephan. "All I want is to see the guys continue to do good. I want to see them make a good living and take advantage of what's left of that 45-year-old baby," Buie smiled. Now in its fifth decade, the band continues to draw adoring fans who demonstrate that they're still so into the Atlanta Rhythm Section.

Visit http://www.atlantarhythmsection.com/ for touring, recording, merchandise and additional information.

The members of the Atlanta Rhythm Section gathered for this photo on August 16, 2014, when they performed at Dosey Doe restaurant's The Big Barn in The Woodlands, near Houston, Texas. In the front row, that's bass player Justin Senker at left, alongside keyboard player Dean Daughtry). In the rear, left to right: guitarist Steve Stone, lead singer Rodney Justo, guitarist Dave Anderson, and drummer Jim Keeling (photo by Courtni Meadows).

ATLANTA RHYTHM SECTION U.S. SINGLES ON THE *BILLBOARD* HOT 100 CHART

Debut	Peak	Title	Label
10/5/74	35	Doraville	Polydor
2/22/75	79	Angel (What In The World's Come Over Us)	Polydor
6/5/76	82	Jukin	Polydor
8/21/76	85	Free Spirit	Polydor
1/29/77	7	So In To You	Polydor
6/4/77	42	Neon Nites	Polydor
9/3/77	64	Dog Days	Polydor
10/15/77	68	Georgia Rhythm	Polydor
3/4/78	7	Imaginary Lover	Polydor
6/10/78	14	I'm Not Gonna Let It Bother Me Tonight	Polydor
9/16/78	43	Champagne Jam	Polydor
5/26/79	19	Do It Or Die	Polydor
8/11/79	17	Spooky	Polydor
8/29/81	29	Alien	Columbia

Billboard's pop singles chart data is courtesy of Joel Whitburn's Record Research Inc. (www.recordresearch.com), Menomonee Falls, Wisconsin.

Epilogue: Buddy Buie

Producer and songwriter

January 23, 1941 – July 18, 2015

Buddy Buie did many things over the course of his 74-year life. He was a restaurant worker, a reef shell inspector, a band manager, a concert promoter, a booking agent, a road manager, a recording session producer, a studio owner. But more than anything else, he loved composing music, and he was hugely successful at it. "Songwriters are born, they're not made. I believe I was born to be a songwriter. It's all I ever wanted to do," said Buddy, who registered 340 songs in the Broadcast Music Incorporated (BMI) catalog. Of those, he amassed 14 *Billboard* Hot 100 hits, three Recording Industry Association of America (RIAA) gold album awards and one platinum album. In 1984 Buie was inducted into the Georgia Music Hall of Fame, and in 2010 he was awarded a spot in the Alabama Music Hall of Fame.

Perry Carlton "Buddy" Buie was born January 23, 1941, in Marianna, Florida, and raised in Dothan, Alabama, where he lived until his career in music took him to Atlanta, Georgia. "My daddy was always called Buddy, and I was called 'Little Buddy.' But I was always 50 pounds heavier than my daddy," Buddy said. "My daddy was a very slight man. If my momma got mad at me, she'd say 'Little Buddy!'"

Buddy's sister, Gloria Jean, is six years older, and his brother, Jerry, is six years younger. "My momma told me that from the time she got pregnant with each one of us, she was turned green sick, so it took six years between each to get up the nerve to do it again. Momma also said I was born at suppertime and I've been hungry ever since," he said with a chuckle.

Buddy compared his childhood in the neighborhood where he grew up to a fabled figure in American literature. "It was like Tom Sawyer's story. My wife [Gloria Jane] always said, 'Everyone didn't have a Tom Sawyer life like you did.' I lived on Irwin Street in Dothan [pronounced DOE-thun], and we played in the backyard. I couldn't have asked for a better childhood," Buddy said. Although nobody else in his family played musical instruments or sang, music began to weave its spell on Buddy by

Buddy Buie in a 1970 publicity photo (courtesy of Gloria Jane Buie).

25

the time he was 9 years old, in 1952. "I remember as a child the first song that I fell in love with was 'High Noon (Do Not Forsake Me)' by Frankie Laine. I thought that was the coolest song."

Buddy's parents, Grace and Carlton, operated Buie's Restaurant at 119 S. Foster Street in downtown Dothan for 42 years beginning in 1938. Buddy recalled, "I worked at the restaurant and it seemed every time I had a date on Friday night, my daddy would call and say, 'Buddy, so-and-so didn't show up. You've gotta work tonight.' The restaurant stayed open 24 hours a day, and it had great food. After 10 p.m. policemen would come in, and I was the only person there besides the cook that late at night. The other people started coming in at 5 a.m. That's when breakfast started. That restaurant had quite a business. At lunch you had to stand in line to get in, and it held a couple hundred people. I would take food orders and they'd ring a bell, and I'd come get it and take it out to the table." The restaurant did not serve alcohol. Houston County, where Dothan is located, was then a "dry" county. "When I grew up there was never any alcohol in our home. I'm trying to make up for that now," Buddy laughed.

When Buddy was 16, he had a summer job with the state of Alabama as a "processed reef shell inspector." Buddy explained, "They were building a highway from Dothan to the Florida line, and they had trucks full of oyster shells for the bed of the highway. When the trucks came in, they had this little card that I had to punch and, at the end of the day, I had to tell them how many truckloads they had. You talk about a boring job – it was two hours between trucks."

At the age of 17, he started hanging out with disc jockeys at a pop radio station called the "Big BAM," WBAM in Montgomery, Alabama. Although Montgomery was 110 miles distant, WBAM's 50,000-watt signal at 740 AM covered much of the state, including Dothan. "We didn't call it rock and roll back then, we just called it music," Buddy said. Although Buddy liked Elvis Presley's singing as much as the next guy, he was particularly intrigued by the people and process behind the hit songs of the day. "I was more interested in the song lyrics, and my heroes were the songwriters. I was a huge fan of Burt Bacharach and Hal David. I said to myself, 'I can do what they do. I can write this song.' Once I started writing songs, I would write pretty much 24 hours a day. I've always been very musical but I've never played in a band. It's all in my head. I constantly had music in my head. I believed if it's not good enough to remember, it's not good enough to keep. If I got an idea, I would pursue it. If I couldn't remember it the next day, I figured it wasn't worth a damn."

Buddy had a special bond with a Dothan childhood friend, John Rainey

Adkins, guitarist for Roy Orbison and the Candymen. "John Rainey is one of my heroes, God rest his soul [John died in 1989 at the age of 47]. We would sit out in front of my house in my 1956 Chevrolet, and I would sing these melodies that I had in my head, and he would pick them out on the guitar. That's pretty much the way I started writing. But it took me a long time to get up the nerve to tell anyone that I was a songwriter. That was kind of uncool back then."

The first song that Buddy wrote, called "It Seems So Strange," was the product of his anguish about lost love. "Gloria Seay [pronounced 'see'] was the one I was singing about. I've known her since she was 5 years old. Both of us grew up in Dothan, and attended the same church. Her family had a pool table at their house and I'd go over there and shoot pool, and in high school Gloria and I started dating. But her parents didn't want us to keep going together because they didn't think I could earn a good living in music, so she started dating this other guy. Next thing I knew, they were married. It just killed me. It almost destroyed my mind," Buddy confided. "I got inspiration as a songwriter from heartache. That's what made me such a good song writer. You've got to suffer. But I was making everything personal. You'll find my angst in the early songs I wrote." When Bobby

Gloria and Buddy Buie in the 1970s (photo courtesy of Gloria Jane Buie).

Goldsboro sang "Honey Baby" (which he wrote with Buie and Adkins, the flip side of "Molly"), he was really singing about Gloria Seay. The same was true for Buddy's compositions "If She Was Mine" (which Chad and Jeremy recorded in '64), "Afraid to Sleep" (which Roy Orbison recorded in 1964) and "Movies in My Mind" (which Billy Joe Royal recorded in 1967).

Songwriting was Buddy's passion, but he decided to leave the guitar work to the best in the business. "I'm a guitar owner, but not a guitar player," he said. "I've worked with some of the best [guitar players] in the world. People want to know why I don't play guitar and sing. I just didn't want to be a guitar player. I know how to play chords, but I wanted to hear other guys play. I wanted to hear John Rainey play. I decided to do something else in the music business, and that turned out to be a wise move on my part."

While still attending Dothan High School, Buddy served as a booking agent for a band called the Webs, which included not only Adkins as lead singer, but also Buddy's good friend Bobby Goldsboro (whose story is told in *Where Have All the Pop Stars Gone, Volume 2*). "I told them, 'What y'all need is someone who can talk for ya.' They were all bashful, so I said, 'I'm going to get you some jobs.' There was a place in Dothan called Porter's Fairy-Land, which sounds weird today. It had a different connotation back then – it was an entertainment park with a swimming pool. I got them booked there, and Goldsboro was so bashful. The dance hall had support pillars in the room, and Bobby would try to hide by standing behind the pillars. After I booked them at Porter's, then I booked them for dances."

Bobby and Buddy both started attending Auburn University after graduating from high school in 1959. Buddy's mother had encouraged him to go to college, so he stayed at Auburn for two quarters, then transferred to Troy State College for another two quarters before music consumed all of his interest and time. Buddy took his first financial gamble in 1961. "I wanted to branch out from dances to do concerts, so I found out who booked Roy Orbison, which was Acuff-Rose. I finally got hold of the guy at Acuff-Rose. He had Roy's booking agent call me, and we booked a date at the Houston County Farm Center in Dothan. I was the concert promoter. My folks helped me with the finances. As a matter of fact, my mother did all of the accounting and made sure everyone was paid. I sold it out," Buddy said.

Roy needed a backup band, so in the weeks before the concert performance, Bobby Goldsboro and the Webs studied Roy's records and learned how to play his songs. "They sounded like you put a quarter in the jukebox; they could play the songs so good. The booking agency told me on the phone that he was bringing his music director with him, and asked, 'Does the band read music?' I said, 'Sure, they all read,' but none of them read music. So they passed out the music, and Roy would say, 'Let's go over "Cryin'."' And the Webs played it just like the record. Later on, Roy said, 'Buddy, I've got to have this band!' Roy was from a small town in Texas, something like Dothan, and we all related well to each other. I said, 'The only way you get that band is if I go with them.' So the whole band crowded into my '56 Chevrolet and hit the road with Roy Orbison. The Webs were all great natural musicians, and Roy was just so totally blown away with them. It was five guys in a car, and lovin' every minute of it. Now I wouldn't do it for anything."

Buddy's job as road manager for Orbison and the Webs was to call the concert promoter for each upcoming show and make sure the venue was booked and ready, and then to meet with the promoter at the site the morning of the concert to make sure the sound system was right. "Things were so different then. I had to get the artist to trust me as a road manager, and Roy was wonderful and gave me that kind of trust. He loved the band and they loved him."

Buddy recalled a funny phobia of Roy Orbison's that many people probably don't realize he had. "There's a really long bridge in Tampa, and Roy was deathly afraid of going over bridges, so we had to negotiate with him. He would have to get down on the floor and close his eyes until we got over the bridge." Back in those days, recording artists made relatively little money, despite the rigors of traveling and performing night after night. "The first time I brought Roy to Dothan, I paid him $500," said Buie.

When Bobby Goldsboro signed with United Artists Records, the record label hired Buddy as a songwriter – for $75 per week. But Buddy had bigger things in mind, and to that end he made one of the most important connections of his life in Nashville in 1965, when he met recording entrepreneur Bill Lowery for the first time. "In Nashville there was a place called The Alley. Gambling was not legal, and they would look through a little peephole to see you before they let you in. Bill loved to play craps. I met someone who got me in. Bill was over playing craps, and we started talking. He had heard of me because I had been on the road with Orbison, and some of his writers had told him about me." That initial introduction would soon lead to a new phase in Buddy's life.

Buddy added another link in what would become the ARS chain in Clearwater, Florida. That's where he met Paul Cochran, a recreational director who had hired Roy Orbison to perform in concert there. Buddy recalled, "Paul had a great job, but one day he and I were talking and I said,

'Let's do something together.' We got in the car and drove, and on the way out of town we passed by this dealership and saw this green Oldsmobile Toronado. We went into the dealership and, on Paul's credit, we bought the Toronado and left town in it. We made all the payments on it and everything was cool, but the only reason we got credit was because Paul was known in the area. When Paul and I decided to make our break, we didn't know where we were heading, but we were going to do shows. He and I became partners in the Buie-Cochran Management Company, and remained friends." The duo first signed the Florida band the Classics IV to a management contract, and Buddy began writing songs with the band's guitarist, J.R. Cobb. Then as Buddy's contract with United Artists was coming to a close, he contacted Lowery and told him about the Classics IV. Lowery was interested.

Buie and Cochran moved to Atlanta in 1965 and formed Low-Sal Publishing with Bill Lowery. At the same time, Buddy and J.R. signed on with Lowery as songwriters to create material for the Classics IV and for Lowery's publishing ventures. "Bill was excited about signing me as a songwriter because I had been with United Artists," Buddy said. Although Joe South initially was assigned to produce Classics IV recordings, he already had too many irons in the fire. He willingly stepped aside for Buie to try his hand at producing Classics IV sessions – giving Buddy his first opportunity to call the shots in the engineering booth. He had success almost immediately as the band's singles on the Imperial Records label over a four-year span beginning in 1968 became hits.

Buddy and J.R. Cobb co-wrote "Spooky," "Stormy," "Traces," and "Everyday With You, Girl" – the biggest hits for the Classics IV. "'Traces' was a very big song and still is. 'Spooky' started out as an instrumental by Mike Sharpe [Shapiro] and Harry Middlebrooks. J.R. and I were riding down the road, and I said, 'God, I love that song!' J.R. said, 'Bill published that.' So I called up Bill and said, 'You've got a song called "Spooky," right?' He said, 'Yeah, Mike Sharpe.' I said, 'We'd like to take it, write lyrics to it, and change it around a bit.' Bill said, 'Go ahead. Let me know what you've got.' So we wrote the lyrics and then we went in and recorded it. I love Mike's version of it, and he was so gracious to let us take it and mold it into what we wanted."

Buddy also attributed creativity on Classics IV sessions to bass and keyboard player Emory Gordy Jr. "He was fooling around on the piano, and I asked, 'Emory, what is that? Do you mind if J.R. and I take that and do something with it?' And he said, 'Go ahead.' So we started writing the song 'Traces,' and I knew it was going to be a big song, and we were proud of it. Basically, everything I wrote was about Gloria. I could make up a story in my mind, and it turned into a song. If you're a real songwriter, stories in your mind turn into a song," Buddy said.

"'Spooky' had six letters. I wasn't into numerology, but it was hip at the time, so we made sure all the song titles had six letters: 'Spooky,' 'Stormy,' 'Traces,' and then we broke out of it with 'Everyday With You Girl,' which is the least popular of all those songs. Maybe we should have stayed with six letters," he laughed. "But the inspiration for 'Everyday With You Girl' was a church song with the lyrics 'Every day with Jesus is sweeter than the day before.'"

Buie described the recording process: "The Classics IV, as such, never played on a record. J.R. was the only member of the band who played on the records. The Classics IV touring band sang on the records, but they didn't play the instruments on the records. J.R. would play guitar, and Emory Gordy [who in the 1980s produced recordings for Patty Loveless and married her in 1989] would play bass, and we had a drummer. The drummer on the first record was Dennis St. John, and after that it was Robert Nix from the Rhythm Section. Then we would add to it, with guitar sounds, and that's how we got the Classics IV sound. That's how we started out writing and producing songs, for the Classics IV. We had a Scully three-track [tape recorder], we dubbed tracks over each other, and we left one track for the vocal," Buie explained. "We tried to perfect each single. Each song took at least a couple of weeks to produce. The Classics IV always recorded in Lowery's studio, so there weren't any studio costs."

Buie quickly learned the ropes of producing, and attained mastery of his craft. In 1970, only three years after Bill Lowery gave him his first opportunity to sit in the producer's chair, Buie joined with Cobb, Cochran, and Lowery in launching Studio One, which gave birth to the Atlanta Rhythm Section. "There was nobody else like Bill," Buddy said.

Buie never wrote songs alone, and he explained why. "I've always written songs with a co-writer because I didn't play an instrument well. I do the music in my head, and I find a guitar or piano player, and I say, 'I've got this song, here's how it goes,' and I sing it. They ask, 'Is this right?' and I say, 'No, go up.' It's that primitive. My songwriting usually started with me having an idea and sharing it with someone, usually J.R., who was my principal co-writer. Besides writing all of the Classics IV stuff, we wrote many of the songs for the Rhythm Section. We wrote them together, but there were times when he would have a musical idea and it would spawn a lyrical idea for me. J.R. was a great lyricist, too. Not only is he a great guitar player, he's just a great co-writer. I don't think J.R. gets the credit he deserves

31

for his guitar playing."

Buddy and Robert Nix wrote "Mighty Clouds of Joy," which became a hit for B.J. Thomas (a chapter in this book) in 1971. Buddy explained the inspiration behind that song. "There's a black gospel group called Mighty Clouds of Joy. We loved that and wrote a song around their name. B.J. is one of my favorite artists and one of my best friends, and he's got a voice that's just unbelievable. J.R. and I wrote the song 'Most Of All.' We were in the studio with B.J., and I said, 'B.J., I want to show you something.' J.R. played the guitar and I sang the song to him, and B.J. said, 'I love it!' He sang that song in the first take from front to end without one punch in [an editing technique to rectify a flaw], without anything. He's one of the greatest singers from that era who is still around." B.J. and Buddy remained good friends and kept in contact throughout the remainder of Buddy's life.

Gloria Seay, the object of Buddy's longing, was married to someone else, and didn't have any inkling that Buddy was writing songs about her. "When she married that other guy, that just broke my heart. Gloria was out in Texas, but we really must have been meant to be together because after she got a divorce in 1971, she went to my daddy and mom's restaurant, and said, 'Where's Buddy?' I had just broken up with my first wife. My mother gave her my number. When I answered a phone call I was shocked to find out it was Gloria. Each of us had been married to other people for seven years. Gloria said, 'I'm getting a divorce,' and I said, 'I'm getting a divorce, too.'" I flew her to Atlanta in January 1972, and we haven't been apart since. We were married June 18, 1972." Gloria soon took on important roles in Buddy's publishing, ARS and Studio One operations and financial management, including dispersing performance royalty payments.

Buddy did much of his songwriting in a mobile home along the shore of Lake Eufaula, about 15 miles northeast of Abbeville, Alabama. In our conversation with him in January 2014, he described the Lake Eufaula property. "It's on a huge reservoir lake, many miles long. My sister's husband said to my dad, 'Mr. Buie, if you buy the trailer, I'll buy the land.' So my daddy found a trailer, and at the time, the lots on the lake cost $500. Now they're worth $200,000 apiece. When mom and dad weren't using it as a fishing trailer, we'd come down there to write music. J.R. and I loved it, because it looked out across the lake, and it was out in the middle of nowhere. The only air conditioning it had was a window unit and, in the summertime, it gets really hot down here. During the summer, we would have to turn the air conditioner off because it made so much noise that we couldn't hear each other. It was two bedrooms, but I liked the smallness and the closeness that we had there."

In February 1978 Buddy teamed with Polydor music marketing specialist Arnie Geller to establish the Buie/Geller Organization talent management agency and BGO Records, a production company that worked with other labels for product distribution. Gloria Buie was involved in operation of the company, which had a staff of 15 people and was based at the Studio One building in Doraville. In addition to managing ARS, the firm achieved success almost immediately with Alicia Bridges and her autumn 1978 top-5 disco smash hit "I Love the Nightlife (Disco 'Round)," which earned a gold record for the Polydor label. They also were behind the scenes for Jerry Buckner and Gary Garcia's early spring 1982 top-10 Columbia Records novelty hit "Pac-Man Fever," which also went gold.

Following the hit-making years of ARS, Buie bought all of his partners' shares of the business and sold Studio One to Georgia State University. After Columbia Records acquired Buie's publishing interests, he and J.R. secured a three-year writing contract with Nashville CBS. During that time they wrote Wynonna Judd's hit "Rock Bottom." They also wrote "Homesick" for Travis Tritt, and "Mister Midnight" for Garth Brooks. Buie shared some special memories about his experience with Garth Brooks. "One day, J.R. and I were in Nashville and the head of CBS Nashville music affairs came in and said, 'Hey guys, Garth Brooks is over at his studio and wants to talk to ya'll.' We had sent him a copy of a song we wrote called 'Mister Midnight.' So we went over to his studio, knocked on the door and Garth came out and there was nobody else in the building, but we didn't know that. He got down on one knee and said, 'Boys, I love your song, but I want to make a few changes.' We went over the changes, and said, 'Fine. We like them.' But Garth is a person who is so nice that you can't even believe it's genuine. But it is. So that song was on his album and later on, it was on a special box set they did. [Garth's wife] Trisha [Yearwood] lived in a little town outside of Atlanta, and J.R. lived in Mansfield, which is right down the road, so I'm sure Trisha knew who we were and probably helped him decide to record one of our songs. He's the most genuine person you will ever meet, and he makes you feel like you're the star and he's the audience."

Other notable artists who have covered Buie's songs include Gloria Estefan ("Traces"), David Sanborn ("Spooky"), and Carlos Santana ("Stormy"). Most recently, John Legend used "Stormy" as the backing track on the single "Save Room," earning Buie a writer's credit. Buie's music also has been used in films. "So Into You" was used in *Lost in Translation,* a 2003 comedy-drama starring Bill Murray and Scarlett Johansson; and "Spooky" was used in *Just Like Heaven*, a romantic comedy fantasy film starring Reese Witherspoon, Mark Ruffalo, and Jon Heder.

Gloria and Buddy have one child together, Ben (born in 1974), and Gloria has a son, Hunter (born in 1963), from her first marriage. They have three grandchildren: Ben has a daughter, and Hunter has two sons. Hunter lives in Tampa and Ben lives in Atlanta. Ben is an IT systems professional, and Hunter has a law degree and works with a software firm as a client representative. After Buddy retired, he and Gloria built and moved into a home on the Lake Eufaula property northeast of Abbeville, Alabama. "This is the lake that my daddy and mom had a trailer on. I told Gloria every time I was here writing that I wanted to stay, so I finally talked her into moving down here, and she loves it now. I live a half mile from the trailer we used to write songs in. A beautiful home that my niece owns is now where the writing trailer was," Buddy said.

Over the years, Buie produced countless records and wrote more than 30 songs that became hits, but few of them have been as heartfelt and emotional as the song he and Ronnie Hammond wrote one cold January day in 1983, called "The Day Bear Bryant Died." Buie explained, "We had rented a cabin on Lake Lanier near Atlanta with the intention of writing another hit for ARS, but the funeral procession carrying [coach Paul] 'Bear' Bryant's body from Tuscaloosa to its final resting place in Birmingham stopped us in our tracks. We were taking a break and turned on the television as Keith Jackson's haunting voice narrated the scene of thousands lining Interstate 20 and I-59 to honor their hero. Every overpass was packed with mourning fans and onlookers as we watched mesmerized and misty eyed. Ronnie began softly playing a hymn-like melody on his guitar. At that point we forgot about our mission to write another rock and roll masterpiece and spent the rest of that sad day composing 'The Day Bear Bryant Died.'" While Buie always wanted someone to sing their song in the University of Alabama stadium, he said he never could get it cleared.

Buddy Buie and Chips Moman
(photo courtesy of Gloria Jane Buie).

Over the course of 47 years, Bill Lowery published more than 5,000 songs. Sony/ATV Music Publishing purchased the Lowery Music Group in January 2000. Buddy's old friend and former business partner Bill Lowery died four years later, on June 8, 2004, after a four-month battle with cancer.

Buddy and Gloria enjoyed inviting friends to their home outside Abbeville for casual get-togethers. "I like to cook, and I watch all the cooking shows. Remember, I grew up in the restaurant business, so I come by it naturally," he said. For one such gathering on Saturday, July 18, 2015, Buddy and Gloria's next door neighbor arrived about a half hour before the other guests. His dog tagged along with him and began frolicking with Buddy and Gloria's dog, a goldendoodle named Hampton. The dogs' play cracked up Buddy, who was laughing uproariously as the pooches wriggled around on the floor with their paws wrapped around each other. Suddenly the neighbor summoned Gloria from the kitchen. In the midst of laughing, Buddy went limp as his head slouched down. They were gently lowering Buddy to the floor to prevent him from falling, just as other guests rang the doorbell. Gloria called for an ambulance, which rushed Buddy 45 miles to Southeast Alabama Medical Center in Dothan. He died there that evening of cardiac arrest without regaining consciousness. At 74 years of age, Buddy Buie had literally died laughing.

Medical Center Barbour, a Eufaula (Barbour County) affiliate of Southeast Alabama Medical Center, has named a fundraising event in Buddy's honor. The nonprofit acute-care medical facility in Eufaula hosted "Buddy Buie's 'Faula Fest" May 13 and 14, 2016. Activities included a daylong golf tournament at Country Club of Alabama and a day of music outdoors in downtown Eufaula. "The director of the Southeast Alabama Medical Center Foundation, which is the fund-raising arm of the hospital, wanted to find a way to memorialize Buddy because he was so loved in this area. Buddy had been involved previously with supporting fundraising for this small-town hospital. We felt it benefitted all of us who needed to use it," Gloria said. "Medical Center Barbour already was doing a golf fundraiser every year, but she wanted to put Buddy's name on it and add music to it as well. So, I contacted Rodney Justo and the Atlanta Rhythm Section, and the band graciously agreed to be the headliner for the day of music."

ARS keyboard player Dean Daughtry retains deep gratitude for Buie. "I owe everything to Buddy. He taught me how to write music. I would call him if something was bothering me. He was like a father to me – he was like a father to all of us in the band," Daughtry told us in March 2016.

Buddy, who said that his guiding philosophy was the Golden Rule – Do unto others as you would have them to do unto you – was most proud of the early part of his career. "When 'Spooky,' 'Stormy,' and 'Traces' became hits, I knew I was succeeding in a very competitive and long-shot field. After that, it seemed like everything I touched was successful. I've never had any thoughts of losing, or 'What am I going to do next?' in my life. I really believe in the power of positive thinking."

Of all the songs that he wrote and produced, he remains most fond of two: "'So In To You,' because it spawned the Rhythm Section, and 'Traces,' because of Gloria," Buddy said. "Those are the songs that mean the most to me."

Buddy's passing was a staggering loss to his longtime composing collaborator J.R. Cobb. "It is difficult for me to talk about Buddy Buie without being emotional. He was my friend and business associate for 50 years. We shared so many experiences that I could write about them all night and never even come close to mentioning all of the wonderful times we had. He had a way of bringing out the best in people, and I certainly benefited from his influences in every part of my musical life," J.R. said. "There would never have been an ARS without Buddy. From the writing of the songs to the producing of the records to the management of the band and the relationship we had with record companies, he played an integral and vital part. I'm sure that I would have never become a successful songwriter or, for that matter, a songwriter at all, without his help and support. He was my dearest friend and brother, and I will miss him as long as I live."

Epilogue: Barry Bailey

Lead guitarist and composer

After more than thirty-five years of laying down expressive, inspired riffs with the Atlanta Rhythm Section, lead guitarist and composer Barry Bailey decided in 2006 that it was time to take his signature Les Paul Deluxe Goldtop home and retire. His distinctive style and phenomenal guitar playing helped to shape the Rhythm Section's unique sound.

Fans may not know that Barry was not his proper given name, but rather was derived from his middle name. He was born Joe Barrett Bailey Jr. on June 12, 1948, in Atlanta, Georgia, the second child of Joe Barrett Bailey Sr., and Virginia Rogers Bailey. "My father started off as an independent businessman – he was a printer and had a huge printing press and a printing business in the basement of our home. He printed business cards and letterhead, and I remember he did some work for Coca Cola," Barry said. After serving in the Army, his father joined the U.S. Postal Service, becoming superintendent of vehicle operations. The family moved around the Atlanta area until they settled in the mid-1940s in the southwestern Georgia town of Decatur – which then had a population of about 28,000 – and built the family home on a half-acre lot on Coventry Road.

Barry Bailey uses an all-terrain vehicle to patrol the land surrounding his home (photo courtesy of Barry Bailey).

Music was an integral part of Barry's childhood. "Big bands gave me my first exposure to music, and my parents said I reacted to music at a young age. My father had a very extensive collection of old 78 rpm records – mostly big band stuff and music going back to the '30s and well into the '40s," recalled Barry. "We had a baby grand piano in our home, and my father played one song and he played it well. It was called 'Indian Love Call,' made famous by Jeanette MacDonald and Nelson Eddy. He also played an accordion, which I still have in my possession. My mom and dad shared musical tastes. My dad sang a little, and whistled a lot. They were very supportive and understanding of my musical pursuits."

Barry remains close to his two sisters. Myra Bailey Kay, who is five years older, lives in Jacksonville, and is widowed. Beverly Bailey is a year younger than Barry and lives in Atlanta. They both play piano and sing. "My younger sister is still in the church choir," said Barry. "Playing and singing Christmas carols together is kind of an annual tradition with us."

Barry began playing the guitar at the age of 12. "I got a Sears Silvertone for my 12th birthday in 1960. My parents gave it to me. I took guitar lessons for a year from a teacher in Decatur. His name was Bill Galloway, and I think he played more lap steel than anything else, but I never saw him play it. When my father became widowed, he would go hang out in places where Bill was playing," said Barry. "The guitar was the first instrument I learned to play, but not the first instrument I owned. I owned a clarinet that I think was assigned to me in grammar school, but it didn't work out. Elvis Presley was a big influence and made me want to play guitar. My father actually taught me the first two songs he knew on guitar. I had some country music exposure. I remember Eddie Arnold's singing, and some country music TV shows, but I didn't like it as much then as I do now."

While attending Decatur High School, Barry joined the chorus in his senior year. "You had the option of sports, the band, or music," he said. "I was in ROTC, and actually enjoyed carrying an M1 rifle around. I don't think I ever fired it. The ROTC had their own armory in the basement of the stadium, and they would raise the colors [the U.S. and Georgia flags] in the morning and take them down at the end of the day. But I ended up in the chorus because my hair got too long for ROTC, and chorus was a little more lenient about things like longer hair."

Barry recalls listening to music on the radio at night, when distant AM signals can be received. "I listened to WLAC, which was out of Nashville. The DJ was John R, whose real name was Richbourg. He had a rhythm and blues show late at night, mostly blues. The Kings – Freddie, Albert, and B.B. – and Jimmy Reed were some of my favorites of that genre. I was

listening mostly to black music. Before the black stuff, I was listening to
Bill Haley and the Comets and Buddy Holly, but the black music was what
I wanted to emulate, or at least it's what influenced my music," Barry told
us in February 2014. "In early high school I also had a little jazz phase, and
I'm still very fond of jazz in the more traditional sense. I liked listening to
guitar players like Kenny Burrell with Jimmy Smith, Grant Green, Wes
Montgomery, George Benson, and Hank Ballard and the Midnighters. I was
eventually attracted to the British Invasion."

During Bailey's high school years he was a member of what he called
"garage bands" that played at dances after football games and at teenage
nightclubs. In the mid to late '60s he performed with a variety of bands,
including the Imperials, the Vons, Wayne and the Kommotions, and St.
John and the Cardinals, led by drummer Dennis St. John. After graduating
from high school Barry performed mostly in nightclubs, and did some
backup work for popular artists traveling through Georgia and the
Southeast. "About that same time I was doing a little independent work
with kind of thrown-together bands for radio station shows. I remember the
Who headlining a show we were in, and the group I was in backed up Billy
Joe Royal [about whom this book includes a chapter]. If a vocalist needed

Barry playing a sitar in 1968 (photo courtesy of Barry Bailey).

a backup band, we were often the ones they called. This would have been either the Cardinals or a group of players put together as a backup group."

In late 1964, Bailey joined Wayne Logiudice (pronounced Locka-dee-cee) and the Kommotions. The group consisted of Bailey on lead guitar, Emory Gordy Jr. playing bass, saxophonist Al Sheppard, trombone player Harry Hagan, drummer Rick Bear, and Wayne as vocalist. Barry recalls, "The first time I went on the road in high school for a three-day weekend, we opened for the Yardbirds with Jeff Beck. Jeff Beck has always been a favorite, ever since then. One show was in Memphis, and one in Little Rock. We did a few dates, but mostly stayed in the Atlanta area. We went up to Louisville, Kentucky, and a couple of summers we did mostly black places because Wayne was considered one of the blue-eyed soul brothers. He was a James Brown imitator and very good dancer. He passed away in May 2013. We played at a place in Atlantic City, New Jersey. We did two- or three-week stays at the place, which was really an experience. It was not exclusively, but very much a black nightclub. We were the only white act performing any length of time there."

Barry and his father, Joe B. Bailey, at a party following an ARS performance at the Chastain Park Amphitheater in Atlanta, ca. 1977 (photo courtesy of Barry Bailey).

After graduating from Decatur High School in 1966, Barry attended DeKalb College (since renamed Georgia Perimeter College). In 1967, Barry got to know the Candymen because they were competing bands playing the same types of venues around the Atlanta area. "I remember the first time I met the Candymen folks, particularly Robert Nix, I was playing in a band that was backing up Rufus and Carla Thomas at a club in Atlanta, and the Candymen were on the same show. They invited me to join them in a hotel room after our show and we became friendly." The Candymen went out on their own, which led to a new opportunity for Barry while he was a member of St. John and the Cardinals. "I was at DeKalb for about 1½ semesters when the Cardinals got a call from the Roy Orbison people to do some backup work for him. We ended up going on the road with Roy several times for the better part of a couple of years, and I dropped my college ambitions."

Barry subsequently focused on recording and working as a session musician. "A lot of my introduction to recording was through Emory Gordy Jr., the bass player with the Kommotions and the Cardinals. Emory got me on the session that Buddy Buie was producing with John Rainey Adkins, who was the guitar player with the Candymen. We did a bunch of instrumental things showcasing my playing. They used some of the instrumental tracks that we cut to approach record companies to get some attention to at least be aware of the band. This was before ARS had a vocalist, before Rodney Justo became the singer, and before the band was a band."

Bailey's distinctive style is an amalgamation of influences from all of the guitar players he has admired, including Chet Atkins, the jazz players mentioned earlier, Duane Eddy, Les Paul and Mary Ford, and others. "As I graduated from high school and began attending college, Jimi Hendrix came along, Cream came along, and Eric Clapton was doing the same kind of stuff that I'd like to do. I was more into the melodic guitar style. I'm pretty much a chord, melody person. I loved Glen Campbell. He was playing bass with the Beach Boys in one of the shows I did with the Kommotions around 1965 or '66."

All these years, Barry has kept musicians' union records from 1967, '68, '69, and '71 showing dates of gigs, sessions, and artists with whom he worked. "For a lot of the sessions we had union contracts. In fact I was the leader on the sessions, and we were actually billing the artists that were signed to record companies," he said. "It was contracted through the local Atlanta musicians' union, which is 148-462 (AFM-American Federation of Musicians). The reason it's 148-462 is that there used to be a black union and a white union. I joined the union when I was with the Kommotions. I remember going down to the black union office because the dues were not as much to join. Later the unions merged and it became 148-462.

"Most of the outside session work and the first ARS album sessions took place in 1971 or, at least, the union contracts that I filed were dated

1971," said Bailey. "The artists we backed that year included Dee Clark, Richard 'Supa' Goodman, Al Kooper, Billy Joe Royal, Joe South, the Tams, Donna Theodore, B. J. Thomas, Wilbur Walton, and Dennis Yost with the Classics IV."

Some of the more memorable dates from 1967 that Barry recalled were July 12 of that year, when he recorded "Hush" with singer Billy Joe Royal and producer Joe South in Nashville; September 1, the date of the first live show he performed with Roy Orbison's Candymen at the Crazy Horse in Birmingham, Alabama; and December 5–16, 1967, when Barry took his first trip to the West Coast to record at a session in Los Angeles. Jim Valley, one of several former Paul Revere and the Raiders guitarists, recorded an album with Bailey, but it was never released. In addition to session work for albums, Barry recorded some jingles for local car dealerships, and national spots for Coca Cola, and BellSouth, which became part of AT&T. The national spots paid royalties.

As co-writer of the Atlanta Rhythm Section's "Doraville" with Robert Nix and Buddy Buie, Bailey recalls the sequence of creative events that led to composing the 1974 hit song. "When we were in the studio in Doraville, sometimes we would set up and play and they would start the recording tape and let it roll. This particular afternoon – we never worked in the daytime – we were just jamming and I started playing the melody, which became the lead melody for the chorus of 'Doraville.' As we were listening to the tape, Robert Nix and Buddy said, 'We can make a song out of that.' So I tried to develop more of the chord progression and the melody from what had been laid down on the tape during the jam session. But the lyrics and ideas were all Buddy and Robert."

A song that he says has the strongest personal meaning for him is "Angel (What In The World's Come Over Us)," which he co-wrote with Nix and Buie. "It was the first time I actually wrote chord changes and melody lines for a song, performed on it, and heard the final results." The song remained on the *Billboard* Hot 100 pop chart for five weeks in 1975.

Barry said that during his years with ARS and after, he preferred his Les Paul guitar for live performances, but for a lot of the recording he played a Telecaster. "On basic tracks, I was more likely to play a Fender. I used the Les Paul for solo work – not exclusively, though – and heavier-type sounds." The amplifiers he used on stage were generally Marshall 50-watt or 100-watt units. "In the studio we used a variety of amps – mostly the Marshall with an Echoplex for a little echo and pre-amping. Back then, the acoustic guitar was just miked."

Barry met his first wife, Dawn Vanderlip, in high school. "We went to competing high schools. I was playing with the Vons at her high school, and our drummer, who went to the same school that she did, introduced us. We married in October 1970." Dawn was a certified master gardener, working for nurseries and landscapers. In 2001 they built a house in Madison, Georgia, a picturesque city with a population of about 4,000 about 60 miles east of Atlanta. Barry explained, "Where we came from was getting so developed, and Dawn did the legwork of trying to find property. I thought we'd just find another house and move in, but we ended up finding a nice piece of property. It's a custom-built home, and I have a music room. I haven't done much recording, and I do most of my playing in the living room, but I have a dedicated area that's an office with music memorabilia on another level of the house."

But the couple, who did not have children, faced crises in 2005. That's when Barry was diagnosed with multiple sclerosis, and the same year Dawn was diagnosed with lung cancer. "I had a little cancer scare myself around the same time. It certainly wasn't anything like lung cancer, but it was my first experience with melanoma." Dawn's disease was advanced and aggressive, and despite efforts to save her, she died on July 6, 2006.

Barry still lives in the home and he has a few animal friends to keep him company. "I've got a few acres and a couple of dogs that are basically pound rescues, and a cat that was a stray, more or less. I've also got a couple of horses that I've had for a long time now. They came with me from my previous home and they're just kind of pets, too. They were never even broken to ride. I'm on my own with the animals, but I have a lot to tend to that keeps me busy."

Barry rocks it in an Atlanta Rhythm Section stage performance (photo courtesy of Barry Bailey).

He keeps his Taylor guitar very close to his favorite chair. "I can still play, but not as well as I did in the past because I've lost some dexterity and grip. It's mostly a mobility issue." While he had been thinking about retiring from ARS, the MS diagnosis was the final deciding factor.

In 2010, he married a woman who was a writer for a Georgia publication called *Southern Distinction Magazine*. "She did a story about ARS and it was published. Besides writing, she's also an interior designer. We stayed together for about two years, but we're no longer together. I think I make a better widower than I did a husband in trying to replace the unreplaceable. But anyway, everything is fine now."

The ARS concert performances that stand out most strongly in Bailey's mind include the Dog Days Rock Fest and Champagne Jam, and the White House performance for Chip Carter's birthday. He also fondly recalls the ARS performance for 60,000 fans at the Knebworth Festival in Hertfordshire, England, in June 1978. The grounds of Knebworth House had been a major venue for open-air rock and pop concerts since 1974. Accompanying ARS in the 1978 show, called "A Midsummer Night's Dream," were Brand X, Devo, Genesis, Jefferson Starship, Tom Petty and the Heartbreakers, and Roy Harper.

Barry remains an avid gardener in spite of his physical limitations. "I stay very active outdoors. I've got about 3,000 square feet of highly fenced garden area. If it wasn't highly fenced the deer would eat it all. I like to grow vegetables. Dawn was really into ornamental stuff, which is still here. Because of her expertise, we've got a nice landscape here. I'm maintaining the ornamental stuff. I grow the usual crops around here – tomatoes, peppers, eggplant, okra, potatoes, onions. I still fish a little. I've got a pond, an area I had dammed and stocked for a fish pond. Dawn and I always entertained each other by cooking together or going out to eat together. I don't get too exotic anymore, but I enjoy cooking, and eating."

Barry regards persistence as one of his defining characteristics and greatest strengths. He said with conviction, "I feel an obligation. I don't know where it comes from, but if I'm going to do something I prefer to do it completely and correctly." With a note of pride in what he has accomplished in music and other aspects of his life, he added, "If it was easy, anybody could do it."

Epilogue: J.R. Cobb

Rhythm guitarist and songwriter

J.R. Cobb could boast about his accomplishments as a musician, lyricist and musical composer, as well as being a member of three well-known bands – the Classics IV, the Atlanta Rhythm Section, and the Highwaymen. He has written or co-written 14 *Billboard* Hot 100 hits, ARS was awarded three Recording Industry Association of America gold albums and one platinum LP, and he individually was inducted in 1993 into the Georgia Music Hall of Fame, and in 1997 into the Alabama Music Hall of Fame, from which he received the Music Creator Award.

J.R.'s humble reaction to such honors: "I'll be honest – that Hall of Fame stuff was kind of uncomfortable for me. For one thing, when they start putting you in the Hall of Fame that means you're old. I never thought of myself as any kind of hero. I don't think any of us in ARS did," said Cobb. "Some people live and breathe music, and they never stop being on stage. We never did that. When we got off the road, we were just plain ole people. We didn't think of ourselves as being all that special. I've got a lot of respect for people who have a job, and work hard every day doing something that they don't get a lot of exposure for. I think they're just as much a hero as I was."

J.R. Cobb's spirited playing energized the ARS 25th anniversary celebration on January 14, 1997, at the Hard Rock Cafe in Atlanta, coinciding with release of the band's album *Partly Plugged* (photo courtesy of J.R. Cobb).

All of those accolades came after J.R. was well on his way to becoming a journeyman steelworker.

James Barney Cobb Jr. was born February 5, 1944, in Birmingham, Alabama, to James Barney Cobb Sr. and Rose Ellen Hutchins. When J.R. was about 4 years old the family moved to Jacksonville, Florida, where other members of his father's family lived. J.R.'s father was a truck driver – a trade he picked up in the Army – and his mother, a housewife. "My parents thought it would be really cool to call me J.R. because I was a junior, and I guess it might have been popular at the time. I've spent many years trying to explain why my name is James Barney, but everybody calls me J.R."

He was 7 years old before the first of his five sisters and brother came along. His siblings (in birth order) are: sisters Janice, Bonnie, Juanita, Jewel, Irene; and brother, Curtis. "I grew up in what was then a middle-class household, with one bread winner, one car, one telephone, and a pretty simple lifestyle," J.R. said. When he was 9 years old, his parents divorced and his mother placed him in Baptist Home for Children in Jacksonville for seven years. At 16, he was of legal age to obtain a work permit and got a job at the local Winn-Dixie grocery store as a bag boy, stock boy, and cashier. He was able to move back home to help his mother with household chores, watch his siblings, and contribute to household finances.

"You know, I enjoyed it at the Home for Children. I can't say enough about it," said J.R. "Two of my sisters were there with me. The rest were young and with my mother, and she just struggled on with them by herself. The Baptist Home had separate houses for older boys and younger boys, older girls and younger girls. They separated the boy side and the girl side, and we met in the middle to eat meals and stuff. It was run in somewhat of a military fashion, but you know if you've got that many kids in one house, you almost have to do that. There were house parents for each house, a man and a woman, and they oversaw everything and made sure we did our chores and stuff like that. I think it was a good thing for me to go there, but I didn't appreciate it as much when I was there as after I was grown and away from it."

Thinking back on his experience in the Baptist Home, he recalled the various sports-related activities it offered him, including football and baseball, along with a dairy farm where the kids learned how to milk cows and raise their own food. "I was happy to do that because when I was home, I was the oldest and I didn't really have a whole lot of friends to play games with and stuff, so it was better for me at that time in my life."

J.R. received his first guitar from his uncle William Crago. "I would play around with it for awhile, then put it away and not touch it for another month or two. But a friend was a pretty good guitar player in a band, and he showed me some stuff. I would go out and watch his band, and I got more interested in playing guitar during my junior and senior year of high school. I knew a couple of simple chords, but for a long time, that's all I knew," J.R. said. That was enough for him to begin a brief stint with a high school band called the Emeralds, which performed at school dances. "A lot of the records coming out then were really guitar-oriented. Of course, rock and roll was big-time guitar-oriented."

While J.R. was still attending Paxon High School in Jacksonville, he wanted to enlist for military service. "I tried to join, but I was under 18 and my mother wouldn't sign for me. The Vietnam thing was getting started and a lot of my friends from high school went into the service, and some of them didn't come home," J.R. said. But enlistment after he turned 18 wasn't an option for him either. "I was really involved with supporting my brother and sisters, and the Army said it would cost them too much in allotments for me to join, so I was exempted for that reason. I wasn't really happy with that, but I guess it turned out all right."

After J.R. graduated from high school in 1962, he took a job working at Florida Steel as apprentice welder. "My parents were blue collar folks and I couldn't wait to get a job and earn my own money. When I was in school, people would ask me, 'What are you going to do?' and I said, 'Well, something with a paycheck at the end of the week.' I didn't really care what it was. My mother insisted that I finish high school, which I did. I lived close enough to the steel company to walk to work, so that was mainly why I went to work there. They made big I-beams – really huge beams they pick up with a crane – for construction, and materials for bridges and stuff. I worked in the plant. I was welding plates on beams and sometimes they put me on the drill press, and I would drill holes. The first thing I started doing was tack-in plates. I never got to be a master welder, but I was good enough to do that."

J.R. also was interested in music, but he hadn't thought about earning a living at it until Joe Wilson, a friend from Paxon High School, approached him in 1965. Joe, who played in a band called the Classics (prior to the Classics IV), asked J.R. if he would like to join the group. "It was like twice the money I was making as an apprentice welder," said J.R., who quit his job at the steel plant. "The Classics played R&B, and they had an organ and some horns. When I got in the band and we started going on the road, the booking agent said, 'You guys should get some original material.' So Joe and I started trying to write some songs. Roy Orbison was on the radio a lot. He was one of the first singer-songwriters, and I was really interested in songwriting and trying to learn how to do it."

While J.R.'s mother was a bit skeptical about his making a career of music, she supported her son. "To tell you the truth, it was hard for me to imagine making a living playing music, but that's what we were trying to do. I guess we did all right at it. In the early days we had just a couple of cars to travel in. We'd put all our instruments in the back of the car and drive to Louisiana, or somewhere, for two weeks. When that was over, we hoped we had something else lined up."

The Classics had some recurring gigs in a couple of clubs in Jacksonville, but when members of the band decided they wanted to go on the road, they learned pretty quickly that a group of five or six people couldn't make enough to survive. "One of the saxophone players got married, or drafted, I can't remember which, so we decided four of us would try to be just a vocal band. Dennis Yost, who played drums, was the lead singer, and we all liked the Four Seasons, the Beach Boys, and the Four Preps, and we learned some of their songs. We were able to work and make a living at it. About that time, we changed the name from the Classics to the Classics IV."

Consisting of lead guitarist J.R. Cobb, keyboard player Joe Wilson, bass and rhythm guitar player Wally Eaton, and lead singer and drummer Dennis Yost, the Classics IV moved to Atlanta in 1966, after promoters Paul Cochran and Buddy Buie became the booking and management team for the band. Buie, in turn, introduced the Classics IV to recording entrepreneur Bill Lowery, who had a publishing business and recording studio in Atlanta. "We had written a couple of songs and we showed them to Bill Lowery, who was kind of a mentor for the songwriters that worked around his offices. We would write stuff and take it in to him and he'd tell us if he thought it was any good and how we could improve it. Some of the stuff he told us was really valuable," said Cobb. "Joe South was working around the studio at the time, and he was going to produce a record on us. He produced our song 'Pollyanna,' which was in four-part harmony, kind of like the Four Seasons. It was on Capitol Records and it did a little bit locally, but never got any widespread airplay. The studio was called Master Sound, and it was in an old Atlanta schoolhouse that Bill had taken over for his offices. There was a booking agency in one part, and a studio up front. I think the studio used to be the school's auditorium."

In order to concentrate on songwriting with Buddy Buie, J.R. had left the Classics IV in the autumn of 1967, before their first hit, "Spooky," on Imperial Records started climbing the charts. "I got married in 1967, and it just wouldn't work for her to go on the road with me. So I wanted to be around home more and, to be honest, performing was a thing I did as an outlet for the songs that we wrote. The group needed a vehicle for the songs, and going on the road was a natural progression. I think a lot of groups were like that at that time," J.R. said.

But after "Spooky" was released in late 1967, the Classics IV asked J.R. to come back and tour for a year to promote the record. And when "Spooky" became a hit, Imperial Records asked Cobb and Buie to write another song like "Spooky." J.R. recalled, "Buddy and I went to Callaway Gardens [a resort in the Appalachian foothills in Pine Mountain, Georgia], rented a room there and stayed four or five days and tried to come up with something that was like 'Spooky' but not exactly like it. That's when we came up with 'Stormy.' At the time Callaway Gardens was like a resort with a golf course. It was just getting started and it had a lot of gardens and flowers. It wasn't really established back then like it is now."

The hotel at which the Classics IV performed at a show in 1966 required the band members to wear tuxedos. They were, from left, lead guitarist J.R. Cobb, lead singer and drummer Dennis Yost, bass player Wally Eaton, and keyboard player, guitarist, and trumpet player Joe Wilson (photo courtesy of J.R. Cobb).

49

In early 1968, J.R. and singer-songwriter Ray Whitley co-wrote "Be Young, Be Foolish, Be Happy," which charted on the *Billboard* Hot 100 for the Tams. Both Whitley and the Tams were part of Bill Lowery's stable of talent. Whitley also had written the Tams' late 1963 top-10 hit "What Kind Of Fool (Do You Think I Am)." Joe South produced the recording of "Be Young, Be Foolish, Be Happy" in Bill Lowery's studio. J.R. described the process he had for songwriting back then. "We'd get together at somebody's house, or in the studio and say, 'Here's what I've got.' I might have had a title and a couple of lines, and maybe a guy would add some lines to it, and it would grow from there."

J.R., Buddy Buie, and Ronnie Hammond conceived Atlanta Rhythm Section's huge hit "Do It Or Die" in 1979 much the same way. "We were sitting in the studio late at night trying to come up with something. Ronnie Hammond had a couple of lines, and we just added to them. I don't know where the inspiration for songs comes from. Sometimes it's from your experiences, and sometimes it's just complete fiction that you make up. I think when you're trying to be a songwriter, just about everything that happens to you, everybody you meet, or every situation you're in – somewhere in the back of your mind, you're thinking, 'How can I make this into a song? What's musical about this?'"

For "Traces," session musician Emory Gordy Jr., who primarily was a bassist but also played keyboards, started off with a melody for the beginning of the song. Cobb explained, "Once again, we were all sitting around trying to come up with something, and Emory played a few bars of a melody, and Buddy had the idea for the lyrics. I might have written a verse or two on it. It was a collaboration, but Emory Gordy had the beginning of it."

J.R. told us the biggest thrill and career boost for him was the first time he heard "Spooky" on the radio. "That's when I found out I could be successful at songwriting, and later on I found out you can make money at it," he said. "I had gone back with the Classics IV, and we were on the road playing clubs and stuff. We weren't playing concerts yet. We were riding along in the car up north to a gig, and we heard 'Spooky,' and thought, 'Great!' Somebody changed the radio station, and it was on the other radio station, too. That's when it struck us that it could actually be a hit song. When I first started writing songs, we really concentrated on songs that the radio would play and people would like. We weren't too concerned with art, although we didn't want to write crap. Back then, it was pretty restrictive. It was unusual for a record to be three or more minutes long. There were some exceptions. We had to be economical and say what we wanted to say quickly."

As a session musician in the studio, J.R. played for B.J. Thomas, Billy Joe Royal and on a couple of albums with Roy Orbison. "Anybody who came in and needed a band, that's what we did. We even made a couple of commercials, including a Dr. Pepper commercial and some local stuff. Primarily, I'd play rhythm and Barry Bailey played lead, but once in awhile, I'd play lead."

During performances, J.R. had a collection of guitars on stage – each of which was tuned differently or set up for slide. "I had an Ovation acoustic I used on some stuff, but mostly I started off with a Fender Telecaster. I did have a couple of Les Pauls, and I used one for slide and another for drop-D tuning, but primarily my main guitar was a Stratocaster," he said. "Barry [Bailey] is a Marshall and Les Paul player, and he played most of the leads. I was looking for a sound that wasn't real close to his, so that's why I chose the guitars I played." J.R. used one amplifier on stage, starting out with an Ampeg until the band received an endorsement from Peavey. He preferred to use a Fender amp in the studio but said it wasn't loud enough for the stage.

In 1987, J.R. left ARS to focus more on songwriting. "I was in Memphis working with Chips Moman, who had a publishing company and recording studio. "When I first went to work for Chips, he was in Nashville and then after about five months he moved to Memphis and built another studio. When I worked in Memphis, I would go home for the weekends, but I was commuting back and forth. After about a year and a half, Chips sold his publishing company, and they didn't need me, so I moved back to Atlanta."

During that time, Cobb performed as a session musician on recordings by Bobby Womack, Ringo Starr, and Carl Perkins. "We finished the Ringo album and it had some really good songs on it, but Chips and Ringo had some sort of disagreement or a record company got involved, and it was never released. I thought it was good, but Ringo said he didn't think it was his best work. Thank God the politics of things like that were out of my hands."

Chips also did a session at the old Sun Studios with Carl Perkins, Johnny Cash, Roy Orbison, and Jerry Lee Lewis. "It was for an album called *Class of '55 – Memphis Rock & Roll Homecoming,* and I got to play on that. A lot of local acts came to the Memphis studio, and my primary job was to listen to songs that people sent in to see if I thought anything was good enough to bring to Chips' attention," said J.R. "That was the main thing I did, but I played on several sessions, too. I listened to probably 25, 30, or 40 songs a day. I worked for Chips in that capacity for about a year and a half. I left after he sold the publishing company to Warner Bros."

J.R. also performed on the recording session for another Chips Moman project. "I was home for probably four or five months, still writing with Buddy Buie, and Chips called me one day and asked if I'd like to come up and play on a session for an album with Johnny Cash, Waylon Jennings, Willie Nelson, and Kris Kristofferson, and I said, 'Yeah. I'd love to.' So I went up and did it in his Nashville studio. Jimmy Webb wrote the title track 'Highwayman.' Glen Campbell came and showed us the song because he and Jimmy Webb were friends." Webb had written a lot of Glen Campbell's hits. Released as a single in May 1985, the song "Highwayman" hit No. 1 on the country chart and inspired the quartet of country superstars to begin calling themselves the Highwaymen. Sales of the single drove the *Highwayman* album to No. 1 on the country LPs chart, and it made a respectable showing on the general albums chart as well.

Cobb went on the road in 1990 with the Highwaymen. "We played two or three United States tours, and we worked overseas quite a bit, maybe four or five times. We would be gone for a month or six weeks. It was one of the best jobs I've ever had. I knew all of the guys who were playing in the band, because most of them I had recorded with. It was a lot of the Memphis musicians, and we all got along great. All we had to do was show up, smile, and play the chart, or the chord sheet, and we weren't involved in any of the politics. It was like a vacation, and I loved it."

After the Highwaymen, Cobb resumed his focus on songwriting with Buie. They would get together at Buie's picturesque property in Eufaula, Alabama, and spend quality time writing and composing songs. One of the songs they wrote was "Rock Bottom," which peaked at No. 2 for Wynonna Judd in 1994. "When we wrote that song, we were thinking of it for the Atlanta Rhythm Section. I wasn't in the group any more, but they were a natural outlet for the songs we wrote. They were planning to do another session. But we played the song and tried to get a record deal for Atlanta Rhythm Section with that song and some other songs. [MCA Nashville producer and president] Tony Brown said he couldn't do a deal with the band, but he liked the song and wanted to cut it on one of his other artists. We didn't know who at the time, but he played it for Wynonna and she liked it. They changed the feel of it around some, but it was basically how we wrote it. We had no idea she was going to do it," J.R. said.

For three years beginning in 1999, Cobb and Buie were under exclusive contract as writers with Sony Music. "We were with Bill Lowery Music and several other subsidiaries under that for almost our whole career. Sony came along and offered Bill a whole lot of money for his publishing company, and he was about ready to retire, so he sold that publishing company and along with the deal was to sign me and Buddy for three years. We were supposed to turn in so many songs a month, good, bad, or indifferent. For the most part we met our quota, but I had never written under that kind of situation, and it's hard because you can't afford to wait for inspiration, you've got to sit down and write, and make yourself do it. I'm glad I did it, but it's not my favorite way to write," said J.R.

"There are two schools of thought," he continued. "If you have a deadline and you have to come up with a song, you'll come up with a lot more songs and your percentages will go up, and there's something to be said for that. The other school of thought is that you write a lot of stuff because you want to meet your deadline, and it may not be exactly what you want to say and you probably need some time to think it over and mull it around in your mind. I've had songs that went on for two or three years, we couldn't get it right, and then one day we'd see how it should be and finish it up. You don't have that luxury when you're writing under a deadline."

Cobb is particularly proud of "Mr. Midnight," which he wrote with Buie and Tommy Douglas. That song is included on Garth Brooks' *Scarecrow* album, produced in 2001. By 2006 the album was designated "5-time multi-platinum" by the Recording Industry Association of America (RIAA), selling more than 5 million copies in the United States. "We were

at Sony in Nashville one day, and we were told that Garth Brooks wanted us to come over to his studio to talk to us about a song we wrote," recalled J.R. "So we went over and Garth said, 'I like your song ["Mr. Midnight"], but I'd like to change a couple of lines in it. Would you let me do that?' Of course, we almost fell down saying, 'Yeah!' We were so happy to have him do one of our songs because Garth sells a lot of records. He couldn't have been a nicer person. He was there at the studio with maybe one other person, but he's just like a regular guy."

J.R. Cobb performing with ARS in the 1970s (photo courtesy of Gloria Buie).

J.R. first met his wife, Bertha "Bert" Ann Absher, when he was

53

performing with the Classics IV at the now-defunct Whisk à Go-Go in Atlanta, Georgia, in 1965. At the time, that franchise of Hollywood's famous Whisky à Go-Go had go-go dancers in a cage, and Bert was one of them. A few months later, Bert moved to Daytona to work at another club, and J.R. happened to be performing in Daytona at the Plaza Hotel. As fate would have it, they met again and began dating, married in 1967, and settled in Covington, Georgia, about 35 miles east of Atlanta. They have one son, Justin, who was born in 1973, and he has two boys of his own – the oldest is John, and the youngest, Michael.

"My son works for Sprint. He helps them install equipment, and he goes around to new stores and helps them get started. John started college this year at Valdosta State University, and Michael is in high school," J.R. told us in 2014. "I gave both boys guitars and showed them a couple of things, but music really hasn't caught on with them. John took his guitar with him to college, so I guess he's still interested. Michael was at our house a year or so ago, and he was looking at some pictures on the wall, and I was in one of them. I looked a lot different because I had long hair, and he asked his mom, 'Who is that?' When she told him it was me, he kinda did a double take."

Those days that the photo captured were enjoyable, but being a member of the Atlanta Rhythm Section wasn't all fun and games. And composing good songs involves far more than inspiration; it involves a lot of concentration. "Even though I enjoy it, composing is demanding because nothing is more intimidating than a blank sheet of paper. When the Atlanta Rhythm Section was really hot, it was a lot of work," J.R. told us. "The hour or two you spend on stage is a lot of fun, but the other 22 or 23 hours, not so much fun. I had a wife and a kid, and I hated being away from them. They understood and were okay with it, but I wasn't okay with it sometimes. I realized when your kids grow up and you lose a year or two, you don't ever get it back."

J.R. and Bert now live outside of Mansfield, Georgia, about 45 miles southeast of Atlanta, and Justin and his family live about 40 miles away in Dacula, Georgia. J.R. explained, "When Justin was a youngster, we were looking for a place in 1974 or 1975 that was out in the country. We lived in Covington, Georgia, at the time. We wanted a place with a little more land and a pond on it to go fishing, and I think it's a better place to raise a child. We enjoy it out here. We've been here since 1980. I've got a pond and it's got a lot of fish in it, but you know how it is, you live on a lake, you stop fishing. It seems like something takes up my time and I don't spend as much time at it, but I do go occasionally."

Besides being involved in the Presbyterian church in Mansfield, J.R. enjoys riding his Harley-Davidson motorcycle. The couple has three dogs, and J.R. said, "We had to make a deal around here that we can't accept any more dogs. I also keep chickens, and I went through a phase when I first moved out here – I had some Angus cattle, we had quarter horses, but I got over that, and I'm kinda glad I did. It was a lot of work and they had become pets more than anything else."

Just as J.R.'s marriage to Bert changed his life and appeared guided by destiny, so was his career in music ordained by Joe Wilson's invitation for him to join the Classics in 1965. "I probably otherwise would have stayed with Florida Steel and became a foreman, worked 20 more years, and got my gold watch. But once I got into music and decided that's what I want to do, I didn't have any other interests," J.R. said.

He reflects on some of his finest moments, including writing a hit song, his marriage to Bert, having a son, and becoming a grandfather. "I regret the times I was gone while my son was growing up. But because of my wife's diligence, he turned out to be a fine young man. Maybe I would have messed that up, I don't know. I've been married for almost 50 years now. A lot of people ask me how I stayed married for so long. I tell them that it might have been because I was gone for so long," he laughed.

Individuals who influenced his life include Bill Lowery, whom he described as an old-school publisher. "He would actually try to help writers along. He would listen to our stuff and give us suggestions about how he thought it could be better and to 'go back and try this again, this is a good idea, but you didn't quite get it.' Chips Moman was that way, too. Chips is a great producer and he doesn't have any musical training but he could hear a song or an artist and think of putting those two things together."

Another person who made a difference in Cobb's life was Silas M. Bishop, the superintendent of the Baptist Home For Children, where J.R. lived for seven years. "He was a rather stern man, but he was a kind man, too. I was scared to death of him sometimes, but he did a lot for me when I was growing up. I didn't like it so much at the time."

J.R. said that songs composed with the most inner reflection have the strongest personal meaning for him. "The ballads, like 'Traces,' have an emotional connection with me. I think it would be hard to write songs like that if you didn't have the connection," he said. "You can sit around and write an up-tempo song, and it's not really hard, but you have to draw on your experiences a bit to write the other kind of music."

Epilogue: Dean Daughtry

Keyboard player and composer

Among all the members of the Atlanta Rhythm Section, the one constant has been the presence of keyboard player and composer Dean Daughtry. Throughout all the years, Dean is the only musician who never left the group. Dean, who began as a member of Roy Orbison's Candymen and was in the Classics IV before joining ARS, prophetically was voted "most likely to succeed" by his high school graduating class. Daughtry achieved that accolade over and over again. But he nearly shunned music for a different vocational path. "During career day at the high school, I talked to a representative from the Columbia School of Broadcasting. I was thinking about becoming a deejay," Dean said. "I was interested in music, and radio would have allowed me to be involved in music, but in a different way. I'm glad I wound up being a musician and did what I have done."

William Dean Daughtry was born September 8, 1946, to William E.C. Daughtry and Alean Daughtry, née Davis, in Samson, a southern Alabama town of about 2,200 people. "I always went by Dean because

Dean Daughtry thrilled Texas fans with his virtuoso keyboard playing April 11, 2015, at the Main Street Fort Worth Arts Festival (photo by Courtni Meadows).

my dad was Bill or William. My dad was a big baseball fan, so he named me after Dizzy Dean [a celebrated Major League pitcher in the 1930s and '40s]." Daughtry's parents divorced before he was a year old, and he and his mom lived with her parents, James Oscar William Spears, and Gypsy Netty Spears. His grandmother had 14 children.

Dean recalls that his introduction to music came by listening with his mother to Montgomery, Alabama, radio station WBAM. "The station was 50,000 watts, and she listened to Hank Williams Sr. and the country music people of the early 1950s. I was raised on Hank Williams. He's the greatest writer and best singer in the world. As I got older, I was listening to Ray Charles and Jerry Lee Lewis. Another influence was Dave Brubeck and his 'Take Five' and 'Blue Rondo à La Turk.' I learned that when I was in the Army with a guitar player."

When Dean was in first grade, Alean enrolled him in piano lessons with a private instructor. She had attended a church revival and was impressed by a man playing piano there. "My mother said to me, 'I thought that was the prettiest thing I've ever seen in my life – a man playing a piano.' She just wanted me to play in church, which I did quite a bit." Alean sang in the choir. "She sang real loud. I guess I got my loud voice from her. It didn't always sound good when she sang, but she was enthusiastic and loud. I just wanted to crawl under the bench in church when she sang," laughed Dean.

Dean lived in Samson until he was about 12 years old, and then with his mother moved to a few other small towns within about a 20-mile radius, including Opp, Alabama. "My mother worked for the cotton mill, and we lived in mill housing. Some of the houses didn't even have hot water heaters. We had to put water on the stove to heat it up to take a bath. Some of the houses didn't have bathrooms. In Opp we had an indoor bathroom, but in Samson, we had an outhouse." His mom also worked at the shirt factory in Florala, Alabama.

Young Dean took piano lessons beginning in first grade and stayed with it throughout high school. When he was about 13 years of age, he started performing with bands in small clubs. "I played all kinds of places when I was still in school. I'd go to school sometimes and fall asleep in class. The teacher would say, 'Just leave him alone, he was up late.' My mother always went to the bars with me because I was underage. The Bungalow is the name of one of the bands I put together, and sometimes I played with other local musicians in Dothan, and other places." He also performed on a WTVY channel 9 TV show in Dothan called *The Used Car Supermarket Jamboree* while still in high school. "I bought a beautiful car from them. I wish I had that car now. It was a 1955 fire gold two-door Pontiac Chieftain.

The Used Car Supermarket was the main sponsor of the program – it was their show."

The family ultimately settled near Kinston, Alabama, the population of which was little more than 300. Dean and his family lived on a farm outside of town. "The neighbors were a mile or two away. We farmed crops, we had hogs, and we had one cow that my grandma milked. I picked cotton, but I never did get 100 pounds a day. You would only get $30 for 100 pounds of cotton, but I was just doing it for a little bit of change," Dean said. "My grandpa worked the farm in halves. He would have somebody farm it for him. He would take half the profits and the guy that farmed it would take half. It was fun being in the country like that. But I sure learned how to play the piano so I could get out of it," he said with a chuckle.

The piano Dean used when he was first learning how to play was his family's upright, which was tuned a step lower than standard tuning because, he said, "the strings were so old they couldn't tighten them. That made it hard to learn perfect pitch. I don't have perfect pitch, but I can guess around it pretty much. I think I can say that's what happened to my perfect pitch, because it was an instrument that was a whole step below standard, but I still loved it and learned how to play it."

The full-sized piano traveled to gigs with him. "I've had a lot of people gripe at me because of my keyboards," he laughed. "When I was in high school, my friends and I would take the piano from the house and deliver it to wherever I was playing, and that thing was heavy! It took about five or six of us to move it. One night I played for the Samson square dance, and a guy named 'Pappy' Neal McCormick was playing steel guitar. He was one of the early steel guitar players with Hank Williams Sr. He didn't seem to be that impressed with me, though. He was much older, and probably thought this young whippersnapper thinks he can do something."

Neal McCormick, who was born in 1909, was an early pioneer of country music and an innovator in the development of the steel guitar. He was the first musician to play an electrified guitar on 650 AM WSM radio in Nashville. McCormick also was known for inventing his patented revolving steel guitar with four necks that could be tuned to different keys. While Neal and his band, the Hawaiian Troubadours, were performing in Pensacola, Florida, 16-year-old Hank Williams seeking his first regular job asked Pappy if he could join the band. Williams worked with McCormick for a few years before becoming a major star, but the two remained friends until Williams' death at age 29 on January 1, 1953. McCormick ultimately owned several recording studios and played on recording sessions with many of the early greats of country music.

The February 17, 1963, edition of the *Anniston Star* newspaper ran an article about young Daughtry, a high school student in FFA performing for a series of business meetings. Dean recalls, "I joined FFA because I needed it for credits to graduate. I was in FFA band, and we entered a contest for WSFA, channel 12 in Montgomery, Alabama. It was called *Search For Talent*. A friend and I did this Paul and Paula song. The TV station called and said we won. They wanted me on the TV show to play the song 'Alley Cat,' but they didn't want her. I had a person who played stand-up bass, who really couldn't play it, but I guess I made up for the other people."

While still attending high school in 1963, Daughtry enlisted in the military at the age of 17. He served for eight years as a medic – six years with the Army National Guard in Enterprise, Alabama, and two years on inactive reserve, achieving the rank of Specialist 5. "I joined the National Guard with Roger Johnson, who was the roadie for the Candymen. It was kind of scary because Vietnam was starting. We were on alert a few times, but never got called. I had to go to summer camps. The last one was when I was playing with the Candymen. When I got off duty, I'd go play and get back at 4 a.m. Then we guardsmen had to get up about 4:30 a.m. I was young, so I could take it. What the medic did at summer camps was have the beer. Nobody ever got hurt. I once stopped bleeding for a cook who stabbed his finger. But we did have the beer at the first aid station."

Dean received his training to become an Army medic at the Medical Education and Training Campus at Fort Sam Houston in San Antonio, Texas. "That's where Brooke Army Medical Center is located, which is the one they use for war injuries. I trained at Brooke General Hospital. I had an uncle and aunt there who owned a store, and my cousins that I've known all my life. I was fortunate to be sent there. My duty went all the way to 1972. They would let me attend meetings when I was off the road. It was actually harder than going to the regular meetings – they work you to death – but I got through it with an honorable discharge. My dad would not have accepted any less. We were put on alert quite a few times, so it was a little edgy. I have these dreams, or nightmares, that I re-up and have to go to Vietnam. I had an uncle in the Air Force who went to Vietnam, and my wife's father was a lieutenant colonel in the Army, who retired here from Redstone Arsenal [in Huntsville, Alabama], and he was going to be sent to Vietnam if he made general. His wife said, 'No. You are not going to Vietnam. You're not going to be a general.' She was a little bitty woman, about 90 pounds. My father-in-law was about my size, about 250."

During his senior year in high school, Dean also was a member of a five-man band called the Kidnappers. "We played in Bossier City, Louisiana, and in Panama City, Florida, a lot, too. A group I formed that played at the Oasis Club in Dothan, Alabama, was called the Exotic Five Wonders, which was the same group of people as the Kidnappers. I was on my jazz kick then, but we played pop music. We were good. I wouldn't have played with them if they hadn't been good," Dean said. "My first real recording session was a song demo in Bossier City, Louisiana. The person I was doing the recording session with was Percy Mayfield, who wrote 'Hit The Road Jack.' The person who got me the gig in 1964 was Mickey Newbury" [who later was inducted into the Nashville Songwriters Hall of Fame].

As Dean graduated from high school with his 38 classmates in 1964, he received a scholarship to attend Huntingdon College in Montgomery, Alabama. His music teacher, Mrs. Collins from Samson, Alabama, was instrumental in getting him the scholarship. He declined it, however, because the Candymen pulled him in a different educational direction. "I said that I could learn more from going on tour with Roy. Plus, I could make money," Dean said. "My mom loved Roy Orbison and thought it would be a great thing, going on the road with him. Roy influenced all of us, as far as our writing goes. It was the greatest thing in the world being on stage with him. The drummer in that FFA band was our first road manager in the Candymen."

Daughtry joined the Candymen, Roy Orbison's backup band, when "Little" Bobby Peterson was drafted for military service. He explained, "John Rainey Adkins [of the Candymen] was in Dothan, Alabama, and I was playing at the local juke joint, the Oasis Club, there. He would come out and see the Kidnappers, or maybe it was the Exotic Five, and he liked the way I played, and Buddy Buie saw me and they asked me to join. Little Bobby

In 1964, when Dean Daughtry (at far left) was a high school senior, he performed with the Kidnappers at the Amvets Club in Andalusia, Alabama. That's Claude Bell on bass, Windell Bell playing guitar, and Jerry Stinson on drums (photo courtesy of Dean Daughtry).

Dean Daughtry loosened up for a Kidnappers gig in Panama City, Florida (photo courtesy of Dean Daughtry).

taught me all the songs the Candymen played. I learned them all in one day and played them exactly, note for note, like Bobby, and it freaked them out. I was so anxious to learn because the Candymen were my favorite group. They were incredible. You don't find a group as good as the Candymen – ever. It was such a great honor to play with them."

The band was scheduled to go on tour with Roy Orbison to New Zealand and Australia in 1965. Dean had to get a passport for the tour, so his father helped him get one where he was stationed, at Fort Gordon, near Augusta, Georgia. Dean's father, who served in World War II and the Korean War, spent 26 years in the Army before retiring as a sergeant major in 1966. "It was quite a thrill to tour with Roy. We had our own personal jet. So I started out getting spoiled," he said. "My dad retired right after that, and I saw him very seldom."

Daughtry found Roy Orbison to be "the nicest, kindest, most gentle person you would ever meet." He said, "Roy put me right at ease. He called me 'Olly Oxen Free.' We were on a bus when we were first going to Canada. The Candymen were doing their tour because we had an album out, and then Roy met up with us in Nashville, and we played poker. I didn't play with them because I didn't have enough money to play with Roy. But Buddy was on that particular tour, and Paul Cochran, who was Buddy's partner, and Robert Nix – they played poker. Roy was definitely an easy person to be around."

Daughtry recalls a trip to England with Roy Orbison and the Candymen. "We met up with Graham Nash from the Hollies, and he produced four cuts on the Candymen. We went to Abbey Road and guess whose equipment we used? The Beatles. Graham called 'em up and they said 'we're not working tonight. Y'all go ahead and you can use all of our stuff.' Paul McCartney had three Höfner basses, they had all kind of Vox amps, and I played the Mellotron that was used on 'Strawberry Fields.' Graham is a great person, and he loved the Candymen.

"We didn't have any trouble using the Beatles' equipment because we were Roy's backup group. And we saw John Lennon and Paul McCartney at a club in London. The Candymen were all there one night at a place called the Bag O' Nails, and Lennon and McCartney came in and sat at a table. You talk about somebody who looks like a star. Paul McCartney shined. We all said hello to him. I got a picture of me and Roy together, and we're both smoking a cigarette. That looks weird nowadays. We ate Indian food at Piccadilly Circus in London. I loved it. It was fun. I wish I could go back to those days."

Dean's father remarried and had a son and daughter. "My half sister, Teresa McPeters, lives in Augusta, Georgia, and she's been married as many times as I have. My mother has had a few, too. I guess it's in my blood," he laughed. "My brother's name was David Wayne Daughtry. He died at 54." David was married to country music singer Terri Gibbs (Teresa Fay Gibbs), who was born blind. She recorded the crossover hit 'Somebody's Knockin'' that peaked at No. 6 on the country chart and No. 13 on the *Billboard* Hot 100 in 1981. "They've got a son who has a band and he is very talented. He's about 6-foot-5, and he takes after his mother. He plays piano, guitar, and writes and sings. I keep in touch with him through Facebook, because they live 380 miles from me. I talk to my sister every week or two on the phone. She has two children."

Daughtry remained with the Candymen until joining the Classics IV in 1968, at Buddy Buie's request. "It was really fun to tour with a group with three big hits: 'Spooky,' 'Stormy,' and 'Traces.' We were treated like stars. We played the Cow Palace in San Francisco, we did the *Tonight Show* twice with Johnny Carson, we did the *Joey Bishop Show,* two or three *Mike Douglas* shows, and the *Phil Donahue Show.* John Denver was on *Phil Donahue,* and I got to meet him, and I also got to meet Eartha Kitt. The Classics IV played some shows with the Temptations, and one of the best shows we did was with Sly and the Family Stone. You talk about a band that rocks. They were incredible!"

Performing for commercial jingles enabled Daughtry and the other musicians to pick up a few extra bucks. "I remember doing the Atlanta Braves theme, and the Coca-Cola theme that Billy Joe Royal sang. And, of course, the Atlanta Rhythm Section did a Dr. Pepper spot. I did one for Old Hickory House Barbecue. I was living in the studio, and the producer came in and said, 'Do you want to make $40?' Yeah, sure. So I played it and sang it: 'Put some South in your mouth at the Old Hickory House.'"

Daughtry said he began dabbling around with writing songs in high school and ended up as musical co-writer on numerous songs for the Classics IV and hits for the Atlanta Rhythm Section with Buddy Buie, J.R.

Cobb, and Robert Nix. He recalls the inspiration behind three of the songs he co-wrote:

"So In To You" – "The best I can remember is that Robert Nix and I were just kinda foolin' around. I was playing this and that on the piano, and then Buddy came in with lyrics, and he and Robert put 'em together, but Buddy always took 'em back home and perfected 'em." He regards "So In To You" as an important milestone. "I remember when I heard WLS radio in Chicago play it. They played only about 20 songs in rotation. They didn't play anything unless it was a hit."

"Dog Days" – "I wrote the music by myself. I was in the studio at 8 o'clock in the morning, and I was playing the grand piano there working on 'Dog Days,' and the first chair violinist came in because they were going to do a session – I think it was a B.J. Thomas session – and he started jamming with me. I had it on cassette, and it took about two or three years to get Buddy to finally came up with 'Dog Days' lyrics, but I had written the music a couple of years earlier."

"I'm Not Gonna Let It Bother Me Tonight" – "Buddy usually took care of the business, and he was going through all of the business hassles, and he said, 'I'm not gonna let it bother me tonight. I'm gonna have a drink' – that sort of thing. Elton John influenced the music for me a little bit on that one."

Dean also contributed to arrangements for numerous songs the band recorded; they annotated their chord charts with arrangement cues. He has owned several different keyboards, for the various sounds he was trying to achieve. For example, he played a Wurlitzer electric piano on the recording of "So In To You," and on his tour with Roy Orbison and the Candymen, he played a more portable Farfisa. "Roy bought the Farfisa; I never gave it back to him. He never asked for it back. And Barry Bailey still has the amps that Roy bought for him. I used to do the piano parts and the string parts on the Farfisa at the same time. When the Atlanta Rhythm Section came around, I had about four keyboards on stage. I had a Fender Rhodes suitcase Rhodes [piano], which was a great instrument. I was endorsed by Fender Rhodes. And I had a [Yamaha] CP-70, which is an electric grand. Then I had a Wurlitzer. Then I had a [Hohner] D6 Clavinet. I used all of them, too. That CP-70 electric grand weighed 300 pounds. I got cursed many times by the road crew."

Some of the concert appearances that stand out most in Dean's mind include a riot in Harrisburg, Pennsylvania, and the huge Texxas World Music Festival (nicknamed the Texxas Jam) at the Cotton Bowl stadium in Dallas on July 1, 1978. "Head East was opening the show for us in

Harrisburg. They set their stuff up, and once they got it up it started raining. So we didn't set ours up, and they called the concert. Well, the people did not like that. There were thousands of them there, and they chased us all the way back to the hotel. I thought they were going to kill us. So we got out of town in a hurry," said Dean.

The lineup for the July 1, 1978, Texxas Jam included Walter Egan, Van Halen, Eddie Money, Head East, Journey, Heart, Aerosmith, Mahogany Rush, Ted Nugent, and ARS. "The picture inside the cover of the *Champagne Jam* album is a picture of the stadium at Texxas Jam. We got up on stage, and Paul Goddard, who weighed about 350 pounds at the time, put on a cowboy hat. And it was 126 degrees on the stage, and he made it through the show and I made it, everybody made it. But when Ted Nugent, 'Mr. Health Nut' and 'Mr. Hunter,' no drugs, no drinking or anything got up there, he fainted on stage. And us in not real good shape made it, and he didn't. I think Ted Nugent fainting might have been about the best thing."

Also in 1978, the ARS performance at the White House for the birthday of President Jimmy Carter's son Chip left a memorable impression on Daughtry. "We had the bus, and our bus driver had left and gone somewhere, and the bus was locked, and there were just thousands of congresspeople's young-uns, and to try to get to the bathroom there on the south lawn part of the White House there was near impossible. So Ronnie Hammond decides, 'well, I've got to go to the bathroom,' so he pees on the White House lawn. I wonder if that grass has grown back," he laughed. "We went up to the living quarters where Chip lived, and all we could drink there was beer and wine, and I drank a *lot* of beer. The Secret Service agents were real nice. We had met Jimmy before because we did a fund-raising gig for his presidential run." Dean met First Lady Rosalynn Carter also. "I don't remember shakin' her hand or anything, but it mighta been after those beers. We had a good time. They made us feel right at home."

Following the Atlanta Rhythm Section's hit-making days, Dean worked with Timothy Collins "Tim" Wilson, a comedian, songwriter, and country music artist, whose act combined stand-up comedy and original songs. Wilson recorded on the Southern Tracks label with Bill Lowery as publisher and Dean Daughtry as producer. "I produced five Tim Wilson albums for the Southern Tracks label," Dean said. Wilson later recorded extensively with the Muscle Shoals Rhythm Section and the Atlanta Rhythm Section. He died of a heart attack on February 26, 2014, at the age of 52. "Tim led a stressful life. He traveled constantly. He could buy a brand-new car and have it worn out in a year, bless his heart. He was a good guy. I'd known him since he was 18 years old. I was with ARS and we were playing with

38 Special in Columbus, Georgia, when I met Tim. He was in high school and he was doing an interview with us, and he interviewed me, and we were friends from then on. I let him borrow my car one time to go out on a date. I had a brand-new Eldorado at the time." Daughtry also played on a Tim Wilson album on which Keith Urban played guitar. "Keith Urban had just signed with Capitol, and Tim was on Capitol."

Dean continues to compose new music through his own publishing company, called So Into You Music, which Tim Wilson named for him. "I've been doing a lot of composing for the past two or three years," Daughtry told us in 2014. "Just about every day, I sit at the piano and work on things, and I've got quite a few tunes basically finished."

Dean and his first wife, Dianne, were married in 1967. They had two sons together – Scott and Chad. "I met Dianne when I just finished high school. She was a year younger than me. She came to the Oasis Club where I was playing with the Kidnappers," Dean said. The couple divorced in 1972, and Dianne died in 2001. Scott became a fireman paramedic, and Chad is a supervisor at a large dairy.

Dean married his second wife, Roxie, in 1973. They remained together until '79, when they legally separated. Their divorce was final in 1982. He then wed Jacque Perry, a marriage that lasted for 11 years. "We should have split up a lot sooner. Times were rough and I just really couldn't afford to get a divorce."

The love of his life is Donna Watson, to whom he has been married since 1997. "She is the one I should have been married to all along. I met her in 1969, but I was on the road at least 150 or 200 days a year, and it would have never worked out. She was going to Bauder College in Atlanta, which specialized in programs in modeling and fashion merchandising. I was with the Classics IV at the time, and a roadie just happened to go by their dormitory, and he came back with a van full of girls. They were all beautiful. They were all models. That's what they were learning. Then I picked her out immediately when I met her, and we kinda saw each other for a while until she moved back to Huntsville, Alabama. We got back together in 1973 just temporarily, after Dianne, my first wife and I, divorced. Donna's grandparents lived in Hampton, Georgia, which is right outside of Atlanta. She'd go visit them, and then she'd come by to see me."

Dean and Donna again lost contact and married other people. Then in September 1993, as ARS was about to get on stage at the Big Spring Jam Music Festival in Huntsville, where Donna lived, Dean spotted her in the crowd. Donna had recently divorced and Dean was separated from his wife. Dean and Donna began spending time together, and friendship blossomed

65

into romance. "It took us a long time – 28 years – but on August 8, 1997, as soon as my divorce from Jacque was final, Donna and I were married," Dean said.

Dean moved to Huntsville after he and Donna were married, because of all of her family ties there and because of her job there in employee benefits for a missile systems engineering defense contractor. "Donna's father is a retired lieutenant colonel here at the U.S. Army Redstone Arsenal, and her family has always lived here. Her nieces and nephews and her sister all live here. Her family traveled in her younger days. For instance, they went to Thailand when she was like 12 years old. Her dad was a Third Army adviser and that's where he was stationed, in different places. I love Huntsville better than any place I've ever lived, because it's a moderate-sized city, and it has a low crime rate."

Dean has long enjoyed bowling, his game began to suffer as increasing pain afflicted his shoulder. He had rotator cuff surgery in 1998, but a decade later the shoulder began bothering him again, and the pain became debilitating. In 2013 he underwent orthopedic surgery again. "I had to get a total shoulder replacement because the rotator cuff was completely gone. The doctors said that all those years of playing the piano probably wore it down," Dean said. "They put a spike down my bone in my bicep. It looks like just a big ol' nail. My surgeon was one of the best as far as shoulders go." Dean's bowling strength and endurance are not as good as they previously had been but, of far greater importance to Dean, he was able to resume piano playing, eventually without pain. Dean continues to write music at least three to four hours a day.

"I put songs down on my Clavinova [Yamaha digital piano]. I can put strings and a few other things with it, just enough to get the melodies, and I record them. Donna is very musically inclined, and she listens to the things that I write. Donna is honest about everything. When she says something, I know that it's right."

Thanks to Donna, Dean is now content. "If I had it to do over again, I would not have married anybody until I married Donna." He philosophically observes that patience is a virtue – in careers, in relationships, in life. To that end, Dean points to the ARS song that holds the strongest personal meaning for him: "Dog Days," a slow ballad album track. "I worked on 'Dog Days' for three years before anything was ever done lyrically. Sometimes it takes a long time to get things just like you want 'em."

Epilogue: Paul Goddard

Bass player

June 23, 1945 – April 29, 2014

Paul Goddard was as popular with musicians as he was with his fans. A lead-guitar-turned-bass player, Paul had a distinct style that set him apart. *Rolling Stone* magazine voted Goddard's bass solo on "Another Man's Woman" from the 1979 Atlanta Rhythm Section live album *Are You Ready!* as one of the top five bass solos of all time.

Paul Bennett Goddard Jr., was born June 23, 1945, in Rome, Georgia, to Paul "Buck" Bennett Sr. and Madge Goddard, née Smith. "They called my dad 'Buck' because he was a football hero in his home town of Harriman, Tennessee (near Knoxville). One of his big disappointments was that I couldn't care less about football. I'm not into sports at all," Paul told us in March 2014. "Mom was from a mill town suburb of Rome called Lindale. The whole town was owned by Pepperell Manufacturing Company. Every house looked the same, and the employees got to live there for free.

Paul Goddard joyfully performed with ARS aboard the cruise ship Norwegian Pearl on the Simple Man Cruise to the Bahamas in October 2013 (photo by Courtni Meadows).

My father came to Rome looking for a job, and both of my parents went
to work at what was known as the general store, also owned by Pepperell
Manufacturing." Paul's dad later became an assistant manager in the
electronics department at the K-Mart store in Rome, and his mom was a
teacher at Project Head Start, and a substitute teacher in the Rome school
system. Equidistant from Atlanta and Chattanooga, Rome had a population
of about 30,000 in the 1950s.

Even though Paul's family struggled financially, they lived comfortably.
"My parents rented a very nice house in Rome and paid very little for it
because the woman who owned it was an invalid and wanted us next door
to her. So we were fairly poor people living in a great house," he explained.
"We lived there until my sister left for college. It was very near downtown
Rome, but it had a huge backyard. It was three bedrooms with a full attic
and basement. I loved growing up in Rome, Georgia, because it was one
of the most innocent, sweet places at the time. I wish I could get in a time
machine and go back there. The downtown area was the hangout – all seven
blocks of it. The population of Rome is about 70,000 people now."

By the age of 4, Paul already was enamored with music. Paul's dad loved
classical music, and his mom was very involved with her church, sang with
the choir, and loved religious music, especially Tennessee Ernie Ford's "A
Closer Walk With Thee." When Buck played classical records, young Paul
would sit next to the metal heater stove and whack the vent pipes in time
with the music. Moreover, he memorized the classical pieces he heard. "My
dad bought me a $5 plastic ukulele when I was 4, and two days later, I was
playing along with the radio. In a week and a half or two I was playing
along with classical pieces. My uncle Lanier, who was my mom's brother,
had a lot to do with me being in music. He told my parents that I was a
genius in music and said, 'You need to support him in every way you can,'
so they bought me a wooden ukulele. My uncle was the smartest man I
ever knew, and the sweetest and kindest man I ever knew," Paul said. "He
bought me my first guitar because my family couldn't afford it. He was very
high security in the U.S. Air Force, and was an Air Force fighter pilot in
World War II."

After briefly becoming interested in orchestral music like that of
Mantovani, Paul heard Gene Vincent and his Blue Caps' "Be-Bop-A-Lula,"
and he said his life became nothing but rock and roll. "I have 10,000 45s.
I used to do without lunch to use the money to buy records. My mother
didn't know that. I've still got them, but they're worn out. My whole
thing was sitting with my record player and playing my guitar along with
the records," he said. "The first record I bought was 'Love Is Strange,' by

Mickey and Sylvia. It was the Groove green label, and they changed it over to a label called Vik, which was RCA. Buddy Holly was my idol, Gene Vincent was rockabilly. If it got too country, I didn't like it. I liked Carl Perkins. Johnny Burnette made good middle-of-the-road pop songs for Liberty Records with violins on them."

Paul's attraction to the aural medium of music is likely attributable in part to his congenital visual deficiencies, which went undetected for years. He was born with cataracts, which turned into glaucoma at the age of 12. By then doctors said they couldn't do anything to stop the deterioration, especially in his right eye. "That means I can't judge distance, and I have trouble with stairs that don't have railings, so I could not play sports, and could not do anything that involved catching balls because of the depth perception problem," Paul explained. Since playing sports was out of the question, he joined the chorus in school. "There were nine boys in the chorus and you wouldn't be kidded about anything more than being in the chorus. Two out of the nine boys could carry a tune," he laughed.

He told us that when he was a kid, Madge was overly protective of him, particularly after he lost all vision in that eye. "As a kid I loved my bicycle, but sometimes I'd drive it into a curb. I've been driving a car for years, and I've never had an accident. You learn to compensate for things like that. With glaucoma, the eye fills up with fluid like a balloon and can't drain. My right eye became very huge, very ugly, and very painful, so in 2011 I had it removed, which I should have done 40 years ago."

Paul's first guitar was a Silvertone from Sears. "That guitar was almost impossible to play, but after I went blind in my right eye, my mother and dad said, 'We're going to buy you any guitar you want,' and so they bought me a Fender Stratocaster at age 12. I was the only person in North Georgia who had one." His mother refused to allow him to get a newspaper delivery route, as many of his friends had, so he immersed himself in learning how to play that guitar.

Paul Goddard was one of those gifted musicians who played by ear, and when his parents enrolled him in formal lessons, he immediately clashed with the instructor's rigid methods. "I took one lesson, but the guy kicked me out, saying, 'You're not trying to read the music, you're just playing the song.' He was actually quite angry about it. I said, 'Well, who needs you? If I can play the song without reading the music, then why do I need to learn to read the music?' I did try to learn how to play clarinet in school, but that was an absolute joke. I could play without reading music, so I suppose you could say I was just jamming. I never learned to read music, but I learned to do what's commonly known in the recording business as writing number charts. That means that if you're in the key of E, then E is a 1, so 2 would be an F sharp, G would be a 3, A minor would be a 4 minor, and I could read chord charts as we all could. But I didn't want any music written out for me in the studio, because I wanted to create it myself. I had a little map of what the song was going to do."

Everything that Paul learned about the guitar he taught himself by practicing alone. "I played, and played. When I was first learning guitar, I would tune my guitar down and also play bass on every song I did." He excelled, and word about his talent spread around Rome. "When I was 12, this bunch of guys from North Georgia College had a band, and somehow word about my ability to play had reached them. A 23-year-old guy named Dale Stone called me and asked if I would play with his band. He played bass and organ, and at times his group, which was called the Dale Stone Trio, had four people, but they never changed the name. So there I was, a seventh grader, playing with a bunch of college kids. I went from a total nerd that nobody liked, or knew, to being one of the 'in' crowd, which I really didn't handle very well. That's when I was playing all these gigs with these college guys," Paul told us.

Paul (third from left) performing with the Valiants on WRGA radio, Rome, Georgia, in the early '60s (photo courtesy of Nan Goddard).

When Paul was a 15-year-old student at East Rome High School in 1960, he formed his own band, called the Valiants, which consisted of three guitarists and a bass player. "Back in those days there weren't that many musicians around, so for three years we tried to find a drummer but couldn't find anybody. We played dances at the gym after the basketball games. All four of us played through one Silvertone amp.

One of the guys was a folk music freak who wanted to play acoustic music. We were like two bands in one: the Kingston Trio, and the Ventures," Paul said. "For those that liked folk music, we would put down the electric instruments and do acoustics to every song the Kingston Trio had ever done. I enjoyed that too. I don't like to sing, but I can. Even with this horrible little high school band, I won most talented in ninth, tenth, eleventh, and twelfth grades. My little local band was playing things when we could, and I was making more money than my father was."

As keyboard player Dean Daughtry had been fascinated with radio, so was Paul. "I always wanted to be in radio, in my dreams, more than being a musician. But I was way too shy to be in radio. When ARS became big, when they wanted to do an interview I'd say, 'Let me do it.' I ended up becoming good friends with all the top DJs in Atlanta – the legendary guys from 'Quixie in Dixie' [WQXI 790 AM], like Tony Taylor, and Paul Drew. I knew all these people. I used to go there when Tony Taylor did the Sunday show, and every other song he played was an oldie. He'd say, 'Paul, go back in the library, and you pick the oldies.' I thought I had died and gone to heaven. These were the disc jockeys that ruled, and they were friends of mine."

Paul said he found high school to be very easy, and that even though he never took a book home he was a straight-A student. As he graduated from East Rome high in 1963, he received a scholarship to Georgia Tech but later transferred to Georgia State College (later renamed Georgia State University) with a major in psychology – but soon switched to another major. Paul was, more than anything else, an individualist. While Madge was heavily involved with church functions, Paul went in a divergent direction. "The head of the philosophy department was a Jew named Herman Munster [actual name: Ralf Munster], who had escaped from Hitler. I was so sad when I heard a couple of years ago that he had died. He gave me a test one time, and I was sick and didn't know it was coming up. Well, everybody just about flunked it, and I made 100 percent. He said, 'I'd like to talk to you,' so we started having visits after class and he explained to me that philosophy is not a great thing to make a living at, but he said, 'You apparently love it.' I said, 'It's everything I've always wanted to study.' Some of the philosophers would really get me mad, because they would start off being very logical, and then they would all try to prove there was a God, which is unprovable. They started off so smart and then just self-destructed. He agreed with me on that."

While attending college, Paul joined in a band called St. John and the

Cardinals, founded by drummer Dennis St. John, who later spent 10 years as part of Neil Diamond's musical entourage. Paul played lead guitar in the Cardinals, which also included guitarist Barry Bailey, bass player Emory Gordy Jr., and saxophone player Charlie DeChant (who became part of Hall and Oates' backup group in 1976). Paul hadn't previously met Barry, but he knew of him because Barry had played in a local band called Wayne Logiudice and the Kommotions. On the recommendation of Tony Taylor of WQXI, the legendary Kitten's Korner nightclub at Peachtree and Sixth streets in midtown Atlanta hired St. John and the Cardinals as the house band for a three-year run beginning in 1965. "It was while I was in college for the most part. At that time in Atlanta, you could stay open until 3 a.m., and then I had to try to make an 8 a.m. class at Georgia State. I generally skipped school on Wednesdays, and I slept all day. We backed big acts, like the Coasters, the Drifters, and Lenny Welch. There was no rehearsal. I knew the songs, note for note. Dennis St. John was real good at picking up stuff, and all I had to do with the other guys was to play it for them once and they would pick it up. It was a really good band."

When Roy Orbison's touring band the Candymen embarked on their own recording career, Roy hired St. John and the Cardinals as a replacement for a few gigs. "We had one of the ex-Candymen playing keyboards with us. That's why a lot of people think I was in the Candymen, but I was not. We went on the road, and at that time Barry Bailey was playing bass and I was playing guitar," Goddard told us. Roy decided to try an experiment. "Roy asked me if I can play bass, and I said, 'Sure.'" So Paul and Barry switched instruments. "Barry let me use his Gibson EB-0. There were lots of good guitar players in Atlanta, but very few good bass players. When we came back from the Orbison tour, and returned to Kitten's Korner, I was the bass player and Barry was the lead player. It was a great move for me, and less pressure. About a year later, I bought a Fender Precision bass."

In 1965, St. John and the Cardinals performed as studio musicians on the 1965 single "Jerkin' The Dog" on the Shurfine label with R&B, soul, and funk singer James Timothy Shaw, better known as The Mighty Hannibal. "'Jerkin' The Dog' was a dance record. It was so big that it got bought up by Decca. I remember the first time I heard it on WQXI radio in Atlanta, I said, 'Well, I made it! I am on the No. 1 station in the South with a hit record.' Wendell Parker, who produced it, was a little independent guy. So that was how I got in as a session musician," Paul said. Gordy, who already had been doing session work in various Atlanta studios, had recommended Paul for recording jobs. "The engineers at Master Sound said, 'Emory was telling the truth. This guy is just as good as he says.' So a lot of times it would be the engineers at Master Sound who referred me as one of the regular studio musicians."

Paul wrote a song called "Rampage" that St. John and the Cardinals also recorded and released in 1965 on the Shurfine label, along with "The Rise," which Goddard co-wrote, on the B side. Paul recalled, "We were in Master Sound studios cutting some things for a disc jockey for sound bites, and we had extra time. I knew the engineer and I said, 'Hey Bob, can we just lay something down for fun?' He said, 'Yup.' I had written 'Rampage,' a very strange song. It has jazz chords in it, and it's like a surf song. We recorded it and didn't think anything was going to happen with it, and Wendell Parker heard it and said, 'I'm gonna put that sucker out.' It was a pseudo hit in Atlanta and North Georgia, mainly because I got in the car and went to every radio station in North Georgia and gave them one. Being a hit in that area might have meant it sold 8,000 records, but it's a very good song."

During the period when Goddard and Bailey were playing cover versions of current hits at Kitten's Korner with St. John and the Cardinals, the duo occasionally also performed in Piedmont Park with a band they called Joint Effort. "During the hippie days, Barry and I and Charlie DeChant, who played sax, keyboards, flute and sang, would go to the park and just play for fun [with horn players Harry Hagan and Al Seppard, and drummer Mike Nepot]. We absolutely blew the hippies' minds. At Kitten's Korner we usually ended up playing a lot of rhythm and blues, which I didn't really like, but I liked making $200 a week when I was 20 years old. They would have all-day music. Roy Orbison had given us Marshall amps," Paul said. Members of the Who, the Small Faces, Led Zeppelin. Deep Purple and Cream used Marshall amps, which were manufactured in England. "[Roy] had a deal with Marshall. I'm sitting there with a bass rig the size that Jimi Hendrix's bass player had. First of all, the musicians were looking at the Marshalls and drooling

Paul Goddard was front and center in this photo with St. John and the Cardinals (photo courtesy of Nan Goddard).

because they had never seen one in person. We did every Jimi Hendrix song, every Cream song, a lot of Traffic, and we became legendary for that. One weekend I was driving down Piedmont Avenue, and this guy pulled up and said, 'Are you the bass player that played in the park?' I said, 'I'm a bass player, and I played in the park.' He said, 'Your band is better than Cream.' I said, 'Well, I don't think so, but thank you.' So we had two audiences: the hippie hip crowd, and the coat-and-tie rich people who liked to go to Kitten's Korner."

After the Kitten's Korner gig ended in 1968, St. John and the Cardinals became the house band at Big Hugh Baby's Hoparooni nightclub on U.S. 41 in Marietta, 20 miles northwest of downtown Atlanta. Big Hugh Baby Jarrett was the bass singer with the Jordanaires, the backup vocal group for Elvis Presley's early RCA Victor hit recordings. Jarrett also had been a disc jockey on WLAC Nashville before moving to Marietta, Georgia, station WFOM, where he and Paul Goddard met. "I used to go out to the Hoparooni with Big Hugh Baby, and he would have a bottle of Jack Daniel's, and I would sit there and play while he sang," Paul told us. "Hugh Baby knew everybody in the business, and he was very, very influential. When someone would ask him to suggest a bass player, he'd recommend me. Buddy Buie might never had heard my name if it hadn't been for Hugh. Tony Taylor and Hugh Jarrett turned our band into a local legend, so Buddy knew who we were, and he'd come see us."

Paul became acquainted with many of the working musicians in the area. "I knew Robert Nix, and he and I played weddings and parties," Paul said. "I also knew Rodney Justo and Barry Bailey, before I started doing Buddy Buie sessions at Master Sound with the Classics IV." Paul had lots of offers from other studios and producers, but turned down many of them because he considered them either unscrupulous or hypocrites. "Remember, I was a philosophy major, so ethics, ethics, ethics has always been important for me. I don't do drugs, so I would not have fit in at some of those places," he said. "I'm not trying to tell you I'm some angel. I do like to drink," he chuckled.

In 1968 Paul graduated from Georgia State with a degree in philosophy, the curriculum of which reinforced his personal ideology. "I'm a total atheist. I was an atheist by age 11. I was one of the biggest disappointments in my mom's life. I've never been known to follow the normal path. I took a little psychology in college and found out that what they considered good or normal was taking a test and scoring in the middle – that was good. I'm off the deep end in some things, and I think most musicians are. I was very proud of being not normal in their definition. On the phone I'm great, but

I'm actually very shy. I could have been valedictorian of my senior class, but I deliberately lowered my grades because I could not have given a speech under any circumstance."

Paul's only sibling, his sister Nan Goddard Jacobs, majored in music at Jacksonville State University in Alabama. While she studied music for several years, she took a different career path as assistant to the vice president of a large manufacturing company in Birmingham, Alabama, and is now semi-retired and living with her husband in Florida. Jacobs described her brother as brilliant, humble, kind, and generous to a fault. "He was a great brother," she said. "Growing up with him, when you're that close to it, you forget how great he was. We were close, but different as night and day."

As a studio musician, Goddard performed on numerous recordings for Joe South, Billy Joe Royal, and B.J. Thomas. "In 1971 I cut a whole album with Joe South, who won a Grammy for 'Games People Play.' That was when he was on Capitol. My bass part was incredible on this song called 'Fool Me,' which was a single, but I don't think it sold much. Billy Joe Royal came and cut a song called '(Don't Let The Sun Set On You In) Tulsa,' which was on Columbia and was a minor hit. The strangest thing about that is Barry Bailey played bass on that, and I played rhythm. That was the only time that has ever happened that I can remember. We cut four or five records with B.J. Thomas, one called 'Most Of All' that Buddy and J.R. wrote. We recorded 'Mighty Clouds Of Joy,' which was performed on the *Ed Sullivan Show*, and we had to re-cut a track here in Atlanta and send it to them so it wouldn't sound just like the record. It was a re-recording of the instrumental track by us and B.J. singing live to it. And B.J. was and is an incredible singer. He's what we call a 'one take guy.' He doesn't have to do it over and over again. We opened for Charlie Daniels many times, and I made him so mad that he said he'd never work with us again because he had a rug that he set his band up on that he had for 20 years, and I burned a hole in it with a cigarette. It could have been J.R. or Barry, but the only one he saw was me."

Many bass players who became fans of the Atlanta Rhythm Section idolized Goddard's unique style – the product of starting out as a lead guitar player before switching to bass – and tried to replicate it. "I play with a pick, and at that time it was very unusual," said Paul in 2014. "Bass used to be just felt and not heard. It was like a drum instrument, it was something people felt and could dance to. I play bass like a lead guitar."

Paul said that he intentionally avoided sounding like any other American bass player. Playing with a pick (also called a plectrum) rather than plucking with his fingers gave his playing the presence and attack he

Backstage at an Atlanta Rhythm Section concert performance: Ronnie Hammond, Paul Goddard, and Sammie Ammons, ARS road manager (photo courtesy of Nan Goddard).

sought. "Chris Squire [bassist for the band Yes, died of leukemia in June 2015], who became my idol, plays with the same kind of pick I use. It's a Fender medium triangle. I order them by the gross online, because music stores don't carry them. So part of the sound was me playing with that pick. Part of the sound was that I'm a sound freak, so I knew how to get the sound I wanted. I would do things like play with hard rock bands when there was nothing else going on, just to have fun. When you grow up playing the Classics IV ballads – for me that's kind of like a chess champion playing checkers. Don't get me wrong, I love some of that stuff. I love the beauty of the melodies. J.R. was an incredible melody and chord writer."

One particularly memorable date for Paul was July 18, 1975, when ARS performed in a concert appearance with the Atlanta Symphony at the Chastain Park Amphitheater in Atlanta. "That came about because *Third Annual Pipe Dream* had some violins and symphonic passages on it," Paul explained. "My parents were in the audience. That was the first time they ever heard me with the Atlanta Rhythm Section, and they nearly fainted. Chastain Park was mainly used for outdoor musical theater, like *The Sound Of Music*. I think we were the third rock 'n' roll band that ever played there."

Paul played a 1957 Fender Precision Bass from 1971 to 1976, then switched to a Rickenbacker 4001 that he used until 1983. "I had two custom built Peaveys that I used from 1980 to about 1983, and I still have them. They're still my favorite basses, but they're heavy, and I have a bad back. My true love was Rickenbacker, and still is, because they're so light,"

Paul explained. "I used my Rickenbacker for *Champagne Jam.*"

ARS guitarist J.R. Cobb admired Paul's talent. "Paul Goddard was an integral part of ARS's personality. He was a great musician and bass player, although he was an unconventional bass player. He approached the bass from the perspective of a guitar player, which he was, and made it work in a very unique way," Cobb told us in March 2016. "His tastes ran to what I suppose you would call progressive rock, and he had very strong opinions about music in general. He was a very able and talented person, and I consider it a privilege to have known him and been able to play with him."

In 1984, Paul and ARS drummer Danny Biget formed a progressive rock band they called Interpol. The band made some demos and gave them to Eddy Offord, a record producer and recording engineer who was especially well known for his work with Emerson, Lake & Palmer and the band Yes. Offord had moved to Atlanta. "After listening to my demos, he said, 'I'm going to produce you for free because this is great music.' Eddie was the total opposite of Buddy in that he believed in the musicians having the freedom to do what they want. I was still playing with ARS, but when they decided to go with Chips Moman as a producer, cutting a country album, that's the day I told them I never wanted to see any of their faces again, and I said, 'I'm working with someone who knows something about music,' and I walked out and didn't speak to any of them for about 10 years." Interpol members also included Terry "T" Lavitz, versatile keyboardist for the Dixie Dregs, and Pat Buchanan, one of Nashville's top session guitarists. Unfortunately, Interpol's music was never released.

Paul decided to make a radical career change. "After music, I started out selling audio equipment for a Georgia retail chain called Stereo Village. The store, in the Buckhead area of Atlanta, sold stereos, TVs, and microwaves. I was no good at it. I knew the equipment backwards and forwards, but that's not how you sell. You sell by manipulating people, which I don't want to do and never learned how, so I was damn near starving to death," he told us.

In 1987, after being unemployed for a year, Paul joined ABC School Supply in Duluth, Georgia, as a software tester and help desk representative. There he attained much greater success. "I went in with absolutely no IT training and became the top guy in the department within four years. We used very difficult software and my job was to teach people how to use it. I had to test the programming to make sure it worked and didn't tear anything else up. I loved that job because it was very much like learning music. It was a very creative job. You made up scenarios and tried to think up every possible scenario, run it through the system and see if it made any mistakes. But in 2003 we were bought out by School Specialty of Appleton,

Wisconsin. Everyone in the Duluth company was phased out."

Again unemployed and depressed, Paul finally got some good news in 2004 when two of his former colleagues from ABC School Supply bought out another company called DirectoryNet. "They called me and said, 'Would you like to go to work for us?' I was kind of legendary at ABC; I was the guy who was not socialized, but was a genius. Our head of sales and head of marketing would come to me because I knew things that nobody else could do, and I'd give it to them. They wanted me to be their customer service guy, along with another guy. Two months later they put him in sales, and I was customer service. There's nothing I would have wanted less, but I had no choice. I got where it didn't bother me much because we didn't get many calls, because once I started cleaning up all the messes, there weren't problems to solve. I worked there until 2007, when my right arm quit working due to pinched nerves in my upper spine. I was able to type with one hand, but I couldn't even put a coat on. I had some good friends who helped me, and I was still doing my job incredibly well, just slower." In June 2007 at Emory Johns Creek Hospital, neurosurgeon Florence Barnett performed spinal surgery that eased Paul's pain, immediately restored the use of his arm, and enabled him to resume playing the bass.

Paul met his wife, Phyllis Raye Karlip, in 1973, when she was attending the Barbizon School of Modeling. "She wasn't the model type. She had inherited some money, and her parents said she could do whatever she wanted. She had gotten to know an English girl at Valdosta State College who started seeing our singer Ronnie Hammond. The girl and Phyllis went to Atlanta State to see Led Zeppelin. We were playing in a folk rock place and in walks this English girl with Phyllis, and I couldn't take my eyes off of Phyllis. She looked a bit like a young Barbra Streisand and was very shy. She didn't say a word. She started to leave and our drummer said to me, 'PG, I can tell you're crazy about her, aren't you?' I said, 'Pretty much!' He said, 'Go catch her, you idiot.' So I ran out after her, and it scared her to death. She said, 'Well, I have to tell you I don't like your band.' I said, 'Neither do I.' So we got to be really good friends. We saw each other off and on, and then she would get scared and move. I'd find her, and we'd get back together for a couple of weeks, and she'd move and hide again. She was so shy, and so afraid of me. She finally let me move in next door to her in her apartment complex, and then we bought a big house in Norcross together."

Phyllis worked as a bank teller for a couple of years, then she went to work for a company called Curtis 1000, which was a printing company, and she stayed there for 23 years. "But she never made a good living. I was making about six times what she was. She was a descendant of a Russian-

Jewish father and a New York Jewish mother. Her parents said, 'If you marry him, we'll disown you.' After they died, in 1999 we finally had a little ceremony because there was nobody left to disapprove except her brother, and we didn't care what he thought." Paul and Phyllis did not have any children.

In 2009 Dr. Barnett gave Paul the difficult diagnosis that Phyllis had developed a tumor on her spinal column. "She had four kinds of cancer that started as colon cancer and just ate her alive. The last year was so miserable that my wife wanted to die. I was basically her nurse and caretaker, and I didn't have time to breathe. I had to carry her to the bathroom, and I wasn't that strong. It got where I would try to pick her up and fall, and I'd have to somehow call 911. They got where they knew me." Phyllis died in 2010.

In May of 2011, Paul re-joined ARS after an absence of 28 years. "Dean Daughtry would call me about every two months and beg me to come back. I'd say, 'Dean I'm making more money than you do, and I never leave home. Why would I do that?' But he would keep begging me, and keep begging me, and finally Barry Bailey quit because he couldn't play anymore, and Phyllis passed away, and I had nothing to do except sit here and be depressed. Dean found out about it and said, 'Will you come back now?' I said, 'Let me sit in with you a couple of times, because I don't know if I can still play.' I sat in and the audience went crazy. It was a little outdoor thing in Woodstock, Georgia, sponsored by the city. I played on two songs: 'Champagne Jam' and 'Spooky.' I had my old beat-up Trace Elliot amp that was making all kinds of noise, but it got me through it. I sat in again

That's Linda Blair, star of the 1973 motion picture *The Exorcist*, sitting on Paul Goddard's lap (photo courtesy of Nan Goddard).

with them in the summer in a big club here called Wild Bill's, and I did the same thing, played two songs. Then they begged me to come back. I said, 'But I love Justin Senker [their bass player] – he's such a sweetheart.' Justin came and said to me, 'I know you're probably going to replace me. I just want you to know that I won't hold that against you.' He said, 'My father's got money. I don't even need to work.' Dean wanted me and Rodney Justo to come back, and I said, 'You got it!'"

After a 27-year absence from ARS, Paul was back in the lineup, and Dean couldn't have been happier. "Paul was one of the best bass players in the world. We all loved him," Dean said.

"We needed to rehearse, which ARS has never liked to do, but we went to Huntsville for a week and rehearsed, because that's where three of them lived," Paul said. "Justo and I went on stage a little shaky because we hadn't played in thirty-something years, but every show got better and better, and now I'm almost as good as I was in the late '70s."

Once Paul decided to resume playing with ARS, he bought a new solid-body Rickenbacker 4003 bass guitar. "I modified it slightly because I have no use for a pickup selector, because you can hit it by accident and mess up. I still have my two custom Peavey guitars," Paul said. "Right now I have a setup of a little of everything, just like I like it. It's two Peavey Power Heads, one 750 watt and one 450, two Peavey 15-inch Black Widow bass cabinets with horn tweeters in them, and on top of that a Trace Elliot made in England that has four tens [10-inch speakers] and two horn tweeters. I can totally separate what I'm feeding them with the two bass heads. I have a very unusual rule that sound people hate. They love to plug the bass in what they call a direct box, which bypasses everything and allows them to control the sound. If I find that done, I will stomp the direct box until I have ruined it. They can mike me all they want, but don't skip my equalization out of my amp. That's how I get this trebly English sound. They call my rig the thermonuclear bass amp, and it will part your hair."

We spoke with Paul Goddard for the last time on March 5, 2014, less than two months before his death on April 29, 2014, when cancer that he had ignored worsened and overcame him. He was 68 years old. Paul had told us that he was excited and looking forward to be playing in his hometown of Rome, Georgia, at the Forum Civic Center that March 8, and that he hadn't performed there since 1978. He told us, "I'm hearing from people from my high school class that they're all coming as a big group." Dean Daughtry told us that Paul really enjoyed himself. "Paul was very happy and proud to play in his hometown after all those years," Dean said. Little did anyone know it would be his last performance.

Not even Paul's sister, Nan, knew how acute Paul's condition had become. He had been diagnosed with cancer of the parotid gland, a salivary gland; as a result of delaying treatment, the cancer had metastasized to his lungs. "After talking with his cancer specialist, Paul was aware of his illness, but was in total denial," Nan told us. "As close as we were, I was not aware of the severity of his illness until he called from ICU and told me he was scared. They were talking with him about end-of-life issues that needed to be addressed."

Throughout his life, Paul Goddard was proudly nonconformist. "Money is not important to me – happiness, pride, and self-respect are," he said. Paul did things only if they made sense to him, and steadfastly refused to mold himself to anyone else's notions of who they thought he should be or how they thought he should behave. "In the '70s people would tell me that I dress like I'm going to work at a retail job," referring to the slacks and buttoned shirts that he wore on stage. "I was there to be heard, not to be seen. I did not dress like a musician, and I still don't. I don't own a pair of blue jeans, and I don't own a T-shirt. I dress how I want to dress, which upset Buddy Buie. I was always the black sheep, and always proud of being the black sheep."

Paul likened his worldview to that of a beloved analytical science fiction character. "I'm basically like Mr. Spock, absolutely torn between two contradictory things," Paul said, matter-of-factly. "Logic is the only thing I can depend on, yet logic will never help you get along with 99.9 percent of people." But during the final months of his life, Paul had become enchanted by a woman for whom he had developed strong emotional feelings. Their budding relationship had given him reason for hope anew. Referring to theology, Paul confessed, "She has almost made me believe again." Nan told us, "although that woman took advantage of Paul's generosity, she made him happy – almost giddy. I could never fault that. He was near the end of his life, and she gave him hope and joy. That was worth whatever she took from him. I am convinced that he left us as a believer."

Epilogue: Rodney Justo

Lead singer

Rodney Justo, the original Atlanta Rhythm Section lead singer, is a man of contrasts. Although he has lived in the South nearly all of his life, he was born a Northerner. He is not an animal lover, despite being raised in a household that kept a menagerie of pets – including a skunk. The proper pronunciation of his surname differs from the way he came to be known – and most of his friends address him by a name other than Rodney. He was the first ARS member to leave the band, yet he has returned – not once, but twice. And after he left ARS the first time, his lack of knowledge about wines didn't deter him from landing a job with a wine wholesaler. That's because Justo is gifted not only with singing talent, but also with an engaging personality and a snappy wit. "I was very fortunate. I had no education, no skills, no trade. Somehow or another, I was just lucky I was born friendly," Rodney said. He's also a quick study and he has an airtight memory.

Rodney can tell you, for example, the date on which he met his future wife, Shirley Ann Alvarez. It was October 31, 1959. Shirley was 13, and Rodney, then 14, was playing drums at a party. That's yet another

Rodney Justo is seen here performing with ARS in August 2015 at a corporate event in Beaumont, Texas (photo by Courtni Meadows).

contrasting aspect of Rodney's life. He was intent on being a drummer, until the leader of another teen band realized that Rodney was a much better singer than he was a drummer. Although Rodney and Shirley dated for more than four years, they each married other people after graduating from high school. And although Rodney moved 1,100 miles away for a time, their paths crossed and brought them back together for good a few years later.

Rodney Cameron Justo was born on February 8, 1945, in New York City, the first child of Ena and Enrique Justo. Rodney's parents hailed from Tampa, but all four of his grandparents are from Spain. When Rodney was 2 years old, his folks returned to Tampa, where his father advanced in his law enforcement career as a criminal detective and became head of the criminal department with the Hillsborough County Sheriff's Office.

When Rodney was 4 years old, his brother, Brian – his only sibling – was born. The boys and their parents lived in an apartment in Ybor City, a quaint, colorful sector of Tampa with one principal industry.

"Ybor City was the cigar capital of America. Just about all of the people there were cigar workers," Rodney said. "Ybor City was a Latin community. It was all Spanish, Cuban, and Italian. In this area of Florida, all of the Italians came from one of two places, either Alessandria della Rocca or Santo Stefano Quisquina, Sicily." Ybor City (pronounced EE-bor) flourished beginning in the late 1800s with a multicultural population that coalesced around mutual-aid societies. "We had local social organizations. Every month somebody would come to your house and collect $1 or $3 or whatever it was, and you went to the Cuban club or the Italian club, and they all had hospitals and all of your medical bills were taken care of. Tampa had more Cubans than Miami. My wife is Cuban-Italian. I grew up in a truly diverse neighborhood. Theaters in Ybor City showed Spanish or Italian movies." After a period of decline that the Great Depression instigated, Ybor City underwent substantial urban renewal and preservation during the 1980s and '90s. These days it's a tourist, dining and arts and entertainment sector that has earned designation as a National Historic Landmark District. "Cuesta-Rey is the only big cigar factory still operating there, though. Ybor City looks just like Bourbon Street in New Orleans," he added.

After Rodney turned 7, his family moved to suburban North Tampa because they were able to buy a small house there, even though the mortgage payment was a financial stretch for the family. "My father was scared to death about that $50 per month payment," Rodney said. But while his parents successfully made the transition to home ownership, Rodney was unprepared for the hostile reception he encountered in his new surroundings. "It was a totally different world. There were no Latins up there. When we moved to North Tampa, people in the neighborhood said, 'It sure was a nice neighborhood until the ni**ers moved in.' They were talking about me and my family," Rodney said. He was forced to assert himself. "There was one kid named Jimmy Kline, and I used to whip his ass every day right in front of his father. His father would say, 'You know I like that Rodney. He don't take no shit off of nobody' – while I was whipping his son's ass." The family members acclimated, to the point of altering the way they pronounced their surname. The correct Spanish pronunciation of the family name is "HOOS-toh," but because many non-Latins butchered either the spelling or pronunciation, the family relented and Anglicized the pronunciation: JUST-oh.

"My mother was an extraordinarily beautiful woman, who my father met when she was 16 years old. He was about 27 at the time. They knew each other for three months and got married," Rodney said. Ena (pronounced EN-na) was the office manager and bookkeeper for a veterinary clinic. "She worked there for 40-something years. I'm not an animal lover, but we had all kinds of animals at home," Rodney said. "We even had a skunk, which I didn't tell a lot of my friends about. I knew that if they came to my house and saw a skunk running around they would panic. A skunk might be the worst pet ever – you don't cuddle with it, you don't pet it. It just hides underneath the bed."

Rodney's academic performance in school was lackluster. He didn't lack the aptitude, though; the problem was that he was distracted. He had dreams of becoming a singer. Or a drummer. "I was scatterbrained and disruptive. I behaved like an imbecile. I was a terrible student," Rodney acknowledged. "I thought my future was going to be selling shoes at Thom McAn, if I was lucky. Maybe I'd work myself up to a manager someday. But at the same time, I have to tell you, I always thought I could succeed in music." By the time Rodney was 5 years old, his enjoyment in singing became apparent, but that was soon supplanted by an affinity he developed for drums – which conflicted with his father's sensibilities. "My father was a very typically Spanish person who didn't like noise. We ate fish for dinner as often as possible. The idea was to keep my brother and me quiet. My father would say, 'No talking, because you might get a bone caught in your throat.' But after I told my mother I was interested in drums, my parents bought me a drum set, which I beat on constantly. It took awhile for me to realize what a sacrifice that was for my father – especially because for much of my young life, he worked nights, so we had to be quiet during the daytime."

To earn spending cash as he approached his teen years, Rodney signed up for a paper route. "That didn't last long because when it came time for people to pay me, they were never home. So I quit that." Rodney instead decided to go into business for himself. He put together a shoeshine kit, walked a block to the Northgate Shopping Center on Florida Avenue near Busch Boulevard, and set up shop. He immediately encountered competition – and displayed an entrepreneurial flair in the solution he devised. "This black kid named Jerome also was shining shoes there. We both charged 15 cents a shoe shine. I said to Jerome, 'Hey, instead of competing with each other, we can pool our money and split it at the end of the day.' We became partners instead of competitors."

Rodney initially was exposed to his parents' favorite musical performers: Perry Como, Frankie Laine, Frank Sinatra and music of the big bands, including that of Artie Shaw. "I still love Nat 'King' Cole, Tony Bennett, and other singers from that era," Rodney said. But what 11-year-old Rodney saw and heard on television one evening in 1956 hit him like a lightning bolt. "The first time I heard Elvis while watching TV at my aunt's house, I went 'Oh my god!' I thought that was the most remarkable thing I'd ever heard," Rodney said.

At George D. Chamberlain High School, Rodney formed his first band with a classmate. "Well, it was just me playing drums with another guy named Blair Mooney, who was a guitar player. That was the whole band," Rodney said. "We would pretend that we had a singer. We would stop playing at the times when a singer would have been singing, and then we'd start again." In 1959, when Rodney was in 10th grade, he auditioned as a drummer for a band called E.G. and the Hi-Fi's, but when the band's leader, Emilio Garcia, heard Rodney's singing voice, he dismissed the band's singer and hired Rodney in his place. Although E.G. and the Hi-Fi's played a lot of dates, Rodney realized before long that neither he nor the other musicians in the band took home as much money as Emilio did. So in 1960, Rodney and most of the members of the Hi-Fi's teamed with a newly formed trio, and the result was an 11-man group called the Mystics. "We had a big horn section, and all the guys were really good musicians who could read music," Justo said. After the group pared down to a more economically viable six members with Justo out front, the earnings per musician became better.

The Mystics got a big break when they performed in a "battle of the bands" competition at the Clearwater Municipal Auditorium in nearby Clearwater, Florida. They had gone directly there after playing a gig in Tampa, and because they were tired, they didn't win the competition. But

Paul Cochran, the manager of the auditorium, liked the Mystics and saw star quality in Rodney. "Paul signed me to a management contract when I was 16 years old. He had to talk to my parents about it, and he was wonderful. He was the only manager I ever had, really. He and Buddy Buie became partners and my co-managers, but the only person I physically signed a piece of paper with was Paul Cochran," Rodney told us. "Buddy and I became friends from the get-go." Cochran immediately changed the name of the band to Rodney and the Mystics, and signed them as the house band at the Clearwater Municipal Auditorium, for which they gained recurrent mentions on St. Petersburg "top 40" radio station WLCY. As the house band, they backed big-name solo artists who made concert tour stops at the auditorium.

"Back in those days the artists with hit records were solo singers," Rodney explained. "We worked with virtually every big-name performer who had chart records between 1960 and 1965. Ray Stevens, Freddy Cannon, Jimmy Clanton, Del Shannon, Brian Hyland, Neil Sedaka – we backed all of them there. Some of them brought their own arrangements with them. They put their charts out, and my guys could all read." Even though Rodney never had taken any formal musical or voice training, his course was set. "After I slept in following a late-night gig, my father used to wake me up in the morning, saying 'Come on, get your ass out of bed, you've got to get a job.' I told him, 'Pop, I make more money than you.'"

After Rodney graduated from Chamberlain High School in 1962, he and his band became increasingly known in the local live music bar scene. "I got a bit of a big head because I was the cool guy around town and I had a band and I was hanging out with strippers, but my girlfriend's family was very strict," Rodney said. So after four years of dating, he and his girlfriend, Shirley, parted and went their separate ways. She met another guy, whom she eventually married.

Roy Orbison was among the performers Rodney and the Mystics backed in Tampa. The next time Orbison came through town, he had his own backing group, an Alabama band that on its own had been known as the Webs. Rodney became acquainted with Roy and the members of his band, and developed friendships with them. The band members included Bobby Goldsboro, who played guitar and sang. Impressed by Rodney's voice, Roy decided to try his hand at producing a Rodney Justo recording session. "On February 8, 1964, my 19th birthday, I sang at a show as a single artist in Dothan, Alabama, with Roy Orbison, Ray Stevens, Bobby Goldsboro, and the Newbeats. After the gig we drove to Nashville, and that next night, I watched the Beatles on the *Ed Sullivan Show* on TV. I thought,

'Uh, oh! I'm screwed with this record I'm getting ready to make. It's out of date already.' On February 10th, Ray Stevens took me to watch a recording session because I had never seen a session and didn't know what to expect," Rodney said. "It was a Jerry Lee Lewis session, which I took for granted. Now I look back and say, 'Holy smoke, I was at a Jerry Lee Lewis recording session.' He recorded a song called 'I'm on Fire,' and he was killing it.

"My session was the next day, and Bill Justis was the arranger," Rodney said. "When I started singing, he said, 'Rodney, I like the way you sing, but you sound a little too soulful. Try to sound a little more like Bobby Rydell.' So I sang four songs, including one called 'Miss Brown,' which a guitar player named Fred Carter, a friend of Roy's, had written. When Roy listened to the playback he declared, 'This song is a smash,' but I knew that record would not be a hit." Rodney was right. Sound Stage 7, a subsidiary of Monument Records (for which Roy recorded) released "Miss Brown" without success. "But all in all, I was grateful that someone had an interest in me."

After Bobby Goldsboro's solo recording "See The Funny Little Clown" hit the national top 10 in early 1964, he left Orbison's band to tour on his own. Roy and Buddy Buie – who managed Roy's band – recruited Justo to replace Goldsboro in August 1964, shortly after Monument Records released Roy's huge hit "Oh, Pretty Woman." By then Roy had renamed

Rodney Justo gives the "thumbs up" sign as he and the other Candymen, along with Roy Orbison (center, wearing glasses), hang out with the Small Faces (photo courtesy of Rodney Justo).

87

Candymen: From left, William Dean Daughtry, Robert Nix, John Rainey Atkins, Rodney Justo, Bill Gilmore.

his backup unit the Candy Men (after his 1961 single of that name) – soon to become shortened to one word: Candymen. The band members included drummer Robert Nix; after keyboard player Bobby Peterson was drafted in 1965, Dean Daughtry became the Candymen keyboardist.

Rodney meanwhile met Jeanne Feiner, and in 1965 the couple married. In November 1966 they welcomed the birth of their first daughter, Kim. That milestone moment brought about a major change in Rodney's life. "Until then, I had been a big drinker. I was drunk most of 1966. But when I saw Kim for the first time, I literally quit drinking right then. I felt this air of responsibility. I didn't want the name 'drunk' associated with my name," Rodney said.

With his new sense of responsibility, Rodney was enthusiastic when the Candymen stepped out on their own during the intervals when they weren't on the road with Roy. "We needed to be able to make a living when Roy wasn't working," Rodney said. The Candymen were more than capable; that was an excellent, albeit far underappreciated band. As the vocalist for the Candymen, Justo came into his own as a showman, swinging the mike around his head with its cord, working the audience into a frenzy. "I would tip the microphone stand forward toward the audience, but I kept one foot on the base, and just before it hit the ground I would step down on the base, and the mike would snap back to me," he grinned. To give him something else to do on stage during instrumental passages, he began learning how to play guitar and worked that into his stage routine. "I never got any good at it; in fact, I think I'm getting worse. Kinda like my golf game," he joked.

At Master Sound recording studio in Atlanta, Buie produced two Candymen albums for ABC Records. The label released the first album, *The Candymen,* in 1967, and then *The Candymen Bring You Candy Power* in 1968. Over the course of a couple of years, the label released several singles, the most successful of which was "Georgia Pines," which Buie wrote with Candymen guitarist John Rainey Adkins. Unfortunately, the band's recordings did not attract the attention they deserved, and insufficient earnings led to the breakup of the Candymen in early 1970.

Rodney and Jeanne by then had a second daughter, Holly, who was born in 1969. A new opportunity presented itself for Rodney when his old high school pal (and duo sidekick) guitarist Blair Mooney along with a guitar player named Buddy Richardson formed a band called Noah's Ark with drummer Bobby Caldwell (who went on to play with Johnny Winter and Captain Beyond). The biggest thing that Rodney got out of Noah's Ark was a nickname that would stick to him from then on. "Blair Mooney would say 'let's do something.' And I'd say, 'all right. Let's rock.' In other words, let's do it. And the next thing, my nickname became 'Rocker,' then 'Rock,'" Justo said. Noah's Ark played enough dates to keep food on the

Graham Nash (right foreground) demonstrates John Lennon's Mellotron as Candymen (from left rear) Bill Gilmore, Rodney Justo, and Robert Nix (behind Nash) take it all in (photo courtesy of Rodney Justo).

Justo family's table, but not much beyond that. Then Buddy called again.

"It was June of 1970. Buddy told me, 'Rock, I wanna put a band together. I've been listening to this album called *Super Session* [Columbia Records, 1968] by Mike Bloomfield, Al Kooper, and Steve Stills. And if they can have a super session, I don't know why I can't have a super band.' So I asked him, 'well, who you gonna get?' And he said, 'some of the Candymen. I've got Dean, Robert Nix, Paul Goddard on bass, J.R. from the Classics IV, and Barry Bailey.' So I said, 'sure, I'll do it,' because I wasn't going anywhere with Noah's Ark," Justo told us. "I was trying to make a house payment, y' know? So my wife went to Puerto Rico while I moved to Atlanta and got set up there."

Construction already had begun on Buie's Studio One. "I literally helped build the recording studio with the other guys in the band," Justo said. Having performed in three bands that had not attained their full potential, he had his sights set on success for the Atlanta Rhythm Section, in the studio as well as on the road. He had every reason to be optimistic. "ARS was Buddy's dream. That's what he wanted more than anything – he wanted a band to be a vehicle for his songs," Rodney said. When the band returned from a brief tour following release of its debut *Atlanta Rhythm Section* album, Buddy perhaps sensed Rodney's unease about finances, and had a conversation with him. "Buddy said to me, 'Rock, you won't believe what I did today.' I thought he was going to tell me we were going to tour with the Rolling Stones, who were about to resume touring in America after a break since 1969. I was thinking, Rolling Stones, here we go. But instead, Buddy said, 'I signed a deal with Hanna-Barbera. We're gonna do the soundtrack for a TV show called *Butch Cassidy and the Sundance Kids* [a cartoon series about a pop music band]. So I wondered where little Rodney fit in this picture. Buddy said, 'we'll put you on the contract singing background vocals.' I thought to myself, not more studio work," Rodney said. "My youngest daughter had two lung operations, and like most musicians, I didn't have insurance, and I had to pay the hospital back. I figured that if I was going to sing background, I night as well go someplace where I can make some good money singing background. That's why I moved to New York."

Relocating to Manhattan was a big gamble for Rodney, and breaking into the recording scene there took time, patience, and persistence. It also was an emotionally tough time for him, as his marriage was disintegrating. But in New York, Rodney had the support of three friends: singer B.J. Thomas (about whom this book contains a chapter); record producer Steve Tyrell, who produced most of B.J. Thomas's recorded output in the early

'70s; and B.J.'s drummer, Allan Schwartzberg.

"When I first moved to New York, I stayed with Steve Tyrell for a while. But you can stay at someone's house for only so long. I told him I had to go on my own, but I had nowhere to go. I was essentially homeless," Rodney told us. "B.J. Thomas allowed me to stay in his office suite. I slept on a sofa in one of the rooms in his office. I got a hotel room every three days or so, so I could wash my hair and bathe. Then I became friends with Allan Schwartzberg, the No. 1 studio drummer in New York who also was B.J.'s drummer. He and his fiancée, Susan, adopted me. They had a one-bedroom apartment, they let me sleep on their sofa, and they gave me a key to the place."

Justo intended to stay with them only one night, but they beseeched him to stay until he got on his own two feet financially. "So I wound up staying about seven months with them in their one-bedroom apartment. I'm still very close to them to this day. They've got a nicer place now," Rodney chuckled. "But I was the original Kato Kaelin. I set the bar for Kato on being an extended-stay houseguest. From the '70s to the 2000s, Allan played on every record, every jingle you could imagine." Schwartzberg played drums on Meco's "Star Wars Theme / Cantina Band," and has performed on sessions for Barbra Streisand, Harry Chapin, Roberta Flack, James Brown, the Spinners, Kiss, Peter Gabriel, Alice Cooper, Roger Daltrey, and other performers. "Allan and Steve Tyrell recommend me for jobs. They got me into a lot of stuff," Rodney said.

Recording jingles was lucrative, and Rodney recorded many, for advertisers that included Coca-Cola, Pepsi-Cola, Mazda, Flagg Bros. Shoes, several regional banks, and Hardee's Restaurants. For a while he was booked as an accompanying singer on a European tour with guitarist Roy Buchanan. "At that time the studio scene in New York was very intense, and most musicians didn't want to go on the road because they were scared that while they were away for a few days, someone else would take their place. So I went to his label, Polydor Records, and dropped off a demo reel of my singing. They called me up and offered me the gig," Rodney said. But he and Buchanan didn't mesh well. Justo was accustomed to rehearsals; Buchanan was less disciplined and preferred to wing it. Justo often didn't know what to expect from Buchanan on stage. "Roy Buchanan was a masterful guitarist. We went to Germany, Switzerland, and all over England. But I gotta tell you, by the time we finished that tour, I couldn't wait to get home."

Rodney learned one important lesson from Buchanan. "Roy was remarkable – probably one of the world's best rock and roll guitar players at that time," Justo said. "One day when we started talking about style, he told me, 'When you can't figure out how to do a song the way someone else does, you figure out your own way to sing it. That's how you develop style.'"

The next time Rodney headed out on the road, it was as a backup singer and musical director with the top-notch troupe of New York studio musicians who toured with B.J. Thomas. "B.J. was riding high, so his traveling band consisted of guitar player Teddy Irwin, bass player Will Lee, Allan Schwartzberg on drums, and his arranger, Glen Spreen. But sometimes these musicians had conflicts with other dates. So in the spring of 1973 I told B.J. about a guitarist friend of mine, John Rainey Adkins, who I used to play with in the Candymen. Since the breakup of the Candymen, John Rainey had a new band in Dothan, Alabama, called Beaverteeth. I told B.J. that the members of Beaverteeth also could do background vocals, which he didn't have with his group of New York studio musicians, and he said, 'OK, I trust you.' So I flew down to Dothan for about 10 days and rehearsed those guys, and then we went on the road with B.J. And that was a very good band."

Indeed, Beaverteeth consisted of pros who by 1972 already had recorded some tracks, including "Texarkana Sunshine" (which John Rainey Adkins wrote) and the anthemic ballad "Georgia Pines" (composed by Buie and Adkins), both of which Musicor Records released in 1974. Unfortunately, neither of those singles generated much action outside of the South. Beaverteeth continued playing their own gigs when not on the road with B.J. When the band's singer, Charlie Silva, was diagnosed with cancer and was unable to continue performing with the band, the other band members asked Rodney to fill in for him. The six-man band ended its relationship with B.J. during the summer of 1975. Rodney, who continued performing with Beaverteeth, left New York and returned to Tampa, but before he did, he made one more important connection.

"While I was living in New York, I reconnected with my old girlfriend, Shirley. She had divorced after being married for seven years. I always had feelings for her, even though we were both married to other people. And after I returned to Tampa we ran into each other, and we knew that we were going to be together," Rodney said. He and Shirley married in 1974, and Rodney gained a stepson, James Freece, who was born in 1969.

In 1977 Beaverteeth signed with the RCA label, which released two albums: *Beaverteeth* (1977) and *Dam It* (1978). Neither album (which Rodney produced in association with Paul Cochran), nor either of two singles – "Sing For You" and "Mystic Notions And Magic Potions" – attracted sufficient attention from radio programmers.

"I loved those guys, and I thought we had a future. But I was pining for my children, and luckily we weren't that successful, so I left the band in 1978," Rodney said. "I moved back to Tampa, called my first wife, and said, 'If you will move back to Tampa with the girls, I will give you everything – the house, the cars.' And she agreed. So she and I moved back to Tampa in 1978, and I left the music business."

Determined to earn a steady income in a field other than music, Rodney began looking for employment. "I was resolved that I would work like other people do. But I couldn't find a job. No one would hire me. Not only would they not hire me, they wouldn't even talk to me about not hiring me. I couldn't get an interview, which I didn't understand, because I thought I was a celebrity. Now I understand. What the heck were they going to hire me for? I didn't know anything other than music," Rodney acknowledged. "It was brutal. For six months I'd been doing nothing, except for cooking. My wife was working for The Hartford insurance company, and when she arrived home, I would have dinner ready."

Then Justo got an unexpected break by virtue of a friend of his, John Maniscalco, who was a sales representative for Southern Wines & Spirits, a wholesale liquor distributing company. "John called me up one Thursday and asked, 'what are you doing, Rock?' I told him, 'aw, nothing, just sitting around getting ready to start cooking.' He said, 'well, I'm going on my [sales] route. You want to come with me?' I said, 'sure, but I've gotta be back home around like 4 o'clock so I can start cooking.' He said 'all right,' and I went riding with him. We went into one account and John said, 'hey, Bill, how you doing?' Bill says, 'I'm good, John, how about you?' John said, 'what about those Bucs, huh? They suck, and they'll never make it as long as they've got John McKay as the coach.' And after a little more chatter, John asked him, 'what do you need today?' And Bill said, 'uh, give me a case of Dewar's liters, two cases of Dewar's one-seven-five [1.75 liter], a case of Kahlúa, six bottles of Grand Marnier, and that'll do it.' John says, 'all right, see you next week.' Then we went to the next account. John says 'Hey, Frank.' Frank says, 'Hey, John, how ya doing?' John says, 'What about those Bucs? Do they suck or what? They'll never make it with John McKay as the coach.' So he does this six or seven times. I said, 'John, I'm not trying to be nosy. What kind of money do you make for writing product names and numbers down on a piece of paper?' He said, 'I make $25,000 to $30,000 a year.' That was really good money in 1978."

Rodney was incredulous. He put those numbers into his perspective. "For a musician to make $25,000, you've gotta generate $100,000, in order to pay your manager, your agent, travel, rooms, other expenses, and the government. I said, 'John, you gotta tell me where the line forms for this job.' He said, 'there's nothing available in the liquor department. But there might be something in the wine department.' He told me the name of the wine department manager. I called the guy, Don, on the phone, and I told him I'd like to come by and talk to him about a job. He said, 'we don't have anything right now, but if you'd like to come by and fill out an application....' I said, 'Don, let me be up front with you. If I fill out an application, you're going to think I never worked a day in my life. I got only one chance, and that's to come and talk to you and let you see that I can put sentences together.' He started laughing, and I went to his office and he interviewed me." The wine division had no jobs available, but when an opening occurred a week later, Don called Rodney.

"It was probably the lowest job in the company, dusting bottles in grocery stores. It paid $150 a week. I didn't know anything about wine. I didn't know a red from a white if I was looking at them. But I told him, you give me something to read, and by the time a week is over, I'll know more about wine than anybody in this place. I got the job. And I said to myself, I will never let anybody in this place outwork me. So I was dusting bottles like an eleven-piece suit." Rodney was resolved to wait for an opportunity for promotion. That came sooner than he expected, when a sales rep became greedy at the company's expense.

Atlanta Rhythm Section in 1983. From left, Dean Daughtry, J.R. Cobb, Roy Yeager, Barry Bailey, Paul Goddard, and Rodney Justo (photo courtesy of Rodney Justo).

"Sales reps were supposed to receive a commission check once a month. Something went wrong with the paperwork for one guy, and he was paid this money every week," Rodney said. The rep was being paid four times as much as he should have been. "This had been going on for months, and he didn't say anything. He just kept the money." The accounting department finally discovered the unreported overpayments. "To the company, that was the same as stealing. So that outside sales route became available, and I took it. I called on little independent convenience stores and grocery stores. But then people in the company realized that the future was going to be in restaurants because it's more profitable – you don't discount the merchandise. So I became part of a team of seven who called strictly on restaurants. I worked really hard and I did pretty well."

In 1983, Beck's Brewery recruited Rodney as regional sales manager. Just as he began his new job, his old friends from the Atlanta Rhythm Section called him. "Ronnie Hammond had left the band, and they asked if I would help out with a few dates. I didn't really want to do it," Justo told us. But he agreed to fill in temporarily as long as his ARS gigs would be confined to weekends. "So I would work all week at Beck's, then I would leave the office early on Fridays, get on a plane, and perform with ARS Friday, Saturday, maybe even Sunday. I originally had planned on doing only about six dates or so with them, but I ended up staying almost a year." Rodney's stay with Beck's didn't last much longer than that. In 1984 he returned to Southern Wines & Spirits, where over the next two decades he rose to a sales management position as the company became the nation's largest wine and spirits distributor.

Rodney retired in 2007 from Southern Wines with plans to take it easy. A few acquaintances had other ideas, though. "I had no intention of ever singing another note again. I was done," Rodney said. Then three other "R" guys – guitarists Robin Sibucao and Roy Garcia, and drummer Rodger Stephan – along with bass player Danny George – got the idea of starting a local band just for the fun of it, playing the early rhythm and blues songs and '60s American and "British invasion" tunes they enjoyed. All were successful in various careers. They named their band Coo Coo Ca Choo (http://coocoocachooband.com), in reference to a nonsensical refrain in Simon and Garfunkel's "Mrs. Robinson" and to the Beatles' "goo-goo-ga-joob" in "I Am The Walrus." And just like that, Rodney was back on stage, singing and playing guitar at Tampa and St. Petersburg clubs about a dozen times a year.

Then in the spring of 2011, Dean Daughtry – the only remaining original member of ARS – and Buddy Buie each asked Rodney to consider returning to the fold. "Buddy said, 'Rock, you may not have been part of the band that had the hits, but there's no denying that you're part of the legacy of the band.' And I felt flattered that he would say that to me. So I agreed to do it," Rodney told us. "Paul Goddard and I had left ARS on the same day, and we both came back on the same day." Rodney continues to perform with ARS. Shirley has retired from her job as a clerical supervisor at The Hartford insurance company after working there for 39 years.

Rodney's daughter Kim has one child, and his other daughter, Holly, has three children. "Having grandchildren is a blast," Rodney said. Shirley's son, James, is a firefighter in Augusta, Georgia. Rodney's brother, Brian, is still working, in the alcoholic beverage business – a field he entered before Rodney did. Visitors at the Salvador Dalí Museum in St. Petersburg are likely to run into Rodney there, where he volunteers as a docent.

Today, Rodney and Shirley live in a comfortable home in Lutz (pronounced Lootz), a suburb about 15 miles north of downtown Tampa. "About three times a year," Rodney said, "I drive by the little North Tampa house that my family and I lived in when I was a kid – just to stay humble."

Billy Joe Royal's "Cherry Hill Park" was written by Robert Nix and Bill Gilmore, arranged by Buddy Buie, J.R. Cobb and Emory Gordy, Jr., produced by Buddy Buie and Bill Lowery Productions, and recorded at Master Sound studio in Atlanta.

As the members of Love stood on the rear deck of lead singer Arthur Lee's Hollywood Hills home in June 1967, Michael Stuart-Ware accidentally kicked and shattered a ceramic vase of dead flowers, which Arthur picked up and cradled. The photo that captured that moment appeared on the jacket of the band's *Forever Changes* album. From left, Johnny Echols, Bryan MacLean, Ken Forssi, Arthur Lee and Michael Stuart-Ware (photo by RHM).

CHAPTER

2

Alone Again Or

Love

As the baby-boomer children of the "greatest generation" headed into adolescence in the 1960s, their seemingly safe world began to crumble around them. That decade was fraught with conflicts and tensions that exposed deep-seated, painful fractures in society. In response to strained relations between the Soviet Union and the United States, American school children practiced "duck-and-cover" bombardment drills while many parents dug underground "fallout shelters" in their backyards in a frantic effort to protect themselves and their families from annihilation in a nuclear attack. America came to the brink of war in October 1962 as Cuban-based missiles with nuclear warheads were aimed at targets in the United States. Thirteen months later, America's beloved and youthful President John Kennedy was assassinated, sending the entire nation into shock.

The decade of the 1960s dawned with college students staging spontaneous "sit-ins" as a form of civil disobedience to protest racial segregation, injustice, and brutality. U.S. Food and Drug Administration approval of Enovid as the first oral contraceptive – "the pill" – gave rise to recreational sex without fear of pregnancy. Meanwhile, the presence of American military "advisers" in South Vietnam quietly increased during the first years of the decade; 16,000 U.S. troops had been deployed there by November 1963. In August 1964, at the urging of President Lyndon Johnson, Congress passed the Tonkin Gulf Resolution, dramatically elevating the U.S. role in combat against North Vietnam, and the Pentagon dispatched the Seventh Fleet to Vietnam. As the Selective Service ratcheted up and began drafting tens of thousands of young men every month, protests against the war began to mount. Defiant anger reached the breaking point at the University of California, Berkeley, where protests that began as the "Free Speech Movement" in the autumn of 1964 mushroomed into turbulent antiwar demonstrations that spilled off campus and spread to protests and blockades at military draft boards and military induction centers not only in the San Francisco Bay Area, but across the nation. In the summer of 1965, Johnson asked Congress to authorize induction of more than 180,000 males for military duty in Vietnam. Many young men of draft age symbolically burned their draft cards in public, as crowds of

young people adopted the peace symbol – which had been conceived in England in 1958 to promote nuclear disarmament (it consists of overlapping semaphore signs for the letters "N" and "D"). As the generation gap widened, young people increasingly turned to hallucinogenic drugs out of frustration and fatalism, and embraced the mantras of sexual liberation: "free love" and "make love, not war." Those were the sentiments and cultural forces that gave rise to the band Love amid the youth culture seedbed that was Los Angeles rock scene of the mid-1960s.

Johnny Echols caressed his twin-neck guitar while Arthur Lee blew his harp during a Love performance at Bido Lito's in Hollywood in the autumn of 1965 (photo courtesy of Johnny Echols).

The trendy Hollywood and Sunset Strip nightclubs that became hotspots for the youth culture provided a platform through which numerous bands ignited the passions of newfound fans. Some of these bands, such as the Byrds and the Leaves, sculpted folk-rock;

some specialized in straight-on rock, as the Standells and the Seeds did; some groups, notably the Doors and Iron Butterfly, plied their trade in psychedelia; others such as Buffalo Springfield wove their spells in tender ballads with acoustic guitars and delicate harmonies while serving up lyrical content seething with thought-provoking social commentary. The L.A.-based band Love deftly spanned all those musical genres, producing during its mercurial lifespan a catalog of starkly divergent musical works, including *Forever Changes,* which many fans and critics regard as one of the most brilliant rock albums ever recorded. *Forever Changes* is an apt title, describing the character of the band itself.

Love in some senses was the consummate L.A. band, fused from elements of Southern California pop, surf music, jazz and rhythm and blues, and it remained rooted in L.A. throughout the changes in personnel and musical styles it has forever endured. Ardent fans insist that the band's magnetic and mystifying leader and lead singer, Arthur Lee, personified Love – that *he* was Love and that Love was Arthur Lee, because the band's rotating personnel all revolved around him. But the fact remains that Love was a band of five – and at one point seven – gifted musicians, the initial configuration of which consisted of Lee accompanied by lead guitarist Johnny Echols, rhythm guitarist and composer Bryan Andrew MacLean, bass guitarist John "Fleck" Fleckenstein (replaced in 1966 by Ken Forssi) and drummer Alban "Snoopy" Pfisterer – superseded by Michael Stuart (Michael Ware's pseudonym, which he began using on a fake ID as an underage musician, to enable him to play in nightclubs that served alcohol).

After attracting a strong following in the Hollywood club scene, Love began its recording career with a hard-rock version of a song almost improbably written by one of the world's most prolific ballad writing teams. "Alfie," "The Look Of Love," "(They Long To Be) Close To You," "Raindrops Keep Fallin' On My Head" and "Do You Know The Way To San Jose?" all came from the pens of composers Burt Bacharach and Hal David, who frequently wrote scores and songs for films, including the 1965 motion picture *What's New Pussycat?* That film, a wacky comedy starring Peter Sellers, Ursula Andress, Peter O'Toole, and Woody Allen, included a club scene with the Manfred Mann band performing a tune in a mopey, languid key. When the film opened in theaters in Los Angeles, Arthur Lee and Johnny Echols went to see it because they liked the singing of Tom Jones, who recorded the title track. But when the bar scene flickered onto the screen, Arthur and Johnny paid less attention to the dialog than to the recurring background music. The Bacharach-David tune "My Little Red Book" caught their attention.

"Arthur and I were both intrigued by that mysterious song. After I went home I tried to play it from memory, but I mistakenly omitted the prevalent minor chords," Echols said. "A couple of days later, I taught the song to the rest of the group and they played the wrong chords as well, and with a much faster beat. We added it to our live set list and played it that way. But every one of us agreed that 'our version' was much cooler, so we decided to continue playing it the wrong way." It turned out to be the right way for Love and the fans who latched onto the song. With a driving drumbeat and a persistent bass line, Love transformed "My Little Red Book" into a throbbing top 40 hit in the spring of 1966.

Arthur and Johnny had known each other since they were kids growing up in Memphis, Tennessee. Arthur's mother, Agnes, was a school teacher, as was Johnny's mother, Dora Echols. The families of both boys coincidentally relocated in the early '50s to the Jefferson Park section of Los Angeles. Arthur became heavily involved in sports, while Johnny developed a deep interest in playing the guitar. By the time Johnny had turned 14 years old in 1961 he was earning money playing guitar in his own band, the House Rockers, the members of which included Billy Preston. When Arthur saw the House Rockers perform at a high school assembly, he couldn't help but notice how much attention girls were paying to the band. Arthur asked to join the House Rockers, which welcomed him. He initially played bongos and congas, then eventually took lessons to play the organ. Over time, the band worked under various names, depending upon the type of gig (weddings, bar mitzvahs or fraternity parties) and the kind of music that was requested. When they played rock they called themselves the House Rockers, the American Four or any of several other names, but they performed rhythm and blues and surf instrumentals as the LAGs (the Los Angeles

Love in 1967, when the band consisted of, from left, Michael Stuart-Ware, Johnny Echols, Ken Forssi, Bryan MacLean and Arthur Lee (photo by RHM).

Group, a name inspired by Booker T. and the MGs). "As mixed-race individuals who grew up in a diverse neighborhood, Arthur and I wanted our group to reflect who we were," Echols explained.

With youthful brashness the band's four teenagers headed across town to Vine Street in Hollywood, and walked into the Capitol Records building. "Adam Ross and Jack Levy of Beechwood Music liked some of our songs, and got us signed to a record deal with Capitol," Johnny said. As Arthur Lee and the LAGs, the group recorded an instrumental single consisting of an organ-driven surf tune called "The Ninth Wave" backed with R&B-flavored "Rumble-Still-Skins" that Capitol released in 1963. The American Four landed another record deal in 1964 with Selma Records, a subsidiary of Del-Fi. "Arthur and I had been hired by [Del-Fi founder] Bob Keane to work with several local groups the label had signed – Little Ray, Ronnie and the Pomona Casuals, the Sisters, and a couple of other groups," Echols said. Keane had discovered Ritchie Valens and signed him to a recording contract. The American Four cut a novelty tune that Arthur wrote called "Luci Baines" – a tribute to Luci Baines Johnson, the younger daughter of President Lyndon Baines Johnson. Johnny and Arthur co-wrote "Soul Food," the song on the flip side. "Luci Baines" was intentionally derivative of the Isley Brothers' "Twist And Shout."

Arthur, who was two years older than Johnny, gradually assumed leadership of the band. As their high school band mates went their separate ways, Johnny began performing with other bands. Among them was the Chuck Daniels Band, a jazz and R&B band that had landed an extended booking over several months at the Sea Witch nightclub on Sunset Boulevard in West Hollywood. The members of the Chuck Daniels Band included bass player John Fleckenstein. One evening in early 1964 Arthur went to see the band perform. "That's where Johnny introduced me to Arthur Lee, who said to me, 'We're gonna start a new group, man, and I want you to come in. We're gonna all wear wigs, and we're gonna be called the Weirdos.' I didn't know what to think about him," Fleckenstein recalled, "but I agreed, and Johnny and I left the Sea Witch gig and we started working with Arthur." Fleckenstein, in turn, recommended a Hollywood High School classmate of his – drummer John Jacobson, who joined the Weirdos-American Four. Beginning in February 1964, the group with Arthur as lead singer and three members named John (Echols, Fleckenstein, Jacobson) began playing Los Angeles area nightspots, including the Cinnamon Cinder on Ventura Boulevard in Studio City, attracting attention with their offbeat getups. "We wore these wigs with bangs. They were ridiculous," Fleckenstein said. "Everybody except Arthur usually called me 'Fleck.' Arthur always called me by my whole name: 'Johnny Fleckenstein.'"

Arthur, in his handwritten memoirs, explained the inspiration for the wigs. "I don't think I would have had the wig idea at all if I hadn't turned my TV that night to the *Ed Sullivan Show* and seen that group from England – 'Here they are, the Beatles.' While sitting in South L.A., in front of my television, I saw something that changed my way of thinking about playing music a lot. The feeling I got from seeing them play was phenomenal, the dedication to the songs, the girls screaming. The show blew me away as much as the first time I saw Elvis Presley play '(You Ain't Nothing But A) Hound Dog.' These guys showed me what a four-piece band could really do. The look, the style, and the music was a brand-new thing," Arthur wrote.

After Jacobson enrolled in college that autumn, he found that performing in the band conflicted with his studies. The American Four turned to Don Conca, who was another school acquaintance of Fleckenstein's. (Although Don's name commonly was shown as "Conka," his Italian surname was properly spelled Conca.) A performance by the Byrds at Ciro's nightclub in the spring of 1965 spun Johnny, Arthur, Fleck, and Don around and prompted them to embrace folk rock. By April 1965, the band had dropped the Weirdos and American Four monikers after adopting a new name: the Grass Roots, which Echols said was inspired by the "Message to the Grass Roots" speech that civil rights activist Malcolm X delivered in November 1963. The band began billing itself under the new name before Dunhill Records founder Lou Adler created another band called the Grass Roots (as the "Grass Roots" chapter in our book *Where Have All the Pop Stars Gone? – Volume 2* describes). Arthur Lee's Grass Roots alternated drummers, performing at various times with Carl Byrd (who had been a member of the Chuck Daniels Band), Roland Davis, or Don Conca.

That spring of '65, after playing one nighters at various nightclubs around Hollywood, the Grass Roots became entrenched as the house band at the Brave New World, a nondescript out-of-the way club at 7207 Melrose Avenue that had scarcely any signage but attracted in-the-know young hip patrons. Frank Zappa and the Mothers of Invention also performed at the club. Arthur, who also had been playing organ and rhythm guitar, relinquished the rhythm guitar role for a few weeks that summer, after guitarist Bobby Beausoleil (pronounced BO-so-lay) approached the band at the Brave New World and asked to sit in with them. Beausoleil was a competent rhythm guitarist, but his tenure with the Grass Roots was temporary, lasting only a few weeks. Beausoleil's name emerged four years later, after he had become a member of the murderous Charles Manson "family." (Beausoleil was convicted and sentenced to be executed for savagely stabbing guitarist Gary Hinman to death for a claimed unpaid debt to the Manson family, but when California repealed the death penalty in 1972 his sentence was commuted to life. Beausoleil remains in prison, where he has recorded music and created paintings and drawings sold through his website that friends maintain for him.)

In late summer 1965 Bryan MacLean, who frequently played guitar at a West L.A. folk club called the New Balladeer and did a stint as equipment "roadie" for the Byrds, introduced himself to the Grass Roots and sat in with them to play a few tunes. With his considerable talent, he was hired to replace the unreliable Beausoleil as the Grass Roots' rhythm guitarist. He also was a serious songwriter. Hullabaloo nightclub management associate Paul Diamond, another high school friend of Don Conca's, recalls the selection of MacLean as a smart strategic move. "Bryan had the right look – long hair, hip clothes, and he was a good-looking guy. Arthur hired Bryan, I believe, because he saw him as a good visual fit for the band. And Bryan progressed right away," Diamond recalled. Arthur's memoirs coincided with Diamond's impressions. "We were drawing a good crowd at the Brave New World, but Bryan was like the new kid on the block, and he brought a lot of Byrds groupies with him," Arthur wrote. "Bryan had that baby face; he wore pin-striped pants, a red handkerchief around his neck, and was about as arrogant as they come. I might add that Fleck and Echols also had no problem with the ladies. If anything, the problem was keeping the girls off the stage and choosing which one we wanted. I used to think of Bryan as the Byrds' reject, but he drew from the Byrds' crowd. Pretty soon the Brave New World was getting too small for us." While performing at the Brave New World, Lee, Echols and their band mates heard some unexpected news.

"One of the regulars at the Brave New World told us that she had just heard the radio play our new record, 'Ballad of a Thin Man.' Of course, that wasn't our record. So after checking it out, we learned that Lou Adler had brought together some studio musicians and called them the Grass Roots, which was no coincidence, since he had been to the club where we were playing on a number of occasions," Echols told us. "I was among many people who believed that he was banking on the fact that our fans would rush out and buy the record, thinking it was us, which is exactly what hap-pened. By the time it became widely known that it wasn't us, the damage – from our perspective – had already been done. The record skyrocketed up the charts and became a hit. We could have challenged his 'borrowing' our name, but after much discussion we decided to find a new name."

While driving along Beverly Boulevard in Hollywood, Arthur, Johnny, and Bryan got the inspiration for their new name from an advertising billboard for Luv brassieres. Arthur had once worked in the shipping department for that manufacturer. Bryan said 'man, that would be a fantastic name for the group.' Arthur said the name 'Luv' was perfect. The band members decided unanimously on that name, with the conventional spelling 'Love' to avoid potential copyright infringement problems. The name resonated with their club patrons as well.

As Love, the band earned a month-long booking in October 1965 at Bido Lito's at 1608 N. Cosmo Street in Hollywood. Meanwhile Fleckenstein received the call he had been awaiting: an opening for an optical production job in motion pictures at Columbia Studios. Because of the camera guild union benefits, he took that job, and the band temporarily filled the gap with bass player Michael Dowd before auditioning and hiring Kenneth Raymond Forssi to replace Fleckenstein. (In 1967 Fleckenstein joined the Standells, as this book's chapter on that band describes.)

At that time, the band also was undergoing another transition – from playing primarily "cover" versions of hit songs to performing original material. "Our set lists reflected the transition, and we began adding more and more of our own songs. We were among the first rock groups to play extended jams, a tradition in jazz," said Echols, who impressed audiences by playing a dual-necked guitar. (The double necks allowed him to shift between six and 12 strings to achieve different sounds without changing guitars. He also was fond of the Gibson Les Paul Standard.) Frontman Arthur Lee was a dramatic presence on stage. Just as the band's music was eclectic, so was the mode of Arthur's apparel. He favored paisley or ruffled shirts, colorful scarves or strings of beads around his neck, fringed jackets, leather capes, small, dark rectangular or diamond-shaped wire-frame rose-tinted sunglasses, and leather knee-high boots or well-worn combat boots – one of which he intentionally kept unlaced. He sometimes wore only one shoe, a high-topped moccasin. To fans, he was as magnetic as he was mysterious, and on stage Love was powerfully hypnotic.

Don Conca's unreliability due to persistent drug problems prompted the band to enlist a backup: Ken's roommate, Alban "Snoopy" Pfisterer – so nicknamed because of his curiosity as a young child. Ken and Snoopy met as college classmates majoring in commercial art. Snoopy was first a pianist and harpsichordist, but also played drums. "Don was the nicest, most outgoing person one could ever hope to meet. He was fun to be around," Johnny told us. "Unfortunately Don succumbed to drug addiction, which robbed him of his personality and most of the qualities that made him so endearing. His skills as a drummer never diminished – he was absolutely fantastic. Sadly, though, he could not pull himself together."

That autumn, Frank Zappa introduced the band members to his manager, Herb Cohen, who had expressed interest in also managing Love. Although the band didn't hire him to manage their career, they did appoint Herb and his brother, Martin "Mutt" Cohen, an entertainment lawyer, to manage the band's publishing arm, Grassroots Music. Herb's business associates included Jac Holzman, founder of Elektra Records.

Herb invited Jac to see Love perform one mid-December evening at Bido Lito's. "By the end of the evening, Jac was absolutely over the moon – he was ready to sign the group on the spot. We, on the other hand were a bit wary," Echols said. Since its establishment 15 years earlier, Elektra primarily was a folk and blues album-oriented label based in Greenwich Village, New York. Elektra had never released a hit single, but Holzman was eager to break into the rock music market. Arthur, Bryan, and Johnny – the core members of the band – headed with Jac to Canter's Deli on Fairfax Avenue to discuss what a record deal with the label might entail. But no contract was signed that night. "Jac returned to the club the next night, and he was even more enthusiastic after hearing us for a second time, so we resumed our discussions at Canter's." That meeting led the band members to sign the contract. "But we did not realize until much later that Herb Cohen would receive a percentage of our royalties, as a finder's fee for introducing our group to Elektra."

Artistically, Love was a collective as much as it was a rock band, communal in nature. Although individual group members (primarily Arthur) were credited for writing the various singles and album tracks the band recorded, song compositions and arrangements really were the result of collaboration among all the members of the band. "The vast majority of our songs resulted from a total group effort. Everyone worked out their own parts, offered suggestions, initiated changes, created those signature flourishes. In effect, each of us wrote the parts of the song that we played," Echols said. "So in fairness, each group member should have received songwriting credits. For Love's first album, members received nominal writing credit for their contribution. Arthur, Bryan, or I would introduce a song idea, usually consisting of a few words and rudimentary chords. The group members would create their own parts, often completely changing the song. But due to the undue influence of the Cohen brothers, there was no such acknowledgement of their contributions on subsequent releases, which caused deep rifts within the group later on."

Don Conca and Snoopy Pfisterer had continued rotating on and off the drum stool for a while, until one evening in late 1965 as Love performed at the cavernous Hullabaloo nightclub (formerly the Earl Carroll Theatre and the Moulin Rouge) at 6230 Sunset Boulevard. Paul Diamond, who was working at the Hullabaloo that night, recalled the incident that led to Don's severance from the band. "When Don Conca showed up, he was not in any condition to play, due to either drugs or lack of sleep, and during the second song he slipped off the drum stool and landed on the floor," Diamond recalled. "Arthur became really mad at Don about that because getting high apparently meant more to Don than the band did. Don was a striking visual presence with his long black hair and hip style of dress, and he was perfect for Arthur's vision of what a hip band would look like. Arthur was hurt on many levels by Don's lack of seriousness about the band." Arthur's composition "Signed D.C.," a somber tale about the lonely desperation of a heroin addict, was an ode to the drug struggles of Don Conca. "But Don hated 'Signed D.C.' because it stamped him as a loser for the rest of his life," Diamond said.

On January 24, 1966, in Sunset Sound recording studio at 6650 Sunset Boulevard with engineer Bruce Botnick at the controls, the band members began recording their first album. Bryan MacLean, Johnny Echols, and Snoopy Pfisterer were 19 years of age. Arthur Lee was 21; Ken Forssi was 23. Jac Holzman and Mark Abramson were credited as producers, but the album consisted essentially of Love running through their frequently performed set list for live gigs. Because they already had the arrangements worked out and everyone knew their parts, they completed the album in only four days.

Preceding the release of the band's first single, Love built a strong Southern California fan base not only at Bido Lito's but also with bookings at clubs throughout the region, including It's Boss (8433 Sunset Boulevard) and the Hullabaloo, as well as in San Francisco clubs – the Avalon Ballroom (1268 Sutter Street) and the Fillmore Auditorium (1805 Geary Boulevard). In March a band called the Sons of Adam, on a night off from their normal gig as the house band at Gazzari's, played a set at Bido Lito's. "We marveled at what an exceptional drummer Michael was. The man could righteously play," Echols said. "Michael was on fire, he was in the zone, the dude had everyone's attention. So after the show, we were all sitting around shooting the breeze, when Arthur just blurted out 'man, you've just got to be our drummer. You would be perfect for us." But Michael declined because he had a comfortable income with the Sons of Adam. As Love and the Sons of Adam members became friends, Arthur persisted in asking Michael to join Love (which Michael did five months later).

In March 1966 Elektra released the band's 14-track debut album, titled *Love,* with the striking red stylized "Love" lettering that Elektra art director Bill Harvey designed and that the band adopted as its logo. Leading off with their gruff version of "My Little Red Book" (which became the band's first hit single), the *Love* LP spanned hard rock (including a searing rendition of Lee's composition "My Flash On You" and Dino Valenti's "Hey Joe," which the Leaves turned into a hit single), folk-rock ballads (Bryan MacLean's love song "Softly To Me," and Lee's gentle compositions "No Matter What You Do," "You I'll Be Following" and "A Message To Pretty") and psychedelia (Lee and Echols' trippy dreamlike instrumental "Emotions"). Some of the lyrics were dark and disturbing, angry or forbidding. The Lee-Echols-Fleckenstein composition "Can't Explain" warned a girl about waking in the morning and finding her boyfriend dead. "Mushroom Clouds," which Lee, Echols, Forssi, and MacLean wrote collaboratively, pondered the fate of humanity against the specter of nuclear annihilation. The album also included Lee's grim composition "Signed D.C.," a stark portrayal of addiction painted with the forlorn wail of Arthur's harmonica. In the photos taken for the album cover, Snoopy had a short haircut and preppy-looking duds, in sharp contrast to the hip appearance of his bandmates; he attributed that to the strict dress code of the art and industrial design college he had been attending.

All of the band members except Snoopy moved into "The Castle," their name for the creepy 21-room, 8,000-square-foot mansion that would become part of the mystique of Love. The rambling mansion, at 4320 Cedarhurst Circle in the Los Feliz sector of Hollywood downslope from the Griffith Observatory, had been built in the 1920s for early film producer Maurice Tourneur. He had sold the home, named The Cedars, to motion picture actor Madge Bellamy, in the late '20s, and it changed hands several times after that. "A realtor who managed the property offered us a fantastic deal to rent the humongous old mansion," Johnny told us. "If we would pay the property taxes and maintain the premises, which amounted to around $1,200 per month, we could all live there for as long as we wanted. Each member of the group had an adjoining suite of rooms." Vacant for years, the place had become decrepit, creaky, and plagued with plumbing problems. Some people said it was haunted. But with a continual stream of stoned rock musician friends, dazed groupies, and hangers-on letting themselves in through the unlocked doors, the dumpy place became a den of decadence, a haven for sex, drugs, and rock and roll. "We loved it there," Johnny added. "It was *the* place to be, and the parties there were notorious."

These were the days before youth-oriented music had gravitated to the FM radio band; rock was confined to AM "top 40 stations" that played primarily singles. Despite the lack of initial album airplay, the Southern California fans that the band had attracted snatched up copies of the *Love* album. Wallichs Music City, a prominent locally owned group of record stores, published a weekly "hit list" that ranked records by sales. By April 18, the *Love* album already was No. 2 on the Wallichs chart of best-selling albums, locally outselling popular albums by the Rolling Stones, the Righteous Brothers, Sonny and Cher, Barbra Streisand, and the Tijuana Brass.

As the band's following grew and the debut album began selling, Herb Cohen concluded that Love needed someone to administer and promote a fan club. He called Elmer Valentine, principal owner of the Whisky à Go-Go (8901 Sunset) and The Trip (8572 Sunset) nightclubs. Valentine referred him to his staff member Ronnie Haran, who did promotion work for both clubs and was in charge of booking talent at the Whisky. When Cohen called, she told him that she was unfamiliar with Love. "I'd never even heard of them, but he told me they were great. So I called Arthur that very afternoon, and I said, 'Hi, Herbie Cohen asked me to call you about running your fan club. And the first words out of Arthur's mouth – and this I'll never forget – were 'Oh, yeah? Would you fire Herbie Cohen for me?' And I just fell in love with Arthur right then," Ronnie told us. She immediately went to his house to meet him. "It was like I had known him for a hundred years. And we got along like a house on fire." Haran wound up being hired as the band's manager, even before seeing them perform. And when she did catch their stage performance, she was impressed. "Love was packing them in at Bido Lito's, and the lines to get in went around the block. I started booking them into the Whisky, and when I did, the whole place [figuratively] exploded."

Copies of the "My Little Red Book" single were still warm at the pressing plant in early April when L.A. "top 40" radio stations KHJ, KFWB, KRLA, and KBLA jumped onto it. Kids blasted it from their car speakers as they cruised the boulevards: Van Nuys, Hollywood, Hawthorne, Sunset, and other popular hangouts. The Wallichs hit list of April 25 showed that "My Little Red Book" soared from No. 20 to No. 6 in only one week. Jump-started by the Southern California crowd, "My Little Red Book" (with "A Message To Pretty" on the flip side) premiered April 30 on the *Billboard* Hot 100 chart. Although it peaked nationally at only No. 52, it ranked much higher in individual metro areas, reflected in the fact that it persisted on the *Billboard* chart for 11 weeks. It also fared better on the *Cash Box* magazine chart, on which it hit No. 35. The *Love* album reached

No. 57 on the *Billboard* Top 200 albums chart. Love's admirers included members of a then-obscure band: the newly formed Doors. Jim Morrison and Doors drummer John Densmore often watched Love perform and began hanging out with Arthur and the guys. Forty years later, in an article in the *Los Angeles Times* memorializing Arthur Lee, Densmore wrote about Morrison's reaction upon hearing "My Little Red Book" on the radio. He reported that Jim told him, "If we [the Doors] could make a record as good as that, I'd be happy." The two bands soon would dramatically influence each other – to the great benefit of the Doors, and, unfortunately, to the detriment of Love.

Ronnie Haran's search for a new house band in May 1966 brought her to the London Fog, a seedy joint at 8919 Sunset Boulevard. The place was nearly deserted except for a few drunks, and the Doors were literally singing for their supper there, but Haran saw potential in them and booked them into the Whisky beginning May 23. Although initially unpolished, the Doors began working out and evolving their set list, improving all the while. Ronnie Haran, Arthur Lee, and Johnny Echols all thought that the Doors deserved a recording contract. Ronnie called executives of numerous labels on their behalf; she also brought the Doors to the attention of Jac Holzman of Elektra, as did Arthur and Johnny. Holzman disliked the Doors the first time he saw them, but after being persuaded to return three more times to watch them perform at the Whisky, he finally understood. "He realized how mesmerized the kids in the audience were," Haran said. That's when Holzman signed the Doors to a recording contract. "Before that, the biggest thing Elektra ever had was the Paul Butterfield Blues Band."

Meanwhile, spurred by the rise of "My Little Red Book" on the charts, Love made a guest appearance June 18 on ABC's *American Bandstand,* giving "My Little Red Book" and "A Message To Pretty" nationwide exposure. Five days later, the band appeared on the ABC TV program *Where the Action Is.* On June 25 Love was part of the lineup in the Beach Boys Summer Spectacular concert on the big stage of the Hollywood Bowl, in a billing shared with the Byrds, the Lovin' Spoonful, Neil Diamond, the Sir Douglas Quintet, Percy Sledge, Chad and Jeremy, the Leaves, the Sunrays, and Captain Beefheart and his Magic Band.

But as popular as Love was becoming in L.A., the band suffered from lack of awareness elsewhere. "I realized that we had a problem when I put Love on the road. Wherever we went, I would call up the local record stores and I would ask, 'Do you have Love's album?' And they would say, 'Who? Never heard of them.' Then I would ask, 'Do you carry anything from Elektra?' Their answer usually was 'Who? Never heard of them.' My big beef with Jac and everyone at Elektra was that they had no distribution," Haran said. "So why should we break our necks showing up in godforsaken places and not even sell albums and make $1,500 a night, and it would wind up costing us more than that to get there?"

The band also encountered other problems with touring. "We would show up in Tempe, Arizona, with some funky stupid sound system that wasn't capable of producing enough volume even for the 500 kids that had shown up there. And Arthur would say, 'I'm not going out on stage until they get me a better sound system. I don't want to sound like shit.' And I would totally agree with him," Haran said. "Every time we did go somewhere, we encountered that kind of thing, because the promoters were just hungry to make money off the kids."

Rather than looking to one of their debut album's other tracks for the band's second single release, Love returned to Sunset Sound on June 20 to record another Arthur Lee song, "7 And 7 Is," with the flip side, "No. Fourteen," culled from among the outtakes of the first album. On "7 And 7 Is," for which Jac Holzman served as producer, Echols' brilliantly frenzied guitar playing and Pfisterer's impossibly frenetic drumming synchronized with Forssi's feedback-infused bass lines driven like a speeding locomotive. On July 30, only five weeks after it was recorded, "7 And Seven Is" made its debut on the *Billboard* Hot 100 on its way to becoming the highest-ranking single for Love. In the ensuing weeks it climbed to No. 33, and remained on the chart for 10 weeks.

Despite Snoopy's Herculean performance on "7 And 7 Is" and other tracks on the first album, he lacked confidence in his drumming, and he seemed out of his comfort zone with the band. As accomplished drummer Michael Stuart became a member of Love in late August 1966, Snoopy shifted to organ and harpsichord. ("Stuart" was Michael Ware's stage name; in later life, he blended his professional and legal names to form the name Michael Stuart-Ware, as the epilogue section about him in this chapter describes.) "Michael immediately fit in. He was the perfect addition, a fantastic drummer and a really intelligent person with a great personality," Echols said. Love also recruited saxophone and flute player Tjay Contrelli (whose real name was John Barberis, and who also had been a member of the Chuck Daniels Band). "He pronounced the first name 'Jay' – the 'T' was silent," explained Michael, adding that Tjay was a jazz musician who admired John Coltrane.

By the time Michael joined Love, its members had vacated the Castle, and headed farther west, to the bohemian haven of Hollywood's Laurel Canyon. There, Arthur, Bryan, and Snoopy moved into a spacious home on Brier Drive. "Arthur and Snoop lived in the upstairs portion of the house, and Bryan lived alone in a smaller unit downstairs," Michael recalled. Johnny and Kenny roomed together in a house on Lookout Mountain Avenue, near Wonderland Avenue. "Tjay lived by himself, in a pad farther up Lookout Mountain where it becomes Appian Way." Michael remained for a time in the house he shared with the Sons of Adam.

Elektra assigned producer Paul Rothchild and accomplished recording engineer Dave Hassinger for the album *Da Capo,* which the seven-member configuration of Love (Arthur, Johnny, Bryan, Kenny, Snoopy, Michael, and Tjay) began recording September 27, 1966, at RCA's Hollywood studios at 6363 Sunset Boulevard. With remarkable efficiency Love laid down all of the album's tracks within five days. "Paul Rothchild was someone with whom we could relate, who also possessed the skills necessary to help bring out all of the nuances and complexities of *Da Capo,*" Echols said. "The difference in sound quality between our first and second albums is night and day." In musical notations, "da capo" is an instruction to repeat a phrase from the beginning. The album was a symbolic restart for the band. *Da Capo,* which veered sharply away from the folk-rock sound that had dominated the first album, was a panoply of Baroque-tinged ballads, psychedelia and rock with intricate arrangements, and wispy woodwind fills that Tjay wrote. MacLean's "¡Que Vida!" was a refreshingly airy counterpoint to the band's sometimes grim lyrics, and Snoopy's harpsichord playing flavored Arthur's delicate jazz-rock composition "Stephanie Knows Who." (The real-life Stephanie Buffington had been Bryan's girlfriend before devoting increasing amounts of her attention to Arthur, then becoming Bryan's girlfriend once again – thereby straining the friendship between Arthur and Bryan.) The hit "Seven & Seven Is" (with an ampersand and numbers spelled out on the album label, as opposed to numerals for the single) was included. The second side of the album was dedicated entirely to one 19-minute track called "Revelation," a freeform jam that Love recorded at Sunset Sound with the intention of capturing the spontaneity of the band's live performances, but within the controlled environment of the recording studio. A novel concept at the time, it may have helped inspire numerous other bands to record long tracks, such as the Doors' "The End" (1967), Iron Butterfly's "In-A-Gadda-Da-Vida" (1968), Lee Michaels' 20-minute, five-song jam on his eponymous 1969 album, and Jethro Tull's "Thick As A Brick" (1972).

"After *Da Capo* was recorded, Snoop moved out of the place where he had lived with Bryan and Arthur, I moved out of the house I had shared with the Sons of Adam, and Snoop and I moved into a house on Durand

Drive, up past the top of Beechwood Drive in Beechwood Canyon, near the Hollywood sign," Michael said. Arthur, meanwhile, changed addresses to a spectacular home, higher up in the hills on Sunset Plaza Drive. "It was at the top of Kirkwood, a narrow dirt road off Laurel Canyon. The home, which had an indoor-outdoor pool, was used for filming *The Trip* starring Peter Fonda and Dennis Hopper," Michael added.

Johnny Echols thought highly of Tjay Contrelli. "Though he was at least 10 years older than me, we became good friends. So when Arthur and I decided to experiment and change directions for *Da Capo,* we thought of Tjay," Echols explained. "Even though he was an 'old school' jazz and R&B saxophonist and flutist, he definitely had the chops to play the type of music we envisioned, and he proved to be a fantastic addition to the group."

But the seven-member configuration did not endure because it was not viable economically. "Later, Blood, Sweat and Tears and Chicago proved that it could be done, but we were unable to make it work. Tjay, being older and more experienced than the rest of us, was the first to realize that," Johnny said. By late 1966, Contrelli and Pfisterer were dismissed, thereby solidifying Love's lineup with Arthur Lee on vocals and keyboard, Johnny Echols on lead guitar, Bryan MacLean on rhythm, Ken Forssi on bass, and Michael Stuart playing drums. But the band struggled with disappointing record sales. *Da Capo* went no higher than No. 80 on the *Billboard* album chart following its release in November. A combination of insufficient promotion by Elektra and inadequate touring stood in the way of additional chart success for the band's singles releases. Love had plenty of bookings in L.A. clubs, and Arthur, who disdained long-distance touring and disreputable concert promoters, was content to reign supreme on his home turf.

"We were musicians, and playing music was our job, our only job. None of us was independently wealthy, so if we didn't play, we didn't eat. We each had cars and later, houses and myriad other expenses, all of which required money. The majority of our income was derived from performing, not from record sales, but promoters in the majority of the country would not even consider booking us. To them, we were off-limits," Echols explained. "A bunch of racially mixed California hippies were most unwelcome. Out of necessity, we played mostly on the East and West coasts. We were able to earn a fairly decent living, but not playing the majority of markets severely limited our exposure and record sales. Add to that the less than adequate promotion by our record label, and Love labored under a huge disadvantage compared to other comparable groups."

Operationally, Love was an autocracy, with one man in charge. "I worked with the whole band, but Arthur ran the show. There was just no question about it. It was Arthur's trip," Ronnie Haran said. "He let certain people into his circle that I would have kicked out, but he was very intuitive about people, as I am, and he instinctively knew who was cool and who wasn't."

The band's follow-up to the "7 And 7 Is" single was "Stephanie Knows Who" (backed with "Orange Skies"), released in October 1966. It did not register on the Hot 100. Elektra then substituted "She Comes In Colors" (produced by Paul Rothchild) as the "A" side (with "Orange Skies" again on the flip), but that didn't help. "We regularly played 'Stephanie' in front of live audiences, with Arthur and Bryan standing next to one another on stage – one the winner and one the loser, which of course only twisted the knife," Michael recalled. "In fact, I remember vividly, the beautiful raven-haired Stephanie in the audience one night at the Whisky, standing right down front at the edge of the stage with her motor running, and all the while making goo-goo eyes at Bryan, while Arthur sang his heart out. That must have just plain hurt."

Ronnie Haran was the architect of Love's most successful promotional event. She worked endless hours coordinating promotional activities for a late December concert appearance by the band at the Dallas Convention Center. She capitalized on the event with a fan reception at the city's airport, Love Field, and an album autograph signing session at the elegant Neiman Marcus department store. In the days leading up to the performance she called Dallas radio stations to drum up excitement, and made sure that record stores were stocked with Love recordings. "When we landed at Love Field, there were 8,000 to 10,000 kids at the airport to meet us," Ronnie recalled. "And we had a police escort from there. It was fabulous." Ronnie hoped the success of the event might persuade the band to tour more regularly, but that didn't happen.

Meanwhile, Elektra was orchestrating a major promotional campaign to launch the Doors. That band got a big jump out of the gate when Casey Kasem premiered the first Doors single, "Break On Through," on the *Shebang* TV program the first week in January 1967. Elektra splashed a big Doors billboard on the Sunset Strip, and obtained a succession of bookings for the band at the Fillmore in San Francisco, Ondine in New York and Gazzari's in Hollywood.

"The Doors would be much more marketable than your average jam band. They were dark and cerebral. College kids would love them," Echols observed. "The lion's share of the recently acquired resources which the label had slated for promoting Love instead went to the Doors. We were basically put on the back burner. From that point on the marketing strategy for us was, for the most part, word of mouth. The Doors, on the other hand, received world-class promotion, including teen magazine covers, interviews, joint promotional ventures with all of the major radio stations, and sponsored tours. The Doors wound up selling huge numbers of records, while we were left in the dust, hoisted by our own petard."

Love's dry spell continued through 1967 with a succession of singles: MacLean's "Softly To Me" (with Lee's "The Castle" as the "B" side); "¡Que Vida!" (what a life) with "Hey Joe" on the flip side; and Lee's "The Daily Planet" (with his song "Andmoreagain" on the flip side), but none of those reached the chart either.

Despite the band's continuing disenchantment with Elektra – a relationship that would become even more strained – Love's greatest and most enduring achievement still lay ahead. In the spring of 1967 the band members had begun preparing for their third album, *Forever Changes,* which they believed was to consist of two discs, with Arthur assuming the role of producer, working out orchestrations with noted arranger David Angel. Arthur had written much of the material for disk 1; Bryan and Johnny had worked for months, meanwhile on compositions and arrangements for disk 2. But the band members as a whole hadn't been disciplined enough in rehearsing the songs, spending too much time getting stoned and partying at Arthur's place on Brier Drive and not enough time practicing together. As the band prepared to enter the studio at Sunset Sound, Elektra stunned Love with two sucker punches: Jac Holzman had sidelined Arthur as producer, instead assigning Neil Young to produce *Forever Changes.* And it would not be a double album, after all; Holzman has stated that Elektra never intended to press dual LPs, because two albums with orchestral backing would have been too expensive to produce. Misunderstanding or not, half of the material that the band members had written, arranged, and rehearsed would have to be shelved for release the following year as a separate album. When everyone, including Young, decided that the project would not be a good fit for him, Arthur was designated to produce the album, in collaboration with recording engineer Bruce Botnick. But one more demoralizing blow was still to come for Love.

"We were devastated by the cruel turn of events, especially Bryan and I. This was to be our magnum opus," Johnny told us. "The two of us had worked for months, writing and working out arrangements for 12 songs that all of a sudden would be excluded from the album. So to show his extreme displeasure in not having more of his songs included on *Forever Changes,* Bryan chose to engage in a minor mutiny. He decided that he wouldn't play the songs written by Arthur with the same verve he had on previous recordings. He sulked and became so disruptive that it seemed the whole project might be in jeopardy of self destructing." The other band members were out of synch with each other as well, provoking Arthur's displeasure. The atmosphere in the studio was tense and unproductive, as expensive studio time ticked away. Something needed to be done to shake up the band and get them back on track.

When the band members showed up at the studio the next day, they found "Wrecking Crew" members Billy Strange on guitar, Carol Kaye on guitar and bass, Don Randi on piano, and Hal Blaine on drums. The band members not only had to endure watching other musicians play their parts, but had to suffer the indignity of teaching them how to play certain licks. "They were fine studio musicians who have played on scores of hit records – but they were not us, and they sounded nothing like us," Echols said. "They didn't even try to do the intricate finger picking, the Spanish flourishes, or any of the myriad signature touches that were the reason that Love sounded the way we sounded. When Kenny saw that Wrecking Crew bass player Carol Kaye was having difficulty grasping the song 'The Daily Planet,' he valiantly tried to teach her the nuances of the bass lines he had worked out for it. When Arthur noticed that, out of total exasperation he said, 'man, this is a bunch of bullshit. Why does Kenny have to teach her his part? He wrote it, and *he* should play it!'"

The experience had shocked the band from its funk – and sent a message to Jac Holzman as well. "If it wasn't clear before those sessions, it was abundantly clear afterwards. Each member of Love was implicitly involved in the creation and performance of the songs and sound associated with Love. Further, these exceptional musicians could not be easily replaced by anyone," Echols declared. (The eventual *Forever Changes* album contained only two tracks on which Wrecking Crew members played: the songs "Andmoreagain" and "The Daily Planet.")

With a renewed focus, Love spent the next several weeks rehearsing the album's content to perfection. When the band members were ready to resume recording in mid-August, Sunset Sound was occupied with someone else's session, so Botnick found an opening three-quarters of a mile east at Western Recorders at 6000 Sunset Boulevard. Convening there, the members of Love performed with precision, determination, and artistry. *Forever Changes,* completed in mid-September and released in the United States in November, would become recognized as the band's masterpiece. The songs expressed the discontent and anxieties, the anger, and sense of helplessness and isolation, that young people were feeling as the Vietnam War escalated, racial tensions seethed, and distrust between young people and authorities deepened and widened. *Forever Changes* led off with the exquisitely beautiful "Alone Again Or," a Bryan MacLean composition that Love embellished with Johnny's gossamer flamenco guitar licks and a wistful trumpet solo. The intricately textured album probed themes of love ("Andmoreagain"), the bloody casualties of war ("A House Is Not A Motel"), the tensions of urban life ("The Red Telephone"), our roles in life and the inevitability of death (the episodic "You Set The Scene"), and the toll of drug abuse ("Live And Let Live"). In this collection of sophisticated, exquisitely orchestrated songs, augmented by strings and brass instrumentation performed by members of the Los Angeles Philharmonic Orchestra, the five members of Love artfully interlaced delicacy, power, and passion. Although *Forever Changes,* released in November 1967, sold briskly in regional markets, it reached only No. 154 on *Billboard's* albums chart. It performed much better in the United Kingdom, where it drove up to No. 24. In January 1968, Elektra issued a "Alone Again Or," backed with "A House Is Not A Motel," as a single. The album version of "Alone Again Or" was 3 minutes 15 seconds long, but for that single it was edited to 2:49 to encourage radio airplay. It became a top-10 hit in Los Angeles, but did not penetrate *Billboard's* national Hot 100.

Michael Stuart-Ware believes that fans were slow to embrace the orchestral *Forever Changes* because its sophisticated contents diverged so radically from prior Love recordings. "It was different from other music that was being played on the radio at the time and even quite a bit different from the music we had previously recorded. People need time to become accustomed to drastic change. They needed more time than the group was together, apparently," Michael said. "Elektra did the best they could with what they had, but they were still a relatively small label at that time, so the promotion and distribution capabilities were probably only somewhere between moderate and good. I think Elektra's main difficulty was that geographically, their promotion was spotty. The result was that in some places we were well known, and in other places, people had never heard of us. Finally and most unfortunately," Michael added, "our willingness to tour and help promote the album ourselves would have been rated as poor. Touring to promote the album was a power that was under our control, and it was a power that we failed to exercise. In order to promote an album properly, a band has to work hard and often, and we didn't. In fact, after the abbreviated 'Forever Changes East Coast Tour' had concluded, we hardly ever played together anymore at all, even in L.A. The problem was that Arthur booked the gigs, and he seemed disinterested in, and even downright opposed to, playing live anywhere. So we sat home quite a bit."

Michael said that booking agents began calling him and Ken Forssi, telling them that Love was committing what they called "professional suicide." Earnings declined. Michael said when Kenny fell behind on payments for his Jaguar, he moved out of the house he had shared with Michael in order to evade repo agents, and for $50 per month rented a garage as his room, parking his car next to his bed. From Michael's perspective, that was the beginning of the breakup of the band.

In late January 1968, Love returned to Sunset Sound to record two Arthur Lee compositions for a single: "Your Mind And We Belong Together," a hard-rocking outcry against a couple's relationship that turned corrosive, twisted into a frenzy by a jolt of psychedelia from Johnny Echols' screaming guitar. The flip side, "Laughing Stock" opened with an eerie chant that gave way to a burst of folk-rock about making music as a form of refuge from an otherwise ponderous life. Because Bruce Botnick had refused to work with Arthur again due to friction between them, John Haeny engineered the session. It was the last session at which that configuration of Love recorded. The single did not reach the charts.

Promotion of *Forever Changes* suffered because Elektra was allocating the bulk of its resources to the Doors. Relationships among the members of Love were fraying, in proportion with their growing antipathy to Elektra Records. "The Elephant in the room was our copious use of drugs. There was indeed a lot of drug usage by all of us – especially during the last months of the group's existence. Drug usage was not the proximate cause of the group's problems, but a response to an untenable situation that had already reached the breaking point," said Echols, who blames Jac Holzman for precipitating the July 1968 breakup of Love.

"Jac was well aware of how unhappy we all were with Elektra, and the situation was growing worse, with little hope of improving. One day, out of the blue, Jac phoned Bryan and offered him the opportunity to record a solo album for Elektra. Of course, Bryan was elated, because that would be his chance to step out of Arthur's shadow," Johnny said. "Bryan excitedly phoned me with the news, even gloating a bit. Then he told Arthur, who replied, 'that's great news Bryan. You're fired.' And it ended with that perfunctory note." The remaining band members carefully deliberated what to do next. "Arthur and I briefly discussed replacing Bryan, but neither of us felt the group would be the same without him. We even discussed the two of us re-forming the group and starting over, but our hearts were just not in it. Maybe it was time for a change. After a great deal of soul searching, we decided mutually to call it quits."

Michael Stuart-Ware has a different view about the dissolution of Love, believing that Arthur was more complicit. "Honestly, I always thought Arthur started taking baby steps toward breaking the group up right after Bryan won the battle for the affections of the beautiful Stephanie Buffington," Michael told us. "Sounds trite, I know, but Love's song 'Stephanie Knows Who' was all about the girl who knows who she wants to be with, once and for all, written by Arthur during a time when the much sought-after Stephanie had chosen him over Bryan. So 'Stephanie Knows Who' was Arthur's victory anthem. But then, lo and behold, after the song had already been designated song number one on side one of *Da Capo*, Stephanie abruptly changed her mind again and went back with Bryan. Bad pie, that little deal was."

Although Ronnie Haran remained a lifelong friend of Arthur's, she also dissolved her official relationship with Love. Her relationship with the band soured not long after one of its greatest triumphs. "It was shortly after the Love Field thing. I had never taken any money from them in the beginning. There just was no money to take. But technically, I was supposed to be getting 10 percent," Ronnie told us. "When we did the gig at Love Field, that was the first time we made some serious money, and when I paid everybody their shares, I took my 10 percent off the top. And Bryan went nuts. 'You're getting more money than *me*,' he said. I'll never forget it. That was the beginning of the end. I felt 'how fucking *dare* you when I had done *all* of this work for *all* this time and had never taken a dime? I was still very close to Arthur, but from then on everything started falling apart. And yet Bryan and I were very close. I really loved Bryan. He was like my kid brother. But just because of not being able to promote his songs and put more songs on the albums, there was this bitterness under everything."

After the dissolution of Love, Lee immediately set about assembling a new Love band, consisting of lead guitarist Jay Donnellan, bass player Frank Fayad, and drummer George Paul Suranovich. For some of the Southern California performances that followed, the band was billed as "Love With Arthur Lee." The new band recorded an LP for Elektra titled *Four Sail* (released in August 1969). It contained some fine tunes, including Arthur's jug band-like "Your Friend And Mine – Neil's Song," fondly lamenting a departed friend, but the album sat dead in the water; it did not sell well. "Elektra immediately realized where things were headed without Bryan, Kenny, Michael, and me, and Arthur soon found out the hard way just how fickle the music business can be," Echols said. "Where there were once huge, standing-room-only venues, he was now reduced to playing tiny, half-empty clubs. While the original Love could easily fill the Santa Monica Civic auditorium with several thousand people, his new group could barely bring 50 people to the Whisky." Arthur subsequently landed a contract for the band with Blue Thumb Records, for which they recorded the 17-track double album *Out Here* (released in December 1969). For the album jacket, Arthur chose to have his name spelled "Arthurly." Before the album was complete, a disagreement led to Jay Donnellan's dismissal. Frank Fayad and George Suranovich recommended his replacement: Gary Rowles, and Nooney Rickett was added on rhythm guitar. Still, Blue Thumb urged Arthur to reassemble the *Forever Changes* complement of Love. Although Kenny, Johnny, and Michael were agreeable, Bryan declined. Johnny, Kenny, Michael, and Arthur performed together on November 7, 1969, at the Santa Monica Civic Auditorium, but after stepping off stage again following a mediocre performance they went their separate ways. "Without Bryan, it just wasn't the same group," Echols said, and the four split for good. "By the way, Elektra never even attempted to record Bryan's solo project, so all of that drama and turmoil was for absolutely nothing."

The new Love was booked beginning in February 1970 for several performances in the United Kingdom, including dates in London, Manchester, West Midlands, and Leeds, and Copenhagen, Denmark, Stockholm, Sweden, and Wiesbaden, Germany. While in England, Arthur met up with his old friend Jimi Hendrix, with whom he had been friends since 1965. Just for fun, Hendrix and Love booked time in a London recording studio and performed a song called "The Everlasting First," which Arthur had written. That September, Hendrix choked to death in his sleep after consuming an excessive quantity of prescription sleeping pills with red wine. In the summer of 1970 Elektra reissued "Alone Again Or," and unlike the 1968 release pressed Arthur Lee's composition "Good Times" from the Four Sail LP on the flip side. Derived from the compilation album *Love Revisited*, this 45 rpm release of "Alone Again Or" managed to reach the *Billboard* chart, but just barely, reaching no higher than No. 99 after its September 12 debut. As with the prior "Alone Again Or" single, radio programmers overlooked the brilliance of the song and failed to give it sufficient airplay.

A subsequent Blue Thumb album, *False Start* (released in December 1970) opened with "The Everlasting First." Although several prominent reviewers gave high marks to *False Start,* it generated little radio airplay and managed to go no higher than No. 184 on the album chart, even though the band toured nationally to support it. Upon Arthur's request, Blue Thumb released him from his contract. Columbia signed Love to record an album in 1971, but the label's expectations differed from Arthur's, and the tracks were shelved indefinitely.

Arthur went solo for a 1972 A&M Records album called *Vindicator,* which he recorded with guitarist Charles Karp, bassist David Hull, and drummer Don Poncher. Radio programmers largely ignored the intensely hard-rocking, blues-influenced album. In early 1973 he signed with independent Buffalo Records for which he recorded another solo album, *Black Beauty,* with a group of sidemen: lead guitarist Melvan Whittington, bass player Robert Rozelle, and drummer Joe Blocker; Arthur played rhythm guitar. Arthur was energetic and forceful on this album of funk and soul, infused with Hendrix influences, but the label shut down before releasing the LP, and it remained unreleased for nearly four decades, other than bootleg copies that managed to circulate.

Every Love album differed from every one that preceded it, and every one that followed. That's just what Arthur intended. "Change is nothing to me. I'm a walking example of change. To adapt and be able to profit from some gift that God has given you is something to be taken advantage of," Arthur wrote. "My trip, when I first started out, was to do different types of music and not be categorized and labeled. I wanted to accomplish my dream of playing all kinds of music. I fulfilled it enough by going from punk-rock and folk-rock to rock; from rock to classical; from classical to a jazz orientation and R&B. All of my albums are different, and I try to use the voice that goes with the music. The voice I used on 'My Little Red Book' isn't the same voice I used on 'Andmoreagain.'"

The final Love album, released on the RSO Records label in December 1974 and titled *Reel-To-Real,* was the product of Arthur Lee and two of the *Black Beauty* musicians, Melvan Whittington and Joe Blocker, along with slide and rhythm guitarist John Sterling, bass player Sherwood Akuna, and conga player Herman McCormick. The soul music album, which seemed reminiscent of Arthur's LAGs and Memphis rhythm and blues roots, did not attain commercial success. Lee subsequently disbanded Love.

Meanwhile, the band members of Love who had recorded *Forever Changes* with Arthur in 1967 had scattered. "After the break-up, I along with Bryan, Kenny, Michael, and Arthur, became seriously involved with drugs. What had been experimentation, even self-medication, morphed into full-blown addiction. Arthur was deeply involved with cocaine, and the rest of us became heroin addicts," the brutally honest Echols acknowledged. "When we tried to re-create that which had been lost, the drug usage was a factor, but not the overriding factor, by a long shot. Even without the drugs, putting Love back together, the way it was – the genuine friendship, camaraderie and trust – could not be easily done. Bridges had not just been burned – they had been blown to hell."

Johnny Echols tried without success to establish a jazz fusion group with Tjay Contrelli and John Fleckenstein, then in 1971 relocated to New York, where he worked steadily as a session musician. Johnny retired from music in 1984 when he bought property in Sedona, Arizona (which the epilogue section about him further in this chapter describes).

Tjay Contrelli was a member of the rock band Geronimo Black in the 1970s, and L.A. recording studios kept him busy as a session musician. He left behind a daughter, Vana Barberis, when he died in 1989.

Following the dissolution of Love, Ken Forssi found some work as a session musician, but not enough to sustain him. Ken had been an art student before joining Love, and he landed a job with the Hanna-Barbera Productions animation studio as an artist, but he didn't hold that position long. After serving a drug-related sentence at the California Rehabilitation Center in Norco, Riverside County, Forssi moved in the mid-1970s to Florida, where he had lived during his pre-adolescent and teenage years. In Sarasota he found resumption of a music career elusive and instead worked in a variety of jobs. He died of a brain tumor in Tallahassee at age 54 on January 10, 1998.

After Elektra rejected Bryan MacLean's solo demos, and an attempted deal with Capitol Records in New York City disintegrated, desperation overcame Bryan until one day in December 1970 when he experienced a revelation and became a Christian. He developed a following performing contemporary Christian music, and had begun discussions with Arthur Lee in the early '90s about resurrecting Love, but that didn't work out. UFO and the Damned recorded versions of Bryan's composition "Alone Again Or," and Patti Loveless turned Bryan's song "Don't Toss Us Away" into a top-5 country music hit in 1989. While sitting with writer Kevin Delaney at a Fairfax Avenue restaurant on Christmas Day 1998, Bryan said he felt ill. There he collapsed and died from a heart attack. Bryan MacLean was only 52 years old.

Donald Michael Conca remained ensnarled in the grip of drugs for the remainder of his life. "He was never in another group that I'm aware of, though he did play with Arthur and me from time to time," Echols said. Don and Prudence McIntyre became a couple beginning in the early '70s after she and John Fleckenstein divorced. Prudence, John, and Don all knew each other as students at Hollywood High School. During their adolescence Prudence and her sister, Patience, had recorded two 1956 hit records: "Tonight You Belong To Me" and "Gonna Get Along Without Ya Now." Paul Diamond had lost contact with Don in 1970, but their friendship resumed after they bumped into each other several years later at

Santa Anita Racetrack. By then Don and Prudence had a daughter named Paige. "At the time Don was working as a service man for a fire extinguisher company, cleaning, recharging, and tagging the fire extinguishers of clients. Then he started his own business servicing extinguishers," Diamond said. "Don was like a magnet who everybody liked. He was a funny guy, he was a hip guy, and even in his darkest moments, he could be pretty funny and entertaining." When Diamond bought Perry's Pizza, a restaurant in Redondo Beach, he employed Don as a kitchen helper. "When I got out of that business I went to work at a motion picture catering business, and I put Don to work as a fixit man there." But Don again got picked up and sentenced on drug charges. Despite undergoing treatment in a methadone clinic he remained incurably hooked on heroin, and died at age 57 on September 26, 2004. "Arthur and Don were always very close. He loved Don so much," Arthur's wife, Diane Lee, said. "Don spent many, many hours with Arthur. When Don died in 2004 Arthur said to me 'I don't have anyone to talk to anymore.' Don truly didn't have a mean bone in his body."

Between 1968 and the mid-1990s, nearly 40 musicians rotated in and out of bands that Arthur dubbed Love. Beginning in June 1993 he paired with a band called Baby Lemonade whose members knew and appreciated Love's repertoire. In gigs with Arthur, the Baby Lemonade combo – consist-

Arthur Lee performing on October 21, 2003, at the Birchmere concert hall in Alexandria, Virginia (photo by Daniel Coston).

ing of lead guitarist Mike Randle, rhythm guitarist David "Rusty Squeeze-box" Ramsay, bassist Henry Liu and drummer David Green – was billed as "Arthur Lee with Love." Irritated in June 1995 by a neighbor's complaint that he was playing his stereo too loud, Arthur purportedly fired a gun into the air from the balcony of his Van Nuys apartment. The validity of that claim was in dispute; a guest who was in the apartment at the time told responding police officers that he, not Arthur, had fired the gun. Despite uncertainty over who pulled the trigger, Arthur was charged with unsafe discharge of a firearm compounded by illegal possession of a firearm because of prior convictions on other charges. He consequently found himself up against California's rigid "three strikes" law, under which he was sentenced to a 12-year prison term, which he began serving in July 1996 at Pleasant Valley State Prison in Coalinga, Fresno County, California. "The whole prosecution was a travesty, since they never actually proved that he was in possession of a gun," Echols said. Throughout Arthur's time in prison, an appeal was slowly working its way through legal corridors. Arthur was released in December 2001 based on a finding that he had been deprived of due process, due to questionable behavior by the prosecutor during the trial. His sentence was revised to the amount of time he already had served.

While in prison, Arthur had withdrawn from friends and music; he kept his identity to himself and blended anonymously into the prison population. Upon his release from prison, Arthur immediately reconnected with his former manager, Gene Kraut, and embarked on a self-imposed regimen of physical exercise and song rehearsals. Arthur resumed performing in April 2002 and was booked for gigs throughout the United States and Europe with Baby Lemonade, whom Arthur dubbed the new Love. For decades Arthur had shunned performances of songs from *Forever Changes,* preferring to concentrate on new music. But with his comeback, he experienced a change of heart. His return to performing began with two triumphant L.A. shows. Backed by guitarists Mike Randle and David "Rusty Squeezebox" Ramsay, bass player Dave Chapple and drummer David Green, Arthur played an unannounced set on April 2 at Club Spaceland at 1717 Silver Lake Boulevard for a surprised audience, and then appeared in a billed performance before a packed house of ebullient fans on May 1 at the Knitting Factory nightclub at 7201 Hollywood Boulevard. Those were the warm-up gigs for a 26-date European tour in which Arthur Lee and Love (the members of Baby Lemonade) performed for wildly enthusiastic fans in Denmark, Sweden, Norway, Germany, Holland, Spain, the U.K., France and Ireland over a six-week span that began May 16. A separate summer tour encompassed cities throughout the United States, as well as the U.K.

and Greece. In January 2003 Arthur and Baby Lemonade (as Love) returned to Europe for what became known as the *Forever Changes* tour, re-creating the album live, song by song, accompanied by horn and string sections, for euphoric audiences. With dates added in Australia and in several cities across the United States, Arthur and Baby Lemonade performed the *Forever Changes* concert in more than 40 cities over the course of the year. He then reunited with his old chum, original Love member Johnny Echols. For several years they toured as "Love with Arthur Lee and Johnny Echols," often re-creating the entirety of *Forever Changes* with a tour de force stage presence. In 2004 U.K. music periodical *New Musical Express* honored Arthur with a "Living Legend" award, and *Mojo* magazine presented a Hall of Fame Award to him for his collective contributions to music. On the 2004 European tour Arthur noticed that he fatigued more easily than in prior years, but he shrugged it off, attributing it to the rigors of the road.

Arthur mustered up the strength for another 16-date U.K. tour with Johnny Echols that began in late March 2005, but was too exhausted to return to England for another tour that went on in July without him. After resting for two months, Arthur managed to recharge sufficiently to move to Memphis in September 2005. He had not lived in Memphis since he was a child, but he was driven by his plans to live there for a year while putting together a new band. His failing health overtook him again, though, as he inexplicably continued to lose weight. Feeling ill and weakened, he was hospitalized for 13 days with pneumonia. When Diane accompanied him in a follow-up outpatient visit to his doctor in January 2006, he was dealt a harsh blow: diagnosis with acute myeloid leukemia. Despite aggressive treatment, he died at age 61 in Methodist University Hospital in Memphis on August 3, 2006.

Michael Stuart-Ware had hoped to remain in music by becoming a recording engineer, but dogged by drug abuse habits, he careened through a series of pursuits; after becoming a law clerk while in law school, he took a job as a shipping and receiving dock worker for a department store chain, then became a telephone line installer. After marrying, he and his wife, Susan, bought a catering business and moved to South Lake Tahoe (as his epilogue later in this chapter describes).

Snoopy Pfisterer, who was born in 1946 in Switzerland, spent his childhood in Maryland and his adolescence in Costa Rica before relocating to Los Angeles. After his departure from Love he sold home heating and air conditioning systems for a while before deciding to resume his pursuit of a college degree; he enrolled as a music student at Evergreen State College in Olympia, Washington. These days he divides his time between residences in

Washington state and Costa Rica.

Under her married name, Ronnie Haran Mellen has since 1979 lived near Santa Barbara, California. There she operates Santa Barbara Location Services, a film and advertising photography location-setting and event-planning business serving San Luis Obispo, Santa Barbara, and Ventura counties. "I'm not a musician, but I knew I was in the presence of greatness with Love. Arthur was such an amazingly brilliant talent," she said. "Even though I didn't work with Love in any kind of official capacity after 1968, I remained in touch with Arthur. He would call me for advice, and I was always there for him. We were like joined at the hip. We thought a lot alike, and there was never anything that we had a disagreement about – *ever*."

Love led fans on a wide-ranging exploration of music, each album carving unanticipated pathways through an adventurous landscape, rendering the band difficult to categorize. "I can only somewhat and partially categorize the genre of the music from the group's first three albums as, 'psychedelically enhanced folk-rock, jazz-rock, and symphonic-rock,' although none in the strictest sense," Stuart-Ware told us. "Each album was somewhat all over the place and each contained elements of 'furious garage-rock.' It was my band too, as well as Kenny's and Johnny's, and Bryan's and Arthur's. We had unfinished business, and I always held out hope that we could work through our differences and just play music."

Numerous compilations of Love's recordings have been released over the years, including reissue specialist Rhino Records' *The Best Of Love* in 1980 and the *Love Story* box set in 1995. Other Love releases reflecting continuing fan interest over the years include *Studio / Live* (with studio recordings on

Arthur Lee and Johnny Echols at the State Theatre, Falls Church, Virginia, on October 16, 2004 (photo by Daniel Coston).

one side and live tracks on the other) on MCA in 1985; *Out There* on Big Beat in 1988; *The Blue Thumb Recordings* on Hip-O Select in 2007; and *Love Lost,* 14 previously unreleased tracks from the 1971 Columbia sessions, which Sundazed Records obtained and released in 2009.

Love made an indelible impression not only on fans but also on fellow musicians. Guitarist, singer, and composer Syd Barrett credited Love for strongly influencing the early musical career of Pink Floyd. When Led Zeppelin was inducted into the Rock and Roll Hall of Fame in 1995, Robert Plant in his acceptance speech acknowledged the influence of Love on his musical career. On May 22, 2002, as Arthur was engaged in a European concert tour, the British House of Commons welcomed him as Parliamentary members voted to pay tribute to him as the "frontman and inspiration of Love, the world's greatest rock band and creators of *Forever Changes,* the greatest album of all time." High Moon Records obtained masters and acquired rights for the December 2012 vinyl release of Arthur Lee's final solo album, *Black Beauty,* which received rave reviews from critics, who hailed it as a recovered lost masterpiece; *Black Beauty* subsequently was released on CD.

"We had what I would call the perfect band," Arthur Lee reflected in his memoirs. "No one else like us in the world – the look, the crowd, the songs, the youth, and the Hollywood scene. And what made us stand out the most was that we were of different races and we were accepted. That is why we were so unique. We sounded and looked so good it didn't seem to matter what color we were, and that, in this life, is as good as it gets."

In 2008 *Forever Changes* was inducted into the Grammy Hall of Fame, which honors recordings of lasting qualitative or historical significance. In *Rolling Stone* magazine's 2012 compilation of the "500 Greatest Albums of All Time" *Forever Changes* ranked No. 40, ahead of the Doors' eponymous debut album, Pink Floyd's *Dark Side Of The Moon, Meet The Beatles,* the Jimi Hendrix Experience's *Electric Ladyland,* Stevie Wonder's *Songs In The Key Of Life,* the Rolling Stones' *Sticky Fingers,* and Van Morrison's *Moondance.* In 2012 *Forever Changes* was added into the National Archives, Library of Congress' National Recording Registry, recognizing it as "culturally, historically, or aesthetically significant."

LOVE'S U.S. SINGLES ON THE
BILLBOARD HOT 100 CHART

Debut	Peak	Title	Label
4/30/66	52	My Little Red Book	Elektra
7/30/66	33	7 And 7 Is	Elektra
9/12/70	99	Alone Again Or	Elektra

Billboard's pop singles chart data is courtesy of Joel Whitburn's Record Research Inc. (www.recordresearch.com), Menomonee Falls, Wisconsin.

Epilogue: Arthur Lee

Lead singer, composer, band leader

March 7, 1945 – August 3, 2006

Ask just about any diehard Love fan, ask just about anyone who knew Arthur Lee personally, and most will agree: as brilliant as he was in deciphering and musically articulating the anguish and despair of his generation, Arthur also was enigmatic and mystifying. Arthur recognized that, and acknowledged it.

"I wanted to be original, and my originality left people in dismay or wonder about 'what's this guy doing?'" Arthur told an interviewer in 2002. "I never wanted to sound like I copied from anyone." His insistence on originality and channeling his views through the music of Love tested the limits of collaboration. "I wanted Bryan MacLean, my guitarist who passed – God rest his soul – I wanted to be a co-writer with him like Lennon and McCartney or Bacharach and David. I admired that and I wanted that. But somehow, some way, it just didn't – it was a personality clash."

No one would ever accuse Arthur Lee of anything but originality. He was one of a kind: a man who communicated through the realm of music

Arthur Lee at Glastonbury Festival, Somerset, England, 2004 (photo by Doug Potoksky).

on his own terms, conveying his perceptions about life, love, paranoia, violence, despair, and desolation.

Tension commonly arises among creative, competitive people. Just as electrical friction within thunderclouds results in high-energy discharges of lightning, creative tensions among Arthur Lee and the members of Love resulted in brilliantly explosive flashes of inspiration that have endured throughout the past five decades. Arthur's music ran the gamut of emotions from ferocity to tenderness, conveyed through a variety of genres encompassing folk-rock, blues, pop, psychedelia, jazz, and symphonic musical styles. He used whatever form was at his disposal to communicate the ideas that emerged in his mind.

Arthur was a man of considerable contrasts who was forever undergoing changes. He initially was immersed in sports in high school and had considered a career as a pro athlete, but the power of musical performers to attract the attention of girls was enough to persuade him to become a singer and musician instead. Influenced by his friend Jimi Hendrix, Arthur shunned meat for several years (although he eventually relented). Accounts of his prolific use of drugs are legion, yet he was strongly religious; he was raised as a Christian Scientist. And while some of his bandmates and associates have characterized him as, at times, demanding, inflexible, brooding, idiosyncratic, or intimidating, he also could be reflective, considerate, and thoughtful.

"Arthur was a very sensitive person – *very* sensitive, and very caring, even though sometimes he could come off as harsh. It's true," his widow, Diane Lee, told us. "I won't say he was the ideal, always sweet, always wonderful person. That wasn't Arthur Lee. He could be hard. There are different sides to him. When it came to music, he was demanding. He wanted the band members to play music the way he heard it in his head. And if they didn't get it, eventually he'd get upset. Yes, he would. But he really was a very sensitive person. He was easily hurt, sensitive to others' feelings, and he was tuned in to the universe."

Two months before the end of World War II European conflict, he was born Arthur Porter Taylor in Memphis, on March 7, 1945. Nicknamed "Po" (short for "Porter"), Arthur was the only child of Chester Arthur Taylor, a cornet player with the jazzy Jimmie Lunceford Orchestra, and Agnes Taylor (née Porter), a teacher at Memphis's Manassas High School – where Lunceford also had been a teacher of language, physical education, and music in the 1920s. Agnes's aunt Susie had a son, James Crawford, who played drums with Lunceford. As a young child, Arthur lived on North Bellevue Boulevard in a working-class Memphis neighborhood called New

Chicago, where he had a close relationship with his aunts, uncles, and cousins. "Arthur and his parents lived together in the two-story house where Arthur was born, until they moved into their own home across the street. Several of his Porter family relatives and relatives by marriage lived in the general neighborhood. Physically they were close; he was also emotionally close. Arthur loved his mother's side of the family," Diane said.

Chester and Agnes had a rocky relationship, and Arthur Taylor's life underwent its first dramatic change as he turned 7 years of age. Agnes and Arthur, along with Agnes' aunt Susie, packed up in 1952 and moved to Los Angeles. In 1955, after Agnes' divorce from Chester had become final, she married carpenter and plumber Clinton Lee, and settled into a nice home on 27th Street in the Jefferson Park neighborhood. Clinton adopted Arthur, whose name legally became Arthur Taylor Lee when he was 15 years of age. In L.A., Agnes resumed teaching. School did not appeal to Arthur, however, as much as it did to his mother.

"Arthur was not very academic. He didn't care for school very much," Diane said. Arthur was drawn more to sports, playing softball competitively in elementary school. He also developed a reputation as a scrapper, the toughest kid in the neighborhood who became used to getting his own way by fighting for it with his fists – all the while regularly attending church on Sundays. He even thought of becoming a boxer.

As a teenager, he earned money in a variety of ways, Diane said. "He worked with his dad for a short time just to please him, but that didn't work out. He also worked in a neighborhood market cleaning up after hours. He spilled an entire bucket of water in an attempt to mop the floor, having never done that sort of thing. When that happened he called home, and his dad came to help."

Arthur's music education began when he was an adolescent. After a neighborhood friend of Arthur's signed up for accordion lessons, Arthur's mother enrolled "Po" as well. "Arthur was maybe 12 years old at the time, but that was the only formal training he had," Diane said. His interest in the accordion was short-circuited by his desire to learn to play the organ. "His dad bought him an organ, and he became very good with keyboards." He developed an interest in singing at the same time.

Sports continued to dominate his life, however, through junior high school and at Susan Miller Dorsey High School, where he excelled in track events, played football, and was a standout player on the school's basketball team. In one game he shot baskets for a total of 41 points, which stood as a school record for years. But as he began to acknowledge that at 6 feet, 1 inch he was not tall enough to play pro basketball, he had an epiphany when he witnessed the excitement that a band generated at a school assembly that he attended.

"The idea of forming a band didn't really click until I saw William (Crimson) Crout and Johnny Echols play at one of our high school assemblies. They had a five-piece band and played a [Chuck Berry] song called 'Johnny B. Goode.' Not only did they bring the house down, they blew my mind, too. The idea of putting a band together of my own came from Johnny Echols, the man who would later be the lead guitar player of the group Love," Arthur wrote in his diary. "I was soon playing the organ in my first band, along with Johnny Echols on guitar, Roland Davis on drums, and Alan Goldman and Allan Talbert playing saxes. Crimson Crout played lead and rhythm guitar, Johnny used to alternate between bass and guitar, and I would sometimes play bass using the foot pedals of the organ. After rehearsing at my house, or at Roland's, it finally came time for us to play at the high school assembly. We were on last, and I was as nervous as a snitch at a gangster party. The curtain was pulled back and there we were: One, two, three, hit it! We played 'Last Night' [a song by the Mar-Keys]. The crowd went wild. I went wild. We played loud. The audience was loud. I think I was playing the right notes, but all I know is the feeling that I had was better than breaking the high school record in basketball and winning first place in the fifty-yard dash in junior high all together. I made up my mind I was going to be a musician – and not just a studio musician, but a star."

The hook was set. The band of neighborhood friends practiced and improved, and they began performing paying gigs at parties in the area, sometimes as the American Four, sometimes as the LAGs. Arthur was so enthused about playing for audiences and so convinced that music was his destiny that in 1962 he dropped out of high school in order to focus on developing his songwriting and singing talents. "He told me that he enjoyed making music, and he always found ways to have a good time," Diane said. Before long the LAGs / American Four were performing in nightclubs. Influenced first by the Beatles and other "British invasion" bands in 1964 and then by the folk-rock style of the Byrds in 1965, Arthur began to see new musical horizons that he hadn't imagined before. He recognized the potential of music as a dimension for social commentary and introspection. In his handwritten memoirs, Arthur described the revelation he experienced one night in the spring of 1965 on the Sunset Strip when he first saw the Byrds perform at Ciro's nightclub. "Their music sounded a lot like what I had been writing but had yet to record. After I heard them play and saw the response of the people, I knew exactly what I was going to do. I was going to join in and help create a new kind of music called folk-rock. The Byrds blew me away. Their music went right to my heart. They played loud and they looked like barbarians with their long hair and freaky clothes."

As the LAGs evolved into the Grass Roots and then became Love, and Arthur began learning to play rhythm guitar, the band took on a higher sense of purpose for him. "In our band, there we were, two black guys from Memphis, raised in L.A., and three white guys from California," Arthur wrote in his narrative. "The more I thought about it, the more it seemed that this was the way the world should be, with everybody getting along with one another. I'm glad I tried to show unity in the world."

The lyrics that Arthur wrote were derived from episodes in his own life and his observations about his surroundings. "No song I have ever written has been about something other than what I have experienced," he declared. "I write songs like a letter. If you take away the music and leave just the words on a piece of paper, they'll probably tell you something you already know. That's all I'm here to do, to remind you. If you took most of the songs I wrote and put them together it would be a book. They all tell a story. They are what I've seen and lived. They're honest lyrics from what I've seen in life." Arthur wrote three songs, for example, about his high school girlfriend Anita Billings – with whom he was forced to break up. "When Arthur was a teenager, he wrote a song called 'My Diary' about Anita. She was beautiful, from what I understand, and they were in love," Diane explained. "They were young, and having a wild relationship. The mother of one of them – I don't know if it was her mother or Arthur's mother – found a diary and put an end to the relationship, and that's why Arthur wrote that song. He was heartbroken. Singer Rosa Lee Brooks recorded that song with Arthur, and with Jimi Hendrix playing guitar. That likely was the first time that Jimi Hendrix recorded in a studio. Arthur and Jimi took to each other. They were both black in a predominantly white rock and roll musician world." The Revis Records label released that recording of "My Diary" in 1965. "I remember hearing that song on the radio when I was a teenager, long before I met Arthur. He also wrote 'Message To Pretty' about Anita." The title of Arthur's composition "7 And 7 Is," Love's second chart record, also refers to Anita Billings, who like Arthur was born on March 7.

Arthur had numerous girlfriends and lovers over the years. The woman who would remain a constant throughout his life, however, came his way through his bedroom window on New Year's Eve 1970. Her name then was Diane Bardezian. She had met Arthur briefly earlier that year. Diane had a boyfriend, Gary Hearn, and was good friends with Gary's sister, Samantha. "Although Samantha had a boyfriend, she *really* liked Love and particularly

Arthur. We were young and a little wild, and she was gorgeous," Diane told us. "When she found out that an acquaintance of mine named Tommy knew Arthur, she asked him if he would take her to Arthur's house and introduce her to him, and he said, 'Oh, OK.' And then she asked me to go with her – you know how girlfriends are. So I agreed and we drove up the hill in Samantha's car to Arthur's house on Avenida del Sol, off Coldwater Canyon [in Studio City]. Arthur's house was full of people, and I thought to myself, 'this is crazy. He just lets anybody in his door.' Tommy introduced us to Arthur, and music was playing, and people were sitting all over here and there."

Arthur Lee in the late '60s (photo by RHM).

Samantha was absolutely smitten by Arthur, much more so than Diane was. "I just liked him as a friend. After all, I had a boyfriend," Diane explained. That New Year's Eve, Samantha and Diane impulsively drove to Arthur's house at about 3 a.m. "We knocked on his bedroom window, and he let us in through the window." Arthur and the girls just hung out. The incident inspired Arthur to write the song "Love Jumped Through My Window," which he recorded for his 1972 solo album *Vindicator*. By then Diane was married to another man. "For years I pretended I had no idea that 'Love Jumped Through My Window' was about me and Samantha, but I knew," Diane smiled. Born in Detroit, she had spent her childhood years in Fresno, California, before she moved with her mother, stepfather, and grandmother to the San Fernando Valley. There, as a family of Armenian descent, they felt isolated in their neighborhood that lacked other people from their culture. "People would ask us, in these exact words, 'what *are* you?' It wasn't even 'what nationality are you?' When I'd tell them I was Armenian, they'd say, 'what's *that*?'" Her friends were unaware of the 1915 Armenian genocide that her ancestors had survived and the financial hardships they endured after fleeing to the United States. From that experience, Diane developed an understanding of racial and ethnic bias.

Arthur was on a continual quest to explore new territory, to try new things musically and personally. Many people had trouble keeping up with his pace, puzzled about where he was heading. After Arthur became a vegetarian in 1970, he refused to be in the company of other people while they were eating meat. "When I was vegetarian, no one around me could eat meat. I didn't even let my dogs eat meat. I really went on that whole veggie trip. I didn't eat meat, fish, or fowl – no flesh at all for five years," Arthur wrote.

Arthur's compulsion to create is what drove him to press on, after the breakup of the original band and the disappointing public response to *Four Sail, Out There,* and other albums with other musicians after 1968. The personnel changes in Love were relatively inconsequential to Arthur. While fans clung to the original Love lineup, he sought musicians who could fulfill his *next* vision – the music that had not yet been created. "There might have been a falling out of musicians who participated in the band, but Arthur never quit. *Love Four Sail* is a pretty good album but that was with the second Love, and it was not received very well. And that was not easy, to go out in the public eye, and to keep on keeping on. Arthur never gave up. He was that kind of a person. He almost always eventually accomplished what he set out to do," Diane said. "Arthur's passion and the love of his life was music. How could he, or anyone with such a passion, give that up?"

The magnetism of *Forever Changes* became troublesome for Arthur. "Once he was finished with something, he was finished with it. Arthur always had new and different kinds of music going through his head," Diane explained. "The fans always wanted another *Forever Changes.* As great an album as that was, Arthur wanted to move past that and do different things, but the fans really didn't accept that."

Arthur lived in a succession of luxurious homes, but in 1977 he made the compassionate choice of moving back to his parents' modest home on 27th Street in L.A. to perform home care for his adoptive father, who had been diagnosed with colon cancer. He remained there until Clinton Lee died in August 1978. Arthur subsequently moved to a North Hollywood home, where Diane joined him in 1979 after she and her then-husband separated. "Arthur was quite charming. We had a wild, crazy relationship for a few years," Diane said. Quarreling led to their breakup, however, in 1983. Later that year a companion of Arthur's intentionally started a fire at an apartment building in Arthur's company. Arthur took the rap for it, and his conviction resulted in a short stint in jail. As a result of a misunderstanding he also found himself in trouble on an unjustified charge of automobile theft after a car that he had borrowed from a friend was stolen from him.

After Agnes moved back to Memphis in 1985, Arthur relocated there as well. He missed Diane, called her regularly, and serenaded her over the phone with songs he had written – a tender ballad called "Five String Serenade" that he composed on a guitar that was missing one string, and

"You're The Prettiest Song," which he wrote about Diane. He returned to L.A. and reunited with her in 1989. Three years later, he committed "Five String Serenade" and "You're The Prettiest Song" to tape among the tracks he recorded for a new album with guitarist Melvan Whittington, bass player Robert Rozelle, keyboard player Tony Mikesell and drummer Gary Stern. (New Rose Records, a French label, released the 10-track album, titled *Arthur Lee and Love,* in 1992.)

Arthur and Diane remained together until his undisciplined ways and roving eye again drove the couple apart, as Arthur began a relationship with another woman. "Arthur and I were separated when he went to prison in 1996. He had another girlfriend, who actually ended up being a friend of mine. Sometimes she would put together a package for him and I would help her, or I would put together a package. We would buy him books and other things," Diane told us. During the five and a half years when Arthur was imprisoned, Diane legally managed Arthur's finances. The bond between them persisted. While in his cell, Arthur learned the devastating news that his beloved mother, Agnes, had died of pneumonia at age 96 in February 1999; prison officials declined to furlough him to attend the funeral in Memphis. "That hurt me more than any sentence. I didn't cry. I wasn't going to cry in prison. In there, you can't show weakness," Arthur wrote in his memoirs. "I would have to say that being in prison is the hardest thing I've had to face so far. It was really hard not to be able to touch or share in any part of what was happening on the outside."

As Arthur entered prison, he began to notice a tremor in his left arm, and a physician concluded it was the onset of Parkinson's disease, for which he was prescribed medication. It was the wrong diagnosis. By the early 2000s, following his release, he had developed diabetes, and knew something else was wrong with him because he didn't feel good – but because he had been raised as a Christian Scientist, he resisted seeing a physician. As much as performing before audiences electrified him, he progressively lost strength and endurance. He was tired and was losing weight. Even though he had another girlfriend, he confided over the phone to Diane that he felt lousy and he didn't know why. Over the years Arthur had been stricken several times with pneumonia, but when she saw him, she was startled by the pallor of his skin and his gaunt appearance. "I could see he needed me – not so much that he needed me to be his girlfriend. I have to tell you: Arthur could always rely on me, and I was always out for his best interests, no matter what the relationship was. I realize that in life I'm a caregiver," Diane said. "I've been able to take care of a few people who I love. I am grateful that I was able to take care of my mother for 14 years when she needed my help, and I took care of Arthur, too."

Despite Arthur's illness, he consented to be interviewed in 2005 for a documentary about Love that the British company Start Productions was making. The footage for the documentary, titled *Love Story,* included Arthur driving the filmmakers around his old neighborhood in L.A., and touring them around "The Castle" mansion in which members of Love had lived together in the '60s. The production crew also had conversations with Love members Johnny Echols, Michael Stuart, and John Fleckenstein, as well as Elektra Records founder Jac Holzman, recording engineer and producer Bruce Botnick, and Doors drummer John Densmore, who greatly admired the artistry of Arthur and Love. Excerpts of Bryan MacLean's interview footage also are included.

The final song that Arthur recorded was neither with Love nor as a solo project, but rather as a guest vocalist with the band of jazz drummer Chico Hamilton (whose son, Forest, had managed the Blue Thumb-era Love band). In a sophisticated, mellow, crooning vibe recorded in 2004, Arthur sang the lead vocal for "What's Your Story, Morning Glory," a swinging jazz tune for Chico's 2006 album titled *Juniflip.* The track validated Arthur's vocal versatility.

Arthur had become too weak to travel to England for a tour with Baby Lemonade that was scheduled to begin in July 2005. The band with Johnny Echols fulfilled the performance dates without him as rumors swirled about possible reasons for Arthur's absence. Diane began spending more time with Arthur, to care for him and to keep him company. After Arthur's aunt Edwinor died and bequeathed her amortized Memphis home to him, he decided to spend a year there, where he could live in the house rent-free. "I knew there was something seriously wrong with him, but I didn't know what it was, and he wouldn't talk about it," Diane said. She drove Arthur and his pet dog to Memphis in September. Returning to his childhood neighborhood – where old folks still remembered him as "Po" – somehow rejuvenated Arthur. As Diane returned to L.A., Arthur started making plans to resume performing. He made connections with some Memphis musicians, with the intention of mounting another European tour. But the weakness malaise he had been feeling degenerated into unrelenting pain in his back and legs, and he developed pneumonia once again. When the pain became unbearable in January 2006, a cousin of his took him to Methodist University Hospital, where he underwent initial tests. "I got a phone call from the hospital, but the doctors I talked to couldn't tell me much. They thought they saw a spot on his lung," Diane explained. More complete test results later led to a diagnosis no one had expected: acute myeloid leukemia.

Diane flew to Memphis to support him as he began punishing three-week rounds of aggressive chemotherapy in preparation for expensive umbilical-cord blood stem cell therapy.

"He had a wonderful doctor who worked like a fiend preparing all the paperwork for an umbilical cord blood transplant. He had to submit a protocol and get approved, due to a limited amount of cord blood available," Diane explained. She was still working in the business office of a hospital in Los Angeles, but she flew back and forth to Memphis, spending anywhere from several days to weeks at a time with Arthur. "I hired a caregiver to stay with him when I wasn't there, even when he was in the hospital, so he wouldn't be alone." Howard Lyles, a member of Arthur's extended family in Memphis, also devoted many hours to caring for and keeping company with Arthur.

Acknowledging how much they meant to each other, for legal purposes Diane and Arthur married on March 30, 2006, in a quiet ceremony at the house in Memphis. Arthur had been uninsured until beneficiary coverage under Diane's health plan kicked in. On May 25, Arthur became the first adult in Tennessee to undergo an umbilical cord blood transplant with stem cells, with the goal of rebuilding his impaired immune system. He was released to rest at home for a critical 100-day period to determine if the stem cell treatment had been effective. "If we had gotten married earlier

Arthur Lee performing at the State Theatre, Falls Church, Virginia, October 16, 2004 (photo by Daniel Coston).

it probably wouldn't have lasted. I'm an only child, Arthur was an only child, and we'd both want our way," Diane said. "But I was able to take care of things for him. And he was comfortable with that. Finally, he was comfortable with it."

As Arthur fought his illness, he set music aside. "I don't want to fill my head with music I can't do anything about," he told a reporter from the Memphis *Commercial Appeal* newspaper. But the outpouring of good wishes and donations that he received gratified him. "But for this disease, I never would have known I was loved this much," he said.

Friends organized two benefit concerts to help raise funds for Arthur's mounting medical bills – a performance by Baby Lemonade with Johnny and Michael at the Whisky in Hollywood on June 6, 2006, and one at the Beacon Theatre in New York on June 23, initiated by Arthur's former manager Mark Linn, who was living in Nashville at the time. The lineup of the Brooklyn show included Led Zeppelin composer and lead singer Robert Plant, singer and guitarist Ryan Adams, Mott the Hoople lead singer and pianist Ian Hunter, multi-instrumentalist Nils Lofgren of Grin, Bruce Springsteen's E Street Band, Johnny Echols, and other friends.

Praising *Forever Changes* the night of the Beacon Theater benefit performance, Ian Hunter told an interviewer "It struck me that it sounds like this one guy against the world, in a particular place in a particular time, and it still sounds that way now. And you can't do better than that. And that's why I think it still figures with people who love music." Although Arthur was unable to attend the performance, he knew about it. "What blew him away, what just filled his heart, was the fact that people did this for him. He was so humbled that they all cared so much to do that," Diane said.

Among the many people who visited Arthur to help lift his spirits was Johnny, who concealed the shock he felt at seeing Arthur as frail as he had become. The results of the therapy initially appeared to be promising. "His blood counts were coming up, and he appeared to be doing well," Diane said. "Arthur Lee always overcame everything, and I told him, 'you will not die.' He tried real hard to live, but he didn't quite make that hundred days before he crashed. He got an infection of some sort." After suffering that setback, his body gave out on August 3, 2006. Diane and Howard Lyles were by his hospital bedside when he died. "It was very sad. It was horrible." Diane accompanied Arthur's body on an airline flight to Los Angeles. Arthur was buried August 12 at Forest Lawn Cemetery at the foot of the Hollywood Hills.

Arthur unfortunately had not lived long enough to see the finished documentary *Love Story*, which was released on DVD in 2008. But he did see a preview. "The video production company sent him a six-minute promo video, which he received during one of his three long stays in the laminar flow isolation room in the hospital," Diane said. "He was so pleased with it. Whenever anyone went in to the room, he showed them the DVD clip."

Arthur was philosophical about the transience of human life. "He was very spiritual and religious, as his mother had been. Arthur was brought up that way," Diane explained. "He had a strong belief in Jesus Christ, but he didn't go around preaching it. Arthur was very intuitive about people and things and life. He saw so much more in life than what was on the surface. About life, he'd say to me, 'don't get hung up on things and people dying. This [human form] isn't ours.' He had a very well-worn Bible."

In the end, Arthur was proud of what his band, Love, accomplished. "We were a part of one of the greatest periods in the history of mankind: the '60s. It didn't matter what race, color, creed, or culture you were; we just all seemed to get along," Arthur wrote in his memoirs. "One thing I can also say about my band members is that they came on this Earth and left a mark and were a part of the greatest name of any time period, and that was Love. Though things may not have gone exactly the way I wanted them to, I can honestly say that each and every one of my band members was a pathfinder for us all. It was more than a pleasure sharing my life with Johnny Echols, Bryan MacLean, Kenny Forssi, Snoopy, Michael Stuart, Tjay Contrelli, John Fleckenstein, and Don Conca, the first successfully integrated rock band in the world."

Diane Lee maintains the Arthur Lee website at http://lovearthurlee.com in honor of the music that Arthur and Love created.

Epilogue: Johnny Echols

Lead guitarist

Love was a band that was as visually seductive as it was musically appealing. The band members were captivating – each in his own way. While lead singer Arthur Lee cast himself as the center of attention, the eyes of the audience often were riveted on lead guitarist Johnny Echols. With his signature custom Mosrite six- and 12-string dual-neck guitar or a Gibson twin-neck, his studious focus on his instrument, and his finely chiseled facial features, Johnny was an imposing, regal-looking figure. Whether he was blasting out a song at the speed of a power grinder with sparks flying off his pick, or coaxing out a delicate romantic melody, or decorating a ballad with a lacy flamenco plume, Johnny was a stately presence on stage.

He might have ended up pacing the floor of courtrooms as a trial lawyer rather than striding on stage, if his parents' wishes for him had prevailed. They had hoped that he would be inspired by family friend Johnnie Cochran, who obtained his law degree while Johnny Echols was a high school student. "When my parents realized that I would have been miserable doing anything other than music, they relented and supported my musical aspirations. That was a wise move on their part, I would have been a horrible lawyer," Echols said.

He might more likely have become a teacher, as his grandmother and mother had been. But he was more heavily influenced by his stepfather's love of music. Born on February 21, 1947, Johnny Marshall in Memphis,

Johnny Echols in recent years (courtesy of Johnny Echols).

Tennessee, he became Johnny Echols after his mother, Dora, remarried. Johnny's stepfather, Charles Echols, loved blues, country and jazz, along with a bit of gospel. He would often play records by blues and gospel singer Gatemouth Moore, B.B. King, Howlin' Wolf, Muddy Waters, Hank Williams, blues singer Jimmy Rogers, jazz saxophonist Charlie Parker, and Miles Davis. "Sundays were reserved for the inimitable Pilgrim Travelers, the Five Blind Boys of Mississippi, and other gospel groups," Johnny recalled.

142

Music isn't the only thing that made a big impression on him at a young age. An emotionally scarring incident precipitated his family's relocation from the South to Southern California. "As a small child I went shopping with my grandmother at Lowenstein's department store in Memphis. It was late in 1951, when I was 4 years old. Being thirsty, I decided to have a drink of water from a nearby fountain. Unable at that age to read the posted sign, I unknowingly drank from the 'whites only' water fountain. I don't remember much about what happened, only that I was sworn at and thrown to the floor, by a horrible old man with brown teeth and fetid breath," Johnny told us. "Too young to understand what was happening and too frightened to cry, I just lay there trembling. My grandmother rushed over and slapped the man as hard as she could. It sounded like a gunshot. I've been told that he ran to get his gun, vowing to 'blow that ni**er bitch's brains out.' We immediately left the store, and not long after the 'incident' my parents moved to Los Angeles."

Johnny, who had no siblings, temporarily remained with his grandparents in Memphis until he rejoined his parents after they found employment and a place to live in L.A. The apartment they rented was a few doors away from that of Arthur Lee's family on 27th Street. "My grandmother and Arthur's mother were best friends. Though they were around the same age, his mother was in her late 40s when Arthur was born. My grandmother started her family at a much younger age," Johnny said. "Arthur was a couple of years older than me, and I looked up to him as a kind of a big brother."

Although Johnny enjoyed listening to music, he had not considered playing an instrument until one day in elementary school. "A friend named Danny Okin brought a Harmony Sovereign acoustic guitar to class for 'show and tell.' For some reason he was called to the nurse's office and he asked if I would look after his guitar," Johnny said. "I immediately fell in love with it. I was hooked from the moment I first strummed Danny's guitar. The feel of the strings vibrating through the instrument, into my body, was mesmerizing. I went home and pleaded with my dad to buy a guitar for me. Knowing how short a young boy's attention span is, my father said 'not right now.' But I persisted, even attempting to build my own guitar. After realizing how serious I was, my dad relented and brought home a well-worn Stella acoustic guitar, which I played day and night. He promised that if I stuck with it, he would get me a better one. True to his word, a few months later, he purchased a Guild acoustic-electric guitar for me – a really nice instrument."

While that guitar was a gift, Johnny had to work for other things that he wanted. "I sold newspapers, mowed lawns, washed our neighbors' cars – I even worked for one of my grandmother's friends from church, selling vitamins door to door. My parents believed a boy should earn his own spending money – and I did," Johnny said. No one else in his family played any musical instruments. "My mother was a gifted singer, who sounded very much like Sarah Vaughan. She had a beautiful voice, but sadly never took advantage of that gift." Johnny took music lessons from a neighbor, Adolph Jacobs, who was the guitarist for the Coasters singing group from 1956 to '59. "Adolph Jacobs was my musical mentor. He taught me so much – not only about the guitar, but about life in general. He was a truly wise man and a fantastic musician," Johnny said.

The Echols family's next-door neighbor was the girlfriend of jazz musician Ornette Coleman. "I would often hear Ornette playing. His avant-garde approach to music influenced my interpretation of what is music and what is just plain noise – the difference is not often clear," Johnny said. Wes Montgomery, Kenny Burrell, Gabor Szabo, Freddie King, and Johnny "Guitar" Watson were among the guitarists whose playing Johnny admired.

Studious in school, Johnny skipped two grades over the course of his public school education. He attributes that acceleration to the strong foundation his grandmother gave him by teaching him to read immediately after the water fountain incident in Memphis. "Learning to read at such a young age opened up a whole new world, far beyond the very limited one in which I lived at the time. Reading engendered a fascination with the written word, which has served me well throughout my life," Echols said. Following his graduation from high school at age 16 in 1963, he attended Los Angeles State College (since renamed California Stat University, Los Angeles) for a year with the intention of later transferring to UCLA. "But I decided against that after realizing that my passion lay elsewhere."

That passion flourished in the American Four and Grass Roots, and in Love. "Our shows were a blast, and throngs of people came to see us because they had a great time," Johnny said. "Arthur Lee was a world-class poet and lyricist, with a unique worldview, which he magically expressed in his songs." The band's repertoire, which encompassed ballads, psychedelic free-form music, R&B influences, flower-power, and angry punk rock, reflected the divergent tastes of its members. "We were eclectic," Echols acknowledged. "Our music was as varied as we were. Arthur was into blues, as was I, and we both loved folk music and jazz. Bryan was deeply into Broadway show tunes as well as bluegrass. Kenny was a surfer who was also a hard rocker. Michael was into jazz and R&B. All in all, we just loved playing music. If I had to define our place on the musical spectrum, I would classify us as a Renaissance group."

While Love was in Phoenix, Arizona, for a performance, Bryan said he wanted to see the Grand Canyon. "So we asked the driver to take us there," Johnny said. Because the highway between Phoenix and Flagstaff was undergoing extensive roadwork, they had to take a detour through Sedona. That side trip later would become important in Johnny's life. "On viewing those majestic red rocks for the first time, I fell in love. I had an overwhelming feeling that this was where I belonged."

Johnny was married once. "That was long, long ago in another universe in another space and time," he said. "We met in Hollywood during the '60s, and we were married for eleven years, before mutually deciding to dissolve our union. I haven't spoken with her in many years." They had a daughter, Kemo. "My daughter is a beautiful and intelligent young woman who has carried on the family tradition by becoming a schoolteacher," said Johnny, who also has a grandson who became a college student in 2014.

After the breakup of the *Forever Changes* Love band, Johnny, Tjay Contrelli, and John Fleckenstein attempted to form a jazz fusion group. "But things just didn't work out the way I had envisioned. Drugs were consuming more and more of my life. I wasn't taking care of myself, nor practicing daily as I once had, and my playing was suffering as a result. It was clear that I needed to get my act together first, before attempting to start a new group," Johnny told us. "I moved to New York in 1971, and checked in to the Morris J. Bernstein Institute at Beth Israel Medical Center to receive methadone-based treatment for my burgeoning heroin addiction. With the help of the dedicated staff there, I was able to overcome my addiction."

Johnny Echols in the mid-'60s with Love (photo courtesy of Johnny Echols).

Wrecking Crew pianist Don Randi opened doors and made connections that enabled Echols to establish himself as a full-time studio musician in New York. For 13 years Johnny earned a living there as a session player and guitar teacher, until he decided he needed another dramatic change of scenery. He purchased land in Sedona, and moved there in 1984. "Sedona is a spectacularly beautiful place. I bought a house there, settled in, and made that magical place my home."

When he developed an interest in guitar making, he enrolled in classes. "I had intended to enroll at the Roberto-Venn School of Luthiery in Phoenix, but when I got there I met a couple of graduates who were forming their own school. We chatted for a while and they invited me over to check out their workshop. I was promised personal attention that I would not get at the larger school with over forty students, so I chose to go with the much smaller start-up with ten students. It worked out very well, and after two years of hands-on instruction, I became a competent guitar maker," Johnny said. He makes and repairs only his own instruments. "I would have to charge so much for my time it would be cost-prohibitive to make guitars for sale. Besides, I would hate to give up my guitars after spending so much time on them."

Throughout the 1980s and 1990s Johnny maintained a low profile, disappearing from the public eye. An article about Love in the *Dallas Observer* on March 25, 1999, reported that Johnny's "whereabouts remain a mystery." But his friends knew where he was.

"I had been in contact with both Bryan MacLean and Kenny Forssi over the years. We didn't talk often, but we did keep in touch. We maintained a friendly relationship. There had been a number of attempts to re-unite Love with Arthur. Finally, it looked as though we were actually going to pull it off, following the successful release of the Rhino Records box set *Love Story*. Enough time had passed for old wounds to have sufficiently healed, and everyone was on board, including Bryan," Johnny said. "Unfortunately the universe was not on board. Arthur was sent to prison on a bogus gun charge, before we could make it happen. It just wasn't meant to be." Although Love did not reunite, Arthur and Johnny did.

"After Arthur's release from prison we decided that it was now or never, so I joined Arthur and the guys from Baby Lemonade in 2004, and we hit the road." They toured the U.K. and the United States that year, and returned to the U.K. together in 2005. "Baby Lemonade never tried to be Love, but they faithfully reproduced our songs on stage, while remaining themselves. They were so authentic sounding, people began to accept them, and they began to draw many times the number of people Arthur's other side-groups had. They are fantastic musicians, dependable family men whom I truly enjoy being around."

Another reunion became important in Johnny's life: he reconnected with Georgiana Waller. "I had met her in 1965, when I was 18 and she was 16, and we became friends." And then they went their separate ways. Georgiana had married singer Gordon Waller (of the British singing duo Peter and Gordon, a chapter in our book *Echoes of the Sixties*) in 1999; Gordon died of cardiac arrest in 2009. "After Georgiana and I had not seen each other for many years, out of the blue, a dear mutual friend mentioned seeing her at a social event. I went on MySpace, found her and friended her, she accepted, we chatted, and soon she began coming to my gigs. Georgie and I immediately re-connected and within the space of a few weeks, we began living together," Johnny said. "Georgiana and I are very happy being together, because we love and respect each other. We have so much in common, having shared many of the same experiences. We are truly best friends, who share absolutely any and everything with each other."

Johnny continues to perform the music he loves. "After Arthur's passing, Baby Lemonade and I decided to continue playing together, as Love Revisited – keeping Love's music alive and relevant to a younger generation, as well as our faithful friends from the past," Johnny said. "We are receiving amazing support, in the form of continually sold-out shows. I'm having an absolute *blast*."

Through it all, Johnny stays true to an important achievement: "I haven't used illegal drugs in more than forty years," he declared. And he is political, in his own way. "I am a strong believer in participatory democracy, so I spend quite a bit of my time trying to convince others to vote."

Echols retains great pride in the legacy of Love. "We were a group of five uniquely talented individuals," Johnny said. "We were individually and collectively allowed the freedom, earned through blood, sweat, toil, and tears, to innovate and experiment, which ultimately led to the creation of a body of work that has become timeless."

Visit http://www.love-revisited.com/ for touring and additional information.

Epilogue: Michael Stuart-Ware

Drummer

Michael Stuart-Ware's course for the first three decades of his life was set before he even entered kindergarten. "I got my first drum set when I was four, for Christmas – one of those little red metal jobs. Even the heads were metal. It was kind of like banging on pots and pans, but they looked like drums." He was born Paul Michael Ware on July 29, 1944 in Texarkana, Arkansas. "My mom and dad lived on the Texas side of Texarkana, but the hospital was located over on the Arkansas side, so when it was time for me to be born they jumped in the car and drove over to Arkansas," Michael said. "My childhood was typical. Friends riding bikes, shooting BB guns and seeking adventure in abandoned houses, construction sites, gravel pits, and other dangerous places."

His mother, Jean Barkman Ware, was a legal secretary. His father, Claude Thomas Ware, worked for Dallas-based military fighter aircraft manufacturer Chance Vought Aircraft, for which he wrote proposals and feasibility reports. For enjoyment, Claude played piano with a jazz group called the Salty Dogs, and throughout his 20s and 30s he wrote music and painted fine art under the name "Claudio de Pablo" – the significance of which he never explained to Michael. Jean played piano also. "My mom even accompanied me on my little metal set to the strains of Fats Waller's 'Ain't Misbehavin'. My granddad on my mom's side played ukulele. My grandmom on my dad's side sang professionally." Michael's folks enjoyed popular jazz artists of the day, including Ella Fitzgerald and Dave Brubeck,

Michael in 2008 (photo by Gloria Fletcher).

and they also listened to classical music and Broadway show tunes, but not to country music or rock and roll. Claude and Jean enrolled Michael and his sister, Gloria, in piano lessons. Gloria (who went on to become a classical musician) loved piano lessons; Michael intensely disliked them. "My mom also coerced my sister and me into going to cotillion to learn to dance all the dances that were popular with adults, like the waltz and the foxtrot and the cha-cha. She said that would enable us socially, but I'm pretty sure she was wrong."

148

Michael and his best childhood friend, a kid named Tony Holman, together discovered rock and roll. They listened to tunes by Chuck Berry, Jerry Lee Lewis, and Little Richard – who Michael especially liked – so much so that the first record he ever bought was Little Richard's "Lucille." Michael was fascinated to learn that Little Richard's drummer, Earl Palmer, had first been a tap dancer, which accounted for the extraordinary limber-footed syncopation with which he played the bass drum. That's when Michael began giving serious thought to taking up the drums.

Gloria and Michael left their friends behind in 1957, though, when the family moved to Southern California as Claude joined Rohr Aircraft Corporation, a manufacturer of aircraft engine components in Chula Vista, 10 miles south of San Diego. "All my friends in Texas were envious that I was moving to San Diego, so I figured it must be a pretty good deal, and I had no apprehension whatsoever," Michael said. "Our new home was located in a brand-new upper-middle-class subdivision, geographically a short drive up the hill from Pacific Beach, so it was near the ocean. I built model airplanes, fished a small stream, and shot .22 rifles down in the canyon at the end of my street with my best buddy, Cary Christie." As a student at Marston Junior High, he cut grass and trimmed shrubbery for neighbors to earn money.

At Clairemont High School, Michael joined the school band as a drummer. He found being part of an ensemble exhilarating. He was a skinny kid with skinny arms, but discovered he had "spring-loaded elasticity" in the ligaments of his shoulders, wrists, and elbows that resulted in high energy, yet control. "By the time I was 15, I had my first decent drum starter set and was playing gigs in bands with friends – high school dances, private parties, and the like," he said. "During those developmental years I was listening to a lot of jazz, as well as rock. I emulated Joe Morello [of the Dave Brubeck Quartet], Art Blakey, Elvin Jones, and Shelly Manne because I liked their drumming, of course, and more importantly, I liked the music that came from the groups they played with."

When Michael was in his senior year at Clairemont High, he won the school's "Outstanding Musician of the Year Award," which helped lead to a scholarship to Pepperdine University (affiliated with the Church of Christ) on S. Vermont Avenue at 79th Street in south-central Los Angeles. When he enrolled for his freshman college year in the autumn of 1962, he found out that weekly attendance at chapel was mandatory for students; three absences resulted in loss of scholarship and tuition. Drinking alcohol and dancing also were prohibited on or off campus. Those restrictions individually didn't bother him because he didn't drink or dance, but he recoiled at the repressive, paternalistic atmosphere. In his junior year, Michael transferred to UCLA. By then his father had taken a new job with rocket fuel and engine manufacturer Thiokol Corporation in L.A., writing proposals for government contracts, and preparing feasibility and cost analysis reports. The family moved to the Ladera Heights neighborhood, between Inglewood and Culver City in West L.A.

"I majored in psychology at both Pepperdine and UCLA. In psychology, everything makes sense, so it's pretty easy to understand, and all you have to do is study. Music theory, a highly technical and necessary component of a major in music, was too intimidating and confusing," Michael said. "I never could get it. Plus, knowing how to play the piano really helps if you major in music, and try as I might, I could never read piano music. It's like trigonometry. I read timpani and other percussion music only. Nice and simple, and one note at a time."

Michael's high school pal Cary Christie had moved to Hawaii with his family in 1960. "By the time he came back to Southern Cal in 1963 to attend UCLA, he was playing a mean surf guitar," Michael said. "We formed a band called the Vectors with a couple of his UCLA friends." The Vectors performed at frat parties on weekends, and they also wanted to play at beer bars in West L.A. – but they legally couldn't because all of the band members were under the age of 21. "One of the guys in the group had a girlfriend who worked for the California Department of Motor Vehicles, so she got us the IDs. She explained to us it was better not to raise any red flags, which could happen if we had all the information exactly the same as it was on our real IDs except for the birth date. That would be too obvious," Michael said. "We couldn't change the address, because the driver's licenses were to be mailed to our homes, and obviously the physical description had to stay what it was, so that left it to each of us to pick a last name other than our legal one. I randomly picked 'Stuart.' Stuart-Ware is merely a joining together of my professional and legal names."

In the autumn of 1964 Cary's mother saw an ad in the *Los Angeles Times* inviting rock bands try out for the "Hollywood A Go-Go Tour." Michael was so convinced that was an important opportunity that he dropped out of college to join the tour group, which consisted of members of UCLA and USC rock bands. "It sounded so important because of the name, but really it was just a quickie low-budget tour, thrown together by a couple of shysters, featuring unknown groups like us and a few other college student-types. We toured by bus throughout the western U.S. – Denver and Salt

Lake City and San Jose, California, and El Paso, Texas, and lots of other towns I can't recall. It lasted only a couple of weeks," Michael said.

Still out of school in January 1965, Michael was hanging out with a few tour band mates at The Mirage, a popular beer bar in Santa Monica, listening to the tight-sounding house band, the Fender Four, an outfit from Baltimore. A young woman who sat next to Michael told him that the band was looking for another drummer to replace the one they had picked up in L.A. Michael later auditioned for the band's lead guitarist (and band leader) Randy Holden and bass player Mike Port, and they hired him. The three of them, along with rhythm guitar player Jac Ttanna, moved together into a house in Pacific Palisades as they did gigs in local nightclubs. While they were playing at a college crowd joint called the Beaver Inn in Westwood, Kim Fowley, producer of the Hollywood Argyles studio group (who had recorded the 1960 novelty hit "Alley-Oop"), strolled into the bar wearing a gothic robe and various odd trappings, trailed by an entourage of about 10 hippie girls. At the break he talked to the band members, and said he could get them work in Hollywood – but told them that the "Fender Four" is a "dogshit name" and said they should change their name to the Sons of Adam – which they did. The Sons of Adam followed the Walker Brothers as

the band in residence at Gazzari's on La Cienega Boulevard, then in May 1965, the Sons opened the new Gazzari's at 9039 Sunset Boulevard.

After motion picture director Sydney Pollack saw the Sons of Adam perform at Gazzari's on the Strip, he cast the band members to appear in a nightclub scene in the suspense film *The Slender Thread,* starring Sidney Poitier and Anne Bancroft. At about the same time they got a clothes modeling assignment for G.Q., photographed at the Whisky à Go Go, and then posed for advertising posters for Leslie speakers and Fender guitars. The Sons of Adam learned from one of their fans at

Michael in the parking lot of the Whisky à Go-Go, Los Angeles, in October 1966 (photo by Bryan MacLean).

151

Gazzari's about a band named Love that was drawing crowds at Bido Lito's in Hollywood. On a night off in the autumn of '65, the Sons of Adam went to check it out. The members of Love and the Sons talked, became friends, and started hanging out together. They even shared a billing in a pair of appearances on April 8 and 9, 1966, when Love, the Sons of Adam, and the Charlatans played a dance concert for Chet Helms' Family Dog Productions in the Fillmore Auditorium in San Francisco.

Four months later, Michael joined Love and began a ride on a figurative careening merry-go-round, as he described in his 2003 autobiographical book *Behind the Scenes on the Pegasus Carousel with the Legendary Rock Group Love*. "We were like a multitude of others in the entertainment arts, who came before us and after. Members of a select group whose lives were set adrift by drugs and alcohol; individuals mindlessly absorbed in a desperate quest for that certain something so mythically special. The traveling Pegasus was the method of transport all right, but there never seemed to be a tangible destination. It was just a thing going around and around in circles – a carousel to nowhere, except maybe a long and embarrassing journey downward. We all rode it," Michael told us. Nevertheless he loved performing with the band for audiences in clubs and other venues. And he took what he did very seriously, in the studio and on stage. "I was intent on precision. I didn't engage with the audience, partly because it's kind of hard to interact with anybody from way back there behind the drums and up on a riser. And I'm not real outgoing anyway. When it was right, performing on stage was what it was all about."

Even after the band broke up and Arthur Lee signed with the Blue Thumb label to record as Love with another group of musicians, Michael was willing to participate in regrouping of the *Forever Changes* Love complement. Blue Thumb owner Bob Krasnow thought the new version of Love was lacking, and encouraged Arthur to bring Johnny Echols, Ken Forssi and Michael Stuart-Ware back into the picture. "It was more than 'encouraged.' In fact, the night we met up at the little Italian restaurant below the Canyon Country Store in Laurel Canyon to discuss the matter, Arthur flat out told us Krasnow was quite insistent on it. He wanted Arthur to do everything he could to reassemble the *Forever Changes* group for the Blue Thumb sessions," Michael said. "Actually, I was rehearsing with another band which was signed to Atlantic Records at the time, but I was willing to drop the other group altogether, if necessary, if the payoff were to be a successful re-formation of Love. The reason Johnny, Kenny, and I went for it is this: I think we were all of the same mind – unfinished business, and quite simply, the call of the siren song. Love had always had so much potential, and it was our band. When we played together, the feeling was magical," Michael said. The reunion lasted only long enough for one live performance, but they would never again record together. "If we could have only for a brief time put aside our differences, the product could indeed have been something to behold."

Following the breakup of Love in 1968, Michael did short stints with a new band called C.K. Strong in L.A., singer-songwriter Danny O'Keefe in Seattle, and then considered and declined an offer to join Neil Diamond's tour band as he re-evaluated his decision to be a professional musician in the first place. Realizing that he had come to a crossroads in his life in 1971, Michael had to decide whether to remain a back-up musician for the remainder of his life, or learn how to earn a living another way. A friend recommended Michael for an assistant engineer position at a recording studio, but he found that he didn't like being on that side of the glass. He also knew that he needed to distance himself from the drug environment and its temptations.

Michael decided he needed to make a bold change in direction. He took the entrance exams for law school, was admitted, and began classes. "While I was in law school, I got a job in the clerk's office at the U.S. District Courthouse, at 312 N. Spring St. in downtown L.A., running all the court documents on their offset print machine. So easy and relaxing, yet somehow challenging it was. The idea was to try to get as many copies as possible from one paper master; and my copies were always super clean well up into the multiple thousands, because early on I developed a technique for cleaning the rollers periodically while the machine was still running. It was no easy task and I had to be careful, of course, which only added to the sense of accomplishment," Michael said. "I could just do my thing without any interference from anybody, because I was the only guy who could run it. It was a good job. I enjoyed the routine and the responsibility, and the people I worked with were cool and friendly. Then I dropped out of law school but I kept the job for another couple of years. The problem was that I couldn't see myself staying there in the clerk's office and working my way up the ladder for the next 20 or 30 years until retirement age, and I began to fear getting trapped into just that, so I quit."

He hired on at the shipping and receiving dock at The Broadway department store in Westchester, on Sepulveda Boulevard a mile or so north of L.A. International Airport. "I liked that job as well. It was physical work, consisting primarily of wrestling bales of things and appliances onto and off of trucks, and from point A to point B, usually with hand trucks. I did that for a few months until I got a job with the phone company, climbing poles, pulling cable, and installing and repairing phone equipment – another great job."

Then in 1975 he met Susan Covic. "When I was still working for the phone company, my good buddy and next-door neighbor, Bobby Covic, came over one day and told me his sister, Susan, was about to come out and visit from back east. He said it was a visit that was in preparation for a move to L.A., and she was coming to kind of check things out – to line up a place to live and find a job. While he was telling me about her, he showed me her picture and she was – and still is – beautiful. And I had a spare bedroom, so there you go. After she arrived and moved in, our personalities immediately clicked on multiple levels, that connection soon turned to love – and we were married in 1976," Michael said. "Susan started doing Kelly Girl substitute secretarial work and teaching nursery and preschool in L.A. Working for the phone company was great, but by 1978 I was just tired of living in L.A., so I quit the phone company, and Susan and I moved to South Lake Tahoe, because we thought the snow was beautiful and it's a small town. In a way it was just the opposite of L.A."

While in Lake Tahoe, the couple bought a catering business that they operated for 10 years, during which time Michael took up professional photography. "Tahoe is the kind of place where it helps to have several things going," Michael explained. Throughout the 27 years they remained in Tahoe, Susan taught kindergarten and first grade for a local elementary school. There they raised two children: Kyle, born in 1980, and Brent, born in 1985. "They're both happy, working hard, pursuing their dreams and enjoying life to the fullest. No grandkids for us yet," Michael said.

With their children in adulthood, they decided in 2011 that they needed a change of scenery. "Las Vegas seemed a likely place to thaw out. It's beautiful here, not at all like it's portrayed on TV and in the movies, unless you go down to the Strip – which I don't," Michael quickly added. "Las Vegas has great shopping and restaurants, a strong economy, well-maintained roads, neighborhoods of houses built in the Spanish-modern architectural tradition. It has beautiful parks, stunning desert sunrises and sunsets, clear blue daytime skies, nights filled with a billion stars and lots of palm trees. What's not to love?" Michael has taken pleasure in renovating the couple's house and landscaping the property. "It's been a full-time job but I'm finally starting to get a handle on it."

Michael stops short of saying that he has *conquered* his former drug dependency, but he has kept it in check for three decades.

"It took a while for me to completely turn away from resorting to the chemical non-solution. I guess I must have been in my mid-30s by the time I finally became desperate enough to actually do something decisive about it. However, the characterization of 'conquering drug abuse' – and I include alcohol in the category of 'drugs,' by the way, because it is one – is a little too unrealistically and presumptuously optimistic, for me anyway. I just have the door closed," Michael told us. "But finding the strength to close the door was all about opening my eyes and realizing where true happiness is in life, and then finally learning how to get there. You know, life reprimands you if you do wrong. If you drive drunk or high on drugs long and often enough, then eventually you'll probably get arrested; and even if you don't, it's an unpleasant way to live."

Michael said that the formula for becoming free of the predicament of drug abuse lies in making suitable adjustments in response to negative reinforcement." It's like pulling your hand away from a hot iron. Then you redirect your focus of attention to more constructive endeavors, ones preferably exclusive of getting high, like those traditionally associated with productivity. 'Substitution therapy' is what social scientists sometimes call it," Michael explained. "The theory goes something like this: because you can do only one thing at a time, if you can start replacing bad choices with good choices, then eventually you'll find that you don't have time for the bad ones anymore, because – sorry, no extra space. No room in the inn. All filled up. I'm busy. Sounds simple, doesn't it? I guess it's simple for some people, but for others, maybe not so simple. It's working for me, so far."

He most enjoys what he calls life's simple pleasures. "You know – conversation with a friend or loved one, a good cup of coffee, watching the world awake at dawn, and then occasionally, when presented with a challenge, entertaining myself with the relentless pursuit of perfection during what would be an otherwise mundane activity," he said. "Each day is a gift, and it's up to us to appreciate the beauty the world holds and to contribute to it, as best we can."

Michael acknowledges that he continues to self-identify as a musician, and from time to time travels to southern California to sit in with his band mate, Johnny Echols, and Baby Lemonade at their "Love Revisited" gigs. "I was always partial to songs off Love's first album. 'Mushroom Clouds,' because of its timelessness – the threat of nuclear destruction initiated by warmongers, a concept just as real today as it ever was; 'Signed D.C.,' because his story became all our stories; Bryan's 'Softly To Me,' for its sophisticated phrasing; and 'Message To Pretty,' because it's such a beautiful little love song," Michael said.

If not for the turn-of-fate meeting with other musicians at UCLA, and the "Hollywood A Go-Go" tour that speciously lured him, he might have become an aircraft accident investigator. "The summer following my sophomore year at Pepperdine, I worked at Douglas Aircraft in Santa Monica in the accident investigation unit. My title was 'statistician detail,' but really what I did for two months was write a study profiling the projected negative effects of hyperventilation on the decision-making process in a pilot who suddenly finds himself flying an airplane in trouble. I did most of my research at the Caltech library in Pasadena. It was interesting work, and my job was considered an entry-level career position at Douglas, so after graduation I might have sought work in that field or perhaps gone into some branch of psychology."

But Michael does not allow himself to ponder how different his life might have been if he had taken a different course. "You're talking about 'regret,' and regret is a potentially debilitating form of mental self-flagellation, usually found teetering precariously at the top of a slippery slope. I do my best never to go there."

In the autumn of 1967, Elektra Records sponsored this high-profile billboard along the westbound side of Sunset Boulevard near Selma Avenue in West Hollywood to promote the impending release of Love's album *Forever Changes*. The famed Chateau Marmont luxury hotel looms in the background (courtesy of Johnny Echols).

Anne in the early 1970s (photo by Sherman Hines, courtesy of Anne Murray).

You Needed Me

Anne Murray

Anne Murray always has defied categorization. A singer whose professional career began with a folk music ensemble, she has recorded an expansive catalog of songs that have scored high on the U.S. and Canadian pop, country music, and adult contemporary charts. She has recorded tunes written by a diverse spectrum of writers, including Kenny Rogers, Paul Williams, Gordon Lightfoot, Henry Mancini, Bobby Darin, Dave Loggins, and John Lennon and Paul McCartney. While many of her singles were a godsend to previously undiscovered songwriters, she had a knack for giving new life and a fresh perspective to already well-known songs previously recorded by the Everly Brothers, the Beatles, the Monkees, Dionne Warwick, and Glen Campbell. She became a bellwether for female crossover singers, even though she didn't set out to do so. Before Anne Murray burst upon the scene, Patsy Cline, Skeeter Davis, and Jeannie C. Riley were among the very few female country singers who made the leap to the pop charts – and even after doing so they remained primarily country music performers. Anne Murray, however, would not be pigeonholed into one format or the other, as demonstrated in the disparate styles of her two singles that earned gold records – the bouncy, country-tinged "Snowbird" and the mature ballad "You Needed Me." Anne's success across divergent genres helped pave the way for Crystal Gayle, Olivia Newton-John, Shania Twain, Lee Ann Womack, and Taylor Swift to further blur the lines between country, pop, and adult contemporary.

During her four-decade singing career, Anne was awarded four Grammys, three American Music Awards, three (U.S.) Country Music Awards, three Canadian Country Music Association Awards, and 24 Juno Awards, presented by the Canadian Academy of Recording Arts and Sciences. The week of June 29, 1974, her version of the Beatles' "You Won't See Me" was No. 1 on the *Billboard* Easy Listening chart, and the following week the flip side, "He Thinks I Still Care," was No. 1 on the Hot Country Singles chart. At the 1974 Grammy Awards ceremony, John Lennon told Anne that her rendition of "You Won't See Me" was his favorite cover version of a Beatles song. When Linda Thompson, a former girlfriend of Elvis Presley's, was a guest on Los Angeles radio station KIIS in 1979, she told the host that Elvis' favorite female singer at the time was Anne Murray. Elton John was quoted as saying that he knows only two things about Canada: hockey and Anne Murray.

"I think my favorite song is 'You Needed Me.' It's a beautifully written song. I've never heard anyone say it like that – 'you needed me.' It's always 'I needed you,' which is the approach most people have, and this song was so different. There was no chorus. When I heard it, I was just a goner, and when we were in the studio, it was magical," Anne said. "Listening to it, we were speechless at how good it was. It was one of those really magical moments that certainly doesn't happen with all songs. You might have one or two in your career where you go, 'Oh yeah!' I had to fight for this as a single. I had to go in and do a little talking. I usually went along with just about everything. If the [record production] group thought it was the thing to do, I almost always would go along with it. But with this one, I felt very strongly that *this* was the song. I didn't have to pound on the desk, but I was quite firm that this is what I thought should happen."

By 1978, Anne was such a big star and wielded so much influence that she was able to persuade Capitol to release "You Needed Me" as a single, replacing "Let's Keep It That Way," which had been scheduled at the pressing plant. "Don Zimmerman was the president of Capitol Records at the time, and he said, 'Okay,' because everybody knew that I was a reasonable person. So when I came in so resolved, they knew that I meant business," Anne told us. "Don got on the phone and stopped the presses, and released 'You Needed Me' instead, and we both looked good after that."

Only 11 years before that, Anne, who hails from Nova Scotia, was a high school physical education teacher at Athena Regional High School in Summerside, Prince Edward Island, Canada. As a teenager she had taken classical voice training, and while enrolled in college she had enjoyed glee club. In the spring of 1966, shortly before her graduation from college, she auditioned for and won a spot on a Canadian Broadcasting Corporation (CBC) ensemble television program called *Singalong Jubilee,* a Halifax-based summer replacement for the popular *Don Messer's Jubilee* variety show. She began her teaching job in the fall of 1966, but she had made a big impression on *Singalong Jubilee* production personnel, including host Bill Langstroth, and Brian Ahern, the program's musical director.

Ahern had been traveling back and forth between Halifax and Toronto, where he was trying to move into record production. Arc Records, a small independent label in Toronto, gave him that opportunity. Convinced that Anne Murray had star quality, he prodded her to abandon teaching and pursue a career as a solo performer. He sent numerous letters to Anne, trying to convince her to come to Bay Studios in Toronto to record an album with him for Arc. The label already had released a *Singalong Jubilee* compilation album on which Anne had sung as a member of the ensemble. She finally agreed to record with Brian after moving to Halifax in the fall of 1967 to join the cast of the CBC *Let's Go* television series, signed a three-year deal with Arc Records, and began recording in the summer of '68.

"When I got to Toronto to record the *What About Me* album on Arc, I had to get Brian's guitar out of hock so he could play on the sessions. All the time I thought he was this big producer in Toronto, and I found out he had no money," she said. In addition to the leadoff song "What About Me," written by Scott McKenzie, the 10-track *What About Me* album included Anne's renditions of Joni Mitchell's "Both Sides Now," Tom Paxton's "The Last Thing On My Mind" and country singer Dallas Frazier's "There Goes My Everything." The album initially was issued only in Canada in 1968 and, despite generating good reviews, it didn't do as well as it could have due to Arc's limited promotion and distribution capabilities. It was a start, but Brian and Anne both realized they needed to land a deal with a bigger label to advance.

Ahern began making inquiries with other labels. "We went to several record companies, and they were going to give me the same deal that I had at ARC Records, with no creative freedom, and they would give us an allowance of $5,000 in production costs to make a record. The last label we talked to was Capitol Records Canada – and they said 'yes' to everything we asked. We were in shock!" Capitol Records Canada was an affiliate of the U.S.-based, EMI-owned Capitol Records of Hollywood. Paul White, the A&R (artists and repertoire) director for Capitol Records Canada, signed Anne to a contract in July 1969, agreeing to Anne's stipulation that Brian Ahern would produce her recordings (which he continued to for the following five years). Brian and Anne simultaneously wriggled out of her contract with Arc, and began thinking about new material for her to record.

Canadian singer-songwriter Gene MacLellan had been a guest on *Don Messer's Jubilee,* which Bill Langstroth was producing and directing. "Don had the longest-running show in the country, and it was hugely popular," Anne said. MacLellan, who had been working as an orderly in a hospital on Prince Edward Island, already was familiar with Anne; he had noticed her on *Singalong.* Bill was so impressed with Gene's performance and the songs he had written that he called Anne and arranged for a meeting at the CBC building. "Bill said to me, 'You've got to come and hear him.' So I went over to CBC, and Gene sat there and played a couple of his songs, and I was just floored. He then gave me a tape with the songs on it and said, 'If you like them, would you like to have them?' I said, 'Well, yeah!' Brian Ahern was there and met him, so then Gene became a guest on *Singalong,* and he sang 'Snowbird' on that show," Anne said. "When I played it for my family, they had a kind of a visceral reaction to it, and they wanted me to sing it. Everywhere that I performed it, people had that reaction to it. I mean, I did, too!" MacLellan said that "Snowbird" was the second song that he had ever written.

During August 1969 in Toronto, Anne recorded her first Capitol Records album, *This Way Is My Way.* Brian Ahern multitasked, as guitarist, bass player, and producer. The album, released on November 17, 1969, included Anne's interpretations of John Sebastian's "Sittin' Back Lovin' You" and Bob Dylan's "I'll Be Your Baby Tonight," along with three of Gene MacLellan's songs: "Bidin' My Time," "Snowbird," and "Hard As I Try." Capitol Canada issued three singles that generated no chart action, but landed on the charts with the fourth release: "Thirsty Boots," a folk song by Eric Andersen about a civil rights worker, backed with Gene MacLellan's "Hard As I Try"; it reached No. 36 on the Canadian adult contemporary chart, which was encouraging.

In February 1970 Capitol released a second single (No. 2738) with the ballad "Just Bidin' My Time" on the A side, and "Snowbird" on the B side. Anne, meanwhile, began recording her second Capitol album, titled *Honey, Wheat & Laughter,* which was released in May. "Just Bidin' My Time" got some airplay and reached No. 48 on the Canadian country singles chart and No. 87 on the Canadian pop chart. But that spring, across the international border, a disc jockey in Cleveland, Ohio, obtained a copy of the single, flipped it over and began playing "Snowbird" on the air. Listeners began phoning requests to the station to play the song, and soon began descending on record stores to buy the single. "What were the chances that anyone would even listen to the other side of a record by a new artist? But someone did," Anne said, "and all of a sudden the record stores started stocking it and then it just spread like wildfire." The July 11, 1970, issue of *Billboard* magazine reported Anne Murray's "Snowbird" as a regional breakout in Cleveland. The following week, it premiered on the *Billboard* Hot 100 chart, and it made its debut on the magazine's Hot Country Singles chart on July 25. On August 1, it was No. 69 with a star, indicating rapid ascent up the chart, and broke into the top 40 on August 22 (by which time it was No. 26 on the country chart). By September 7 it was No. 19 on the pop chart, and on September 26 it hit its peak at No. 8 on the Hot 100, where it roosted for two weeks.

Anne found her newfound fame dizzying and intimidating. "I remember being in New York with Bill, and we were in this pub having dinner and somebody passed our table and went to the jukebox and played 'Snowbird.' I just freaked! The two of us freaked! I think I had heard it on the radio, but being in New York City and having that played on a jukebox in a pub was just amazing," she told us. "I had the same reaction in Las Vegas when I looked out and there was Frank Sinatra's name on a marquee up the street from the hotel where I was playing. Sometimes when I'd be coming back out for an encore in Vegas, I'd say to myself, 'What the hell am I doing here?' I'd just shake my head, thinking, 'All the way from Springhill, Nova Scotia, to playing in Las Vegas.' That was pretty heady stuff." Anne's *Snowbird* album simultaneously premiered on *Billboard's* Top LPs chart and on its Hot Country LPs chart on October 3, 1970, and by October 24, the LP was No. 8 with a star on *Billboard's* Hot Country LPs chart.

With sales of "Snowbird" approaching 1 million copies, Anne was invited in September to do a guest spot on the *Glen Campbell Goodtime Hour*, a prime-time CBS television show. "Glen had heard 'Snowbird,' and he had heard my album, and he wanted me on the show. So I flew to California and walked into the studio scared out of my mind. Before the rehearsals, we went up to Glen's dressing room, and the producers, the writers, everybody was there with him. Glen asked if I could sing harmony and I said, "Yes," so he started singing and I just jumped in with the harmonies, and we sang two or three songs. I could see everyone in the room relax, and everybody just went, 'Oh yeah, oh yeah, this is going to work.' Glen was so excited that I could do all of this stuff vocally, because he was such a great singer," Anne said. Beginning with the October 4 episode, Anne was a guest on Glen's show seven times during the 1970–71 season. "I was a semi-regular on his show for three years, and somewhere in there we decided it would be nice to do a duet album [*Anne Murray/Glen Campbell*, which Capitol released in November 1971]." Before the end of 1970, Anne signed on with Campbell's manager, Nick Sevano, to represent her interests in the United States. CBC television, meanwhile, was saturated with Anne Murray appearances on the Friday evening country music-oriented *Tommy Hunter Show,* on *Singalong Jubilee,* and in her own variety specials. Even the Canadian Football League recognized Anne's newly earned stardom; the league chose her as grand parade marshal for its November 28 Grey Cup championship game.

"Snowbird" remained on the *Billboard* Hot 100 for 16 weeks, and immediately established Anne as a three-way international crossover artist. It also was a No. 1 hit on the U.S. adult contemporary (AC) chart, No. 10 on the U.S. country chart, No. 2 on the Canadian pop chart, No. 1 on the Canadian country music chart, and No. 23 in the United Kingdom. On November 16, the Recording Industry Association of America (RIAA) recognized the single "Snowbird" with a gold record award, recognizing sales of 500,000 copies. RIAA certified the *Snowbird* album gold on December 21.

"Snowbird" proved to be a tough act to follow, and her following seven singles garnered only modest action on the Hot 100, although they fared well on the country and adult contemporary charts – particularly in Canada. "Sing High – Sing Low" premiered on the Hot 100 on December 5, 1970, but rose no higher than No. 83; however, it attained No. 53 on the U.S. country chart, No. 21 on the U.S. adult contemporary chart, No. 4 on the Canadian adult contemporary chart, and hit No. 1 on the Canadian country chart. All the while she continued performing on stage to promote her music, charming audiences with her down-to-earth qualities typified by her partiality to performing barefoot. Striding on stage without the encumbrance of shoe leather helped her feel comfortable, and she was more relaxed in her concerts as a result. She continued performing barefoot for years.

Anne unreservedly credits her personal manager, Leonard Rambeau, for helping to shape and guide her career. Before she began working with him in April 1971, he had been a government employee of the Department of Manpower and Immigration's student placement service in Halifax. "I met Leonard for the first time when I was teaching phys ed and he approached me to sing in December 1968 at a youth club fundraising concert in Dartmouth, Nova Scotia, and then again a year later when he asked me to sing at Saint Mary's University carnival weekend in Halifax," said Anne. "He was just such a good organizer, and I was so impressed with the way I was treated, so I said to him, 'If I ever need a manager, I'm going to give you a call.' It was just off the cuff, but then he started calling me. Well, once the first album was out, he would come over to my apartment and say, "We've gotta let radio stations know about this," so he started doing mail outs in his spare time. He was working relentlessly doing phone calls, mailing stuff, and just bugging people. But it wasn't his job. He had a big crush on me, too. But that was over very quickly – he knew where he stood – but he was still very keen to promote this talent. So it was after 'Snowbird' that I finally called him and asked him if he would come and move to Toronto and help me out. And he did."

Bill, Anne, and Leonard established Balmur Investments, the corporate umbrella under which Anne would operate for nearly 30 years. Balmur was a combination of the first letter of their first names, plus "mur," which was Anne's nickname in college. Instead of paying Leonard a commission to manage her career, Anne made him a business partner.

Anne's first single of 1971, "A Stranger In My Place" (written by Kenny Rogers and Kin Vassy), was a track from her third Capitol album, *Straight, Clean, and Simple,* recorded at Eastern Sound on Yorkville Avenue in Toronto. "A Stranger In My Place" did not reach the Hot 100 after its February release, but went to No. 27 on the U.S. country chart, No. 18 on the Canadian pop chart, and was a solid No. 1 hit on Canadian country and AC charts. Anne and Brian had thought that the Gene MacLellan tune "Put Your Hand In The Hand," one of the tracks on the *Honey, Wheat & Laughter* album, should have been the logical hit follow-up to "Snowbird," but when Capitol released it as a single in April, Canadian disc jockeys flipped it over and made a hit of the "B" side, "It Takes Time," written by Shirley Eikhard. It went to No. 26 on the Canadian pop chart, No. 6 on the country chart, and No. 1 on the adult contemporary chart. In early June, Anne embarked on a tour that kept her on the road for two and a half months. The tour began with a two-week stand with Glen Campbell at the International Hotel in Las Vegas.

The title song from Anne's fourth Capitol album, *Talk It Over In The Morning,* put her back on the U.S. chart, premiering on the *Billboard* Hot 100 on September 11. It rose to No. 57, but up to No. 7 on the adult contemporary chart. In Canada it hit No. 1 on the AC and country charts, and No. 12 on the pop chart. From the album Anne recorded with Glen Campbell, Capitol released the medley of "I Say A Little Prayer / By The Time I Get to Phoenix" as a single that premiered on October 23, 1971, but hung up at No. 81 on the *Billboard* pop chart.

Anne recorded most of her material in Toronto, where she and her producer and guitarist Brian Ahern relied on a stable of studio musicians that included guitarists Lenny Breau and Miles Wilkinson; pedal steel guitarist Ben Keith; bass player Charles "Skip" Beckwith, who served as

Anne's musical director from 1969 to 1975; piano and keyboard players Bill Speer and Pat Riccio Jr.; horn players Don Thompson, Rick Wilkins, and Butch Watanabe; guitarist and harmonica player Brent Titcomb; and drummer Andy Cree. Beckwith, Riccio, and Cree doubled as members of Anne's touring band.

Anne toured relentlessly and exhaustively in the U.S., Canada, and Europe throughout 1971 and 1972. She spent most of her hours either on stage, in dressing rooms, driving to and from airports, on airplanes, or in hotel rooms. Rather than sleeping in on New Year's Day 1972, she had to wake up in the predawn darkness in order to ride on the Province of Nova Scotia's float in the nationally televised Tournament of Roses parade. Her first single of 1972 was her version of Gordon Lightfoot's "Cotton Jenny," from the *Talk It Over In The Morning* album. The 45 rpm release of "Cotton Jenny" premiered on the *Billboard* Hot 100 on April 1, 1972, and spent five weeks on the chart, during which time it peaked at No. 71. Capitol turned to her next album, *Annie,* for her subsequent single: "Robbie's Song For Jesus," composed by *Singalong Jubilee* alumnus Robbie MacNeill. Although that single reached No. 17 on the Canadian pop and country charts and No. 7 on Canada's AC chart, it did not reach the U.S. charts.

The first Anne Murray single of 1973 resonated much more strongly with fans in the States as well as in Canada. Her interpretation of Kenny Loggins' composition "Danny's Song" premiered on the *Billboard* Hot 100 on January 6, 1973, shot to No. 7, and spent 18 weeks on the chart. It hit No. 10 on the country chart and No. 1 on the AC chart, and No. 1 across the board on all three Canadian charts. The success of the single prompted recording of a *Danny's Song* album, which became her most popular LP to date, hitting No. 39 on the U.S. album chart and No. 5 in Canada. "Brian Ahern and I were both flying by the seat of our pants, because we were both young and learning. So it was kind of experimental. He was willing to try anything, and he was very creative," Anne said.

From the *Danny's Song* album, Capitol released Anne's rendition of Scott MacKenzie's "What About Me?" as a single that peaked at No. 64 after its May 26 debut. Anne's recording of "Send A Little Love My Way," written by Henry Mancini and Hal David, was featured prominently in the soundtrack of the 1973 motion picture *Oklahoma Crude*, in which George C. Scott, Faye Dunaway, John Mills, and Jack Palance played leading roles. Anne's vocal played during the opening and closing credits, as well as during one of Scott's scenes in the film. Released as a single, "Send A Little Love My Way" premiered on the *Billboard* Hot 100 on August 18, 1973, and rose to No. 72 on the pop chart and No. 10 on the adult contemporary chart. In Canada, it went up to No. 25 on the pop chart, No. 10 on the country chart, and No. 6 AC. Anne and Brian Ahern were the guests of the film's director, Stanley Kramer, at the film's world premiere in Tulsa.

By 1973 she had attained the upper echelons of stardom, winning the admiration and respect not only of her millions of fans, but also of fellow musical performers. To maintain the momentum, she made a radical change in her U.S. management, signing with a hotshot freethinker named Shep Gordon, who had managed the band Alice Cooper. He was adept at staging events to cast the attention-getting spotlight on Anne Murray. After crisscrossing the United States on a whirlwind schedule of concert dates, Anne staged a 17-concert "homecoming" tour that broke all existing house and gross figures in Canada's Atlantic provinces, according to the October 13, 1973, issue of *Billboard.* She was guest of honor at a state testimonial dinner hosted by the Province of Nova Scotia. Such dinners normally are reserved for honoring foreign dignitaries and royalty. In keeping with that protocol, Garnet Brown, provincial secretary, toasted Anne as "the Queen of Nova Scotia." After graciously accepting accolades, she was back on the road. The December 8, 1973, edition of *Billboard* reported that when Anne walked on stage for her opening night performance at the celebrated Troubadour nightclub in Los Angeles on November 21, the audience members included John Lennon, Harry Nilsson, Helen Reddy, Neil Diamond, Mickey Dolenz, and Alice Cooper (Vincent Furnier).

Anne turned another Kenny Loggins tune, "Love Song" (which he wrote with D.L. George) into a No. 12 *Billboard* pop hit that made its debut on the chart December 15. That one went to No. 5 on the country chart, No. 1 on AC, and swept the Canadian charts at No. 1. The Recording Academy recognized it with a Grammy Award for 1974's best country vocal performance by a female. Those successes gave her and her management and legal team a strong position from which to negotiate a more advantageous four-year contract in 1974 with Capitol Records in Hollywood. "The contract gave me complete creative freedom to choose whatever songs I wanted to record," Anne said. The prestigious, revered nightclubs and concert halls in which Anne headlined included Massey Hall in Toronto, where she performed May 3, 1974, with the Toronto Symphony Orchestra.

She earned John Lennon's admiration with a terrific version of the Lennon-McCartney song "You Won't See Me" on her album *Love Song* – the musicians on which included Bill Langstroth playing banjo. Released as a single, "You Won't See Me" premiered on the *Billboard* pop chart on April

20, 1974, and remained for a 20-week tenure during which it peaked at No. 8 – and No. 1 on the AC chart. It also was a top-five hit on the Canadian pop and AC charts. During 1974, Capitol Records issued a compilation album, *Country,* the tracks on which include "Snowbird," "He Thinks I Still Care," "Cotton Jenny," "Break My Mind," and "Danny's Song." Her interpretation of Doris Troy's 1963 hit "Just One Look," from the *Love Song* album, premiered on the Hot 100 on November 9, but stalled at No. 86 on the chart. Anne closed out 1974 with a track from her album *Highly Prized Possession* – her rendition of the Beatles' "Day Tripper," which premiered December 21 and rose to No. 59. That was the 10th and last album that Brian Ahern produced for Anne; they realized that their creative partnership had run its course.

Anne turned to Tom Catalano, who had worked extensively with Neil Diamond, as well as with Helen Reddy, Bill Medley, and Peggy Lee. The richly orchestrated 1975 album *Together* that Catalano produced with Anne in Los Angeles had a stellar list of contributing talent, including Dusty Springfield on backing vocals; Al Casey, Tommy Tedesco, Larry Carlton, and Lee Ritenour on guitar; Michael Omartian on keyboards; Hal Blaine and Jim Gordon on drums; and eight horn players, three woodwind players, and 29 string musicians. "I love that album! It was such a different experience for me because I went into the studio and recorded all that live. Those musicians were all in the studio. Talk about intimidating! I was always there when basic tracks were put down – from day one," Anne told us. "I sang until those musicians got it. Often producers will record instrumental tracks first and the singer will come in and sing to those tracks, but I never did that. I was always there from the beginning as part of the recording process. No one ever recorded a track without me there, throughout 32 albums."

Anne made another change in 1975. When Skip Beckwith decided to focus on record production, she designated her keyboard player, Pat Riccio Jr., as her new musical director. Riccio eventually grew into the role of conductor for her concert performances. Although Anne's loyal fans enjoyed *Together* and her 1976 LP *Keeping In Touch,* both of which Catalano produced in Los Angeles, neither one yielded pop hit singles. She continued to have AC chart success though, with "Sunday Sunrise," "The Call," "Golden Oldie," and "Things" (a remake of the 1962 Bobby Darin hit). And as Anne's Canadian manager Leonard Rambeau had become more confident in his role, Anne thanked and dismissed Shep Gordon as Leonard also assumed U.S. management responsibilities.

Anne and Bill Langstroth had been in love discreetly for several years, and they married on June 20, 1975 – her 30th birthday. In the months leading up to and following the birth of the couple's son, Will, in August 1976, Anne largely withdrew from touring, and slowed the pace of her recording activity to enjoy married life and parenthood. But she began getting pressure from Capitol to produce another album to satisfy her contract with the label. With babies on the brain, and a contract that gave Anne complete creative control over content, she decided to record a children's album. Instead of recording traditional children's tunes, she chose to include songs that adults would enjoy as well. The album's title, *There's a hippo in my tub*, came from lyrics in a song called "Hey Daddy," which was written by Bob Ruzicka (a pediatric dentist from Alberta, Canada, who moonlighted as a singer-songwriter and recorded several albums and hit singles of his own). Pat Riccio did all the arrangements on the album and produced it. When they presented it to Capitol, the label's executives "went berserk," said Anne. They thought it was some kind of joke and rejected it. "One of the great things about that album is that it consists of songs that parents like, too," Anne said. "That's what I had in mind when I recorded it. But Capitol Records was not happy." So Anne took the album to Sesame Street Records, the executives of which loved it and released it. Its sales soared, and Capitol's parent company, EMI Group Limited, repurchased rights from Sesame Street. "Generations of kids have been raised on that album," she said proudly.

Anne in 1975 (photo by Bill Langstroth, courtesy of Anne Murray).

In the autumn of 1977, Anne paired with producer Jim Ed Norman, a working relationship that would yield nine best-selling albums and a string of hit singles over the course of the following eight years. "I was looking for hit records, and Jim Ed Norman helped me come up with those." A member of the EMI staff in England had recommended Norman to Anne and her manager, Leonard Rambeau. "Jim Ed at the time was doing string arrangements for the Eagles. She introduced Leonard to Jim Ed, who asked if he would like to work with me, and he said, 'Yeah, I'd love to.' He had produced the

Jennifer Warnes single 'Right Time Of The Night,' which was his first foray into producing. After that became a big hit he decided he wanted to do more producing," Anne explained. "The first time we met, Jim Ed said that the Catalano albums were too much a departure from what people expected from me. I never thought about that kind of thing. I just sang the stuff – the songs that I like to do. But Jim Ed was more geared to a country audience. He thought that was where my strength was, so he guided me there and I went along with it. I said, 'Okay, let's give it a go.' I was a gamer – what the heck. And it worked."

The first LP that Jim Ed Norman produced for Anne was *Let's Keep It That Way*, which included the Sonny Curtis tune "Walk Right Back," which had been a top-10 hit for the Everly Brothers in 1961. Anne's version, released as a single in January 1978, hit No. 4 on the U.S. country chart, reached No. 15 on the AC chart, and was a pop, country and AC hit in Canada.

But it was another track on the *Let's Keep It That Way* album that returned Anne to the top of all the charts. The song was "You Needed Me," a tender slow waltz ballad about the ecstasy of feeling needed by someone else. Randy Goodrum, who had written Michael Johnson's spring 1978 hit "Bluer Than Blue," composed "You Needed Me." Capitol Records personnel thought it belonged at best on the "B" side of a single, but Anne strongly defended the song and, on her insistence, Capitol released it as an "A" side. The song, richly orchestrated and exquisitely sung, premiered on the *Billboard* Hot 100 chart on July 15, 1978. By August 19 "You Needed Me" pierced the top 40, making it her highest-ranking hit in four years. In a slow but steady climb "You Needed Me" hit No. 1 on November 4. It was perfectly timed and suited for the laid-back "mellow rock" radio format that had emerged at that time. The single, which remained on the Hot 100 for 26 weeks – half the year – also hit No. 4 on the country chart, No. 3 on the AC chart, No. 22 in the U.K., and No. 1 across the board on all three charts in Canada. If anything, that song spoke directly to Anne's fans, old and new; they needed her, and they responded by buying enough copies of the single to earn it RIAA gold record certification on October 26, 1978. "You Needed Me" also brought Anne a Grammy Award for best female pop vocal performance of 1978, and the Academy of Country Music awarded it "song of the year" for 1978. The popularity of the single drove sales of *Let's Keep It That Way*, which earned an RIAA gold record on October 12, and a platinum record (signifying 1 million in sales) on December 19, 1978.

By then Anne already was at work on her aptly named next album, *New Kind Of Feeling*. The first single from that album, "I Just Fall In Love

Again," an achingly beautiful song written by Steve Dorff, Gloria Sklerov, Harry Lloyd, and Larry Herbstritt, was another solid hit. After premiering on the *Billboard* Hot 100 on January 27, 1979, it rose to No. 12 and remained on the pop chart for 16 weeks. Meanwhile it hit No. 1 on the AC and country charts, and No. 1 on all three charts in Canada. On February 5, just weeks after *New Kind Of Feeling* was released, it earned RIAA gold record certification. At the top of her game throughout the late '70s, Anne strengthened her contract with Capitol Records in 1979 and kept turning out hits amid her hectic schedule of concert touring, nightclub shows, and television program guess appearances. *New Kind Of Feeling* also yielded another hit single, "Shadows In The Moonlight," written by Rory Bourke and Charlie Black. (Bourke had written Charlie Rich's 1973 smash "The Most Beautiful Girl," and Black wrote songs that country singers Bobby Bare and Tommy Overstreet recorded.) Anne's single "Shadows In The Moonlight" premiered on the *Billboard* Hot 100 on May 26, 1979, peaked at No. 25, and remained on the chart for 12 weeks. U.S. and Canadian country and adult contemporary audiences loved it, and sent it to No. 1; it hit No. 10 on the Canadian pop chart.

Anne's booking at Carnegie Hall on September 19, 1979, reaffirmed her stature as an entertainer. She performed for a sellout crowd in that venerated musical shrine. Anne's next single, "Broken Hearted Me," came from her Capitol album *I'll Always Love You.* Her tender, mature reading of that Randy Goodrum composition about emotional heartbreak premiered on the *Billboard* pop chart on September 22, rose to No. 12 (No. 15 in Canada) and was on the chart for 17 weeks. "Broken Hearted Me" was a No. 1 hit on the U.S. and Canadian AC and country charts. *I'll Always Love You* also included Anne's first hit of the 1980s, her toe-tapping version of John Stewart's "Daydream Believer" with which the Monkees had held the No. 1 spot for four weeks in 1967. Anne's take on the tune premiered on December 22, 1979, and hit No. 12 on the Hot 100, as well as No. 1 on the U.S. and Canadian AC charts, No. 3 on the U.S. country chart, No. 1 on the Canadian country chart, and No. 15 pop in Canada. *I'll Always Love You* earned RIAA gold record certification on February 7, 1980.

Another Charlie Black and Rory Bourke song, "Lucky Me," became her 30th single to reach the charts in North America. A track from her *Somebody's Waiting* album, "Lucky Me" was sung from the perspective of a lovelorn woman waiting for romance that so far had eluded her. The ballad, which premiered on the *Billboard* Hot 100 on April 5, 1980, rose to No. 42 during an eight-week run on the pop chart, but was a top-10 hit on U.S. and Canadian pop and country music charts. The same album also included

Anne's interpretation of another Lennon-McCartney song, "I'm Happy Just To Dance With You," which Capitol released as a single that premiered on the *Billboard* Hot 100 on June 14. It peaked at No. 64 during its six weeks on the chart, but did far better on the U.S. and Canadian country charts, and for AC audiences it was No. 13 in the States and No. 1 in Canada.

Anne and Bill celebrated the birth of their second child, daughter Dawn, in April 1979. After taking time off, Anne hit the road again with the benefit of a deep repertoire of hits amassed over the previous decade. Typical of her appearances in that era was a headlining performance June 26, 1980, at the prestigious outdoor Greek Theatre in Los Angeles. Backed by a full orchestra, she performed her sophisticated set in a glittering gown, in sharp contrast to her early '70s barefoot-and-blue jeans persona. In a *Billboard* magazine review of the performance, writer Paul Grein declared, "Murray's 17-song, 75-minute set included all 10 of her singles to have cracked the upper half of *Billboard's* Hot 100 in the past 10 years. It demonstrated conclusively that Murray has quietly collected one of the finest repertoires in the field of pop-MOR of any act in the business." The review said the appreciative audience acknowledged her performance not merely with polite applause, but rather with a "lusty ovation." (MOR stands for "middle of the road," a radio programming term for a music format emphasizing adult-oriented pop standards.)

Anne continued to put records on the charts throughout the remainder of the 1980s, but her most prevalent hit of the decade was part of the soundtrack of the hit motion picture *Urban Cowboy*, starring John Travolta (as "Bud") and Debra Winger ("Sissy"). As Bud and Sissy danced during the wedding scene and drove to their new trailer home, Anne Murray sang "Could I Have This Dance" (written by Wayland Holyfield and Bob House). Jim Ed Norman was arranging music for the soundtrack. "Jim Ed brought that song to me because somebody from the film production company had approached him about getting me to record it. They wanted it as a duet with Kenny Rogers," Anne told us. "I was going to sing the top part, but I sang his part – the lead, down below – and I sang a harmony on top of that to guide Kenny. When we learned that he didn't have time to record it, they released it just like that. I said, 'Wait a second, that was just a demo.' So what you hear on that record is the demo track that I put down for Kenny. It was a great song, though, and I've always been a sucker for a waltz." The single premiered on the *Billboard* Hot 100 on September 6, 1980, and spend 14 weeks on the chart, during which time it rose as high as No. 33. "Could I Have This Dance" hit No. 3 on the U.S. adult contemporary chart, No. 19 on the Canadian pop chart, and No.

1 on the U.S. and Canadian country charts, and the Canadian AC chart. The song was included on the motion picture soundtrack album on Full Moon Records, and Capitol issued it on *Anne Murray's Greatest Hits* in November 1980. Concurrent with its release, that album earned RIAA gold record certification on November 10. Two weeks later, on November 28, another presentation ceremony took place when *Anne Murray's Greatest Hits* qualified for a platinum record with 1 million in sales. "Could I Have This Dance" brought Anne her third Grammy Award, this time for best female country vocal performance of 1980.

Anne's album *Where Do You Go When You Dream* took her through 1981 and into 1982, spawning three singles. The first of those, "Blessed Are The Believers," premiered March 28, 1981, and rose to No. 34 during a 13-week run on the *Billboard* pop chart. RIAA certified *Where Do You Go When You Dream* gold on June 29, 1981. Anne's subsequent 45 rpm single, "It's All I Can Do," premiered September 26, reached No. 53 and stayed on the chart for nine weeks. In 1981 Anne recorded her first holiday album, *Christmas Wishes,* side 1 of which consisted of popular holiday tunes (including "Winter Wonderland," "Silver Bells," and "I'll Be Home For Christmas"), while side 2 was devoted to spiritual standards (including "Away In A Manger," "O Holy Night," and "Go Tell It On The Mountain").

Anne began 1982 with "Another Sleepless Night," from the pens of Charlie Black and Rory Bourke; that one made its debut on January 30, 1982, peaked at No. 44, and remained on the chart for nine weeks. The advent of MTV and the rise of new wave, hip hop, techno pop, and heavy metal music signaled a shift in musical tastes in the early '80s, however. As Michael Jackson, Madonna, Prince, Whitney Houston, Lionel Richie, the Pointer Sisters, Def Leppard, Bon Jovi, Duran Duran, and other performers captured the attention of radio programmers, airplay of Anne Murray's singles declined on top 40 radio. But her music persisted as a mainstay on adult contemporary and country radio. Her 1982 releases of "Hey! Baby" (a cover of the 1962 Bruce Channel hit) and "Somebody's Always Saying Goodbye," both of which were from her album *The Hottest Night Of The Year,* kept her prominent on the AC chart. On October 25, 1982, her album *Christmas Wishes,* released the previous year, earned an RIAA gold record.

A recurrent guest on many television shows, Anne hosted a half dozen variety show specials of her own, beginning in May 1979 with the Canadian Broadcasting Corporation production *Anne Murray's Ladies Night,* in which she and Marilyn McCoo, Phoebe Snow, Carroll Baker, and other guests performed songs, most of which were written by women. In December 1981 CBS broadcast *A Special Anne Murray Christmas* with guest Kris Kristofferson. In January 1983 she hosted *Anne Murray's Caribbean Cruise* also on CBS, and fourteen months later she starred in *Anne Murray's Winter Carnival from Quebec.*

Anne ranked well on the AC chart with the 1983 single "A Little Good News," from her album of the same name. On the Hot 100 the single reached only as high as No. 74 after its September 17 debut, but it was a bell-ringer on the country chart, on which it hit No. 1. That earned Anne her fourth Grammy, for best female country vocal performance of 1983. *A Little Good News* and its title track earned Anne the distinction of being the first female recording artist to win both the Country Music Association album of the year and single of the year awards. She continued to do well on the AC charts with her 1984 releases "That's Not The Way (It's S'posed To Be)" and "Just Another Woman In Love" (No. 1 country), both of which were on the *A Little Good News* album. Her autumn 1984 single release "Nobody Loves Me Like You Do," a duet with Dave Loggins, also hit No. 1 on the country chart. That was included on Anne's album *Heart Over Mind.*

By the 1980s Anne Murray's stage persona had taken on a sophisticated air as she performed in revered concert halls, with orchestral backing. When she stepped out on stage in a sequined gown at the Place des Arts in Montreal on January 28, 1985, some of her fans appeared to long for the Annie of old who wore jeans and other casual clothing when performing in public. After Anne had flawlessly performed several songs in the Montreal appearance, a fan yelled, "Take off your shoes!" Anne obliged, and the remainder of the performance took on a relaxed air to which her adoring fans responded with thunderous applause.

Her 1985 singles, "Time Don't Run Out On Me" (written by the legendary team of Carole King and Gerry Goffin) and "I Don't Think I'm Ready For You" did well on the U.S. and Canadian adult contemporary and country charts also. On March 15 of that year, the Recording Industry Association of America recognized her 1983 album *A Little Good News* with a gold record. Three months later, on June 11, her 1984 album *Heart Over Mind* earned RIAA gold record certification. During 1985 she signed another, even more lucrative contract with Capitol Records. *Heart Over Mind* was her last Capitol album working with producer Jim Ed Norman, who joined the staff of competitor Warner Bros. Records in Nashville. Hoping to regain footing in the pop market, she decided to try a different approach – working with several contemporary producers to benefit from their varying approaches.

Her subsequent album, *Something To Talk About,* consisted of 10 songs – one of which David Foster (from Canada) produced, six of which German-born Jack White produced, and three of which Trinidad-born Keith Diamond produced. In 1986 Anne made her last appearance on the *Billboard* Hot 100 with a song from that album, "Now And Forever (You And Me)," which David Foster wrote with Jim Vallance and Randy Goodrum. It premiered on the chart March 1 of that year and remained for six weeks. It rose no higher than No. 92, although it was No. 7 on the U.S. AC chart, No. 7 on the Canadian AC chart, and No. 1 on the U.S. and Canadian country charts. Two more poignantly titled singles of Anne's reached the U.S. adult contemporary charts: "Who's Leaving Who" in the spring of 1986 (from *Something To Talk About*) and "Are You Still In Love With Me" in the late spring of 1987 (from her album *Harmony,* produced by Jack White and Mark Spiro). *Something To Talk About* also yielded two more U.S. and Canadian country hits: "My Life's A Dance" and "On And On," both in 1986.

Anne racked up five RIAA awards in 1987. On March 17 of that year, Anne was presented with a gold record for her album *Country,* which had been released thirteen years earlier. Her album *New Kind Of Feeling,* which had earned a gold record shortly after its early 1979 release, went platinum (signifying 1 million copies sold) on August 19, 1987. On the same date, RIAA awarded a platinum album her 1981 album *Christmas Wishes.* Before the close of the '80s, Anne put six more singles on the U.S. country chart: "Anyone Can Do The Heartbreak" (from *Harmony*) in the autumn of 1987; "Perfect Strangers," a

Anne in the late 1970s (photo by Gord Marci, courtesy of Anne Murray).

175

duet with Doug Mallory (also from *Harmony*) in 1988; "Flying On Your Own" and "Slow Passin' Time," both in 1988 (from the album *As I Am*); "Who But You" in 1989 (also from *As I Am*); and "If I Ever Fall In Love Again" in 1989 (from her *Anne Murray's Greatest Hits, Volume II* album). On September 23, 1987, RIAA bestowed a gold record award for Anne's album *Something To Talk About,* which Capitol had released the previous year. And on October 16 of that year, *Anne Murray's Greatest Hits,* released in 1980, earned RIAA triple platinum certification, signifying sales of 3 million copies.

Country music radio and fans retained their embrace of Anne's music into the early 1990s. "Feed This Fire," from her album *You Will,* hit No. 5 on the country chart in 1990, and her follow-up that year, "Bluebird," reached No. 39. In 1990, Heartland Music licensed and issued a double, 22-track compilation album called *The Very Best Of Anne Murray.* Her 1991 album *Yes I Do* for EMI Music Canada yielded her last U.S. country chart single, "Everyday." But on May 30, her consistently selling 1980 album *Anne Murray's Greatest Hits* went quadruple platinum, earning RIAA certification for 4 million copies sold. On November 22, her 1981 album *Christmas Wishes* earned RIAA double platinum certification for 2 million units sold. She retained her popularity in Canada for another decade, during which 10 of her singles earned radio airplay and rankings on the Canadian country and adult contemporary charts.

Anne's disagreement with Capitol Records over who would produce her subsequent recordings, along with the decision to shift her from the Capitol label to an affiliate imprint, prompted her to depart the label in 1992. Anne always retained fond feelings for the songs that were popular during her childhood, and she became determined to record an album of her favorites from that era. It would be called *Croonin'.* Unsigned to any label, she enlisted producer Tommy West to co-produce the album with her, and in January 1993 booked expensive studio time for which she paid herself. She licensed the recording to EMI Music Canada, which released the album that year. It included her interpretations of songs made famous by Patti Page ("Old Cape Cod" and "Allegheny Moon"), Gogi Grant ("The Wayward Wind"), Doris Day ("Secret Love"), the Lettermen ("When I Fall In Love"), the Four Lads ("Moments To Remember"), Jo Stafford ("You Belong To Me"), and Bing Crosby and Grace Kelly ("True Love"). "*Croonin'* is one of my favorite albums, and I did that on my own. Even though EMI Canada released that album, EMI U.S. wouldn't," Anne said. "Charles Koppelman, the head of EMI, actually told me that he had the album in his car and loved it, but he wouldn't release it because it wasn't his idea. Can you imagine somebody telling you that? He loved it. What kind of thinking is that? As the career goes on, these things happen and you try to revitalize. But I always wanted to do an album like that because I was weaned on those songs of the '50s. Those were very formative years for me, and I sang along with every one of them. When I was in the studio recording them, I didn't even need sheet music with words to those songs. That album was a labor of love."

When Anne's longtime trusted personal manager Leonard Rambeau died of colon cancer at age 49 in April 1995, she contemplated shutting down her career. "Leonard and I had worked hand in hand, and after he died, I didn't think I wanted to go on, because we were a team for almost 25 years. I didn't really think beyond that. I didn't care if I ever performed again. But my friend Bruce Allen called and said, 'If you ever need anything, call me.' So, I did." Allen, another well-respected talent manager whose clients included Bachman-Turner Overdrive, Bryan Adams, Martina McBride, and the band Loverboy, artfully guided her into a new phase of her career. Anne always had been a hard worker who had never become complacent. She had not in her mind attained the juncture at which she thought her popularity had become so solidified that it was no longer dependent strictly on record chart position. "I don't know that I ever came to that realization. I just went out and worked. I made albums and tried to sell them – that was the way we did it," Anne told us. "We would record an album and then we would go on tour to promote the album. Our shows were based on the material in that album, and so I continued to do that. I was very aware that it couldn't go on forever, and I just went out and did my job. I actually enjoyed performing much later in life because the pressure was off. I just had to perform for the folks and enjoy myself and have a good time. By then I had Bruce Allen at the helm, and he made sure I didn't work my ass off – that I took time for myself and for my family. He would say, 'Take time off. People aren't going to forget you.'"

After 28 years as a solo artist, Anne had not yet recorded a concert album. But the Canadian Broadcasting Company captured a performance of hers at the Halifax Metro Centre in Nova Scotia on December 18, 1996, and the following September EMI Music Canada released tracks from that performance on the album *An Intimate Evening With Anne Murray ...Live.* That LP included renditions of several of her hits, including "Snowbird," "You Needed Me," and "Could I Have This Dance," along with favorites of Anne's – the Drifters tune "Save The Last Dance For Me" and "That's The Way It Goes," written by Cyril Rawson, Kerry Chater, and Lynn Gillespie Chater (Kerry had been a member of Gary Puckett & the Union Gap, a chapter about which was included in our first book, *Echoes of the Sixties*). The album performed well on the U.S. and Canadian country charts, and PBS subsequently aired the CBC telecast.

On December 7, 1998, RIAA awarded gold record certification for her 1990 compilation album *The Very Best Of Anne Murray*. And she continued to garner awards into the early 2000s. Her first gold record of the new millennium came on June 20, 2002, for *What A Wonderful World: 26 Inspirational Classics,* which StraightWay (a subsidiary of EMI Christian Music Group) had released in October 1999. "I had to be dragged kicking and screaming to record that one, because I was raised Catholic and for the album I had to sing all of those Protestant hymns," Anne chuckled. "We made a compromise. I agreed to do it if I could include some songs that have an inspirational message, but aren't necessarily religious. So half of the album consists of songs that are inspirational but have no religious connotation, including 'Let It Be' and 'I Can See Clearly Now.' As it turned out, that album did really well."

The 30-song album *Country Croonin'* that Anne recorded in 2002 for the StraightWay label was awarded an American gold record on May 13, 2004. And RIAA simultaneously awarded gold and platinum records on October 25, 2007, for Anne's 1994 20-song EMI Records compilation album *The Best ... So Far*. She recorded two more albums in the new millennium. Collaborating once again as co-producer with Tommy West, she recorded *I'll Be Seeing You,* another album of 1930s, '40s and '50s standards that StraightWay Records released in 2004. The title was Anne's way of saying goodbye to her fans; she had intended that to be her last album. The 15 songs on the album included "All of Me," "As Time Goes By," "Over The Rainbow," "Twilight Time," and "Don't Get Around Much Anymore." StraightWay reissued the album the following year under the title *All Of Me,* packaged with a second CD of Anne's own hits. But EMI executives prevailed upon her for one last project, to which she agreed. That final album, *Duets: Friends & Legends,* was a tour de force of 17 songs that Anne recorded with Martina McBride, Emmylou Harris, Carole King, Olivia Newton-John, Shania Twain, Amy Grant, Céline Dion, and other top vocalists. That farewell album, which acclaimed producer Phil Ramone artfully piloted, deservedly returned Anne to the U.S. and Canadian album charts following its release in November 2007. *Duets: Friends & Legends* propelled Anne on a packed-house 56-concert farewell tour throughout the United States and Canada in the spring of 2008.

Over the course of Anne's prolific hit-making career, she had major success as a recording artist, as a concert performer and in television.

She recorded 37 studio albums that yielded 80 singles, and she won four Grammy Awards. Two of her singles earned gold records, and Anne's albums yielded 15 gold records and nine platinum and multi-platinum awards.

During four decades, Anne received dozens of accolades and honors, including three American Music Awards; 25 Juno Awards from the Canadian Academy of Recording Arts and Sciences, capped with her 1993 induction into the Juno Hall of Fame; three U.S. Country Music Association awards; 16 Academy of Country Music Awards, including "top female vocalist" in nine years; and three Canadian Country Music Association awards, including her 2002 induction into that organization's Hall of Fame. In 1980 her star on the Hollywood Walk of Fame was unveiled.

In addition to the scores of recording industry awards that Anne received over the course of her career, she was presented with the Officer of the Order of Canada award on June 25, 1975, and was invested on April 10, 1985, as a Companion of the Order of Canada, the highest honor that can be awarded to a Canadian civilian. In 1998 she earned a star in the inaugural year of the Canada's Walk of Fame on King Street in Toronto. In 2002 she was as an appointee in the Order of Nova Scotia, and she also was the first inductee into the Canadian Association of Broadcasters' Hall of Fame. Although Anne never did any songwriting, the Canadian Songwriters Hall of Fame presented her with the Legacy Award in 2006 – in recognition of her support of songwriters from Canada by recording their music.

Canada Post issued a limited-edition Anne Murray stamp in 2007 honoring Canadian musical performers. The others for whom stamps were issued were Paul Anka, Gordon Lightfoot, and Joni Mitchell. The University of Prince Edward Island presented her with an honorary Doctor of Laws degree in 2008. She also has received honorary degrees from Saint Mary's University in Halifax, from the University of New Brunswick, and, most recently, from Mount Saint Vincent University in Halifax in May 2016.

Visit http://www.annemurray.com for audio and video clips, merchandise, a photo gallery and additional information.

ANNE MURRAY U.S. SINGLES ON THE *BILLBOARD* HOT 100 CHART

Debut	Peak	Gold	Title	Label
7/18/70	8	▲	Snowbird	Capitol
12/5/70	83		Sing High – Sing Low	Capitol
9/11/71	57		Talk It Over In The Morning	Capitol
10/23/71	81		I Say A Little Prayer/ By The Time I Get To Phoenix	Capitol
4/1/72	71		Cotton Jenny	Capitol
1/6/73	7		Danny's Song	Capitol
5/26/73	64		What About Me	Capitol
8/18/73	72		Send A Little Love My Way	Capitol
12/15/73	12		Love Song	Capitol
4/20/74	8		You Won't See Me	Capitol
11/9/74	86		Just One Look	Capitol
12/21/74	59		Day Tripper	Capitol
11/29/75	98		Sunday Sunrise	Capitol
2/21/76	91		The Call	Capitol
10/30/76	89		Things	Capitol
7/15/78	1	▲	You Needed Me	Capitol

▲ symbol: RIAA certified gold record (Recording Industry Association of America)

Continued...

Anne Murray Hot 100 U.S. Singles (continued)

Debut	Peak	Title	Label
1/27/79	12	I Just Fall In Love Again	Capitol
5/26/79	25	Shadows In The Moonlight	Capitol
9/22/79	12	Broken Hearted Me	Capitol
12/22/79	12	Daydream Believer	Capitol
4/5/80	42	Lucky Me	Capitol
6/14/80	64	I'm Happy Just To Dance With You	Capitol
9/6/80	33	Could I Have This Dance	Capitol
3/28/81	34	Blessed Are The Believers	Capitol
9/26/81	53	It's All I Can Do	Capitol
1/30/82	44	Another Sleepless Night	Capitol
9/17/83	74	A Little Good News	Capitol
3/1/86	92	Now And Forever (You And Me)	Capitol

Billboard's pop singles chart data is courtesy of Joel Whitburn's Record Research Inc. (www.recordresearch.com), Menomonee Falls, Wisconsin.

Epilogue: Anne Murray

Singer

When Anne Murray turned 15 years of age, she began
a weekly regimen to which she conscientiously adhered
for two years. Every Saturday morning at 8 o'clock, she
stepped aboard a bus that stopped in front of her family's
home in Springhill, Nova Scotia, Canada, and rode it on twisting roads 50
miles (80 kilometers) east to the harbor village of Tatamagouche, where her
father had been raised. There she spent the entire day in classical singing
lessons with Karen Mills, a voice teacher whose husband was a pastor. "The
bus took a couple of hours to get to Tatamagouche because it was like a
milk run that stopped everywhere along the way. I got to know the bus
driver pretty well over two years. I had my lesson late in the morning, then
I'd have lunch at my grandparents' home, and return to the voice teacher in
the afternoon for singing with a choral group until 5 p.m., when I'd go back
home," Anne said. "I must have really wanted to sing, but I also wanted
to please my parents. They had set this up and thought it would be a good
idea, so I went along with it, and I quite enjoyed it."

But Anne had not planned to earn her living by singing. Interested in
sports as a youngster, she spent her college years training to be a physical
education teacher, a career in which she
embarked professionally in 1966. She
probably would have spent the following
three decades teaching high school team
sports and fitness if not for a music producer
who relentlessly pursued her in the hope of
persuading her that music was her destiny.

Morna Anne Murray was born on June
20, 1945, to Marion Margaret (née Burke)
and James Carson Murray, in the coal
mining town of Springhill, Nova Scotia.
Her mother was a registered nurse and her
father a tireless physician, who made house
calls, performed surgeries, delivered babies,
and did rounds at All Saints Hospital in
Springhill. The couple married in 1937.
Anne's mother, a devout Catholic, had
prayed to Saint Anne, mother of the Virgin

Anne in 2015 (photo by
Katy Ann Davidson, courtesy
of Anne Murray).

Mary, for her fourth child to be a girl. Her prayers were answered, and her parents named her Morna after her paternal grandmother. "I was always Anne. It was my parents' decision. Anne Morna didn't flow as well as Morna Anne."

Anne says she came from a very happy family with parents who were devoted to one another. Unfortunately, she saw far less of her father than she would have liked because of the demands placed on him as one of no more than three doctors in town. "All of the doctors worked at the hospital, and they had office hours. In those days, they also made house calls after hours, and they worked 18- to 20-hour days. So we didn't see much of Dad. He was a very shy, retiring kind of a guy, so the town was perfectly suited for his personality." Anne's mother loved having children and would have had more if she could have. Anne grew up with five brothers – David, Daniel, and Harold came before her, and then Stewart and Bruce. "They treated me as one of them, so I had to hold my own. They were pretty mean to each other and pretty mean to me. When they had to look after me and they wanted to go play ball, they would tie me to a tree," Anne told us. "We had a bunk room that had double bunk beds and everything was built in. When the boys would start fighting and going at it, mother would just close the door. You could hear the bodies hitting the wall. She just let them go at it. They'd beat the crap out of each other. They were all hockey players, baseball players, soccer players, so they pretty much kept out of trouble. They were all good students and all of that, they just pounded on each other – a brotherly thing." Anne enjoyed playing hockey as much as her brothers did. "Every Friday a bunch of girls would get together in the rink and play hockey. I was a Montreal Canadiens fan with my father, whom I adored, and my brothers were Toronto Maple Leafs fans. There was dissention about that in the house. But you'll never find a closer family. We spent all of our summers together."

Springhill, with a population of about 7,000 when Anne grew up, is nestled in the Cobequid Hills, about 100 miles (160 kilometers) north-northwest of Halifax. For more than 80 years it boasted the biggest and deepest coal mining operations in North America. The city suffered severe hardship as a result of three disasters during a three-year period in the 1950s. An electrical mishap that ignited coal dust underground triggered a powerful explosion on November 1, 1956. Anne, who was 11 years old at the time, recalls that the blast flattened several buildings and trapped dozens of miners a mile below the surface. Most of them were rescued, but the blast and collapse of support timbers killed 39 miners, many of whom were fathers of Anne's classmates. A year later, fire destroyed much of Springhill's downtown area. On October 23, 1958, a third disaster resulting from an earthquake collapsed tunnels in the 14,000-foot-deep mine, trapping 174 miners in the dust-and-methane-choked catacombs. Rescuers brought 99 of them to the surface alive, but the rest perished. Again, several of Anne's friends endured the loss of fathers, uncles, and brothers. School was cancelled for a week, so Anne and her friends kept vigil for hours while her mother and father worked in the armory, where they cared for the injured and set up a mortuary for the dead. The Springhill mines closed down in 1962, drastically changing the economy of the town, although one mine later was converted into a geothermal heating and cooling facility. Much to Anne's dismay, many of her friends whose fathers had worked for the mining company moved away.

Anne's father came from a musical family. Her uncle was a concert pianist and her aunt studied music. "All of us kids sang, and we all took piano lessons, but the boys were not the least bit interested in that. Their idea of doing well was to see how quickly they could play a piece and get it over with. They weren't serious about it. I took piano lessons for seven years, beginning when I was 10 years old. I was never interested in playing piano enough to really want to practice, though. We had recitals and I had to do well, so I had to practice. I'm a perfectionist, so I worked hard on that one recital piece."

At her weekly singing lessons in Tatamagouche, Anne learned and performed semi-classical and classical songs in French and German. The teacher formed choirs of three, six, and nine students, and in those lessons Anne learned to read music and breathe properly, and improved her natural skill in singing harmonies. "I already knew how to harmonize. I sang as far back as I can remember. I sang all the time. I grew up listening to the Everly Brothers, Patti Page, and Les Paul and Mary Ford. I would sing along with the Everly Brothers and I would put in the third part. I did it naturally," Anne said. The training served her well. By the time she completed her voice lessons, she had fully developed her musical range of two and a half octaves. "I didn't always use that range with my professional career. People liked the low part of my range, so I used that most often. I didn't use the top part, and if you don't use it, you lose it." In her early teens, she found an appreciative audience at church when she sang there.

As a student at Springhill High School, Anne formed a singing trio with two schoolmates, and they performed for local civic groups to the accompaniment of Anne's ukulele, which she had taught herself to play. Anne advanced to higher education directly after completing grade 11 in 1962. "In those days, grade 12 was equivalent to first-year university, so I chose to go directly to Mount Saint Vincent College in Halifax. My voice teacher had referred me to a voice coach there named Charlie Underwood," Anne said. "It didn't matter where you took your first year of university. You could still go anywhere else after that. Mount Saint Vincent was an all-girls school and it was like a prison. I didn't have nearly the freedom at university that I'd had at home. It was a dormitory situation run by Catholic nuns, and while there were day students there, I was a live-in. For the first time, I was living with other girls, other women, and it was a revelation to me. I made some really good friends who have endured over the years, and it was a great experience. I was there for a year and then transferred to the University of New Brunswick (UNB) in Fredericton because I wanted to take phys ed."

As part of her physical education major at UNB, Anne took courses in anatomy and kinesiology (the study of the mechanics of body movements). It was there that one of the students noticed that her spine was curved, and she was diagnosed with scoliosis at the age of 18. "My mum said to my father, 'How come you never saw that?' He said, 'I never saw her with her clothes off.' I had so many brothers, I was modest, you know. They would run around half naked, and I would always be covered up." Although the scoliosis was not bothersome then, it would cause her discomfort later in life.

After enrolling at UNB in the autumn of 1963, Anne sang in her room for enjoyment, and she with her roommates and other students often participated in impromptu singalongs. She won a role in a choral group performance in the college's annual student variety show. For the show the following autumn, Anne was chosen to solo with two songs: "Unchained Melody" and "A Little Bit of Soap." During that second year at UNB, a friend of Anne's brother David obtained an application for tryouts for *Singalong Jubilee*, a Canadian Broadcasting Corporation television show. He encouraged her to fill it out and submit it, which she did. She flew to Halifax to audition and returned home feeling that her tryout went well. After receiving a letter saying the show already had all of the altos it needed, Anne was devastated. "There was no doubt in my mind that I was the best one in the auditions," she said. Nevertheless, she had unknowingly captivated the attention of two important people: the show's music director, Brian Ahern, and the producer and host, Bill Langstroth.

Anne tried her best to put that rejection behind her and focused on completing her college degree work. But in the spring of 1966, when Anne was in her senior year at the University of New Brunswick, Bill Langstroth tracked down the number of the pay telephone on her dormitory floor, and he and personnel at the CBC radio station in Fredericton began incessantly

Anne's University of New Brunswick graduation photo, 1966 (photo courtesy of Anne Murray).

leaving messages for her. "We had only pay phones at the end of the hall, and I was getting all these phone calls from Bill Langstroth and people from the local radio stations. Somehow I stuck in his head and in Brian Ahern's head. When I finally talked to Bill, he asked, 'Will you come down and audition again?' I told him, 'No.' I had been hurt by the rejection the previous year. He said, 'Look, if I tell you that your coming down to audition is just a formality, and that you're going to be on the show, will you go through the motions?' I said, 'Of course!' So I went down and auditioned again, knowing full well I was going to be on the show. So I was much more relaxed." With Brian Ahern playing guitar, Anne sang "You've Lost That Lovin' Feelin'" and nailed it. Following her graduation from UNB in June 1966, Anne had a teaching job lined up at Athena Regional High School in Summerside, Prince Edward Island. But she spent that summer as a member of the ensemble singing cast of *Singalong Jubilee,* the musical repertoire of which encompassed folk, country, then-popular songs, and spirituals.

"Talk about a learning experience – that was amazing! The group singing was fantastic. We had these woodshedding rehearsals, and it was amazing having all these really good singers and being right in the midst of it," said Anne, who was given some solo spotlights in addition to singing as a member of the ensemble. Producer and host Bill Langstroth also sang and played long-necked banjo on the show, which originated in the studios of CBHT Halifax and was broadcast on CBC-owned and affiliated stations throughout Canada.

That autumn, Anne began teaching ninth and tenth grade physical education and health at Athena High School. "Teaching there was a great experience. I already was a celebrity when I arrived at the high school, because the students had seen me on television and found out that I was going to go and teach phys ed there," Anne said. "I was hired to teach the girls, and my university classmate and friend Larry Wright taught the boys. He was a great help, because he knew a lot more than I did. I coached basketball, volleyball, and track and field, and I had no idea what I was doing. But the kids liked me," Anne said.

At the school, Anne assembled recreational singing groups. "I didn't sing on my own. I got together with a couple of Athena students, sisters Susan and Carol Perry, and we would sing three-part harmony. I'd play my guitar or ukulele, and we'd sing at assemblies and other school events," Anne explained.

However, Anne was much more dedicated to the music than she was to teaching. "I don't think I had a passion for teaching. It was just something that was there and available to me. I love sports, and I thought teaching would be something I'd like, but the singing was a whole different kettle of fish – *that* was my passion. That was something I had to do, like breathing. So wherever I went, even in the school, I would sing with the choirs. There was a music teacher there, and he invited me to come to choir practices and be part of the school choirs. So any chance I could get to sing, I did," Anne said. During the school year she frequently performed on CBC radio programs that originated in Halifax. "I was still teaching school, and the principal would let me go early on Friday afternoons to drive to Halifax to appear on programs. I had to take a ferry across the strait and then drive another three hours to the studios in Halifax."

In the middle of the school year she was offered an enticing package: a spot on the cast of the national television show *Let's Go,* along with recurring guest appearances on several other CBC television and radio programs. Cast members on *Let's Go* sang renditions of the hits of the day. Acceptance of that offer would require her resignation from her teaching job. Struggling with the decision, she consulted the advice of her parents and Bill Langstroth. "I called Bill and he said, 'There's no doubt what you should do. You should do this show.' And my parents didn't know what I should do, but they stayed up all night talking about it, and the next morning they called me before I had to go to the school to tell the principal my decision about returning to teach a second year. Mum said, 'Your father and I have discussed it, and we think you should give this a go. You can always go back to the phys ed if you need to.' They were really supportive. So, off I went and never looked back."

Anne moved to Halifax that summer of 1967 and started what would become a grueling schedule of performances and recordings. In addition to appearances on *Let's Go* and *Singalong,* Anne was performing on other CBC shows and on weekends in clubs across the Canadian Maritimes – the provinces of New Brunswick, Nova Scotia, and Prince Edward Island.

Disc jockeys, concert promoters and others tried to label Anne as a country, folk, or pop singer, but she never defined herself in those terms. "I just thought of myself as a singer. If I liked a song that happened to be folk music, I sang it. *Singalong* introduced me to country music," Anne said. "Before then I didn't listen to country music stations. What I loved most about country music was singing those harmonies. Freddy [McKenna], the guitar player on the show, was hardcore country." As busy as Anne was during her first year working fulltime as an entertainer, she had no inkling of how chaotic her life would become after she began recording and "Snowbird" flew her into the international spotlight.

After Anne began recording and performing as a soloist, she realized that advancement of her career would be difficult if she remained in Halifax, so in January 1971 she moved to an apartment in midtown Toronto. After Anne received her first substantial royalty check for sales of "Snowbird," she splurged and bought a house for herself in the Forest Hill neighborhood 5 miles (8 km) north of downtown Toronto. Her hectic schedule throughout the early 1970s left Anne little personal time, but somehow romance bloomed. She married *Singalong* producer William "Bill" Maynard Langstroth on June 20, 1975, in a small ceremony at her home, accompanied by her parents and brother Bruce, Bill's father, and a few other family members and friends. Their son, William Stewart "Will" Langstroth, was born August 31, 1976, and their daughter, Dawn Joanne Langstroth, was born three years later on April 16, 1979. In her autobiographical book *All of Me* (written with Michael Posner; Vintage Canada / Random House, 2009), Anne describes her feelings after giving birth to Will: "I had loved pregnancy, but I loved motherhood even more. Long deferred, it proved to be a hugely empowering experience, richer and more fulfilling than I had anticipated.... I had taken a few months off before Will's arrival, and I took four more afterwards, luxuriating in the everyday demands of breastfeeding, bathing, dressing, and playing with the marvelous creature that was young Will. Interviews I gave at the time reported that I hadn't seemed so relaxed in years."

When her children were young, Anne took them on the road with her as often as possible to try to bring some stability to her hectic life and greater normalcy to theirs. She signed an agreement for recurring multi-week engagements at the Riviera Hotel and Casino in Las Vegas, a city in which she never felt at ease. "I'm not a city person, at all. I'm a country person. I lived for many years north of Toronto, but I've never liked the city, and being in Las Vegas, to me, was like living on the moon. It couldn't be any farther from my roots. I never adjusted, and I played Vegas off and on for 25 years," she said. "The money was great – how do you turn down the money when you're raising a family? I could have them there with me for awhile. I never did longer than two weeks in Vegas, but it was two shows a night. It was grueling. There were three hours between the shows, so I didn't go on stage until close to 1 a.m. for the second show. But the money was great, and it was just my job."

Taking the kids on tour with her wasn't always practical or possible, and her heart ached when she had to leave them at home. She also worked hard to shield them from inquisitive reporters and the public. Seeking more privacy and space in early 1979, Anne and Bill bought and moved into a home in Thornhill, a somewhat secluded neighborhood 12 miles (20 km) north of downtown Toronto. On the road,

Anne in the late 1970s (photo by Bill Langstroth, courtesy of Anne Murray).

she sought hotel guest rooms in which she could open the windows. "As a singer, I hate air conditioning. Subjecting your voice to air conditioning is the worst thing you can do to it, because it dries out your throat so much. Of course, I had to deal with that in Las Vegas no matter what, so I took humidifiers with me everywhere," she said.

Despite Anne's best efforts, the dizzying pace of her career interfered with her personal life. "I would have a couple of hit records a year, but the record company would want me to churn out three a year, and it got to be too much. I was a workhorse, and I was working all the time. I worked way too hard, because I thought that's what you had to do. Things suffered, but in those days it was strike while the iron's hot, and it just wore me out," Anne said. She agrees that flooding the market with too many albums dilutes each one. "That was my biggest regret, and it upset me terribly. If I had it to do over again, I would cut the number of albums in half, to make each one count. I don't have a lot of regrets, except I wish I had dug my heels in and said, 'I need some time with my family.' I never would say that for myself, but I would say it for the family. The family really suffered and there were too many compromises. I kept thinking this is my job, and this is what I have to do, and I can't stop." Others even tried to discourage her from having a second child. "People told me, 'Oh, I don't think you should have the second one now, because this is the peak of your career.' My daughter was born when I was at the very peak of my career, and I knew that my kids were going to suffer, and they did."

But Anne found ways to include her family members in her career. Her brother Bruce, who took classical voice lessons from Anne's singing trainer Karen Mills, sang background on Anne's albums beginning in the mid 1970s, and starting in 1980 joined her on tour, singing backing vocals and duets with her. "Bruce had the most powerful voice as a kid. He was on the road with me for six years," Anne said. "He has a master's degree in history, but he wanted to sing. He tried out having a career of his own for awhile, but that didn't work. Because he wanted to sing he came on the road with me. But he was away too much from his two little boys, so he returned to university for a year and got a teaching credential, then taught school for more than 20 years. He was a born teacher, too." Her brother David became a nephrologist; Daniel worked as a geologist; Harold was a gastroenterologist; Stewart, a correctional system administrator, was the only one of Anne's siblings who remained in Springhill.

Anne and Bill's son Will, who became a computer programmer and software developer, also is a talented drummer. Their daughter, Dawn, became a singer, songwriter, and painter. "Will and Dawn performed the background vocals with me on 'You Won't See Me' on the *Duets* album. Having my two kids sing with me in the studio was the highlight of my career," Anne told us. "And they're so good – the two of them. I was always known as a one-take-wonder and they are, too. In May 2014 Will and his wife gave me my first grandchild, and we're just totally smitten. Her name is Piper. She has a sister, who is my step granddaughter, and her name is Keya." Dawn Langstroth recorded and released a CD of her own music, called *Highwire,* as well as a five-song collection called *No Mercy.* Her smooth, rich tones are strongly reminiscent of Anne's voice. "She is gifted with a beautiful, angelic voice," Anne said. "It's just magnificent. I'm glad that she's so good because, quite honestly, I'm a perfectionist and I would have trouble encouraging her otherwise. But Dawn is extraordinary." Dawn also is a painter, and sells her vibrant, stylistic artwork through her website (http://dawnlangstroth.com/).

After 22 years of marriage, Anne and Bill separated in 1997, and divorced the following year. She has not remarried. "I'm quite comfortable with that," she said. Anne's parents remained in Springhill for the remainder of their lives. Her father, James Carson Murray, developed leukemia, which he battled for several years before complications of the disease resulted in his death at age 72 on March 30, 1980.

Springhill struggled economically after the closure of the mines, and did its best to make lemonade out of lemons by converting the old mine shafts into a geothermal energy facility that uses leached groundwater to supply heating as well as cooling for the entire town. However, with a population that is half the size it was during the 1950s, the community lacked the tax base to maintain services, triggering the dissolution of the municipal structure in March 2015. Springhill now is an unincorporated area within Cumberland County. However, the Murray family made two significant contributions to the community.

In the late 1980s when the Springhill Industrial Commission set out to find a way to pay tribute to Anne by constructing a museum dedicated to her achievements, Marion Murray became a champion of the project. With funding from grants and private donations and the enthusiastic organizational leadership of Leonard Rambeau, the nonprofit Anne Murray Centre opened its doors at 36 Main Street in Springhill in July 1989. It has since become an important tourist attraction. "It houses a lot of memorabilia from my career and my life, and it's beautifully done. I'm so proud of it," Anne said. Exhibits in the museum trace Anne's career and celebrate the music of Nova Scotians, and the volunteer-run facility hosts various cultural events.

After heavy snowfall in March 2001 collapsed the roof of Springhill's indoor hockey arena, the city obtained Canadian federal funds toward construction of a new arena. The Murray family made a significant financial contribution toward that project. The town recognized the philanthropic donation by naming the new facility the Dr. Carson and Marion Murray Community Centre. The facility, which opened in September 2004, contains a National Hockey League regulation size ice surface, locker rooms, and other associated facilities, a gymnasium, and a teen center. "The town needed it so badly, and it's really well used. The building is heated and the ice is made geothermally," Anne observed.

Marion Murray, Anne's mother, died on April 10, 2006, at the age of 92 following coronary valve replacement surgery. Bill Langstroth, who became a freelance photographer and president of the sports promotion organization Croquet Canada, remarried in 2000. He died of complications from multiple myeloma at age 81 on May 8, 2013.

These days Anne swims regularly as one means to manage her scoliosis. The disorder did not cause her discomfort until she became pregnant. "I could really feel my back with that extra weight, and it started to bother me then. When I was playing in Las Vegas years ago, I went to a sports clinic there where I was given some exercises to do, and I've been diligent for the past 30 years. I see a trainer twice a week, I swim three times a week, I do aerobics and yoga, so I'm in tip-top shape. I'm doing everything I can do to keep my posture straight, because the scoliosis really bothers me now, and it gets worse with age," she said.

The Springhill home in which Anne and her brothers grew up is still standing, although another family now owns it and lives there. "It still looks exactly the same as it did," Anne said. Now she spends her summers in the Nova Scotia fishing village of Pugwash, with a population of about 750. That's the site of Thinkers' Lodge, where the series of Pugwash Conferences on Science and World Affairs were initiated in 1957. "I have a place on the water, as do the other family members. Four of us are on 32 acres, and the other two are just up the road. All of my brothers are retired now," Anne said.

Anne herself retired from show business in 2008. "Forty years is long enough to do anything. I have kids, and now I have grandchildren, and I wanted to have some time with them. I wanted to have time with my kids and get to know them. And for the past several years, I have. I also play golf, and I do whatever I want to do. It was hard at first. It's hard to retire. I can stop singing, but I can't stop being Anne Murray, so there are charities, and lots of things that I do to keep me busy, so that's what I do now." *Golf For Women* magazine named Anne the world's best female celebrity golfer in 2007. "I've played on a regular basis since I was about 40 years old. My game has slipped a bit since then, though. My daughter is threatening to teach me how to crochet. She's hooked, if you'll pardon the expression," Anne laughed. "I'm trying to relax and enjoy life. I do crosswords and sudoku, I read, and do things I never had time to do before. But it's not easy for me to just sit." Apparently not. Anne also has been active in lending her celebrity to raise funds for numerous public service organizations with diverse interests, ranging from colon cancer research to child protection agencies.

Anne was radiant when she stepped on stage at the Hummingbird Centre in Toronto (since renamed the Sony Centre for the Performing Arts) on May 23, 2008, in her last performance for the public. "Performing live the way I did required 23 of us on the road – three buses and a truck. The way I had to perform was three nights on, a night off, two nights on, a night off, three, two, and so on. With the exception of four or five nights during a tour, my voice was never the way I wanted it, because I never got to rest it," Anne explained. She did one final show, a private performance, in July, after two months of rest. "The beautiful thing about my leaving public performance that May was that when I did the smaller, private show with the same musicians, my voice hadn't sounded that good in so long. What a way to retire. I was singing like a friggin' bird. I hadn't sung that well in quite some time. I was so happy when I came off stage, after singing so well, to leave my career there and go, knowing full well that I would never do it again."

With funding from grants and private donations and the enthusiastic organizational leadership of Leonard Rambeau, the nonprofit Anne Murray Centre opened its doors at 36 Main Street in Springhill, Nova Scotia, in July 1989. Exhibits in the museum trace Anne's life and career, and celebrate the music of Nova Scotians. The volunteer-run facility hosts various cultural events, as well (photo by M.F. Gaul).

Billy Joe Royal in an outtake from the 1965 photo
session for the cover of his *Down in the Boondocks*
album (photo courtesy of Savannah Royal).

CHAPTER
4

Down in the Boondocks

Billy Joe Royal

Music is an aural medium, but it has powers to stimulate much more than our eardrums. Its rhythms can make us sway or shimmy, its beat can make us slap the steering wheel in time or jubilantly punch the air. Poignant lyrics with a tender arrangement can make us pensive or bring us to tears. Beyond that, some songs possess the power to paint pictures in our mind, not only evoking sweet memories but also sparking our imagination to visualize the scenes and characters embedded in narrative lyrics. One such "story record" that emerged from the pack in the summer of '65 transported city kids to the backwoods. Opening with twangy pulled guitar chords, ethereal and vaguely suggesting the muted echoes of a swampy forest, singer Billy Joe Royal's country-influenced recording of "Down In The Boondocks" stood out sharply among the pop-rock hits on "top 40" radio playlists that summer.

Written and produced by Joe South, "Down In The Boondocks" conjured images of a small Southern hamlet with distinct economic and social class divisions. Sung from the perspective of a struggling, working-class young man, it painted a picture of the poverty and desperation that he endured, working hard but consigned to live in a rickety shack in a neglected part of town. The lyrics brought to mind a sagging wooden cabin with peeling ancient paint and a patched roof. It may have lacked indoor plumbing, and in the minds of listeners, the hulks of rusting farm equipment and old pickup trucks up on blocks may have littered the rutted,

195

weed-choked ground surrounding the cabin. At night from the poorly maintained gravel road in front of the old house, the singer could see the shimmering lights of the hilltop mansion of his "boss-man" – who also was the father of the girl with whom he had fallen in love. She loved him as well, but the couple couldn't let her father know, because he would not tolerate her associating with someone out of her wealthy social class. We didn't know how they met, but through the song we learned that whenever she could, she snuck away from the house to spend time with the song's hero. The young man was purposefully saving every dime he could, determined to build a better life for himself – hoping that one day the girl he loves may become a part of his future.

Without knowing how the story turns out, Billy Joe's fans snatched up copies of the Columbia single and within six weeks of its national debut on July 3, 1965, radio airplay and record sales drove the song into the nation's top 10. Like the young man in the boondocks, Billy Joe Royal had spent his childhood in poverty, and ever since age 9 he had been dreaming of becoming a musical star. By the time he turned 23, that dream came true. And he was up against heavy competition. Performers with hits soaring to the top of the charts that summer of '65 included the Beach Boys (with "California Girls"), We Five ("You Were On My Mind"), James Brown ("Papa's Got A Brand New Bag") Sonny and Cher ("I Got You, Babe"), Wilson Picket ("In The Midnight Hour") and Bob Dylan ("Like A Rolling Stone").

While pop music fans are most familiar with Billy Joe's hits of the mid to late '60s, many do not realize that he had a resurgent career in the 1980s. Unlike many "crossover" artists who started in country music or soul music and gravitated to pop, Billy Joe defied convention and did just the opposite, re-emerging as a country music singer with a top-10 hit in 1985 and sending 11 more singles into the nationwide country top 30 during the following seven years.

Georgia-born Billy Joe, who grew up appreciating country, pop, and gospel music, had planned to become a lap steel guitar player. But after gaining experience singing with local bands, he passed an audition at age 14 to appear on the *Georgia Jubilee,* a barn-dance program that was broadcast on Atlanta-area radio. Also chosen that day was country music singer Freddy Weller, and fellow performers that Billy Joe met there included Jerry Reed, Ray Stevens, Tommy Roe and – most importantly for him – Joe South. A talented guitarist as well as a singer, Joe South (born Joseph Souter) became a prolific songwriter and producer, talents that would have great bearing on Billy Joe's career.

Although Billy Joe grew up only 20 miles outside of Atlanta, where he recorded his first hits, his road to fame took him on a ride to Savannah in 1959. Royal and Joe South roomed and worked together as members of the house band at the Bamboo Ranch, a large Savannah club, where they polished their craft as they backed Sam Cooke, Chuck Berry, B.B. King, the Isley Brothers, Jim Reeves, Ray Price, Marty Robbins, George Jones, Roy Orbison, and other headliners. Billy Joe greatly admired the singing style of Tony Williams of the Platters, Clyde McPhatter, and Smokey Robinson. "I wanted to sing like them so, at the Bamboo Ranch, I strained and pushed my voice to sing in the highest pitch I could. Eventually, that became easier for me," Billy Joe said. By then, Joe South already was writing songs, and he and Billy Joe began recording demos in the production studios of cooperative radio stations.

After sending their tapes to numerous independent labels but receiving no response, they pooled their money, rented time in an Atlanta recording studio, and took their resultant tape to music entrepreneur Bill Lowery, a longtime acquaintance of South's. Lowery thought their songs had promise, so he took Royal and South to Nashville, where they recorded several tracks. From that session the independent Fairlane label picked up and released "Never In A Hundred Years" (written by Jerry Reed) in November 1961, and "Dark Glasses" (written by Joe South) in February 1962. With distribution by King Records, "Never In A Hundred Years" earned Billy Joe his first radio airplay. "All of the songs were good because Joe and Jerry could really write," Billy Joe told us in March 2014. "Fairlane Records was owned by a country musician named Dennis 'Boots' Woodall, who had his own TV show, *Boots Woodall and the TV Wranglers,* on WAGA-TV in Atlanta. Then when he switched to distribution by Atlantic Records, he changed the name of his label to AllWood." Woodall also was a partner in Lowery's music publishing business.

Billy Joe's subsequent release caught the attention of *Billboard* magazine, which predicted "strong sales potential" for his recording of a Joe South composition called "Wait For Me, Baby" (AllWood 401). In describing Billy Joe's singing, the October 20, 1962, issue of the magazine reported "Strong vocal work by the lad here," adding "The side is in a good dance groove and features some fine gospel-like vocal choral work behind the singer."

Despite the mention in *Billboard,* the record didn't catch on, and Billy Joe thought his dream of becoming a recording artist was fading away. After meeting Gregory Peck near Savannah during filming of the thriller motion picture *Cape Fear* and working as an extra in a scene in the film, Billy Joe began to think of pursuing a career in acting. He had been playing at the

Bamboo Ranch for four years when a Cincinnati piano player named Marty Mitchell stopped by, caught his act, and urged him to join him in a gig at the Guys n' Dolls Club in Cold Spring, Kentucky, telling him he could make more money there over a weekend than he did all week at the Bamboo Ranch. Billy Joe went to Kentucky, auditioned, and in early 1964 got the gig. Singing pop songs of that early "British Invasion" era, he let his hair grow a little shaggy as English musicians did.

The Guys n' Dolls Club was just across the Ohio River from Cincinnati, and Billy Joe thought seriously about enrolling in drama classes there. But before he had a chance to act on that notion, popular Cincinnati disc jockey Dusty Rhodes of WSAI radio caught his stage act at the club. Rhodes signed Billy to perform in a concert at the Cincinnati Gardens arena to raise funds for the John F. Kennedy Presidential Library and Museum. When Billy Joe stepped out on that stage with his Beatles-style hair, girls in the audience greeted him with a chorus of adoring screams – a reception that he never had experienced before – and some of those fans asked him to sign autographs after the show. Rhodes took notice, and on his WSAI program began talking about Billy Joe and, during the following months, booked him to perform at dances. Soon, Billy Joe Royal fan clubs began forming in the Cincinnati area.

All the while his star was rising locally in Cincinnati, he remained in contact with his old friend Joe South. Joe's association with music entrepreneur Bill Lowery went back to the days preceding Lowery's music publishing and recording enterprises. Lowery previously had been a disc jockey, and as a youngster Joe regularly played guitar on Lowery's radio program on Atlanta station WGST. After Lowery launched his NRC (National Recording Corporation) record label in 1958, Joe South was the first artist he signed.

One day in the spring of 1964, Joe phoned Billy and persuaded him to travel to Bill Lowery's studio in Atlanta to record some new songs he had written. Among them was "Mama Didn't Raise No Fools." With a soulful arrangement reminiscent of Jan Bradley's 1963 hit "Mama Didn't Lie," Billy Joe laid down a strong vocal interpretation. Lowery's friends included Steve Clark, vice president in charge of sales for Vee-Jay Records. Upon Lowery's urging, Clark signed Billy Joe to Vee-Jay's then-new subsidiary Tollie label (which had pressed early Beatles singles in the United States before Capitol Records agreed to release Beatles product). Billy Joe returned to Cincinnati and his loyal following there, not expecting much of anything to come from the small label.

Tollie's release of "Mama Didn't Raise No Fools" did receive a mention in the May 30, 1964, edition of *Billboard* magazine, which said the record had hit potential, but that didn't translate into sales. South had written a couple of other songs with a particular sound in mind. Well acquainted with Billy Joe's vocal range, South said he wanted Royal to sing in a register higher than usual, with a sense of urgency in his voice – like Gene Pitney, who throughout the previous four years had racked up a string of hits about love, desperation, and heartache. One song that Joe wrote with Billy Joe in mind was "I Knew You When." The other was a song that Billy Joe didn't think "top 40" radio programmers would take seriously because of its title: "Down In The Boondocks."

Lowery built his studio in the abandoned Brookhaven School building that he had purchased in northeastern Atlanta. The property included an old, empty septic tank – which, as it turned out, had remarkable acoustic properties. With audio fed into the drained, dry tank, it served as a fine echo chamber for "Boondocks" and other songs. "The septic tank echo chamber worked fine, except for when it rained," Billy Joe said. "Also, a railroad line ran right by the studio, and every time a train would come through we would have to stop recording."

When Billy Joe recorded "I Knew You When" and "Down In The Boondocks" in December 1964 he assumed that they would be released to little fanfare on the Tollie label. But early in the spring of 1965, after Tollie's loss of the Beatles to Capitol Records, Vee-Jay folded Tollie. Bill Lowery was undeterred, though, because he had bigger plans in mind. He pitched Royal's unreleased Tollie tracks to acquaintances at Columbia Records, one of the major recording companies with excellent distribution and deep resources. Executives from Columbia heard a quality in Billy Joe's tenor voice that they liked. Columbia Records at the time was undergoing a transition, augmenting its traditional adult pop catalog with youth-oriented acts. The label offered Billy Joe a contract that he signed, but he remained skeptical. "That didn't mean much to me at the time. Columbia was a major label, and they were signing people right and left – the Byrds, Paul Revere and the Raiders, Simon and Garfunkel."

To Billy Joe's surprise, Columbia put its money on "Down In The Boondocks," and released it as a single. Among the first disc jockeys to play it on the air was Skinny Bobby Harper on WSAI. "Bobby Harper told me he was going to play my record at a certain time. I lived in an apartment complex, and I got everybody to gather at the pool while we listened to it on my transistor radio," Billy Joe recalled. On June 5, 1965,

Billboard listed "Down In The Boondocks" among its "spotlight" singles worthy of attention. On July 3, Billy Joe's phone rang again. A Columbia representative called to tell him that radio stations in additional cities had begun playing "Boondocks," and that it had hopped onto the *Billboard* pop chart at No. 90 and showed signs of climbing steadily. "Columbia called me back not long after that and said, 'Dick Clark wants you for his "Caravan of Stars" tour.' When the folks at WSAI learned that, they gave me a going-away party – Lesley Gore was there. Then I packed up, rented a U-Haul and headed back to Georgia." Columbia wanted Billy Joe to record in Atlanta with Bill Lowery to preserve his Southern roots. The dream to which Billy Joe had clung was turning into reality. But as he left Cincinnati, he glanced wistfully into his side-view mirror. "I will always be grateful for those people in Cincinnati. They gave me a shot in the arm and made me feel like a star before I even had a record out," he told us.

The Caravan of Stars tour that began in late July put Billy Joe on the bill with Peter and Gordon, Tom Jones, the Shirelles, the Drifters, Jackie DeShannon, Ronnie Dove, Mel Carter, and Brian Hyland. By then "Down In The Boondocks" had leapt to No. 27, only five weeks after its debut. The Caravan of Stars troupe zigzagged around the South and the Midwest, making performance stops in Memphis; Greenville, South Carolina; Raleigh, North Carolina; Charleston, West Virginia; Sandusky, Ohio; Chicago; Atlanta; Columbus and Akron, Ohio; Terre Haute, Indiana; then finished with dates in Syracuse, Atlantic City, and Hartford. The record hit its peak, No. 9, as Billy Joe was on the road. "Down In The Boondocks" remained on the chart for 13 weeks, into early October.

Already climbing the *Billboard* Hot 100 chart by that time, though, was Billy Joe's next Columbia single, "I Knew You When." In its September 4 issue, *Billboard* had anointed it a hit, describing it as a "hard-driving ballad to follow up his 'Down In The Boondocks' smash. Great Royal vocal backed by a strong rhythm beat. Winner all the way." Exploding from radio speakers with an opening salvo of nine powerful *Yeah*s, "I Knew You When" was an emotional outburst, with Billy Joe pouring his heart out after a once-lonely girl cruelly used him as a steppingstone. The 45 rpm single powered its way onto the chart on September 18, rose to No. 14, and remained on the chart for 11 weeks, into early December.

Just as that single was fading, Billy Joe sent yet another Joe South composition onto the chart. "I've Got To Be Somebody" premiered on December 4 on its way to becoming Billy Joe's third consecutive top-40 hit. This time, he was singing about hopefulness, determined to rise up from being "a nobody" in order to persuade the girl of his dreams to take him seriously. It reached No. 38 and spent eight weeks on the chart. Columbia packaged those three hits into an album titled *Down In The Boondocks* (the U.K. release of which was titled *Introducing Billy Joe Royal*).

"To me, Joe South was truly a genius – a great writer," Billy Joe said. Despite the spirit of optimism in "I've Got To Be Somebody," however, Billy Joe went into a slump that would last three and a half years. His uptempo dance-beat recording of Joe South's "It's A Good Time," which Columbia released in early February 1966, did not reach the *Billboard* Hot 100. *Billboard* projected that his next release, "Heart's Desire" (yet another Joe South tune), would be a hit, designating it as a top-20 spotlight tune. It was a bright, well-produced tune with a pulsating beat that Billy Joe sang with confidence. But it disappointingly went no higher than No. 88 after its May 21, 1966, debut, and dropped off the chart after only three weeks.

Billy Joe Royal in a 1970 Columbia Records publicity photo.

"Campfire Girls," written by his friend Freddy Weller (who had played guitar on "Down In The Boondocks") and produced by Joe South, had some intriguing lyrical hooks, sung from the standpoint of a jilted guy who told his departing girlfriend that she missed some important lessons about loyalty that she should have learned in the Campfire Girls. The tune premiered on the *Billboard* chart on September 3, but dropped off the following week after reaching no higher than No. 91. His final single of the year, an energetic horn-driven interpretation of Joe South's "Yo-Yo," earned a mention in the November 5 edition of *Billboard* but did not reach the Hot 100. It was four years ahead of its time, it seems; the Osmonds' 1971 version of the song with a nearly identical arrangement hit No. 3 on the *Billboard* chart and earned a gold record.

Billy Joe's first single of 1967 was "Everything Turned Blue," written by Ray Whitley (who had penned "We Tried," the flip side of Billy Joe's "Yo-Yo" single). This was not Ray Whitley the country music singer, but composer Ray Whitley, who also had written the Tams' 1963 hit "What Kind Of Fool (Do You Think I Am)" and Brian Hyland's 1966 single "Run, Run, Look, And See." Unfortunately, Whitley's tune did not return Billy Joe to the charts, and neither did his next single, Joe South's composition "The

Greatest Love," released in April 1967. On August 15, Columbia released Billy Joe's recording of another Joe South song that would send Royal back onto the chart – but would become a much bigger hit for a British power band. On September 30, Billy Joe's version of "Hush" began an eight-week stay on the *Billboard* Hot 100, but reached no higher than No. 52. Covered subsequently by the Woody Herman big band and by singer Donnie Brooks, Joe South's song became a top-10 heavy-metal rock anthem during the autumn of 1968 in the hands of the British quintet Deep Purple.

Capitalizing on Billy Joe's return to the chart, Columbia released his second album, titled *Billy Joe Royal Featuring "Hush,"* which included the title track as well as "Yo-Yo" and "Heart's Desire." Billy Joe turned down another Joe South composition that he regrets. "Joe played it for me one day, and I told him it was okay, but I wasn't interested," Billy Joe recalls. The song he declined was "Rose Garden," which Lynn Anderson turned into a top-10 pop-country crossover hit in late 1970. "Another day Joe got together with me and played some other songs that he had written," Billy Joe recalled. "One of those songs was 'Games People Play.' I went berserk, and told him, 'That's the best thing you've written.' He said, 'You like it?' I said, 'It's great!' So he decided to cut it himself, and it became a Grammy-winning hit for him."

After Joe South signed with Capitol Records as a recording artist in late 1967, Columbia paired Billy Joe with arranger Emory Gordy Jr. and producer Buddy Buie, architect of the Atlanta Rhythm Section (ARS) and a longtime associate of Bill Lowery's (see the chapter about ARS in this book). Very little came of the first four Buie-produced releases: Chip Taylor and Billy Vera's "Storybook Children" (released in June 1968); Joe South's "Gabriel" (released in October '68); and two Buddy Buie and J.R. Cobb tunes: "Bed Of Roses" (released in December '68) and "Nobody Loves You But Me" (released in March 1969). Lightning struck, though, when the production team turned to a song written by ARS drummer Robert Nix and Billy Gilmore, inspired by a place in New Jersey.

"Singers and musicians hung out at Bill Lowery's schoolhouse recording studio like most people hung out at a drugstore. People would go into a room there and write, and I was walking down the hall one day and heard Robert Nix and Bill Gilmore singing 'Cherry Hill Park.' I told them, 'I really like that.' And Billy said, 'Why don't you record it?' I said, 'Sure.' We got Buie to produce it," Billy Joe told us. "I had first met Buie when he was Roy Orbison's road manager. As a producer, Buie was completely different from Joe South. Joe was loosey goosey, satisfied to let me sing the way I wanted to sing, but Buie was more disciplined. I'll bet I sang that song 20 times, and *still* he didn't like the way I was doing it. At one point, after we had been working on it all night long, I really thought I had it down, so I went home. It wasn't long before someone knocked on my door, and when I opened it there was a guy from the studio telling me, 'Buie wants you to sing it one more time.' Looking back, it's one hell of a good record, the production was really good, but I didn't appreciate it at the time."

In the song, Billy Joe sang passionately about a girl who by daytime had been "a teaser" and at nighttime "a pleaser" – before marrying and moving away from Cherry Hill, New Jersey – a song in step with that "free love" era. Released on June 3, 1969, "Cherry Hill Park" initially remained stagnant. "It took forever to hit," Billy Joe recalled. In the August 2 issue of *Billboard,* WLLL in Lynchburg, Virginia, labeled it a "left field pick"; on September 6, KTSA in the much larger market of San Antonio called it a "happening" record. Another month passed before it premiered on the *Billboard* Hot 100 chart on October 4, and then it snowballed. It didn't take long for "Cherry Hill Park" to crack the top 20 and land at No. 15, remaining on the chart for 15 weeks. The success of the single prompted Columbia to issue Billy Joe's third studio album, *Cherry Hill Park.*

But beginning in early 1970, Billy Joe entered another slump. His first two singles of the year, Buie and Cobb's "Mama's Song" and Paul McCartney's "Every Night," failed to reach the Hot 100. "(Don't Let The Sun Set On You In) Tulsa," written by Wayne Carson Thompson, made it onto the chart beginning February 20, 1971, but only for a three-week

Singer-composer-producer Joe South (at left), singer Tommy Roe and Billy Joe Royal posed for this early 1970s publicity photo.

run during which it reached no higher than No. 86. Billy Joe continued singing live on stage without interruption, though. Among his bookings during that period was a weeklong series of appearances beginning August 17, 1970, at the beautiful Greek Theatre in Los Angeles in a show that also included Joe South, Linda Ronstadt, Tommy Roe, and Dennis Yost and the Classics IV. Always a vibrant performer, Billy Joe decided to develop a showroom stage act geared to Nevada casinos. At the same time Bill Lowery became convinced that Billy Joe should sign with prominent talent manager Seymour Heller (who represented Liberace for nearly four decades, as well as the Standells, Frankie Laine, Jimmie Rodgers, and numerous screen actors).

"I really wanted to be a regular in Las Vegas. I told Seymour, 'if you can get me into Las Vegas, you've got a deal.' Right away, he booked me into the lounge at the Flamingo Hotel. I rehearsed that band until their fingers bled. The night before I opened, I met Liberace and Elvis, and I thought, 'I'm not ready for this. I'm just way above my head.' Seymour had the room packed with celebrities for my opening, so it looked good, but I've never been so scared in my life," he confided. "But somehow I pulled it off and then Seymour called me and read the review, and it was like I had written it. Seymour got me great jobs. He got me on the *Ed Sullivan Show, the Merv Griffin Show,* and just about every other show on the air. Seymour did a heck of a lot for me." The Flamingo offered Billy Joe a deal to perform in its lounge several weeks a year, and Heller also landed a recurring gig for Billy Joe at the Sahara Tahoe Hotel and Casino. He moved from Georgia to the Southern California community of Hidden Hills, northwest of Los Angeles.

"Buie by then was working with the Atlanta Rhythm Section, and he was really busy with them. Jerry Fuller had a lot of success with Gary Puckett, and he was still producing Johnny Mathis and Andy Williams sessions, and he was hot as a pistol," Billy Joe said. "Columbia suggested I go with Jerry Fuller. I was appearing in Lake Tahoe, and Jerry went there to see me work. He told me, 'We can work together.' We cut a couple of great records – 'We Go Back,' which he wrote, and 'Child Of Mine' [written by Gerry Goffin and Carole King]. Columbia people thought those were going to be hits, but they never got off the ground. We never had any success together, but Jerry Fuller was a great singer, a great writer, and a great producer." After seven years with Columbia, Billy Joe was released from his contract with the label in 1972.

With Bill Lowery paving the way, Billy Joe signed with MGM South in 1974 and recorded "Start Again," composed by Stephen Hartley Dorff and Richard Merz Mainegra. Dorff produced the recording, but that song did not prove prophetic for Billy Joe. By 1978, Royal was on the roster of the Private Stock label. Working with prolific producer Chips Moman, who nudged him to a rhythm and blues groove, Billy Joe cut a rendition of the Drifters song "Under The Boardwalk," composed by Arthur Resnick and Kenny Young. Billy Joe's version premiered on the Hot 100 chart on June 3, 1978, but it stagnated at No. 82, and after four weeks dropped off the chart.

Billy Joe continued performing on stage, and two years later, signed with Mercury Records, for which he recorded an album titled simply *Billy Joe Royal*. The album, which Robert Nix produced in association with executive producers Joel A. Katz and Paul Cochran, included a Robert Nix and Danny Roberts composition called "Let's Talk It Over" that Mercury released as a single in June 1980. Working again with Chips Moman, Billy Joe recorded a couple of singles for the Kat Family label – "(Who Is Like You) Sweet America" (written by Toni Wine and Irwin Levine) and the Smokey Robinson classic "You Really Got A Hold On Me" (accompanied by Toni Wine). None of those singles reached the Hot 100, however. His career reached its lowest ebb in the early '80s, when he was reduced to playing for peanuts in small, dark, booze-drenched joints.

Come 1985, Billy Joe's recording career was rejuvenated. While "top 40" radio stations gravitated toward REO Speedwagon, Foreigner, Madonna, and the technopop sounds of Duran Duran and Tears for Fears, country music stations and fans were about to welcome Billy Joe Royal with open arms. "Kenny Rogers lived in my neighborhood and we became friends," Billy Joe said. Kenny Rogers had begun his musical career in rock with the First Edition, which gradually shifted to country – as Kenny subsequently did as a soloist. "Kenny had 'Lucille,' which was a mega hit, and B.J. Thomas had three No. 1 records in country, and even Bill Medley had a top 20 hit in country. So I told Bill Lowery that if he could find a good country song, I might have a shot at a hit." Convinced that was the right path for him, Billy Joe packed a suitcase, loaded it into his pickup truck, and drove to Nashville to listen to some demo tracks. He was in the office of country music producer and songwriter Nelson Larkin when they listened to a track by a yet-to-be-discovered Connecticut songwriter named Gary Burr, who went on to write numerous hits.

"Nelson played Gary Burr's song 'Burned Like A Rocket' and I went bananas over it, saying 'That's it! That's it!' No one else there liked it though," Billy Joe said. "I took it to Bill Lowery and he didn't like it either. Bill agreed to have me cut it, but couldn't give it away to any labels. Through the goodness of his heart, Bill put it out on his Southern Tracks label" [as "Burns Like A Rocket" in March 1985]. After a few small-market stations in the region began playing it, Billy Joe contacted his old friend

Emory Gordy, who had come out of retirement to produce Brenda Lee recording sessions with Jimmy Bowen. "I told him, 'Emory, I think I have a hit here.' So the next day he came back and said that they didn't think much of 'Burned Like A Rocket' but that Jimmy wanted me to record an album," Billy Joe said. The offer was tempting, but Billy Joe remained convinced that "Burned Like A Rocket" had hit potential, and he was determined to find a way to make that happen. "I hadn't had a hit in 15 years. But then a disc jockey on a big pop station in Tampa found the record, started playing it, and it went to No. 1 there. I will be eternally grateful for that. When we heard Atlantic Records was starting a country label, Atlantic America, we contacted them and asked them to talk to the radio station in Tampa. They did, then called me back and said, 'You're right, you've got a deal.'"

Finally, "Burned Like A Rocket" lived up to the promise of its title. It began a 22-week residency on the *Billboard* "Hot Country Singles" chart on October 19, 1985, almost immediately after well-distributed Atlantic America released it, and it took off. By December 21 it had cracked the top 20, and on February 1, 1986, landed Billy Joe at No. 10. "Burned Like A Rocket" probably would have gone to No. 1 if radio stations had not stopped playing it in the wake of the horrifying space shuttle Challenger explosion that January 28.

Billy Joe was back and in demand, touring with fellow country stars Ronnie Milsap, the Judds, Conway Twitty, and Steve Wariner. Over the following seven years working with producer Nelson Larkin, Billy Joe recorded 14 country top 50 chart hit singles – three times the number of top-50 hits that he had as a pop artist. "I had a really good string going in country music for a while," he said. He observed that he hadn't changed his singing style though; he was still singing the same way he always had. The recording industry's concept of what constitutes country music had changed, however, and Billy Joe fit right in.

His follow-up country hit was the pretty ballad "Boardwalk Angel," written by John Cafferty, who with the Beaver Brown Band recorded the *Eddie and the Cruisers* soundtrack. "Boardwalk Angel" began a 16-week run on the chart April 26, 1986, and reached No. 41 on the country chart. So confident was Atlantic America that it issued a Billy Joe Royal album optimistically titled *Looking Ahead* – four tracks of which became hit singles. *Looking Ahead* impressively rose to No. 21 on *Billboard's* country albums chart. Beginning on August 23, Billy Joe's heartfelt remake of the 1957 Marvin Rainwater and Faron Young song "I Miss You Already" rose to No. 14 and stayed on the chart for 24 weeks. In 1987 he went higher on the chart with three more hits, the first of which – a song about a disintegrating relationship, "Old Bridges Burn Slow" (composed by Sanford Brown, Jerry Meaders, and Joe South) – premiered February 7, peaked at No. 11 and remained on the chart for 26 weeks.

Billy Joe made a guest appearance in a duet with Donna Fargo in her Mercury Records single release of Larry Addison's saga for the brokenhearted, "Members Only," which premiered June 27, 1987, for a 15-week run during which it reached No. 23. Billy Joe's third country hit single of the year, the powerfully sung breakup song "I'll Pin A Note On Your Pillow" (written by Carol Berzas, Don Goodman, and Nelson Larkin), premiered October 17, rose all the way to No. 5, and stayed on the chart for 23 weeks. That was the lead track on his next Atlantic America album, *The Royal Treatment,* which hit No. 5 on *Billboard's* country albums chart.

In 1988 he sent two more hits onto the country chart. After premiering March 12, the sorrowful ballad "Out Of Sight And On My Mind" (written by Bruce Burch and Rick Peoples) hit No. 10 and held fast on the chart for 22 weeks. He kept the theme of heartbreak when his superb update of the old Johnny Tillotson tune "It Keeps Right On Hurtin'" premiered August 27, went to No. 17 for Billy Joe, and stayed on the chart for 17 weeks. In 1989 he had three country hits. The first was his faithful remake of Aaron Neville's late 1966 hit "Tell It Like It Is" (written by George Davis and Lee Diamond); Billy Joe's version premiered February 4, rose to No. 2 where it perched for two weeks, and remained on the chart for 17 weeks. On the

strength of that single, Atlantic America released what became another brisk-selling album, *Tell It Like It Is,* which rose to No. 15 on the *Billboard* country LP chart. That album included another single, "Love Has No Right," a pretty body-swaying ballad that Billy Joe co-wrote with Nelson Larkin and Randy Scruggs; as a single it began a 24-week run on the Hot Country chart on May 20, peaking at No. 4. Another big hit, the anguished "Till I Can't Take It Anymore" (composed by Dorian Burton and Clyde Otis) first appeared on the chart on September 30, shot up to No. 2, and demonstrated remarkable

Billy Joe Royal recorded from 1985 to 1992 for the Atlantic America label, which issued this publicity photo of him.

207

staying power, remaining on the chart for six months – 26 weeks. Billy Joe received additional validation on November 12, 1989, when the Recording Industry Association of America issued a gold album award for *The Royal Treatment,* acknowledging audited sales of a half-million copies.

Billy Joe wasn't done yet, as 1990 brought him two more country hits, from his album *Out Of The Shadows,* which rose to No. 24 on the *Billboard* country album chart. On May 12, "Searchin' For Some Kind Of Clue" (written by Donny Kees, Nelson Larkin, and Pat Rakes), about a guy trying to get back in his lover's good graces, made its debut on the chart; it rose to No. 17 and stayed on the chart for 21 weeks. His melodic rendition of the tears-in-your-beer tune "Ring Where A Ring Used To Be," composed by Gordon Eatherly, Bob Moulds, and Kris Bergsnes, premiered on September 15 for a 20-week run, during which it rose to No. 33. January 26, 1991, was the premiere date for another hit, "If The Jukebox Took Teardrops," also from *Out Of The Shadows.* "If The Jukebox Took Teardrops," a traditional country song about a lovesick guy, composed by Michael "Dee" Graham, Don Goodman, Nelson Larkin, and Wyatt Easterling), reached No. 29 and spent 14 weeks on the chart. He subsequently recorded *Billy Joe Royal,* another 10-song album for Atlantic. It included a song that became Billy Joe's final country chart single, which went to No. 51 during an eight-week stay on the chart that began on March 21, 1992. That song, by Max T. Barnes and Skip Ewing, was called "I'm Okay (And Gettin' Better)." As Billy Joe really was.

He recorded his final album, titled *Billy Joy Royal – His First Gospel Album,* in 2009. Released on the Gusto Records label, the album was inspired by his admiration of the early gospel music career of Sam Cooke.

Billy Joe never retired. Throughout what he called his "dry patches" – the periods between hit records or recording contracts – Billy Joe maintained a loyal following and continued performing on stage in clubs, lounges, fairs, and other venues for appreciative audiences, recurrently joining concert tours with other country and pop performers, including his friends B.J. Thomas and country music singer Ronnie McDowell.

In the autumn of 2015, Billy Joe was preparing for a series of tour dates with McDowell following a headlining gig that October 10 at the Carl Perkins Civic Center in Jackson, Tennessee, for the WMXX "Kool 103" Caravan of Stars. He was looking forward to appearing on stage at that show with original Rascals lead singer Felix Cavaliere, Ambrosia lead singer Joe Puerta, Kansas singer and keyboard player John Elefante, Bay City Rollers lead singer Kyle Vincent, Beaver Brown Band lead singer John

Cafferty, and Archies and Cuff Links lead singer Ron Dante. But Billy Joe didn't live to take the stage at that show. His fans were stunned to learn that he had died unexpectedly on Tuesday, October 6.

While some performers can point to one pivotal event as their big career break, Billy Joe had two: "'Boondocks,' of course, and 'Burned Like A Rocket' [on the Hot Country Singles chart], because until that became a hit I thought I was washed up," he explained. Billy Joe recounted some favorite memories along the way. "Appearing on the *Ed Sullivan Show* was a big deal for me. So was working at the Grand Ole Opry. Little Jimmy Dickens brought me there. I knew him because he used to work the *Jubilee* all the time. I appeared at the Opry two or three times, and I got a charge out of that each time."

Billy Joe's musical legacy encompasses eight *Billboard* Hot 100 hits, 14 country music hits, and induction into the Georgia Music Hall of Fame in 1988.

BILLY JOE ROYAL U.S. SINGLES ON THE *BILLBOARD* HOT 100 CHART

Debut	Peak	Title	Label
7/3/65	9	Down In The Boondocks	Columbia
9/18/65	14	I Knew You When	Columbia
12/4/65	38	I've Got To Be Somebody	Columbia
5/21/66	88	Heart's Desire	Columbia
9/3/66	91	Campfire Girls	Columbia
9/30/67	52	Hush	Columbia
10/4/69	15	Cherry Hill Park	Columbia
2/20/71	86	(Don't Let The Sun Set On You In) Tulsa	Columbia
6/3/78	82	Under The Boardwalk	Private Stock

Billboard's pop singles chart data is courtesy of Joel Whitburn's Record Research Inc. (www.recordresearch.com), Menomonee Falls, Wisconsin.

Epilogue: Billy Joe Royal

Singer

April 3, 1942 – October 6, 2015

Picture the 1955-era town square in the original *Back to the Future* movie, with a butcher shop, a bakery, a malt shop, a shoe store, a dress shop, a hardware store, and other mom-and-pop shops surrounding the central green. That was Billy Joe Royal's memory of Marietta, Georgia, where in the '50s he spent much of his childhood and adolescence. "We had two movie theaters on the square, and when the movie let out, we all hung out at the drugstore," Billy Joe recalled. Marietta Square also had a bandstand and a gazebo. He and his family moved to Marietta when he was 10 years old.

Billy Joe Royal – that was his true birth name – was born April 3, 1942, in the southern Georgia town of Valdosta. He was the oldest among his three other siblings – his brother, Jack, two years younger, and two sisters, Marilyn and Christine. Their parents, Clarence and Mary, worked hard to scrape together a living for the family.

Billy Joe Royal recorded from 1985 to 1992 for the Atlantic America label, which issued this publicity photo of him.

"My dad and the whole family came up through the Great Depression, and it was tough for them. They picked cotton, then moved to a mill village and they all worked at the cotton mill. Then my dad shifted to construction work, and eventually ended up working for Roadway Trucking Company. He drove a long-haul, refrigerated trailer packed with poultry. He was gone, on the road, a lot," Billy Joe said.

Music captivated Billy Joe as a youngster. He enjoyed listening to various types of music on the radio, and by age 9 began spontaneously singing along and displayed real talent. "The radio stations in Valdosta would play three or four different formats during different parts of the day. We had a daytime-only station that went off the air at sundown, but at night we could pick up the distant clear channel stations. One of them played black gospel music, and I especially loved songs by the Soul Stirrers. At the time I didn't know that the lead singer with that gospel group was Sam Cooke, and he became my favorite singer in the whole wide world," said Billy Joe, who later met Cooke. "I have a picture of me and Sam Cooke."

Billy Joe had two uncles in Valdosta who had blue-collar jobs but who played musical instruments and on weekends sang in a local country music band, Blackie Fleetwood and the Dixie Moderneers. One uncle was a guitarist and fiddler and the other played steel guitar. "The band sometimes let me sing a few songs with them when they performed on the local radio station and played for square dances on the weekends," Billy Joe said. Entranced by the steel guitar, Billy Joe became determined to learn how to play, and enrolled in lessons. "This guy taught Hawaiian steel guitar for $1 per lesson, and there were about 15 students in the class. They were all older than me, but I seemed to get it more than they did. It just came natural to me," Billy Joe said. "My uncle played steel guitar really good, so I would ask him after class how to play this or that, and he showed me, and I learned how to play 'Steel Guitar Rag' [a western swing tune that Bob Wills and his Texas Playboys popularized]. Learning that was a big deal for me. He showed me how to do a walk-up [chord progression], and that got me to the head of the class."

Billy Joe sadly had to leave that behind him when he turned 10 years old, though, because Clarence Royal got a new job with another trucking company for which the family moved 250 miles north to Marietta, a town with a population of about 20,000 in those days. "I thought my world was coming to an end because I couldn't sing with my uncles, or play the steel guitar anymore," Billy Joe said. The Royal family moved into an apartment in the 132-unit Clay Homes public housing project on Roswell Street, near Marietta Square. It didn't take Billy Joe long to adjust to life there.

At the square, he paused every day and looked longingly through the window of a store that had a steel guitar on display. "I didn't want to ask my folks for it because I knew it cost too much, but that was what I really, really wanted. We were all as poor as we could be, but there were a lot of kids there and a playground. At the time, we thought everybody was poor. It was just a great place to grow up. We had a million kids there to play with and everybody was in the same boat, just trying to scratch out a living," Billy Joe said.

Billy Joe Royal

Billy Joe Royal at age 14, when he was a freshman at Marietta High School in Georgia (photo courtesy of Savannah Royal).

Christmas morning 1954 was especially memorable for him. "I was 12 years old, and when I came downstairs at Christmas, my parents said, 'There's something hidden behind the tree.' They knew how much I wanted a lap steel guitar, and they had bought one for me with a little amplifier. It only cost $36, but it was a fortune for my parents. I'll never forget that feeling. I went crazy. That was a heck of a thing for them to do," said Billy Joe, who later in life generously donated that guitar to the Country Music Hall of Fame.

Billy Joe's family subsequently moved into a house a few blocks away on East Dixie Avenue. "My mom was a stay-at-home housewife. Just like on *Leave it to Beaver,* we would eat at 5 o'clock every day. It was wonderful. I had a great time there – a lot of laughs, a lot of friends. I could walk to everybody's house. My best friend lived behind our house." Billy Joe was in 10th grade at Marietta High School when his family moved 6 miles south to Smyrna, where Clarence went to work for the fire department. Billy Joe transferred to Campbell High School in Smyrna and quickly developed a friendship with his next-door neighbor, Mike Cushman, who played guitar. Although Billy Joe initially liked country music, he had by then developed interest in rockabilly, doo wop and rock and roll. "Mike and I decided to get a little group together. We called ourselves the Corvettes and began playing at parties, and pretty soon we won a local contest called 'Stars of Tomorrow' and we were kind of hot stuff in our little town."

By then Billy Joe had his sights firmly set on a musical career. "I wanted to make a living making music. It was all I cared about," Billy Joe told us. "In my own mind, I thought I was a pretty good singer, and maybe I could make a go of it." Good fortune appeared to be on his side. "I tell you, every dream I dreamed as a kid came true for me. It was just amazing." An important step toward realization of Billy Joe's dream came at age 14 when he discovered the *Georgia Jubilee* on WTJH radio, a rebroadcast of a stage show recorded weekly at the East Point City Auditorium in East Point, Georgia, at the southwestern fringe of metropolitan Atlanta.

"The *Jubilee* would bring in a Grand Ole Opry star from Nashville on Friday and they taped the show and played it back on the air on Saturday. Ray Stevens, Jerry Reed, Joe South, and many other talented, talented people were regulars on the show. I knew Priscilla Mitchell, a piano player and singer who was dating Jerry Reed and later married him. I asked her how in the world they got on that show, and she said, 'you go down and audition.' So I went for an audition, and that's where I met [singer and guitarist] Freddy Weller."

Billy Joe and Freddy auditioned the same day. "We both made the cut. This was the rockabilly age, and I went out and bought a pair of Scottish plaid desert boots, and wore them with a pea green coat, a black shirt, and a white tie, and I sang the Conway Twitty song 'It's Only Make Believe,' and they called me out for an encore my first time out. So I went back on stage and sang 'Wear My Ring Around Your Neck,' and I felt so good," Billy Joe said. "The emcee was a guy called the Old Sharecropper, and as I got off the stage he told the audience, 'I don't know who that kid is, but he's going to be around for a long time.' And I thought, 'Man, this is the greatest thing in the world.'"

Billy Joe's mother was supportive of his musical ambitions, but his father initially was less so. "My dad thought it was kind of silly, but I think he changed his mind when he came to the *Jubilee* and saw me on stage. My parents would come to the shows and I knew they were proud of me," Billy Joe said. As Billy Joe developed his singing techniques, he set the steel guitar aside. "I could sing a whole lot better than I could play. And I realized that people pay a lot more attention to the singer than they do the steel guitar player. Of course, I was around such great musicians, I should have sat down with Joe South and asked him to show me how to learn to play the thing better. And the great guitar player Lonnie Mack and I were really good friends, but I never asked him to show me how to play."

Billy Joe performed numerous times at the *Jubilee*, developed a repertoire, and then in the autumn of 1958 decided he was ready to stage his own show. He was only 16 years old, but he boldly approached the manager of the Strand Theatre in Marietta and told him, "I'd like to put on a rock and roll show, and I'll split the take from the door with you." The theater manager agreed. "So I called Freddy and a couple of the guys from the *Jubilee*, and with our quartet, we packed the place, because all of my school friends came." The marquee that November 28 billed him as "Billy Royal" in large letters. "The manager of the Strand thought 'Billy Joe' sounded like a redneck hick, and told me to just use 'Billy Royal.' It just so happened that the guy who managed all the Martin theaters in the area was there, and he asked me if I'd like to do that every weekend. I said, 'Heck yeah!' I paid the guys in the band about $15 apiece for each show. Then one time we had a gig in Griffin, which is about 40 miles south of Atlanta. One

Billy Joe early in his performing career, in a 1962 publicity photo for Fairlane Records (photo courtesy of Savannah Royal).

of the guys, Red Jones, called me and said that Rodney, our guitar player, was sick and couldn't make it. Jerry Reed said he could play, but he wanted $25. I said, 'Okay. He's got me over a barrel, so I'll pay him the $25," Royal said. He and his buddies continued performing through 1958 as they had a steady lineup of gigs throughout the region. "We were all so ambitious, it was ridiculous, and we all became very good friends."

He landed a salaried gig for $75 per week singing and accompanying himself on guitar at the Anchorage Club in the Clermont Hotel in Atlanta in 1959. "Their floor show also included a comedian and an interpretive dancer. I did two shows a night. I had been there for only a couple of weeks when this guy walked in and said, 'I have a club in Savannah called the Bamboo Ranch, and you would fit right in there. He said that he would pay me $125 a week, which was the greatest thing that had happened to me at that point in my life." Billy Joe packed a couple of suitcases, tossed them into the trunk of his 1950 Ford, and drove 250 miles southeast to Savannah, near the Atlantic coast. He had become accustomed to performing as "Billy Royal," but that changed when he arrived in Savannah. "The Bamboo Ranch already had another performer named Billy Brown, so when I told the manager that my name is really Billy Joe, he said, 'Okay, you'll perform as Billy Joe Royal.'"

The Bamboo Ranch was a huge club on Highway 17 South that catered to military personnel from Parris Island Marine Corps Recruit Depot, 40 miles northeast. "The military guys fought all the time at the club. Part of my job was to stand on this little soapbox thing, watch out for fights, and signal the bouncer, who was named Dick. It was a rough place. When I first got down there I was a little skinny guy, and I wouldn't go to the bathroom there. I was afraid I'd get killed. I'd go down the street to use the bathroom. I'd be singing and I'd see a couple of guys fighting and I'd say 'Dick' and point out where the fight was. Then he'd go over and break up the fight."

Billy Joe was one of four singers who each sang five sets each night and worked six nights a week. "Each singer did 20 minutes. None of the patrons ever looked at the singers. We were just background, like a jukebox, and if they danced they never looked our way. I started off trying to play the guitar and sing at the same time, but I wasn't very good. But I learned how to do spins like Jackie Wilson, and when I sang 'Mack The Knife' I did a few moves, and the people actually stopped and applauded. The boss told me, 'That's the first time we've ever had any applause. I want you to put that guitar down and move around like I saw you do. Pretty soon, things started feeling a lot better.'"

The house band at Bamboo Ranch was a popular local outfit, Buddy Livingston and the Versatones. "When the guitar player decided to quit, I told Buddy, 'I know someone that I can get to play guitar – he's famous and he's really, really good,'" Billy Joe said. He was referring to Joe South. "I called Joe and said, 'I'm working this club down here in Savannah, and they need a guitar player. If you want the job, it's yours.' Joe said, 'Yeah. I'll be there.' So he came down from Atlanta. Many people don't realize that besides being to me the greatest writer that ever lived, Joe South was one of the greatest guitar players. To me, Joe South was truly a genius. That's him playing guitar on Aretha Franklin's 'Chain Of Fools' record. He played with Simon and Garfunkel, he played with Bob Dylan." So the manager at the Bamboo Ranch hired him. South and Royal roomed together in the York House apartment building on York Street near Abercorn Street. "It cost us $7 a week to live there, and we had it made. We were on the fourth floor, and my calves looked like Arnold Schwarzenegger's from climbing up and down those stairs. We had our own rooms and a maid, but no heat. We were on a local TV show on WTOC, channel 11, every Thursday night advertising the club."

Working six nights a week, Billy Joe remained a member of the stage show at the Bamboo Ranch for four years, during which time the club booked headliners that included B.B. King's orchestra with Chuck Berry, the Drifters, the Isley Brothers, and Little Richard with a group called the Upsetters. "When the owner booked Sam Cooke in, I was so excited that I was beside myself. Sam flew in from California and had to change planes in Atlanta, so when he got to the Bamboo Ranch, he was dog tired. When I met him, he was whipped but he was really nice – probably a lot nicer than I would have been," Billy Joe said. "He sang like nobody I ever heard sing before in my life. The second time he came to play there, he was rested up, and when I got through singing, he came over and put his arm around my neck and said, 'You just get better, and better, and better.' Man, I almost cried. He had this kind of Eisenhower jacket, a kind of short jacket, and I said, 'Hey, I love what you're wearing.' He sat down and drew a picture of it on a piece of paper. I tried to dress snappy, too, and I took the drawing to a tailor, who made a jacket for me just like Sam Cooke's." During his time in Savannah, Billy Joe also met someone else: a woman named Donna Hammock, whom he married in 1963. The marriage ended in divorce after a couple of years.

Joe South already had been writing songs, and he and Billy Joe began cutting demo recordings together. With music publisher and talent manager Bill Lowery helping to open doors, Billy Joe got his first record deal with the small independent Fairlane label in the autumn of 1961. The series of recordings that followed led to his contract with Columbia Records and ultimately to his national smash hit "Down In The Boondocks."

Billy Joe got his first crack at performing in a major television commercial in 1969, when Coca-Cola was preparing to switch slogans from "Things go better with Coke" to "It's the real thing." A representative from the firm's longtime advertising agency, McCann Erickson, contacted Billy Joe and asked him to travel to New York to record a demo. "In New York, we went into a rehearsal hall that looked like something in a B movie, with an old piano and a 25-watt light bulb hanging down from the ceiling. I was wondering what I had gotten myself into. Then the guy told me what the jingle was – 'It's the real thing, in the back of your mind.' I thought, 'Holy moly, Coke's not going to go for that.' I was embarrassed to sing it, but he had hired me, so I sang it. After I went home he called me and said that the people at Coke really like my jingle." Billy Joe returned to New York to record the jingle with a full orchestra. "While I was in New York I got an agent who told me, 'Whatever they offer you, you say "no." What you want is residuals.' They offered me $10,000, but I did what the agent advised and declined it. So instead the agency signed the Fortunes to record the commercial."

But McCann Erickson remained interested in Billy Joe. In late 1971 another rep from the agency called. "He said they wanted me to film a national TV commercial for Coke in the Grand Canyon. At the time, I was appearing at the Flamingo Hotel in Las Vegas, so I would do my show in Vegas, and they would put me on an airplane and fly me to the Grand Canyon, and I'd ride this mule about halfway down the canyon," said Billy Joe, who was a skilled horseback rider. "These guys from New York would walk down that canyon because they were afraid to ride those mules. They would shoot for a whole day, getting angles so the sun was shining through my lips. Going back and forth, doing three shows a night at the Flamingo and then flying over to the Grand Canyon and fooling with that mule all day was killing me." Recurrent snowfalls interrupted the shooting schedule, which included aerial shots from a helicopter flying over and past Billy Joe at close range, as he crooned "sing along with me" while standing atop the precarious Duck-on-a-Rock formation. "I was scared to death I was going to fall off. We worked on that commercial for days. They shot a bunch of stuff and then pieced it together. They spent so much money, it was ridiculous. We finally got the shots done, and I was pretty excited when that national campaign came out in February 1972."

In 1974, after Billy Joe had left Columbia Records and signed with MGM South, he married for the second time, to an old friend, Georgia Mosley. "She was my high school sweetheart." That marriage lasted 10 years, but fell apart during a period when Billy Joe's career was in decline. Billy Joe was no longer getting bookings into Las Vegas lounges, and he was no longer under contract to a record label. Living in Hidden Hills, an upscale enclave at the southwestern corner of L.A.'s San Fernando Valley, he felt hidden and isolated. "I had some really dark days there, and I had given up by that point. I was going through a terrible divorce, and I wasn't recording. I thought I was finished," Billy Joe told us. Realizing that he needed motivation, he began reading *The Power of Positive Thinking* by Norman Vincent Peale. "That book gave me the confidence and inspiration to get up off my tail and go do something." He transformed that inspiration into action by contacting Bill Lowery and moving to Nashville with the determination to carve a niche for himself in country music – which he did in 1985 with "Burned Like A Rocket" and other hits that followed.

In Nashville during 1995 Billy Joe married Michelle Rivenbark, who had two sons, Trey and Joey, from a previous marriage. Billy Joe and Michelle, who remained married four years, had a daughter, Savannah, in June 1996. "Not to brag, but she's the greatest kid on Earth. She was Miss West Carteret High School, and president of FFA. She excels in anything she tries to do," Billy Joe said. "When she was younger she took piano lessons, and dance lessons. Even though she could play well, she really didn't care that much about music." Her interests lie elsewhere. "She has horses and won all kinds of trophies for showing them. At the North Carolina State Fair she took four first-place awards. She plans to be a veterinarian." She also has been involved in various humanitarian activities.

On September 24, 2015, Billy Joe was in fine form when he performed at the Gwinnett County Fairgrounds in Lawrenceville, Georgia. That would be his last performance. Billy Joe Royal died in his sleep 12 days later, on Tuesday, October 6, at his home in Morehead City, North Carolina. He was 73 years old.

Billy Joe had reminisced about the joy he derived from meeting performers he considered his idols. One of those was Bobby Darin. "Seymour introduced me to Bobby Darin. When I shook his hand, I told him how terrific he was. His recording of 'Splish Splash' was the first record I had ever bought. When I worked at the Bamboo Ranch in Savannah, Fats Domino played there. That came full circle later on when both of us were playing Las Vegas at the same time," said Billy Joe, who never did have any hobbies. "I liked riding horses when I had them. My whole life was work, work, but that was my passion. Most everyone goes through dark periods, but all in all, I've had an amazing life – a crazy, wonderful life."

From left, Larry Tamblyn, Dick Dodd, John Fleckenstein, and Tony Valentino (photo courtesy of Larry Tamblyn).

Sometimes Good Guys Don't Wear White

The Standells

Teenagers in the early and mid-1960s listened to hit records in any of several ways: through the tinny speakers of their AM transistor radios tuned to "top 40" radio stations, in their cars (if they were old enough to drive), or in their bedrooms, on a portable record player with a heavy tonearm that rode the grooves of undulating 45 rpm vinyl records. Most of the hit records of the era were "safe" – kids could invite their friends over to listen to them with their bedroom doors open. Records by the Beach Boys, Herman's Hermits, the Supremes, Freddie and the Dreamers, and Sonny & Cher were all open-doors tunes. If mom or dad happened to walk past, none of the song lyrics or bouncy rhythms gave them cause for concern. But during those relatively innocent times, some records called for greater discretion – listening in private, behind closed doors to avoid agitating protective parents. In most cases, it wasn't what the lyrics overtly said, but rather what they *didn't* expressly say – what the feverish beat or faintly suggestive lyrics intimated. The Kingsmen's "Louie, Louie" was one such record. So were the Rolling Stones' "(I Can't Get No) Satisfaction" and "Let's Spend The Night Together," Paul Revere and Raiders' "Hungry," the Kinks' "All Day And All Of The Night," the Swingin' Medallions' "Double Shot Of My Baby's Love," and Lou Christie's "Rhapsody In The Rain." These were among many songs that brimmed with implied, though not explicit, sexually rebellious energy. Although with a wink these and other lustful, raw-edged songs slid past censors, one band had the unfortunate distinction of being ensnared in a net of overzealous censorship that was far more onerous and punishing than their music warranted. That band, the Standells, was targeted in a coordinated campaign that torpedoed their musical career, all because of one only vaguely teasing record: "Try It."

That song, though, was an anomaly for the Standells. Sexual and drug references were absent from most of their songs. That's not to say that the Standells weren't edgy. To adult ears, the music of this Tower Records band was harsh, shrill, raw, uncultured. Their vocals sounded defiant, rude, unruly, snotty, tough – which was the essence of their appeal to their youthful fans. The Standells didn't start that way; their music was tame in 1964 and '65, when they recorded for Liberty Records, then for Vee-Jay (where their producer was Sonny Bono) and MGM. But the career of the Los Angeles band took a sharp turn after Tower Records released what would become an unofficial anthem of the city of Boston – their top-20 hit "Dirty Water," which has since become a mainstay at Boston Red Sox and Boston Bruins home games because of its prominent reference to the "River Charles." Hailed by some people as the "godfathers of punk rock," the Standells predated the punk rock movement by a dozen years.

Although during more than five decades the Standells endured numerous personnel changes, underwent a change in name spelling, and survived periods of hiatus, the one constant in the band through all the years has been its founder, Larry Tamblyn. The younger brother of musical film actor Russ Tamblyn (best known for playing Jets gang leader Riff in the 1961 Academy Award-winning motion picture *West Side Story*), Larry as a high school senior began his solo singer recording career with independent Faro Records, which released three of Larry's singles between February 1960 and October 1961. After briefly joining a band called the Starlighters (different from Joey Dee's group) as an electric organ player, Larry, along with two members of that group – guitarist Tony Valentino (born Emilio Anthony Bellissimo in Sicily, Italy) and bass player Jody Rich (real name: Jody Ulrey) – formed a new group in 1962 with teenage drummer Benny Hernandez, who performed under the name Benny King. "We started visiting booking agents. We didn't have a name for the group yet and we couldn't figure out what to call ourselves, but we spent so much time standing around at these booking agents' offices, I came up with the name Standels [with only one "l"]. And it just clicked," Larry said. Persistence paid off, as the McConkey Artists Agency agreed to represent the band. After booking the Standels into a couple of local clubs, the agency landed a five-month gig for them at the Oasis Club in Honolulu.

The Standells

Friction arose among the members of the Standels, and upon the return of the band to California in late 1962, Jody and Benny were out. Larry and Tony replaced them with two Garys – bass guitarist Gary Lane (whose real name was Gary McMillan) and drummer Gary Leeds (who later became a member of the Walker Brothers vocal group under the name "Gary Walker." Upon the return of the Standels to the mainland, their agent booked them into a series of California club dates in Fresno, in Sacramento, and in Eureka. As Larry Tamblyn & the Standels, the band recorded a couple of Larry's compositions in doo-wop style – "You'll Be Mine Someday" and "The Girl In My Heart," which the independent Linda Records label released as a single in August 1963. When the band heard in September that the Peppermint West at 1750 Cahuenga Boulevard in Hollywood was looking for a house band, they auditioned and won the gig, by which time they added a second "l" to their name to become the Standells. The club was patterned after New York City's Peppermint Lounge, which was the nucleus of the early 1960s "twist" dance craze. In the early autumn of 1963 few Americans had heard of the Beatles, who already were wildly popular in the U.K. and Europe. But the Standells were hip to the Beatles, and in their stage appearances began wearing long-haired wigs, in contrast to other American musicians who still had crew cuts, slicked-back, or waxed pompadour hairstyles. The wigs soon became unnecessary, as the Standells let their own hair grow long.

"We did get a lot of recognition playing there, and that's where we met Burt Jacobs, who became our manager. Burt had no experience in the business up until then, other than that he was a bookie," Larry said. After watching the band perform, Jacobs approached the band members and asked if they would appoint him as their manager if he were able to get the band a recording deal with Liberty Records. The band members agreed because at the time Liberty was a hit-making independent label with good distribution and an artist roster that included Bobby Vee, Gene McDaniels, Johnny Burnette, Jan and Dean, Jackie DeShannon, the Rivingtons, Bud and Travis, Vikki Carr, Timi Yuro, the Ventures, Si Zentner, the Johnny Mann Singers, the Marketts, and Dick and Dee Dee. The Standells signed with Liberty in February 1964.

"Burt loved the Standells, and there was nothing mean-spirited about him. He was just a great guy, but the only reason he got us signed with Liberty was that he took bets from guys over there, and they were into him for a lot of money," Larry told us. "Liberty assigned us a producer, Dick Glasser, who just wasn't meant for the Standells. He was more like a pop producer. The first recording we did for Liberty was a song I wrote called 'The Shake,' which was supposed to be a wild and raunchy in-your-face fast rocker, something like 'Shout' by Joey Dee and the Starliters." That's not how it turned out. "The arrangement absolutely ruined it. It sounded like a combination of polka and doo-wop. It even had a clavinet in it, and backup singers. I was the lead singer, but I didn't have the experience to tell Dick Glasser that was not acceptable." The flip side of the single, released in March 1964, was a tune called "Peppermint Beatle." By then the band had been wearing long locks for months. "Nobody else had long hair, even in Hollywood," Larry recalled. "I remember going into a real noisy diner with our long hair, and all of a sudden it got really quiet. This was a new concept, even for a rock group. Once the Beatles started catching on, a writer for one of the teen magazines came out to the Peppermint West and interviewed us. The article in the magazine identified us as the first American group with long hair."

The Standells left the Peppermint West for a three-week booking in the Pow Wow Room, the lounge at the Thunderbird Hotel and Casino on the Las Vegas Strip, where they were billed as "America's answer to the Beatles." The band returned to L.A. in late March '64 and began a two-year stint as the house band at P.J.'s, the classy little jazz club at 8151 Santa Monica Boulevard where Trini Lopez had come to fame and recorded two best-selling live albums. P.J.'s management didn't like the long-haired look and made the Standells trim their hair shorter (although it remained longish). But the Standells reciprocated by changing the character of P.J.'s – they made that place rock. "Back then P.J.'s was a small nightclub that seated maybe 150 people, but we started bringing in crowds that filled the place to the brim every night. So while we were there, the owners, Bill Daugherty, Chuck Murano, Paul Raffles, and Elmer Valentine, decided to expand the club. They knocked out the rear wall and added a new 2,000-square-foot room, in an L-shaped arrangement. When it was done, that big room held about 500 people," Larry recalled.

As Liberty made plans to record the Standells at P.J.'s in July for a live album, Gary Leeds split from the band to join the Walker Brothers. "Two weeks before we were to record this album, we held open auditions for a drummer to replace Gary," Larry said. "In walks this kid who was a couple of years younger than me. But boy, once he sat down behind the drums, he was just dynamite." The kid was Dick Dodd, who at the time was the drummer in the touring band of Liberty recording artist Jackie DeShannon, but could do more than play drums. "He sang a song, and I said, 'Wow.' Right away we knew he was the one," Larry said. Joseph Richard Dodd, who had grown up in Redondo Beach, California, was a show-biz kid who played the accordion and took tap lessons at a dance school, where a Disney talent scout recruited him for the *Mickey Mouse Club*. At age 9 in 1955, he put on the ears cap and became a Mouseketeer named Dickie (because the show's producer liked all the kids on the show to have two-syllable names). Fellow Mouseketeer Cubby O'Brien taught drum-playing basics to Dickie, who bought a used snare and cymbals from Annette Funicello. As an adolescent in 1957, Dick played drums on the *Gisele MacKenzie Show* on NBC TV, then worked as part of her Las Vegas stage act. He had been a member of the band the BelAirs, who recorded the 1961 early surf tune "Mr. Moto," and Eddie and the Showmen, who cut a tune called "Mr. Rebel."

When the Showmen worked as the backup band at a gig where Jackie DeShannon was performing, she hired Dick for her own band. "Jackie was the one who got me into the Standells. At that time I just sang a little bit, and she'd been coaching me on that. When I joined the Standells I was just their drummer, and then next thing I'm their lead singer. She made me have confidence in myself. She was really wonderful. I also had a gigantic crush on her," Dodd told a *Los Angeles Times* reporter in 1990. Dodd also had a dancing role in the musical motion picture *Bye Bye Birdie* starring Janet Leigh, Dick Van Dyke, and Ann-Margret by the time he joined the Standells. Larry had been the lead singer until then, but graciously let Dodd take the singing spotlight on a few songs. "He was able to catch on very quickly, and he was such a good singer," Larry said. When the time came to record the live album, Larry Tamblyn, Dick Dodd, Tony Valentino, and Gary Lane were ready.

The Standells in Person at P.J.'s, which Liberty released in September, was a collection of favorite R&B tunes, including Johnny Otis' "So Fine," Jimmy Reed's "Help Yourself," James Brown's "I'll Go Crazy," and Larry Williams' "Bony Moronie," along with Lennon and McCartney's "You Can't Do That," a nod to the British Invasion. "Another genius move by Glasser: he decided to speed up the recording to make it sound more exciting. By doing so, it raised the pitch, and we sounded more like Alvin and the Chipmunks than the Standells," Larry said. "It wasn't until the re-release of the album as *The Standells Live and Out of Sight* in 1966, after the success of our single 'Dirty Water,' that they slowed the tracks back down to their original pitch.

Liberty released "Help Yourself," backed with "I'll Go Crazy," as a single in July '64, but it didn't reach the charts. Neither did the follow-up "So Fine" (with "Linda Lou" on the flip side), even though *Billboard* magazine on October 17 proclaimed that it had "chart potential." After three misfires on Liberty, the band had become restless. "Burt wasn't very happy with Liberty, nor were we," Tamblyn said. When Liberty accidentally failed to exercise its option on the Standells' recording contract, Burt Jacobs took advantage and opted out. A news brief in the November 7, 1964, edition of *Billboard* reported that the Standells had left Liberty and were shopping for a new label.

The Standells' tenure as the house band at P.J.'s had led to cameo rock band roles in television and films. "The first movie we had done was *Get Yourself a College Girl* with Mary Ann Mobley," Larry said. "One of the songs we performed for it was a revised version of 'The Shake.' They asked us to revise the lyrics and call it 'The Swim.' Instead of 'they're shakin' in the East, they're shakin' in the west,' it was 'they're swimmin' in the east, they're swimmin' in the west.' [The "swim" was a popular dance of the era.] And during the movie they also played 'Bony Moronie,' which was another song that we did on the album. It was our first exposure to film, and we were nobodies back then." MGM chose the Standells to record the title song for *Zebra in the Kitchen,* a comedy film starring Jay North that opened in theaters in December '64; MGM released the song as a single that did not reach the charts.

Jacobs landed a contract for the Standells with Vee-Jay Records, a heretofore highly successful independent label that had recently shifted operations from Chicago to Hollywood. The Four Seasons recorded for the label, which had an expansive roster of R&B artists, including Jerry Butler, John Lee Hooker, Jimmy Reed, the Impressions, Betty Everett, Dee Clark, and Gladys Knight and the Pips. It seemed like a good fit for the Standells. "We were all into R&B. Vee-Jay was a huge label in the R&B market, but they had yet to establish themselves much in the rock field. They assigned Sonny Bono to produce us." The Standells recorded several "A" sides that Bono wrote or co-wrote, including a pop ballad called "The Boy Next Door," on which Cher sang background vocals. The January 23, 1965, issue of *Billboard* tagged "The Boy Next Door" as having "chart potential." The weeks of February 6 and February 13 it was "bubbling under" at No. 102 – so close, but it did not reach the Hot 100.

The Standells themselves barely noticed, because they had been anointed for an extended engagement as the first rock band to perform in the Tiger-a-Go-Go Room at the Hilton Inn near San Francisco International Airport. After booking the Standells for a four-week stay spanning the month of January, the hotel extended their contract for six weeks – and then for eight additional weeks beginning in early April.

In the spring of 1965 the Standells were seemingly on every TV channel. They appeared in a guest spot on *The Munsters* CBS TV show on March 18, on *American Bandstand* on ABC television on March 20, and on the ABC show *Shindig* on March 25 – all before the Standells had a hit record. Not long afterward, the Standells were booked to appear on the *Ben Casey* ABC TV drama. The band also appeared in the 1965 teen musical film *When the Boys Meet the Girls,* in which they performed a tune called "It's All In Your Mind."

In April, Vee-Jay released another Standells single, "Big Boss Man" (a hard-driving rocker written by Al Smith and Luther Dixon), backed with "Don't Say Goodbye" (written by Mike Gordon); that single didn't register on the charts. But Vee-Jay was about to say goodbye. The label, which had been entangled in royalty disputes and other legal actions, lost its two biggest performers – the 4 Seasons and the Beatles – and Vee-Jay soon after went out of business.

Jacobs, who was more of a promoter than a manager, realized that the Standells would benefit from more management expertise. So he contacted his friend Seymour Heller, a highly successful personal manager whose clients included Liberace, Frankie Laine, and Al Martino. Heller, Jacobs, Ray Harris, and Ed Cobb agreed to join forces, under the umbrella of a new corporation called Attarack. Its divisions included Greengrass, a music publishing and record production business, and a talent management arm, B-J Enterprises, which Burt Jacobs headed. As the Standells returned to Hollywood for another residency at P.J.'s that summer, Jacobs signed a deal for the Standells with Greengrass Productions. Principals in Greengrass were Ray Harris, who had formerly worked in sales and promotion for Capitol Records and Vee-Jay, and Ed Cobb, a songwriter and A&R (artists and repertoire) man who had been a member of the Four Preps, an easy-listening vocal group who recorded for Capitol for nearly a decade beginning in 1956. Pianist Lincoln Mayorga, a Hollywood High School classmate of Cobb's who had been arranger and accompanist for many Preps recordings, had encouraged Cobb's foray into songwriting; Mayorga and Cobb collaborated in arranging and producing Ketty Lester's bluesy 1962 top-10 hit "Love Letters." Cobb also wrote Brenda Holloway's 1964 hit "Every Little Bit Hurts," and wrote and produced Gloria Jones' recording of "Tainted Love" the same year; the British duo Soft Cell scored a top-10 hit with a synth-pop version of the song in 1981.

Greengrass entered into an arrangement in September 1965 to lease recording masters by singers Ketty Lester and Gloria Jones and the Standells to the Tower Records label, a subsidiary of Capitol Records. (The Tower label had no relationship to the record retailing chain of the same name.) Both Harris and Cobb were instrumental in securing that deal, because of their prior relationships with Capitol. However, the Standells initially wondered if whether or not Ed Cobb would be a good fit for them.

"To be frank, we had our reservations about Ed, because he was with the Four Preps, and they were square. But he had produced soul singers Ketty Lester and Gloria Jones, so that gave us confidence in him," Tamblyn told us. The Standells needed new material to record, and Ed Cobb had a song in mind. He had recently returned from a Four Preps national tour that included Boston. While he was there he went out on a date with a female college student, which ended much sooner than he had hoped because the dormitory in which she lived imposed a midnight curfew. He told friends that as he walked alone back to his hotel, he noticed the pollution in the Charles River and felt threatened by some people he encountered along the way. That experience inspired him to write a song, which he presented to the Standells. He called it "Dirty Water." The Standells initially were ambivalent about it.

"The way Ed wrote 'Dirty Water,' it was a standard 32-bar blues song. We agreed to record it, but only after Ed said that we could rearrange it," Tamblyn said. "I altered the chord structure. Instead of doing a straight seventh, I made it as an extended seventh, so it was part of a combination of an A and a B. It was that extended chord that made it sound different from what Ed had written." It was much in the vein of the Standells' spring '65 release "Big Boss Man." In addition, Dick Dodd worked out his spoken introduction to "Dirty Water," and Tony Valentino devised the gruffly rockin' *ah-room-boom-boom, room-baa-daaa* opening guitar riff that made the song a top-of-the-hour favorite for top-40 radio stations. To record "Dirty Water," the Standells went to a garage – but it was no ordinary garage.

The session was in the home-based recording studio of Armin Steiner, a recording engineer who has since attained legendary stature in the recording and film industries. Steiner, a classical violinist who as a young man had begun training in recording techniques at UCLA, worked as an engineer for a commercial recording studio. Through that line of work he met and became friends with Ed Cobb and Lincoln Mayorga, who gave him technical advice when he decided to build a professional recording studio in his mother's home in West L.A. Steiner's mother allowed him to convert the garage into a soundproofed studio with an isolation room for vocals. He turned a bedroom above the garage into the control room with two three-track recorders, and the basement became a live echo chamber equipped with a reverb unit. The first hit recorded in Steiner's studio was Dick and Dee Dee's 1961 top-five hit "The Mountain's High."

When the Standells set up in Steiner's garage studio in the autumn of 1965, the instruments were recorded on one track, the lead vocal was recorded on another channel, and the background vocals were recorded on the third track. Although three discrete channels were used, it was not a stereo session, because the channels did not represent stereo imaging. Those three tracks were then mixed to produce a crisp monaural master. "Armin to me was a genius," Larry said. Although the Standells substantially modified the arrangement of 'Dirty Water' to suit their bluesy-rock style, they were flabbergasted at what they saw on the label of the 45: Ed Cobb had credited Lincoln Mayorga, rather than the Standells, for the arrangement. "I think very highly of Lincoln as an accomplished composer, musician, and arranger, but when we recorded 'Dirty Water,' he never set foot in the studio." But Tamblyn is quick to praise Cobb for coaxing a perfectly surly, scowling tone from Dick Dodd. "Ed Cobb was able to bring out something in Dick, that raw energy, that I never heard before or since with another producer. Snarly, raw attitude, with snot all over it." The song also had "hit" written all over it – but it took a while to get there. Its release in November 1965 went largely unnoticed. During the void that followed the release of "Dirty Water," Dick Dodd decided to leave the band. His replacement was Canadian drummer Dewey Martin (born Walter Midkiff), who later joined the Modern Folk Quartet and the Dillards before becoming a member of Buffalo Springfield. "Besides drumming, Dewey traded off with me on lead singing. I loved Dewey, but the other two guys didn't care for him that much," Larry said. "He had this really wry sense of humor, like gallows humor, but the other guys didn't catch onto it like I did. Dewey had a pet ocelot that he took with him every place he went. The thing was tame, but it was still a wild animal."

While most "top 40" radio stations, by definition, had short playlists of songs, some stations allowed greater latitude for introduction of new songs on the air. One such station was WLOF "channel 95" in Orlando, Florida. In January 1966, "Dirty Water" caught the attention of WLOF music director and air personality Bill "Weird Beard" Vermillion, who added it to the station's on-air rotation. Listeners loved it, and its ranking on the WLOF survey began to climb. Orlando was a relatively small radio market back then and local sales didn't make much of a dent in national figures, but when "Dirty Water" hit No. 1 on the WLOF playlist on February 5, radio stations in Miami paid attention and began playing it. When Dick Dodd learned that the single was gaining airplay, he asked to return to the

Standells – who welcomed him back. After all, the lead vocal on "Dirty Water" was his.

"Dirty Water" was No. 8 in Miami by March 26, and getting strong airplay in several other cities in other states, when it made its *Billboard* debut, "bubbling under" the Hot 100 chart at No. 132. For three weeks beginning April 2, "Dirty Water roosted at No. 2 in Miami, then hit No. 1 there on April 23 – the same day on which it premiered at No. 98 on the Billboard Hot 100. And then it began climbing – not rapidly, but steadily. It didn't catch fire in markets across the country simultaneously, but the cumulative effect of radio stations in various markets adding "Dirty Water" to their playlists over a period of several weeks that spring contributed to the record's rise on the *Billboard* chart. On May 7 it was No. 69 with a star, indicating rapid ascent. It cracked the top 40, hitting No. 31, on June 11.

The band was in Seattle for a multi-week gig at the Club Esquire when Tower label execs decided to strike while the iron was hot and get a Standells album on the market. Producer Ed Cobb met the band in Seattle, rehearsed some new songs with them, and during three days at Audio Recording Inc. on Fifth Avenue in Seattle recorded all the tracks they needed for an album, titled *Dirty Water.* In addition to the title track, the 10-song album included three other Ed Cobb compositions, "There's A Storm Coming," "Rari," and "Sometimes Good Guys Don't Wear White." The *Dirty Water* album simmered with a rude, fevered, smart-aleck attitude, epitomized by Jim Valley's "Little Sally Tease," and Minette Alton and Ben DiTosti's song "Medication." Also included were Larry Tamblyn's song "Pride And Devotion"; Dick Dodd and Tony Valentino's "Why Did You Hurt Me?"; and Mick Jagger and Keith Richards' "19th Nervous Breakdown." On the album jacket, Cobb shared credit for arrangements with Tamblyn, Valentino, Dodd, and Lane.

Rushed for release in mid-June 1966, the *Dirty Water* album made its debut on the *Billboard* "Top LPs" chart at No. 129 on July 2. By then, the "Dirty Water" single was at No. 16 with a star in its 11th week on the Hot 100 chart. At that time, the Standells were on a five-week U.S. and Canadian tour with the Rolling Stones that had begun June 24 at Manning Bowl in the Boston suburb of Lynn. It was a compatible pairing; the music of both bands crackled with defiance. The Tradewinds and the McCoys also were on the bill. "One night on the tour I had dinner with the Stones in one of their rooms in the hotel," Larry recalled. I don't eat red meat anymore, but at the time I was a red meat eater. We had these beautiful London broil steaks. I was still an immature kid, even in my 20s, and I asked for ketchup to put on it. When Mick Jagger heard that, he said, 'Fookin' yank.'"

On July 9, "Dirty Water" peaked at No. 11 (for two weeks), while the *Dirty Water* album was at No. 93 with a star, rising 12 notches with a star the following week. The single "Dirty Water" remained on the chart for 16 weeks, through the week of August 13. On that date, the Standells' follow-up single, "Sometimes Good Guys Don't Wear White" premiered on the chart. That gave the Standells two records on the Hot 100 that week. "Sometimes Good Guys" was another song that seethed with youthful rebellious attitude. "As far as being the snotty, rebellious type of group, I think that the type of material that we did brought that out. It all had that 'us against them' type of attitude, which really caught on," Larry said.

The Standells thrived on their ambitious touring schedule – all the members except bassist Gary Lane. His wife was expecting a baby, and he disliked spending time away from home on the road. "Gary was a really good friend, and I didn't hold his departure against him, but it put us in a difficult spot. We needed to find a replacement fast," Larry said. "We put out feelers in the venues where we were playing, and with the musicians who we met. We especially liked the bass player, Dave Burke, in a band

Standells (from left) Larry Tamblyn, Tony Valentino, and John Fleckenstein in a 1967 performance (photo courtesy of Larry Tamblyn).

231

called the Tropics that performed with us. He auditioned for us, and we hired him."

Eager to fully exploit the Standells, Tower Records execs urged the band to record another album, and Greengrass obliged. The Standells recorded another 10-song album, this one titled *Why Pick On Me – Sometimes Good Guys Don't Wear White* after two of its tracks (both of which Ed Cobb wrote). Not only was the rushed timing odd, but so was the fact that the song "Sometimes Good Guys Don't Wear White" was included on two successive Tower album releases. The *Why Pick On Me – Sometimes Good Guys* album also included two Larry Tamblyn compositions, "The Girl And The Moon" and "Mr. Nobody," Burt Bacharach and Hal David's "My Little Red Book" (a hit by the band Love), and another Jagger and Richards song, "Paint It Black." Tower Records released it in September, only three months after the band's previous album.

The single "Sometimes Good Guys Don't Wear White" rose to No. 43 and spent eight weeks on the *Billboard* Hot 100. The title may have prevented the song from charting higher. "It wasn't as big a hit as 'Dirty Water' because radio stations in many markets modeled themselves after two stations in L.A., and they called their on-air people either 'boss jocks' or 'good guys.' [KFWB in Los Angeles, WMCA New York, WIBG Philadelphia, KOIL Omaha, WSAI Cincinnati, and WKDA Nashville were among many radio stations that branded their disk jockeys "good guys."] A lot of the stations that were the 'boss jock' stations refused to play our song because it said 'good guys.' That's why it wasn't as big of a hit," Larry said. As "Sometimes Good Guys Don't Wear White" dropped off the chart, the Standells' follow-up single, "Why Pick On Me" (another Ed Cobb composition) was waiting in the wings. Yet another statement of ill-tempered, youthful resentment, "Why Pick On Me" made its debut on the Hot 100 on October 22, beginning a seven-week run during which it peaked nationally at No. 54 – although it performed far better in individual markets around the country. "The reverse side of 'Why Pick On Me' was a song that I wrote and sang, called 'Mr. Nobody.' A lot of people said that should have been the 'A' side. The band members thought 'Why Pick On Me' wasn't a Standells type of song, but we didn't have a say in the decision," Larry said.

Astonishingly in November, Tower released yet another Standells album, titled *The Hot Ones!* It consisted largely of the Standells' interpretations of hits by other bands, including The Monkees' "Last Train To Clarksville," the Troggs' "Wild Thing," Donovan's "Sunshine Superman," the Kinks' "Sunny Afternoon" and the Lovin' Spoonful's "Summer In The City." It closed with their own "Dirty Water." That was the third Standells album to be released within five months. And two Standells songs had been duplicated among those albums. The track "Dirty Water" was on both the *Dirty Water* and *Hot Ones* albums, and the song "Sometimes Good Guys Don't Wear White" was on both the *Dirty Water* and the *Why Pick On Me – Sometimes Good Guys Don't Wear White* album. "I didn't approve of that," Larry said. "Ed Cobb and Ray Harris made all those decisions. They tried to milk it for everything they could."

That included Tower's release of a single with the band's name spelled in reverse order: the Sllednats. Horsing around with a Tony Valentino composition called "Don't Tell Me What To Do," the band recorded it in 1920s crooning style, taking a page from the playbook of the New Vaudeville Band (who recorded "Winchester Cathedral," an autumn 1966 novelty hit). "We were just having fun with it, but it was all just kind of a joke," Larry said.

Nearly six months had gone by since Dave Burke had joined the Standells, and although he was a good bass player, he never did fit in comfortably with the band or its touring schedule. In late autumn, he and the band parted company. "We were back in L.A. and in between concerts, and we auditioned a number of bass players to replace Dave. We took our time," Larry said. The February 25, 1967, edition of the *KRLA Beat* newspaper, distributed to radio station fans in Los Angeles, reported that the Standells auditioned 163 musicians before selecting John Fleckenstein, who had been a member of the band Love until the spring of 1966, when he left to serve his apprenticeship in the motion picture cinematography guild. "A week after I joined the Standells, we did our first gig at the Santa Monica Civic Auditorium – and Love opened for us. I had quit Love to go into the picture business, and then there I was back in music – only this time with the Standells," said Fleckenstein, who shortened his stage name to "John Fleck." Larry speaks highly of him. "John particularly impressed us because, number one, he had been with Love, and number two, he added that extra something that we seemed to be lacking. As it turned out, he was a great songwriter, too. He wrote all the lyrics and the melody for 'Riot On Sunset Strip,' and split writing credit with Tony, who wrote the guitar riff. John is a very talented guy, and he brought in real freshness. He's a great bass player."

The Standells had been commissioned to write the title song for the American International motion picture *Riot on Sunset Strip*. The film dramatized anti-curfew demonstrations that pitted young rock music fans against Los Angeles police officers in November 1966 outside Pandora's

Box, a popular Sunset Boulevard hangout. Stephen Stills wrote the song "For What It's Worth" about the series of confrontations. "We were at the MGM studio, and although we hadn't seen a script of the film, we were very familiar with the riot on which it was based. I had previously performed at the Pandora's Box nightclub with one of the groups I was in," John explained. "Tony Valentino and I went over to one of the MGM sound stages, and I wrote the lyrics from my experience and what I knew about the riots on Sunset Strip. The words just came to me. Tony wrote that guitar lick. We composed 'Riot On Sunset Strip' in about an hour or so." Larry wrote a second song, "Get Away From Here," for the film, which was produced by Sam Katzman – who also produced *Get Yourself a College Girl* and more than 200 other feature films. "We recorded those songs on a motion picture sound stage, and it was a very rough recording. They were set up for orchestras, not for rock and roll," Larry explained. The Standells subsequently recorded another, faster-tempo, more polished version of "Riot On Sunset Strip" in a recording studio for release as a single. "The version on the movie soundtrack doesn't sound a bit like the 45 record." For the stark black-and-white photo on the single record sleeve, the Standells looked brooding and menacing. "We weren't angry. We were just looking snotty," Larry laughed.

Searching for new material for the band to record, Ed Cobb found a song from songwriters Joey Levine and Marc Bellack that played right into that snottiness: "Try It." Its teasing lyrics tingled with innuendo, without explicitly mentioning what "it" was. In the recording session, Cobb coaxed out all of the rawness that Dick Dodd could muster in his singing, and in the band's background vocals. Without being as blatant as the Rolling Stones' "Let's Spend The Night Together," the Standells' "Try It" was tantalizingly covert. It also was a good rock tune, and shortly after its release in February 1967, "top 40" radio stations began playing it. The single was getting strong airplay and enthusiastic listener reaction on stations in Los Angeles and elsewhere. "It was getting played on every 'top 40' station. It was great. It was going to be the next big hit for us," Fleckenstein said.

In Dallas, however, those nebulous lyrics rankled one radio station group owner: Gordon McLendon. A traditionalist, McLendon banned the record from his stations in Dallas, Buffalo, and Houston because of what he deemed suggestive lyrics. Programmers at other stations took notice because of their high regard for McLendon, who instituted the "top 40" radio format in the mid 1950s. While KOWH Omaha owner Todd Storz is recognized as the creator of the hit singles radio format, McLendon refined and popularized it by tightening the playlist and emphasizing personality disc jockeys at his anchor station, KLIF in Dallas. As much as McLendon was a radio innovator, he cared very little about the music itself; he tolerated rock as nothing more than an ingredient in his programming formula. But he held strong views about propriety and virtue.

McLendon decided to make "Try It" the scapegoat in a crusade against indecent lyrics. He launched a nationwide campaign with a large display ad in the April 8, 1967, edition of *Billboard* magazine. Titled "An open letter to the music industry," it began, "Frankly we're tired – tired of today's new releases coming through rife with 'raunchy' lyrics." The ad called on broadcasters to adapt McLendon's code of standards prohibiting airing of songs with reference to sex or drugs, declaring, "In the past month, six records which were on the national charts far overstepped the boundaries of good taste, and we were forced to ban them." The message fired a direct shot at record companies with the statement that McLendon and the programmers on his staff were "tired of policing *your* industry. It is time consuming, not *our* responsibility, and an outright imposition – on all broadcasters." The ad threw down the gauntlet to record companies by saying, "our success, after all, is often dependent on your success as record producers; but conversely, your success is predicated on radio airplay of your product."

McLendon launched a national tour, speaking to any group that would listen to him – even though he obviously hadn't listened carefully to the songs he was criticizing. Records he banished from his radio control rooms included Petula Clark's "Don't Sleep In The Subway," Lou Christie's "Rhapsody In The Rain," and Aretha Franklin's "Respect" (because he interpreted her refrain "sock it to me" as lewd). He preposterously misinterpreted the lyrics of a Beatles song, announcing to an audience at a convention that "the McLendon radio stations will not air records that offend public morals, dignity or taste, either innocently or intentionally. We've had all we can stand of the record industry's glorifying marijuana, LSD, and sexual activity. The newest Beatles record, out next week, has a line of 40,000 purple hearts in one arm. Is that what you want your children to listen to? I certainly don't think so." McLendon had absurdly misinterpreted the lyrics of the Beatles' "A Day In The Life," which contained a lyric about "four thousand holes in Blackburn, Lancashire" – a reference to a newspaper article that John Lennon had read about street disrepair in Blackburn, where a surveyor had calculated that the roads were pocked by 4,000 holes.

Ignoring McLendon's objections, the May 6 edition of *Billboard* selected "Try It" for one of its "top 20 pop spotlights" positions, with this prediction: "Right up the alley of the teen buying market, this hard-driving rocker should put the Standells back in the 'Dirty Water' selling bag. Exposure could skyrocket it up the chart." But McLendon had his say again in *Billboard*; a front-page article in the May 20 edition of the magazine announced McLendon's intention to establish a lyric-testing panel – composed of "prostitutes, ex-prostitutes, junkies, and ex-addicts" to assist in weeding out suggestive records. In his campaign against what he termed "filth" in the music-record industry, McLendon set a May 15 deadline for all record companies to supply printed lyrics with new records if they want them considered for broadcast on his stations. The *Billboard* article reported, "McLendon is seeking to carry this campaign to every radio station in the nation and, so far, is riding a groundswell of enthusiasm, especially at the grassroots level, but also from major stations and broadcasting chains." McLendon played heavily on radio station owners' fear of the Federal Communications Commission, which in those days had much sharper teeth than it does today and inflicted heavy punitive fines on radio stations for content it deemed offensive. In that era, even the mildest profanity – *hell, damn,* or *crap* – could place a radio station's license in jeopardy. FCC officials were equally disapproving of content they considered to be lewd.

Like falling dominoes, most radio stations throughout the nation pulled "Try It" from the air. Only a few stations disputed McLendon's contention about the song. In L.A., for example, KHJ and KFWB dropped it, while it was a top-10 hit on crosstown rival KRLA. "The way Dick sang it, it was pretty sexy, but what wasn't back then? It was just so ludicrous. When that happened, it was like the carpet was pulled out from under us," Larry said. "At the same time, radio stations were playing the Rolling Stones' 'Let's Spend The Night Together' and other songs that didn't seem to bother them. The Standells weren't as big as the Stones, so they could pick on us."

Then Standells seized an opportunity to take on McLendon head-on. Producers from *Art Linkletter's House Party* TV show contacted the Standells about debating McLendon about the propriety of song lyrics on the nationally broadcast show. In the Hullabaloo Club, a Sunset Boulevard landmark that previously had been the Earl Carroll Theatre and the Moulin Rouge (and which later would be the Kaleidoscope and then the Aquarius Theater), the Standells stood face-to-face with Gordon McLendon. John and Larry came well prepared for the debate, which aired on CBS television May 27, 1967. "We creamed him in that debate, because we were pretty well researched. There wasn't anything that he said that we didn't have an

236

This full-page ad for the Standells' Tower Records single "Can't Help But Love You" was published in the November 18, 1967, issue of *Billboard* magazine (courtesy of Larry Tamblyn).

answer to. We asked him, 'what about lyrics from your day, Mr. McLendon, like *birds do it, bees do it?* What did they mean by that?' But the show's producers edited out a lot of our responses, such that on the TV show it ended up looking pretty even," Larry recalled.

The members of the Standells had urged Ed Cobb and others at Greengrass Productions to file suit against McLendon for damages, but they declined. Tamblyn has no proof, but he believes that Cobb and Greengrass quietly made an agreement with McLendon to avoid suggestive lyrics on future Standells recordings, in exchange for McLendon's promise to play the band's next release as long as he judged it to be "clean." Both Tamblyn and Fleckenstein independently said that Cobb had resolved to steer the band away from its rebellious, "snotty" image, and shift its repertoire toward R&B influences. That next single the Standells recorded was "Can't Help But Love You," written by Ethen McElroy and Don Bennett, session singers who composed R&B songs. Richard Podolor engineered the track at his American Recording Company studio, and McElroy and Bennett were credited for musical arrangement. "It was a good song, but it was quite a departure from the Standells sound," Larry said. "We should have stayed with that snotty kind of sound," Fleckenstein maintains.

Something else was changing, too. When Ed Cobb first became the Standells' producer, he and the band worked collaboratively, and the Standells played the instruments in their recording sessions. Over time, though, the working relationship between Ed Cobb and the Standells began to corrode. "Ed Cobb became increasingly unapproachable and very dictatorial, and started bringing in other musicians for our recording sessions. As it went on it became less and less of us, and more and more about Dick Dodd," Larry explained. "Dick and I sounded pretty much alike. I had sung lead on some of the album cuts, including 'Mr. Nobody' and 'St. James Infirmary,' and fans couldn't tell us apart. But Dick had become the main guy, because Ed Cobb was sold on him." That favoritism began to fracture the band.

Tower released the Standells' *Try It* album in November, with a stark black-and-white cover and a photo of the band looking defiant. The album jacket proclaimed "The most talked-about record of the year!" The only color on the cover was bright red stencil type declaring "Banned!" The album's 10 tracks included the title song, along with the traditional jazzy blues song "St. James Infirmary," "Can't Help But Love You," "Ninety Nine And A Half" (by Eddie Floyd, Steve Cropper, and Wilson Pickett), and "Riot On Sunset Strip." Released as the band's next single, "Can't Help But

Love You" premiered on the *Billboard* Hot 100 on November 25, 1967, but in its three weeks on the chart it went no higher than No. 78. It was the last Standells single to reach the Hot 100. "Some radio stations played it, but it just wasn't the Standells [sound]. Our popularity really started declining at that point. We made some other recordings after that, but by then it was too late," Tamblyn said.

The band's recording of a song called "Animal Girl," written by Mike Moore, became their last Tower single, released in February 1968. In a Special Merit Spotlight for singles, *Billboard's* February 17, 1968, edition described "Animal Girl" as a "Raucous rocker with clever brass-style arrangement" and called it "a discotheque winner loaded with teen appeal." Nevertheless, radio programmers did not pick up on it. About then a disagreement resulted in Burt Jacobs' departure from Greengrass Productions.

"At that time we were pretty disillusioned with Cobb, and he suggested that we leave Greengrass also. So all of the Standells agreed to it, including Dick. But Ed persuaded Dick to stay and convinced him that he would be successful as a single artist," Tamblyn said. Unaware of Dodd's imminent departure, Tamblyn and the other band members were puzzled why many of Dick's relatives were in the audience when the Standells performed at the Ice House nightclub in Pasadena, California. "As we soon learned, they were there to see Dick's last days with the Standells. We didn't know about this until the day we were supposed to perform at a concert at my alma mater high school, and I was so looking forward to it," Larry said. "Then we received this letter from Dick announcing he had quit the band. The letter said that Ray Harris and Ed Cobb hadn't done anything wrong and that we should have stayed with them, but he hadn't mentioned any of that in our group meetings. We tried to call him, but he wasn't home, and we had to cancel that gig. So we brought in a series of new people, but that just didn't work."

In Atlanta, Dodd recorded a solo album titled *The First Evolution of Dick Dodd,* co-produced by Ed Cobb and Buddy Buie (the architect of the Atlanta Rhythm Section, as described in another chapter of this book). Tower released it in April 1968, but it didn't make a dent in the album charts. The Standells replaced Dodd with drummer Bill Daffern, as Jacobs and the Standells formed Big 5 Productions Inc., an independent record production and publishing company. *Billboard* magazine reported that Big 5 signed a band called the Sideshow, and produced a recording by them, but were unable to land a record deal. At the same time, Jacobs had begun negotiations with ABC Dunhill Records to sign the Standells. Tamblyn claimed the deal soured after Greengrass Productions implied the possibility of legal action for breach of contract, a charge that Greengrass personnel denied. In any case, the dispute chilled further attempts to sign the band with any other labels.

Tony persuaded the band to part company with Burt Jacobs. With encouragement from John Fleckenstein, the Standells recruited guitarist Lowell George and began performing in clubs, but tension and power struggles kept George's tenure with the band brief. "Lowell brought a new dimension to us, but it was very far from the Standells sound. He played sitar, and [with his previous band, the Factory] he had worked with Frank Zappa and the Mothers of Invention. He was a very accomplished musician, no doubt about it, but we didn't get along that well," Larry said. Relegated to playing nightclubs again, the Standells broke up in 1970. Larry became an employee of Superscope-Marantz in Sun Valley, California, where he produced children's records and tapes. John Fleckenstein played for a short time with a band called the Night Shift, which subsequently evolved into Eric Burdon's group War. Just before recording with Burdon was to begin, Fleckenstein resumed work in the film industry, in which he remained for four decades. After Lowell George's departure from the Night Shift, he joined Zappa's Mothers of Invention, then in 1969 formed the band Little Feat. Burt Jacobs went on to become part of the management team of Three Dog Night (as this book's chapter on that band details).

Larry, Tony, and Dick resurrected the Standells several times during the 1980s, but all reunions were fleeting due to disputes among the members. Tower Records kept the Standells' masters shelved for more than a decade. But after Rhino Records arose as a successful reissue label, Ed Cobb and Ray Harris acquired the Standells' master tapes and licensed the recordings. Rhino packaged three collection albums: *The Best of the Standells* and *Rarities* (both released in 1983) and *Best of the Standells – Golden Archive Series* (released in 1987). Tamblyn, Dodd, and Valentino regrouped, with the addition of bass player Peter Stuart, for a Standells performance on November 7, 1999, at the Cavestomp "garage rock" festival at the Westbeth Theatre Center on W. 17th Street in New York City. The appearance resulted in a live Standells recording titled *Ban This! Live From Cavestomp*, released on the Cavestomp label. "Then we tried to get serious about it and in 2000 we were contacted by a group in Spain that wanted to bring us over there for a tour. All the guys were for it so we agreed to it, but then Tony and Dick both backed out. They said they didn't want to travel and tour," Larry explained.

One more comeback was particularly memorable. The Standells were invited to perform October 24, 2004, at Fenway Park, home stadium of the Boston Red Sox, for Game 2 of the World Series against the St. Louis Cardinals. The Sox brought the Standells back in each of the following two years, and again in 2007 for a weeklong series of events beginning with the American League Division Championship Series. "We performed with a jet flyover, and we performed the national anthem a cappella," Larry said. "And we sang 'Dirty Water,' of course." The song by then had become a victory anthem for the Sox, just as Frank Sinatra's "New York, New York" became a game-closing theme at Yankee Stadium.

In the 1990s Ed Cobb was performing with a vocal group composed of fellow original Four Preps lead singer Bruce Belland, David Somerville (who had been lead singer of the Diamonds), and Jim Yester of the Association (a chapter in our book *Where Have All the Pop Stars Gone? – Volume 1*). The quartet performed as the New Four Preps. But Cobb left the group in 1998 after being diagnosed with leukemia, from which he died in September 19, 1999, at the age of 61. Dick Dodd later in life managed a restaurant. He also had worked in the office of a construction equipment company, and became a limousine chauffeur. In addition, he fronted an oldies band called the Dodd Squad, which played gigs in Orange County, California, where he lived. He continued to perform with the resurrected Standells throughout the first dozen years of the new millennium, until he became ill and was diagnosed with metastatic esophageal cancer, from which he died at age 68 on November 29, 2013. Bass player Gary "Lane" McMillan, who had left the Standells in 1966 and became a barber but rejoined the band in 2000, was diagnosed with lung cancer in 2013. He died 18 months later, on November 5, 2014, at age 76. "We keep in close contact with his widow, Edie," Larry said.

For many years Tony Valentino operated a pair of Italian restaurants called Cafe Bellissimo in the Los Angeles area communities of Woodland Hills and Thousand Oaks. He continues to perform on his own, with a backup band.

After Larry retired from his job, he became determined to put the band back together as a fulltime pursuit, and phoned John Fleckenstein to ask him to rejoin the band. Larry was unaware, though, that John had just undergone lengthy, critical-care hospitalization and successful treatment for leukemia. John had decided to semi-retire from cinematography, so the timing of Larry's call was good; the idea of rejoining the Standells appealed to John. Also recruiting guitarist Paul Downing and drummer Greg Burnham, Larry resumed his original role as lead singer, and began

241

performing and recording, including a European tour in 2010. Paul Downing left the band, and Mark Adrian replaced him. With that lineup, the reconstituted Standells performed at the Monterey Summer of Love "45 Years On" Festival in September 2012. "That was great. We had a wonderful time. The spot on the stage where Jimi Hendrix stood when he performed in the 1967 festival is circled in paint. It's still there. That was a lot of fun," John said.

On the Standells' 2013 album *Bump,* they rock on their aggressive versions of Love's "7 And 7 Is" and the Seeds' "Pushin' Too Hard." Their songs "It's All About Money" and "Big Fat Liar" have plenty of snarling attitude, and "Let's Go Bump In The Night" picks up where "Try It" left off. At the close of 2014, Sony Music released a CD titled *The 60s: The Standells,* a live recording of the band's stage performance in Chicago the previous May during which they blasted out high-energy versions of their hits and fan favorites. They remain a vital band, not just stuck in the oldies groove, but performing new material with energy and attitude, sharpened by maturity. The Standells still are edgy, after all these years.

"Greg Burnham is fantastic — a very accomplished drummer. There aren't a lot of drummers who can hold '7 And 7 Is' for a whole song, but Greg bangs it out with no sweat. And Mark Adrian has a great voice for a lot of our harmonies. We recorded our new album, *Bump,* entirely in Greg's home studio in Burbank," Fleckenstein said. "We do all of our rehearsals and recording in Greg's studio, which has a huge mixing board and speaker system." Fittingly, Greg built that studio by converting his garage.

When viewers tuned in to CBS television on October 30, 2014, for the premiere of the sitcom *The McCarthys,* set in Boston, they were treated to the Standells' "Dirty Water," the program's introductory music. The song also was used prominently in the 2015 Fox TV series *The Last Man on Earth,* starring Will Forte, in Edward Burns' 2015 TNT series *Public Morals,* and in a TV commercial for Benjamin Moore Paints. And in October 2015, the Standells were among the musical guests on "The Cornerstones of Rock" program that Chicago PBS television station WTTW recorded for broadcast. "We performed with some of our friends – Rick Derringer of the McCoys and Jimy Sohns of the Shadows of Knight," Larry said. The program, which made its debut in Chicago in December and was released for nationwide distribution on PBS in January 2016, also included performances by members of the Buckinghams, the Cryan' Shames, the New Colony Six, the American Breed and the Ides of March.

The Rock and Roll Hall of Fame and Museum identified "Dirty Water" among some 650 songs for an exhibit on "The Songs That Shaped Rock and Roll," a list developed by a panel of museum curators, rock critics, and music historians.

Visit www.standells-official.com/ and www.facebook.com/Standells/ for touring, recording, merchandise and additional information.

The Standells today, from left: Larry Tamblyn, Mark Adrian, John Fleckenstein, and Greg Burnham (photo by Jude Bradley).

THE STANDELLS' U.S. SINGLES ON THE *BILLBOARD* HOT 100 CHART

Debut	Peak	Title	Label
4/23/66	11	Dirty Water	Tower
8/13/66	43	Sometimes Good Guys Don't Wear White	Tower
10/22/66	54	Why Pick On Me	Tower
11/25/67	78	Can't Help But Love You	Tower

Billboard's pop singles chart data is courtesy of Joel Whitburn's Record Research Inc. (www.recordresearch.com), Menomonee Falls, Wisconsin.

Epilogue: Larry Tamblyn

Keyboard player, singer

Throughout his life, Standells leader Larry Tamblyn has resisted acting his age, at times by preference, at times by necessity. As an adolescent, he had to grow up fast and take on responsibility, following the death of his father. As a professional musician in his late teens, he assumed responsibility for running a band after its older leader was deposed. He spent many of his post-Standells years thinking like a kid in order to be effective in producing recordings for children. And now, performing once again with the resurrected Standells, he admittedly does not think of himself as the septuagenarian that he is.

"Being called 'Grandpa' was tough on me at first," Larry said. "I now have eight grandchildren, but to be honest, I don't identify with people my own age. I am kind of in a 'Neverland,' like Peter Pan. On stage I jump around a lot and make a fool of myself. I don't just stand up there and sing. I clown around and go out into the audience and sing to individual members of the audience and get them to participate. We tell jokes on stage, and we get the audience involved. I really believe in entertaining people. That's the kind of shows we're doing now, and we're getting rave reviews." Larry's singing voice still exudes youthful vigor, and he ripples his conversation with inflection and humor.

Larry seemed preordained to devote his life to entertaining people, despite the embittering experiences of his father. Larry and his two brothers were the children of former vaudevillian dancer and actor Eddie Tamblyn,

Larry Tamblyn today (photo by Jude Bradley).

and former chorus singer and dancer Sally Tamblyn (née Tripplet). Eddie got his start in vaudeville at age 14 in 1922 with *Gus Edwards' Review,* then five years later formed the Vernon Trio of dancers, appearing in New York nightclubs until he began to win roles in Broadway musicals.

"In New York my father was in a lot of Broadway shows, which is where he and my mother met each other. They met on stage in a play called *Follow Thru.* Dad was one of the stars of the show, and Mom was a chorus girl. They got married about a year

245

later," Larry said. After being on the road in the cast of several theatrical touring companies, and with the onset of the Great Depression in the early 1930s, Eddie and Sally decided to seek new opportunities in the emerging Hollywood film industry. "He had a walk-on part in one of the first Fred Astaire and Ginger Rogers movies, *Flying Down to Rio* [1933]. But he just couldn't get much work after that," Larry said. Eddie had been typecast in the role of a young man, and as he approached his 30s he had difficulty finding steady work. He landed his last film role in 1937, by which time he and Sally had two sons: Warren (born in June 1933) and Russ (born in December 1934). Eddie decided to learn a trade. He became a tool inspector at North American Aviation in the western L.A. community of El Segundo, a financially sound move as the aircraft industry geared up its production when the United States entered World War II. North American manufactured NA-16 trainers, B-25 bombers, and P-51 Mustang fighter planes.

As the war raged, Lawrence A. Tamblyn was born on February 5, 1943, in Inglewood, where his family lived. Sally focused on being a homemaker, raising Larry and his two older brothers. When aircraft production declined following the end of the war, Eddie took a job with Whittaker Gyro, and the family moved to North Hollywood. "When I was a kid, my family and I used to do a lot of things together. Our folks took the family on lots of camping trips. We went to Yellowstone, to the high Sierra, and Yosemite," Larry recalled. As a kid, Russ was athletic and took gymnastics, which served him well. At age 10, Russ was cast in a play called *Stone Jungle,* which led to other acting roles. "My father told him, 'no son of mine is ever going to be an actor.' I'm very much against stage parents pushing their children into the field, but Russ had a knack for dancing and tumbling," Larry said. "Russ used to clown around, and he would go up during matinees in movie theaters and entertain everybody. He showed an early inclination to acting, as his daughter Amber later did."

In 1948 Russ was cast in his first film role in *The Boy With Green Hair,* with Dean Stockwell, in which he played one of Dean's schoolmates. "After that Russ had a much bigger part in *The Kid From Cleveland* [1949], and in *Father of the Bride* [1950]." His gymnastic skills came to the fore in the acrobatic demands of his role in *Seven Brides for Seven Brothers* in 1954. "He had one of the major parts in the movie *Peyton Place* [1957] for which he was nominated for an Academy Award for best supporting actor," Larry added. Eddie Tamblyn, despite souring on show business, was proud of Russ' success. But he didn't get to see Russ' greatest triumph, playing Riff in the Academy Award-winning 1961 blockbuster film version of the musical

246

West Side Story. Eddie died of a brain malignancy at age 49 on June 22, 1957, when Larry was only 14 years old. Warren and Russ were living on their own by then, and Sally found work as a receptionist and secretary to support her and Larry, who helped around the house as much as he could.

The acting bug also bit Larry at an early age. "I did want to be an actor like my brother. I idolized him," Larry acknowledged. "I had an acting part in an early 1950s TV series called *Big Town*. I had just a couple of lines in it. But I wasn't like my brother. He was into gymnastics. I wasn't inclined that way. I was a skinny little runt. There was nothing that I seemed to fit into, other than choir in school." But when Larry was in eighth grade at Sun Valley Junior High, shortly after his father died, he made a life-changing discovery. "I attended a school assembly with a performance by a jazz band that included a guitarist. I had never played an instrument, but when they took a break, I went up on the stage, grabbed the guitar, and I did an Elvis Presley imitation. The kids all got a kick out of it, and that's when I really started taking an interest in music." That was fine with Sally Tamblyn. "My mother was a great pianist, and she could read music. Russ and Warren also played piano," Larry said.

Russ had a good-sized collection of 45 rpm records, primarily rhythm and blues, and let Larry listen to them. "I was into Little Richard, Chuck Berry, and all the other early R&B artists. I also liked rockabilly – Carl Perkins and some of Elvis' early things, when he was on Sun Records – and I was an avid fan of Gene Vincent and the Blue Caps," Larry said. His mother bought an acoustic guitar for him and enrolled him in lessons. But Larry quickly grew impatient with the guitar teacher's rigid approach. "The teacher told my mother, 'I just can't do anything with him. He doesn't study what I show him.' I was more interested in doing rock stuff, all the guitar riffs." Before long, Larry got a Fender electric guitar, and started his own band, with his garage as the group's practice headquarters. Larry attended North Hollywood High School for one semester before transferring to nearby John Francis Polytechnic High School, which he liked much better. There, he formed a band called the Emeralds with four classmates: singers Darron Stankey and Frank Zworkin, drummer Wayne Edwards, and saxophonist Frank Fayad. Stankey subsequently formed the Innocents, who had their own recording career and also backed singer Kathy Young. Wayne Edwards became a member of the Hondells. Fayad later switched to bass guitar and became a member of Love (as the chapter about that band in this book mentions). "The Emeralds started making money performing at sock hops, *quinceañeras* [15th birthday coming-of-age celebrations for girls] and wedding receptions," Larry said. "Ritchie Valens also used to compete for

some of these weddings and quinceañeras, before he began recording. He
went to San Fernando High School, and I knew him. I was so impressed
with him. What a talent he was."

Although Larry initially had shunned piano, he learned to play as he
began composing songs. "I switched over to the keyboard because I was
writing my songs with it rather than on guitar," he explained. A fellow
named Lorin "Speed" Kopp took notice of Larry's talent, and signed on
as his manager. Kopp arranged an audition for Larry with Eddie Davis,
who owned the independent Faro recording company. While Larry was
a high school senior, Davis signed him to a contract with Faro Records.
Tamblyn recorded the doo-wop tunes "Dearest" and "Patty Ann," both
of which he wrote and which Faro released as a single in February 1960.
Eddie Davis managed to get Larry signed as a supporting act to appear on
stage in the San Francisco Bay Area with Connie Francis, who by then had
attained headliner status with a dozen top-40 hits to her credit. "Connie
was completing a grueling concert tour, and after our show we were at the
airport in San Francisco, when she said, 'Hey, Larry, let's get some sodas.'
So we broke away from the entourage, and as she was walking with me, she
started weaving and fainted, and I caught her in my arms. It was due to a
combination of lack of sleep and pure exhaustion. On tour, you're doing
your shows in the afternoon or at night, and you're doing interviews during
the day, and you're never able to relax and unwind," Larry explained. "So
there I was, with one of my idols in my arms. She did sign a photo for me.
She wrote 'To Larry, my hero. Follow your star.' A few years later, when the
Standells were performing at the Peppermint West in Hollywood, Connie
came to visit us there. She is such a nice person."

In June, Faro released "The Lie" backed with "My Bride To Be," which
Larry wrote. But neither that nor his prior Faro release had sold many
copies, and Larry was having self-doubts. Sally had remarried, and while she
was supportive of Larry's budding music career ambitions, her new husband
was not. "My stepfather was not a very nice person. He was always telling
me 'you'll never amount to anything.'

"While I was in high school I worked in an awful factory with no air
conditioning. They made wooden bases for lamps. I had to dip those bases
in a tub of varnish. The smell could knock you out. I would come out of
there like I was stoned. When I graduated from high school in the summer
of 1960, I was at a real crossroads about where to go," Larry told us. "I
worked as a dishwasher for a while, and then I got a job as a car mechanic.
I knew nothing about it, but my job was to take engines apart, not to put
them back together. I decided to join the Air Force. But I was still 17, too

young to enlist on my own, and my mother wouldn't sign permission papers for me. So I enrolled at Los Angeles Valley College. Counselors there had encouraged me to take music courses. But when things started happening with my music, I quit college."

Larry continued to endure berating at home. "My stepfather was very abusive psychologically. He continually told me that I was a loser, and that my musical career would never amount to anything. He was always trying to prove he was better than me, even though he was a window washer. He and my oldest brother, Warren [who became a real estate appraiser], cornered me one day and they said, 'You're never going to do anything with your music. You're wasting your time.' But by 1961, I was doing monthly concerts at the Rainbow Gardens dance hall in Pomona. I was the leader of the house band, and it was my job to learn the hits of the guest artists, like Conway Twitty, Ral Donner, and the Beach Boys, who back then were a vocal group. Before the concerts, I would teach the songs to members of the band. I also performed in a number of concerts and local California TV shows, promoting my single records," Larry said. "With the confidence I gained from these performances, I finally developed the resolve to confront my stepfather. When he lambasted me with his usual diatribe, I looked him square in the eyes and told him that in six months I would be making a damn good living with my music. And sure enough, six months later I was not only earning a good living, but also making even more money than he was."

After Faro Records released a third Larry Tamblyn doo-wop single, "This Is The Night," backed with "Destiny" (both of which Larry wrote), label owner Eddie Davis connected Larry with the members of the Starlighters. That was not Joey Dee's group, but a different band, in search of a new keyboard player. The band hired Larry in 1962. That group led to formation of the first generation of the Standels [initially spelled with only one "l") and an extended booking at the Oasis Club in Honolulu. "That's when I was able to show my stepfather and my older brother that I was able to earn a living doing music," Larry said. "The Oasis Club had a variety show and a complete Japanese floorshow that we alternated with. They had actors, a comedian, chorus dancers, a singer like Pat Boone whose name was Pat Bueno, and a burlesque show. The Standels came on stage right after the stripper. It was tough to follow the stripper. You had to earn the respect of the audience there, and we finally did to the point that people came to see us, but it took a while."

Although the Standels were working, they watched their money carefully and lived frugally. "We were staying in a two-room apartment in a run-down building on Waikiki Beach. Our guitar player Tony Valentino and I shared one room, and our bass player Jody Rich and the drummer, Benny Hernandez, were in the other room. Tony and I would invite girls up to the room, but there was a major problem: we also shared the room with a rat. We named him Fred, because it rhymed with 'dead,' which is how we wanted him," Larry said. "He got into our food and was a pig about it. Besides that, whenever we had girls over he would run out, make his appearance, and the girls would scream and leave. It happened every single frickin' time we had girls over there. This occurred probably over a month's period. Finally one night, Tony was spending the night out with a girl and I was by myself, in my skivvies, and turned on the radio. Fred must have thought we had girls over there, and he came running out. His home was behind the stove, but we had been unable to slide the stove out to nail his entrance shut. When he ran out that night, I blocked his path to the oven and he couldn't get back there. I got out a butcher knife, and went screaming and hollering, chasing him around the apartment. He went under a table, I overturned that. He went under Tony's bed, I overturned that. The room was a complete wreck, but there was no place left for Fred to go except into the bathroom." That turned out to be a bad move for Fred.

"I ran in the bathroom after him. Fred ran to the bathtub and then had no place else to go. There I was crouching with my knife, and all of a sudden he opened his mouth and flashed his big incisors at me. I started to rethink my strategy – he had a lot more experience with those teeth than I had with that knife. So I slowly backed out and left the door cracked a little bit so I could watch his moves. I swear, this is the truth. Fred made a move for me. He walked around to the side of the toilet, climbed up on a little table, on which an empty Kleenex box was sitting. He crept inside the Kleenex box, probably thinking I would never in the world look for him in there. So I dropped the knife, ran in there, grabbed the Kleenex box and threw it into the toilet. There was Fred in this little cardboard boat, with no place he could go. And I knew this boat wasn't going to float forever because it was cardboard.

"I shut the door, went to bed, and had the most peaceful deep sleep I had ever had. But I was awakened at around 4 o'clock in the morning by a horrible scream. Tony came running through the room. The first thing he had done when he returned to the apartment was head for the bathroom. He had to sit on the toilet, and he felt some movement below him – and it wasn't a bowel movement. He bolted up, screaming and dragging his pants through the apartment."

Larry calmed Tony down and told him that he had trapped Fred in the bathroom. "We both went back in there and saw that during the night the cardboard tissue box had slowly disintegrated until there was only one tiny little corner of the box sticking out of the water. There was Fred, and his two hind feet were on that corner. And he was stretched up to the side of the bowl with his other two feet. He couldn't move or he would have fallen in the water. There were little teeth marks all around the lid of the toilet seat, and I felt completely vindicated. But I didn't have it within me to finish the job. So I grabbed a towel, threw it over Fred, went down the stairs, walked a couple of blocks away, and let him go. We never saw him again."

After the band returned to California as Larry Tamblyn and the Standels in late 1962, doors began opening for them. "We played up and down the California coast in numerous nightclubs," Larry said. During that time Eddie Davis' Linda Records label released the band's single of "The Girl In My Heart" and "You'll Be Mine Someday." As they gained recognition they were booked into Hollywood's Peppermint West nightclub, where the Standells (by then spelled with a second "l") became the house band for a stretch. The Peppermint West manager, a fellow named Mario, gave Larry a glimpse of his promising future. "Mario was a transvestite. I had no problem with that," Larry said. "He approached me one night, and at first I wondered if he was going to hit on me. He asked, 'Larry, can I talk to you alone?' I thought, 'oh, no.' I was hesitant, but I went with him into a hallway, and he said, 'there's something very personal I want to tell you.' And I thought, 'oh, God.' He said, 'not many people know this, but I am a medium, and I get visits by spirits.' This just totally threw me off – a transvestite medium. He proceeded to tell me that he had a visitation from my father, and that my father was my guardian angel and looked after me. He didn't know anything about my father, and he didn't know that my father had died. Mario said that soon there was going to be a big transformation in my life that had to do with my music, and that I would go on to do a lot greater things." Mario was right.

From there the Standells were booked into the lounge at the Thunderbird Hotel and Casino in Las Vegas – where Larry encountered a problem he had not anticipated. "We performed every night, and I was the lead singer. I developed what they called Vegas throat – laryngitis from the very dry conditions there," Larry said. "I almost completely lost my voice. I was so hoarse, it was almost a whisper. I went to a doctor, and was getting shots. Of all things, one of the Japanese girls who I had met in Hawaii happened to be a chorus girl in a show in Vegas. Very sweet girl. I told her

251

about my condition. She told me she knew a remedy – a combination of raw egg and vinegar. She said that the vinegar eats away the mucus, and the raw egg coats your throat. She told me to swallow it, without barfing, if I could. So I drank it that day, and by that evening I had my voice back." From there, the Standells were on a trajectory to success that took them to an extended residency at P.J.'s nightclub in Hollywood, and to their recording deals with Liberty and Tower.

Although Dick Dodd was the lead singer on most of the Standells' recordings beginning in mid-1964, Larry sang lead on several album tracks and "B" sides of singles. He was the lead vocalist on 10 of the 12 tracks on *The Standells in Person at P.J.s.* album. "I sang lead on 'Mr. Nobody,' which was the flip side of 'Why Pick On Me.' And on the earlier songs, before we went with Ed Cobb, I was on most of them – 'Bony Moronie,' 'Linda Lou,' a number of things that Liberty put out as singles," Larry said. "I sang my heart out on 'St. James Infirmary,' a really bluesy song. And Dick and I harmonized on 'Little Sally Tease.' I also wrote and sang 'The Girl And The Moon' [on the *Why Pick on Me – Sometimes Good Guys Don't Wear White* album]. On just about every album we did, I had a song." The Standells worked steadily for seven years, a respectable run for a rock band. At their peak, they were fan favorites throughout the country, and toured extensively for appreciative audiences.

"One night we were driving through the mountains of Tennessee. Tony, who was born in Italy, was driving. All of a sudden we saw red lights behind us. We had been doing at least 70 miles an hour in a 35-mile-an-hour zone. Back then in the South, they looked upon people who had long hair as being the lowest of the scum. A patrol car pulled us over, and a smokey got out and tapped on the driver's window of our car," Larry recalled. "Tony never could understand English very well. The smokey said, 'Whar you goin,' to a fire?' And Tony said, 'yes.' So he took Tony's wallet and said, 'turn around and foller me.' I said, 'Tony, why did you have to be such a wiseass?' Tony said, 'I couldn't understand him.' We followed him into this one-horse town. One building had the justice of the peace, the sheriff's office, and the mortician. We had visions of wearing striped suits while working on rock piles with picks and shovels. When we walked into the sheriff's office, he saw us in the light for the first time. He looked us over and said, 'Are you boys in some kind of rock and roll group?' I thought, 'oh, shit, here it comes,' and I answered him, 'yeah, we are.' So he asked, 'well, what's the name of your group?' And I said 'it's the Standells.' He looked surprised and he asked, 'the *what?*' And I repeated it. He asked incredulously, 'THE

Standells?' I said, 'yes.' And he said, 'well, good golly, my daughter is a big fan of yours.' This is the truth. We got out of there by giving this guy an autographed album for his daughter – no ticket, no nothing."

Although the cop hadn't investigated potential drug use, he wouldn't have found any evidence with Larry. "I didn't do drugs," he said. "Oh, in the '70s, I got into it occasionally, socially. To be truthful, though, smoking a joint did nothing for me. So I figured why bother? Today I don't do that stuff at all."

Larry Tamblyn in 1967 (photo courtesy of Larry Tamblyn).

By the time the Standells dissolved in 1970, Larry was tired of the pop music treadmill, and was ready for a change. Because he enjoyed the recording process and studio production, he intended to become an audio engineer. But an opening at Superscope Inc. in Sun Valley, his teenage stomping grounds, appealed to him. Superscope, which initially developed a wide-screen cinematic projection process in the early 1950s, branched out into consumer electronics by obtaining U.S. distribution rights for Sony tape recorders. In 1964 the company solidified its base by acquiring Marantz, a manufacturer of high-quality home electronics gear. Superscope hired Larry as a product manager, in charge of producing "Tele-Story" series of children's records and tapes, and "AudiSee" science fiction audio stories. Each Tele-Story product re-told a classic fairy tale in a package that included a book and a produced word-for-word cassette tape or vinyl record. "Throughout the decade of the '70s, I produced about a hundred of those things, including doing all the music on them," Larry told us. "Then K-Tel Records, wishing to get into the children's recording market, approached me to produce a children's album, *Lolliwinks*. I invented all the characters and how each one thought. I recorded it in London using British orchestral musicians because it was more economical to do there than it was in L.A. I did all of the voices, and I also produced the national TV commercial for it." Larry is justifiably proud of that accomplishment.

In the '80s, he returned to Superscope to accept an upper-management position. "That turned out to be the worst time of my life. I was hired to manage the company's Pianocorder division, which had been failing," Larry said. The Pianocorder was a new take on the player piano. Instead of traditional punched paper reels, the Pianocorder used cassette tapes to store the commands that played the piano. The recordings captured none-for-note playing of numerous concert pianists, including George Shearing, Oscar Peterson, and Liberace, who encoded their performances on Superscope's concert grand piano equipped with recording sensors. Consumers could hear the technique of famous pianists played on a Pianocorder-equipped instrument in their own home. That was the idea, but it just didn't catch on.

"It was much more sophisticated than a regular player piano. It controlled the same pedals and all the keys, and had the impact definition of the original performing artist. Hearing it play the piano gave you goose bumps. That division of Superscope had been losing money and, as general manager, I turned the business around and increased it by about 150 percent. But it was not satisfying for me at all," Larry told us. "It was a lot of headaches, and numerous people were taking credit for what I did in the corporate structure." Larry left Superscope not long before musical instrument manufacturer Yamaha acquired Pianocorder, and he established himself as an independent recording engineer.

Larry, who had been twice married and divorced, had become accustomed to being a bachelor again. That changed after Russ and his wife Bonnie invited Larry to a party at their home in 1993. There, Larry met actress Glenda Chism, who had played the mother of Macaulay Culkin's character in the 1991 film *My Girl,* which also starred Dan Aykroyd and Jamie Lee Curtis. "Glenda had been friends with Russ for years. They had appeared in a musical theatrical production together. Glenda and I hit it off immediately and became instant friends. We talked and laughed and had the greatest time. We stayed good friends for about a year before we got serious, and then we moved in together. Glenda and I lived together for about six years before we got married in 2000," Larry said. They scheduled the wedding in Las Vegas on the same weekend that the reunited Standells performed a gig at the Gold Coast Hotel and Casino there. "Everything that could have gone wrong went wrong – missing the plane flight to Vegas, having my car towed because someone didn't like cars being parked on his street, having to pay an impound fee. But the wedding itself was great."

Larry is a proud father. "I have a litter of kids – six children altogether," Larry grinned. His first child is daughter, Lisa, who was born in 1970, followed by his oldest son, Shon, born in 1974. Larry's daughter Bleu was born in 1976, followed by another son, Micah, born in 1978. Daughter Sheris was born in 1980, and his youngest son, Joel, was born in 1983.

Speaking of litters, Larry and Glenda love animals, and they have a lot of them at their home in Palmdale, California. "I have dogs and cats. And every one of them has come to us either as a stray or a gift. We have a Yorkie named Chewy. We have cats – one that showed up in our back yard, and one that was either dropped off or showed up on our front porch as a little bitty kitten on Christmas morning. We have another cat that my daughter nursed back to health after finding him in an alley, near death. He's about 11 years old now. Another time right before Christmas we were out for a walk on a drizzly evening, and this thing showed up – this great big ball of fur. I couldn't tell what it was. It was a huge mess. The direction it was walking gave us the only clue where the head was. It walked up to us, and I didn't know what to think. Not until it rolled over on his back did I realize it was a dog. We took him in to the vet for a checkup and a fur trimming. He's a cocker spaniel mix, maybe with Lhasa apso. He's been a good pal of Chewy." The Tamblyns also have winged pals.

"We have two birds – domesticated doves that we rescued. People release doves at quinceañeras and other events, and they become hawk food because they don't know how to fend for themselves," Larry explained. "One of our dogs found the first one in a neighbor's yard and led us to him, and we picked him up. Several years later some neighbors came to tell us they found a female dove. And we have the two of them in a cage. So we have three cats, two dogs, and two birds – and a 'no vacancy' sign out front. Yes, we are animal lovers. For some reason, cats are attracted to me. When I go into people's homes, their cats always wind up on my lap."

As a recording engineer, Larry has developed proficiency in use of Avid Pro Tools audio recording, editing, and mixing software. He also composes orchestral film scores. His retirement from full-time work in 2011 enabled him to concentrate fulltime on the resurrected Standells. He particularly enjoys the hands-on approach he can take now in producing and mixing Standells recordings. "It's such a pleasure to work with the guys who are in the group now. We've been working pretty steadily," Larry said. "I've gotta say that since we rebuilt the Standells, these are the best years of my life."

Epilogue: John Fleckenstein

Bass guitar

On a rocky ridge at the border between France and Germany, the 12th-century Fleckenstein Castle majestically overlooks the forested valley of the River Sauer below. Rhineland aristocratic ancestors of Standells bass guitarist John Fleckenstein occupied that fortress for four centuries. The nobles of the Fleckenstein family included knights, counts, lords, and barons. Generations of Fleckensteins had brewed beer at sources of spring water in Bavaria. Even after French soldiers ransacked and heavily damaged the castle in 1680, the Fleckenstein family proliferated in the region. In 1853 Gottfried and Ernst Fleckenstein emigrated to America and made their way west, settling in Faribault, Minnesota, about 50 miles south of Minneapolis-St. Paul. There they established a brewery. The business thrived, and Fleck's Beer, as it was popularly known, remained a regional favorite for a century, until the brewery was sold to Blatz Brewing Company.

Jimsey and John Fleckenstein in early 2007 at the American Society of Cinematographers awards ceremony, where John received an award. The ceremony is held shortly before the Academy Awards ceremony (photo courtesy of John Fleckenstein).

By remarkable coincidence, when John Fleckenstein was hospitalized in 2010 with a life-threatening illness, the lifesaving tissue match that his doctors identified through a medical database search turned out to be from a donor who lives near the ruins of Fleckenstein Castle. It was as if his ancestors were watching over him.

The Fleckenstein family descendents who grew up in Faribault included John's father, William P. Fleckenstein, who was born in 1903. After graduating from Carleton College, "Wild Bill" (as he became known) carved out a pro football career for himself as a hard-hitting offensive lineman with the Chicago Bears for five seasons, followed by stints with the Portsmouth (Ohio) Spartans (precursor of the Detroit Lions), the Frankford (Pennsylvania) Yellow Jackets (which gave rise to the Philadelphia Eagles), and the NFL Brooklyn Dodgers (for which he played center). Following his last gridiron season in 1931, Bill Fleckenstein bought an automobile dealership and in February 1934 he married Mildred Harris Chaplin, former wife of film star Charlie Chaplin. The couple settled in Chicago, but Mildred developed ovarian cancer, from which she died in 1944.

Bill journeyed to Los Angeles, and there he met Esther L. Priebe, who was born in 1914 in Topeka, Kansas. They began seeing each other, fell in love, and married. Their son John William Fleckenstein was born in Los Angeles on August 2, 1946. "My mother had 14 brothers and sisters, and her family had come from Germany and took part in the Oklahoma land rush. They lined up at the border of Kansas and Oklahoma, and with a cannon shot as the signal, they rushed the land, they picked properties, and put flags down to claim them," John said. "When I was a kid, the family members had about 14 farms outside of Enid, Oklahoma, and in McAlester, south of Tulsa. They drilled producing oil wells on six of the farms, so my mother didn't have to work very much. I still get checks from the oil wells. Of course, it's divided up among 14 grandchildren, and their children, and the great-great grandchildren."

For the first five years of his life, John lived with his folks in an apartment building on Rossmore Avenue in the southern portion of Hollywood. "Mae West lived in the penthouse there. She used to come downstairs and hold my hand," John recalls. Following the birth of his two sisters – Cheryl in 1948 and Julie in 1950 – the family moved to a larger home elsewhere in Hollywood.

"In Oklahoma my mom had studied opera, and when she moved to Hollywood, she got roles singing in movies for all of the studios. That included singing in the chorus of 'Indian Love Call' in the film *Rose Marie* with Nelson Eddy and Jeanette McDonald." Esther stopped working for films when John was born, and then she and Bill bought Movie Center Music Company, which set people's poems to music recorded on disc for a fee. They employed several tunesmiths, piano players, and singers. It was a profitable business. "My mom and my dad ran that company until I was out of high school."

Because of that business, John and his sisters were exposed to music throughout their childhood years. "People were at our house writing songs constantly. We had two pianos, and there was always one of the guys playing piano in the house. In our home we heard everything from show tunes to jazz to opera. I took trumpet lessons, guitar lessons, and tap lessons, and I went with my mother to her exercises with her voice coach. My sisters as little children had ballet lessons, and they danced in *The Nutcracker* at the Hollywood Bowl," John said. "When I was in middle school I loved the Ventures' guitar instrumentals, and that's why I started playing guitar. For the trumpet, Harry James was a big influence on me, and I did play trumpet with the Standells on a couple of tracks we recorded. It was overdubbed four or five times so it sounded like a horn section."

As a teenager John had various little jobs. He had a paper route for the Hollywood *Citizen News,* and he tossed papers for the Los Angeles *Herald Examiner* one summer. In middle school he enrolled in band classes. In addition to playing trumpet and French horn in the school orchestra, he learned to read music, and he tried all the other instruments that his teacher would let him play. "I also took private guitar lessons, and my guitar teacher told me, 'later on if you want to get a lot of work, you should try taking up the bass, because there are a lot of guitar players, but not many bass players.' So I took up the bass," explained Fleckenstein – pronounced fleck-en-STINE (rhymes with "fine").

As a student at Hollywood High School, he was in several party-gigging rock bands with classmates, including guitarist Lowell George – who in the late '60s joined the Standells, and then formed Little Feat. But John declined to join the Hollywood High orchestra because he pursued another interest. "Because my dad played football, I wanted to do that. I tried out for the high school team, became a fullback, and I was an all-city player," John said. "When the Chicago Bears were in town at the Coliseum to play the L.A. Rams, I got to sit down on the bench with the Bears, and went into their locker room." John worked out diligently, and by the time he graduated from high school in 1964, he weighed 215 pounds. The University of Southern California recruited him on a scholarship for its freshman football squad. But by then, John had yet another passion.

Mike Butler, his best friend during high school, was the son of Larry Butler, who along with Don Glouner owned Butler-Glouner Inc., the special effects optical house at the Columbia Pictures film studios. The special effects studio created fades, dissolves between scenes, and titles for TV shows and movies. "I'd go to the Columbia studios on the weekends with Mike. I learned how to use the optical printer, and how to do fades. We did the smoke for the *I Dream of Jeannie* scenes when she went into the bottle and came out. We worked on *Fantastic Voyage*. I was at the studio when *Robin and the Seven Hoods* was filmed, and I got to see Frank Sinatra and Dean Martin. Columbia had a lot going on then." Larry Butler gave John some additional career advice. "He told me that if I stay in music, when I get older, I'm gonna be sorry. He said if I get in the picture business, I'll have a full lifetime career. I listened carefully to that advice."

John played only two games as a blocking back for USC. "I hurt my knee in a game against Notre Dame," he explained. John had not yet chosen a major, and was planning to take photography and cinematography classes. "Making films is what I wanted to do, but that's too expensive to do in school. I realized that the only way to learn the motion picture business was to be in the picture business." Consequently, he left USC after his freshman year ended in June 1965. In order to work in the film industry, he needed to be a member of the International Cinematographers Guild labor union – the International Alliance of Theatrical Stage Employees, Local 600, popularly known as the "camera guild." However, the guild did not accept new applicants unless all guild members already were working on camera crews at the time a studio issued a call for a worker. Guild members are organized into three hierarchical groups, analogous to the "strings" of players on football teams. All guild group 1 members must be assigned to jobs before any group 2 members can be called up, and all group 2 members must be working before any group 3 members can be assigned to jobs. John had to await the occurrence of a job opening when all members of groups 1, 2, and 3 already were on assignments. While he waited for the camera guild's door to open, his music career began blossoming.

"I had a girlfriend whose mother worked as an 'extra' in the movies. In one of the entertainment industry trade magazines, she read a classified ad that the Chuck Daniels Band had placed for a bass player. That was the house band at the Sea Witch nightclub on Sunset Boulevard. I went there and auditioned with them, and they hired me. That was my first professional band gig," Fleckenstein said. "The Chuck Daniels Band was a black rock band. Johnny Echols was the lead guitar player, and I was the only white guy in the band. We played there at the Sea Witch for months.

That's where Johnny introduced me to Arthur Lee, who recruited me to join the American Four – which changed its name to the Grass Roots before eventually becoming the band Love" – as described in the Love chapter in this book. John was with the Grass Roots and Love from its formation, through its rise in popularity in the L.A. nightclub scene, until November 1965. With Arthur Lee and Johnny Echols, John Fleckenstein co-wrote the folk-rock tune "Can't Explain," which appeared on Love's debut album. Fleck also devised the throbbing "do-do-do-do" bass lick that helped distinguish the band's version of "My Little Red Book." In November, shortly before Love signed with Elektra Records, the call that John had been awaiting came.

"My friend Mike called to tell me that all of the camera guild members were working, and he said, 'My dad says he can get you in now. A job opened and the union can't supply anybody, and so you can get in the union to fill that job.' I was only 19 years old, and there I was working at the Columbia studios," Fleckenstein said. That marked the beginning of a distinguished 44-year cinematography career in which he rose to the respected rank of director of photography. To get there, he worked his way through a prescribed succession of jobs. "When I got in the guild, I was a loader for two years, loading the [film] magazines. Then the union required you to spend six years as a camera assistant, and in that job you pull focus. After that you get to be a camera operator, who looks through the eyepiece and does the shooting. After that you could become a director of photography. That's how the union was set up, so that members got their experience. That was 'the school,' and it was structured that way because you can never learn that business unless you're in it and around it. At first, of course, I was in group 3, so I had to stay working at the optical house. I couldn't get calls to go out on production. You had to know the cameraman in order to get hired as an assistant cameraman."

John became impatient with the slow, deliberate progression path. "I was starting to yearn to go back to music again," he said. "I stayed at the optical house long enough to qualify me to remain in the guild. The requirement was to work consistently in the film industry for a set period, nearly a year. And then you were legally in the guild." When John reached that threshold, he became receptive to additional options. When he learned in late 1966 that the Standells were looking for a new bass player, he auditioned and the band chose him from among a reported 163 other applicants. He became a member of the Standells in January '67, joining them on the fly as the band immediately went out on tour. He was on the road with the Standells when he received news that his father had unexpectedly died of cardiac arrest at age 63. "Nobody saw that coming," John said. Immersing himself into his new role in the Standells helped John get through that emotionally difficult time. "We were on the road just about constantly. We played all over the United States." John's mother, who had heart disease, also died of a heart attack on November 15, 1972. She was only 58 years of age.

When the Standells broke up in 1970, Fleckenstein initially planned to pair with guitarist Lowell George in forming a band. But before that got off the ground, John joined an R&B band called the Night Shift. "We played at a place called the Plush Bunny in Pico Rivera. One night we were playing, and some guy in the crowd got mad at somebody else and pulled out a gun and accidentally shot himself in the leg, then shot the other guy," John said. That gave him second thoughts about sticking with music. "We played a couple of other places and then we were picked to do backup on some songs

From left, Larry Tamblyn, John Fleckenstein, and Dick Dodd on a replica of the stage at Pandora's Box, from the 1967 motion picture *Riot on Sunset Strip*. John was playing the EKO bass that he played with the band Love and with the Standells; he still has that instrument (photo courtesy of John Fleckenstein).

for Eric Burdon at Western Recorders on Sunset Boulevard. And then the Night Shift became the group War." But before the band went into the studio, John received another timely phone call.

"My friend Mike Butler called me from Hawaii. He and his brother David were working on the motion picture *Tora! Tora! Tora!* David was a cameraman who did aerials for the movie. He and Nelson Tyler had invented the rig that hung out of helicopters to do the aerial shots. They asked me to come to Hawaii to work on the film. So I did. It was an amazing experience," John said. Hollywood film crews normally have strict hierarchical divisions, each with sharply defined functions. Film loaders insert film into camera magazines, unload exposed film for transfer to the processing lab, and keep an inventory of shot film; second camera operator assistants order camera equipment for shoots and make certain that the right equipment is on the set; first camera operator assistants verify proper operation of cameras before shooting begins, thread film in the cameras, and keep the camera in focus while it is shooting. John blurred those hierarchical divisions on *Tora! Tora! Tora!* as he performed all of those functions. "I got to fly in the back of B-19 bombers. I was loading magazines and pulling focus. We were over there working on that film for about a year."

That experience propelled John to move up to first camera assistant on his next assignment, *The Christian Licorice Store*, a 1971 film starring Beau Bridges and Maud Adams. During the following three decades, he worked his way up the ranks. By 1974 he had his first camera operator job on the film *Harry and Tonto,* starring Art Carney and Ellen Burstyn. By then, he had risen to group 1 in the guild. As a camera operator working immediately under the cinematographer (also known as the director of photography), John composed shots, choosing the proper lenses and angles, planning camera movements, and avoiding unwanted background distractions. During the ensuing 10 years, he worked as a freelance camera operator on a half-dozen other films – *Jaws 2, Wanda Nevada, Death Valley, E. T. the Extra-Terrestrial, Princess Daisy,* and *Flashpoint.* He also filmed numerous national TV commercials. "Most of the commercials I did were music-driven, and I did my scene cuts on the beat," John told us. His musical background also came to the fore in a couple of other assignments. "I was a camera operator on the Michael Jackson music video for 'Beat It,' which won multiple awards, and I also was a camera operator for the video 'Say, Say, Say,' with Paul McCartney and Michael Jackson. The cover of *American Cinematographer* magazine showed me strapped onto the back of the shark during filming of *Jaws II,"* John said.

During his younger years, John had twice been married and divorced. His first marriage, shortly after he had joined the Standells, fell victim to his continual touring; it lasted less than a year. Then while John was working in the studio as a camera assistant, he got together with Prudence McIntyre, a former high school classmate of his. As a teenager she formed a singing duo with her sister Patience, and they recorded two 1956 hit records, "Tonight You Belong to Me" and "Gonna Get Along Without Ya Now," for the Liberty Records label. "I used to play her record when I was a kid, and we ended up getting married. That's bizarre," John chuckled. That marriage did not endure for long, however.

John had camera operator duties and his friend Michael Butler was director of photography in 1978 on *Wanda Nevada,* with Brooke Shields and Peter Fonda in lead roles. "We shot in Marble Canyon near Page, Arizona, and all up and down the Grand Canyon," John said. The production coordinator for that film was Jimsie Eason, daughter of well-

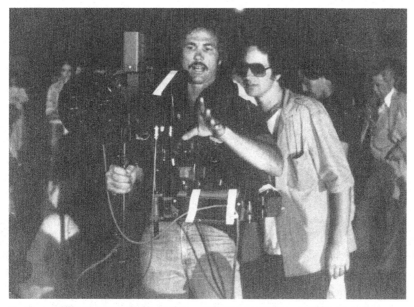

On the set of the 1982 motion picture *ET The Extra-Terrestrial,* director Steven Spielberg (wearing sunglasses) reviewed a replay of a scene that mustachioed John Fleckenstein shot using a steadicam. John took the shot inside an isolation tube through which people in hazmat suits captured ET in the adjoining house in Tujunga, California. The Steadicam stabilizing mount and film camera that John hoisted as he dashed through the tube weighed nearly 60 pounds (publicity still courtesy of John Fleckenstein).

respected camera operator Bert Eason, whose film production career began in the early 1930s. Jimsie, an accomplished horsewoman, also worked as a production associate in the 1980 film *Altered States* and in the 1984 motion picture *Body Double*. John and Jimsie began seeing each other, then moved in together, and got married. "She retired from the picture business after that," John said. "She resumed riding, in which she excels."

John made the leap to director of photography (also called DP) with the 1986 film *The Men's Club*, the cast of which included Harvey Keitel, Frank Langella, and Roy Scheider. The DP collaborates with the director in establishing the visual mood of a film, and oversees not only the entire camera crew, but also the lighting crew and the grips – workers who handle other equipment on the set. Between then and 2008, John was the DP for a succession of theatrical films and made-for-TV movies, as well as the music video for Pat Benatar's 'Love Is A Battlefield' and also several television series – including *Flipper, Any Day Now, Summerland, Waterfront, Windfall,* and *Women's Murder Club*. In 2007 John was nominated for an American Society of Cinematographers award for his work on *Women's Murder Club*.

In 2009 John was preparing for another season as cinematographer for *Women's Murder Club,* and made an appointment for a required routine physical check-up – that turned out to be far from routine. "In order to insure me, the production company required me to get a medical checkup. The medical lab work showed that my blood white cell count was way down. After a weekend of tests in the hospital, I was diagnosed with leukemia," John said. His physicians wanted him to begin treatment right then, but a month of production work remained on the show. "I told the doctors, 'give me some antibiotics or whatever it will take to enable me to finish the show.' I finished the show, then I was admitted into the hospital for induction chemotherapy. I ended up remaining in the hospital for eight months. The doctor had told me he could give me a course of chemo spread out over eight to nine weeks, but I couldn't do that while I was working. Or he could give me a powerful dose in a compressed two-week stint of the chemo, and kill the cancer. I chose the two-week concentrated chemo, which killed the cancer, but it also caused everything else in my body to shut down – my kidneys, liver, everything, and I went into a coma."

John remained comatose for two weeks. "They didn't think I was going to make it. They told my wife I probably would be gone by the weekend. Then all of a sudden, I came to, and I was talking. When I awoke I was one sick puppy. They had me on a dialysis machine because my kidneys had failed. I was so weak from lying down for so long that I had to learn how to walk again. I didn't want to go into a hospital ever again, but my oncologist told me 'you've got to go to the City of Hope and get a bone marrow transplant, because if you don't the leukemia will come back.' And when it returns, it comes back with a vengeance. And after a month or two, it started to creep up again. So in 2010 I went to the City of Hope for a transplant," John said.

This advertisement feted John's cinematic accomplishments and his use of Kodak motion picture film (courtesy of John Fleckenstein).

City of Hope is a nonprofit cancer research and treatment organization that operates a hospital in Duarte, in eastern Los Angeles County. "My doctor at the City of Hope told me that the heavy dose of chemo that I had was like going a hundred miles an hour and running into a brick wall. It was just way too much for me. Doctors at City of Hope administered a drug that temporarily suppressed the leukemia while they searched for a bone marrow donor tissue match. "After two months, they found a donor for me – a 29-year-old medical student in Germany. What was especially interesting was that he was from a village down the hill from Fleckenstein Castle. I was unable to travel, but my sister Julie went there to meet and thank the donor. She said that Fleckensteins are all over the place there." John remained in the hospital for about a month after undergoing the transplant, then continued his recuperation at home. By then he had put in enough years in cinematography to retire comfortably, and he began thinking about what to do with his time. "I was taking all my medications, and getting stronger, and then Larry Tamblyn unexpectedly called to ask me to get back in the Standells. He had not known that I was in the hospital," John said.

John riding his horse "Fahrenheit" in the 1990s (photo courtesy of John Fleckenstein).

John mentally jumped at the idea, but his body wasn't quite as willing, as a result of his immobility during his extended hospitalization. "My knees were in rough shape, due to arthritis, because I hadn't walked for so long while I was in the hospital. So after I was released from City of Hope and regained strength, I had knee replacement surgery on both knees at Ronald Reagan UCLA Medical Center, two weeks apart," John said. "Now I have the bone marrow of a 29-year-old, and two brand-new knees. I haven't felt this good since I got out of high school." Only four months after undergoing the bone marrow transplant, John went on tour with the Standells in Europe. "We went from Spain to Germany to England to France to Greece, then to Norway." And he felt terrific. "The bone marrow transplant was perfect. It took immediately. I'm totally cancer-free now, totally rid of the leukemia," John told us in October 2014. "The City of Hope did a wonderful job on me." He continues to record and perform with the Standells.

After retiring from film production, Jimsie pursued her interest in horses, and became an avid competitor in horse grand prix stadium jumping. "She started competing at all the horse shows, and did very well. Now together we're breeding warmbloods," John said. He and Jimsie keep horses at their home in Burbank. "Jimsie is in such great shape that she can still jump horses. We also have a Labrador retriever, and Jimsie rescued a chihuahua. We're having a ball."

Raise a Fleck's Beer to that.

B.J. Thomas performing in the early 1980s with drummer Richard Gates and bass player John Sterling Francis (photo courtesy of B.J. Thomas).

Hooked on a Feeling

B.J. Thomas

In an era dominated by bands and vocal groups, B.J. Thomas emerged as a soloist who, as his fans would learn, could sing just about any song with conviction and style. Over the course of a recording career spanning more than three decades, a baker's dozen of his singles landed in the national top 40, with a nearly equal number of hits on the country charts, including three that hit No. 1. Gospel music fans embraced him as well, sending 11 of his songs into the top 20 on Christian music charts.

Blessed with a warm honey-toned voice, B.J. Thomas first rose to the national pop music stage in early 1966 as the lead singer of the Houston-area band the Triumphs by resurrecting "I'm So Lonesome I Could Cry," a mournful Hank Williams composition that predated the emergence of rock and roll. B.J. Thomas' anguished interpretation of that 1949 song was a stirring tribute to Williams, who died before many of Thomas' teenaged fans were born. B.J. would put another Hank Williams song on the charts, but just as his newfound followers were beginning to think of him as a country music artist, he charged out of another chute with a couple of top-30 rocking pop tunes, before deftly shifting to a smooth pop crooning style that sent him to the top of the charts.

At the peak of Thomas' career, he was asked to record the principal theme song of one of the most popular motion pictures of the era, and he recorded a song that was among the first singles to prominently feature an electric sitar. Just as he appeared to gravitate toward the gospel market in the early '70s, he shot to the top of the pop and country charts simultaneously with a gently swaying ballad – and then just for the fun of it returned to the top-20 tier of the pop charts with his resurrection of a Beach Boys tune. If anything, B.J. Thomas is a versatile performer.

Billboard magazine has ranked B.J. Thomas among the 50 most-played recording artists of the past 50 years. Over the course of his career, he has received five Grammy Awards, including the first four platinum albums ever awarded in the gospel music category. Although country and gospel music influenced Thomas' musical development, the energy and emotion that he injects into his recordings and live performances germinated from his passion for rhythm and blues during his adolescent years. When he was a youngster in southeastern Texas his parents had listened to the Grand Ole Opry on the radio, and he sang in church. B.J.'s father loved Hank Williams' songs, but when B.J. discovered rhythm and blues music as a teenager in the mid-1950s, it grabbed him by the shirttails and spun him around.

"I loved Bobby Bland, Jackie Wilson, Little Junior Parker, Ray Charles and those guys. Of course, Elvis had real country overtones that I didn't really recognize, but he sang in a blues and rockabilly kind of way. It was a great time for music, with Hank Ballard, the Drifters, and Chuck Berry. To me it was incredible what Chuck Berry and Little Richard were doing at that time, and I loved those guys. I totally was a rhythm and blues guy," B.J. told us.

In the autumn of 1958 some friends of B.J.'s older brother, Jerry, were forming a band at Lamar Consolidated High School in the small community of Richmond-Rosenberg, 30 miles west of Houston. B.J. was introverted but Jerry prodded him to sing a Buddy Holly song and a Ricky Nelson tune at a band rehearsal. The next thing B.J. knew, he was the singer for that band, the Triumphs. The band consisted of two brothers, lead guitarist Tim Griffith and bassist Tom Griffith, rhythm guitarist Denver "Denny" Zatyka, saxophonist Don Drachenberg, and drummer Teddy Mensik. B.J. compensated for his lack of stage experience by patterning his moves after Ricky Nelson, who sang a tune on each episode of the popular *The Adventures of Ozzie and Harriet* television program. Beginning in January 1959, the Triumphs were booked at dance halls in small towns throughout the region, performing their interpretations of pop and R&B hits of the era, with a smattering of country tunes. Along the way, trumpet player Gary Koeppen joined the band.

Now and then, the Triumphs would cut a couple of tracks here or there working with various guys – notably, Charlie Booth, Ray Rush, and

Huey P. Meaux – who had access to a recording studio and had affiliations with small, independent labels. In February 1962 Dante Records released a Triumphs single called "I Know It's Wrong" backed with "The Lazy Man," both of which 18-year-old B.J. Thomas wrote. In 1963, Valerie Records and Lori Records each released the Triumphs' song "Hey, Judy!" written by Mark Charron, a friend of B.J.'s. In 1964, B.J. and the Triumphs hooked up with Bragg Records, a small Houston label that sent B.J. to Nashville by train to record two more Charron tunes, "Never Tell" and "Billy And Sue" – a song about a soldier who goes off to war and receives a "Dear John" letter from his beloved girlfriend. Backing B.J. on those tracks were the "Nashville A-Team" session musicians, with Ray Stevens playing organ and serving as musical arranger. That Bragg single subsequently was picked up by Warner Bros., which didn't promote it adequately. But B.J. and the Triumphs continued to score with Houston "top 40" radio stations KNUZ and KILT, which played those early singles, translating to brisk sales in local record stores. The most successful among those was "Garner State Park," which the small Joed Records label pressed and released in the spring of 1965. It got radio airplay and with strong audience response climbed into the top 10 in Houston – but practically nowhere else. A couple of 1965 Pacemaker Records releases, "Mama" and "Tomorrow Never Comes," stalled beyond southeastern Texas due to limitations in record distribution.

After six years of trying for that elusive breakthrough hit, Billy Joe Thomas – that's his full name – began to consider paths other than music that his life could take. After beginning the process to enter seminary school, he decided instead to enroll at Wharton County Junior College, where he began taking some business courses. When Billy Joe Royal's "Down In The Boondocks" became a hit in the summer of '65, that solidified Thomas' use of the initials "B.J." while he continued performing with the Triumphs on weekends. "Billy Joe Royal was a great guy. He was one of my best friends," B.J. said. Thomas was less than enthusiastic about school, though, as music resonated stronger within him than studying did. He remained in college for only one semester. By the autumn of 1965 the Triumphs amassed enough material for an album, and with producer Charlie Booth, they booked overnight studio time at Pasadena Sound, a small recording studio in the Houston suburb of Pasadena. Half of the tracks they cut were original Mark Charron songs, including "Bring Back The Time" and "Mama," along with cover versions of Wilson Pickett's hit "In The Midnight Hour" and Tom Jones' "It's Not Unusual." They were just about to wrap up the overnight session when a last-minute thought struck B.J.

"It was about 5:30 in the morning. We were tired and everyone was preparing to stop recording, and I said, 'Hey, I forgot to do this thing for my dad. He's going to be upset if I don't do something country on this album.' That's when we recorded 'I'm So Lonesome I Could Cry,' never thinking it would be anything but just something for my dad. So we put it on the B side of what we thought was a hit record," B.J. explained. He and the Triumphs had been performing "I'm So Lonesome ..." at gigs, inspired by the 1964 film *Your Cheatin' Heart* dramatizing the life of Hank Williams. Meaux's Pacemaker Records label released "Candy Baby" with "I'm So Lonesome I Could Cry" designated as the "B" side. In contrast to Hank Williams' country version, B.J. infused the song with a soulful reading, empowered with horns and organ backing.

"Bob White, the program director of KILT radio in Houston, was a real supporter of mine and he would play our records locally. I took the record to the radio station and played him the song that we thought was a hit, and he said, 'While you're here, let's listen to the other side.' I wasn't even that excited, but by the time the second verse of 'I'm So Lonesome I Could Cry' started he said, 'B.J., I love this.' He went directly into the control room and had the disc jockey who was on the air start playing it. The record went to No. 1 in Houston within three weeks and, bang, here I am talking with you," B.J. told us. "If it wasn't for my dad wanting me to do that country song, and Bob White for playing it...." His voice trailed off. "A lot of things came together for that one."

B.J.'s childhood friend Steve Tyrell was watching, and went to bat for B.J. After high school Tyrell had abandoned singing with bands and went to work for a Houston record distributorship that was a wholesaler for several labels, including New York-based Scepter Records. Tyrell was responsible for persuading radio programmers to listen to new singles and play them on the air.

"Steve pushed my early records, and he was very instrumental in Dionne Warwick getting her first record, "Don't Make Me Over," a hit in Houston, where it broke out and then became a national success," B.J. said. Based on that success, Scepter hired Tyrell as a promotion man, soon promoting him to head of A&R (artists and repertoire). Scepter had national distribution and an impressive roster, including the Shirelles, Roy Head, and the Guess Who, as well as Dionne Warwick. When "I'm So Lonesome I Could Cry " hit No. 1 in Houston on the Pacemaker label, Tyrell told his bosses at Scepter Records, and the label agreed to license all tracks on the album of the same name that the Triumphs had recorded.

"Steve was very instrumental in getting me signed to Scepter," B.J. said.

Released as a single on Scepter, "I'm So Lonesome I Could Cry" premiered on the *Billboard* Hot 100 pop music chart at No. 87 on February 19, 1966. Two weeks later it was No. 45 with a star, indicating rapid upward movement. B.J.'s star rose along with it. By the end of March, "I'm So Lonesome I Could Cry" was No. 12 and still climbing. On April 9 it hit No. 8 and remained in the top 10 for three weeks. Scepter quickly released the already-recorded album of the same name, and as B.J.'s follow-up single reissued "Mama," which Pacemaker had released the year before. With the promotional punch of Scepter, "Mama" hit the *Billboard* chart on May 14 and rose to No. 22.

Early validation of B.J.'s star-power potential came in the form of a phone call with an offer for him and the Triumphs to join the Dick Clark Caravan of Stars, a high-profile but grueling concert tour. B.J. said "yes," but the Triumphs declined. "There were about eight guys in the band then, and some were going to college. One guy's father had a big business and he was doing a lot of work with his dad. I didn't have anything to lose; I had no reasons to stay behind. That was the opportunity I had been waiting for, and I went. It wasn't like we had an argument and split up. It was just that I accepted the offer to go on tour, and they didn't," B.J. explained. Later when I began touring on my own, I called my older brother, Jerry, and asked if he would come work for me as my road manager. He said, 'Yeah, I'd love to.' He wound up staying with me on the road for 25 years or so."

As the Vietnam War was escalating in 1966, Wesley Rose, head of Nashville-based Hickory Records, remembered B.J. Thomas and the Triumphs' "Billy And Sue," which Bragg Records had first released two years earlier. Hickory had been a country music label but it began branching out into rock in 1965 by signing the Newbeats and Donovan. Although "Billy And Sue" didn't specifically mention Vietnam, Rose thought the song had become more relevant and purchased the master. Re-released on Hickory, "Billy And Sue" swept onto the Hot 100 on June 18, and during an 11-week run it peaked at No 34. Chart success eluded B.J. for the remainder of 1966, as his reissued singles "Bring Back The Time" and "Tomorrow Never Comes" – an Ernest Tubb country music classic – languished in the lower quarter of the Hot 100. Scepter's hope to re-create magic by releasing B.J.'s interpretation of another Hank Williams tune, "I Can't Help It (If I'm Still In Love With You)," fell flat in the spring of 1967.

B.J.'s fortunes changed, though, in 1968. That's when he became engaged to songwriter Gloria Jean Richardson, whom he married that December. And that was when Mark James, a longtime Houston acquaintance of his, called from Memphis, where he was establishing himself as a songwriter. "When Mark called me I didn't have a current recording, and I was trying to plan what I was going to do next. He said, 'B.J. you need to move to Memphis. A lot of good writers are here, and people are cutting hit after hit out of this studio with a great band," B.J. recalled. In Memphis, James introduced Thomas to recording engineer and producer Lincoln "Chips" Moman, owner of American Sound Studio on Thomas Street, where the Box Tops, Merrilee Rush, Joe Tex, Wilson Pickett, the Gentrys and other performers recorded. Moman previously had polished his skills at Stax Records, where he produced hit records by Booker T. & the MGs, the Mar-Keys and Carla Thomas. At American Sound, Moman had assembled a top-notch studio band consisting of guitarists Reggie Young and Bobby Womack, bass player Tommy Cogbill, organist Bobby Emmons and drummer Gene Chrisman. Moman heard a quality in B.J.'s voice that he knew he could translate into hits. The first prominent result of B.J.'s collaboration with James and Moman was "The Eyes Of A New York Woman," a gentle rocker that hit the chart on June 22, 1968, and propelled B.J. to No. 28 on the chart.

"The American Studio group should be in the Hall of Fame because they've recorded so many hit records. The first time I sang with them, it was like they were my band and I was their singer," B.J. said. "They were just real down-home guys. We fit together perfectly, and Chips was a great engineer and one of the greatest producers of all time – he went on to produce 'Suspicious Minds,' 'Don't Cry Daddy,' 'Kentucky Rain,' 'In The Ghetto' – all those comeback songs for Elvis beginning in 1969."

On a roll with his new creative team, B.J. turned up the heat with his exuberant vocal work on another Mark James tune, "Hooked On A Feeling." Propelled by Reggie Young's radiant opening electronic sitar riff that was a natural for top-of-the-hour radio airplay, the infectiously hummable "Hooked On A Feeling" leaped onto the chart November 16, 1968, soared to No. 5, and remained on the chart for 16 weeks – until the following March. Sales of the record qualified it for a Recording Industry Association of America (RIAA) gold record award. B.J.'s self-confidently titled album *On My Way* included "The Eyes Of A New York Woman" and "Hooked On A Feeling," along with a lushly scored version of "Smoke Gets In Your Eyes," which had been a hit for the Platters in 1958. "That would have been a huge record for me, but no one thought to put it out as a single," B.J. said. Audience exposure of that and other album tracks suffered because Scepter concentrated on its artists' singles, allowing album promotion to languish. B.J.'s next single was yet another Mark James composition, "It's Only Love," which made its debut on March 22, 1969, rose to No. 45 on the pop chart, and put B.J. for the first time on *Billboard's* Easy Listening chart, where it hit No. 37. That was one of the tracks on *Young And In Love,* his most cohesive album to date. B.J. appeared to be losing momentum that summer when one of the other album tracks, a Mark James and Johnny Christopher song, "Pass The Apple, Eve," was released as a single on July 12 and became logjammed in the upper 90s on the chart. But a consequential change in direction was in the wind.

"Ever since I had signed with the Scepter label, Steve Tyrell had been trying to get Burt Bacharach and Hal David to write something for me," Thomas said. "By that time I had a couple of gold records hanging in the

Record producer Steve Tyrell, B.J. Thomas, and his wife, Gloria, with television host Ed Sullivan in 1970 (photo courtesy of B.J. Thomas).

office of Scepter Records, and Dionne Warwick took them into Burt's office. She told him, 'Hey, see these records? You better write something for this guy.' Those gold records put me on their minds, but there wasn't an appropriate song for me until *Butch Cassidy and the Sundance Kid* came along. 'Raindrops Keep Fallin' On My Head' was obviously not a Dionne Warwick song, so they started looking around for singers, and I was lucky to get it." *Butch Cassidy and the Sundance Kid*, a motion picture starring Paul Newman and Robert Redford as two bank robbers at the dawn of the 1900s, included a dreamy sequence with Butch and Sundance's girlfriend Etta (played by Katharine Ross), riding a bicycle through the countryside as B.J. croons "Raindrops." The version of the song that B.J. recorded in the summer of '69 for the film soundtrack, accompanied by a ukulele, a banjo, standup bass, and a rhythm guitar, was more sparse than the eventual single. The bicycle scene had been filmed before it was set to music. "I had just come off the road after three weeks of one-niters in the Midwest and I had pretty much burned the candle at both ends. At the end of the tour the film studio called me unexpectedly to record the song, and I wasn't in very good shape when I got to the studio that Sunday morning, with laryngitis. They had a big screen in there and they ran the bicycle scene as we recorded. Usually I have my way with the melody and do my licks when I record songs, but Burt wanted me to sing it just like he had it phrased – and he was exactly right. There wasn't really room for me to do my thing until the word 'me' on the end."

If anything, the raspy sound of B.J.'s voice that day personified the dustiness of the Old West. "I was so in awe of Burt Bacharach, who is such a cool guy. How many guys get to work with one of the greatest composers of all time? Hal David was probably the greatest lyricist of all time. If you go through the songs he wrote, you become amazed at the simple beauty of what he would do. We had many conversations about 'Raindrops.' They wanted him to write a silly song, a frivolous song, and so that's why the guy's two feet were too big for the bed. But as it turns out, there was such a truism and such a spiritual correctness about the rain falling on me, yet I'm free, and as long as I'm free, I'm all right," Thomas said. "It was just magical, and I was so fortunate to have been involved with that. Hal David was just a beautiful, beautiful man. He was a mentor for me and took me under his wing, so to speak. Those two guys were very different from each other, though. Bacharach was very intense. The music was going through his head at all times. About six weeks after we recorded the film version of 'Raindrops' in California we re-recorded it for the single with about 100 musicians at Columbia Recording Studios on Broadway in New York. Phil Ramone was the recording engineer for that session." In response to Scepter's request, B.J. and Gloria moved from Memphis to New York City to enable more extensive collaboration with Bacharach.

The single version of "Raindrops" made its debut on the *Billboard* Hot 100 on November 1, a week after *Butch Cassidy and the Sundance Kid* was released in theaters nationwide. The song began steadily climbing up the chart and on January 3, 1970, displaced "Someday We'll Be Together" by Diana Ross & the Supremes at No. 1, a position it held for four consecutive weeks. It also hit No. 1 on the Easy Listening chart. "Raindrops" remained on the Hot 100 for a 22-week run – more than five months – and went on to earn an RIAA gold record. Scepter capitalized on the single hit with an album titled *Raindrops Keep Fallin' On My Head,* which included B.J.'s version of another Bacharach and David composition, "This Guy's In Love With You," Joe South's "The Greatest Love," and two Mark James compositions – including an energetically soulful version of "Suspicious Minds," a comeback hit for Elvis Presley.

Bacharach and David, meanwhile, had another song ready for B.J.: "Everybody's Out Of Town." With a loping rhythm, the song stood out with a tipsy trumpet signature. "Burt had to show the trumpet player how to play it. He told him, 'You've got to mash down the keys all at one time to make that sound I'm looking for.' I'm as proud of 'Everybody's Out Of Town' as I am 'Raindrops' because it was unique and it made a good statement: if we keep doing what we're doing, nobody's going to be in town. It had a nuclear devastation suggestion. It was a very futuristic, advanced, a very intelligent song, and I always appreciated getting to do it." Premiering on March 28, 1970, "Everybody's Out Of Town" peaked at No. 26 on the Hot 100 and remained on the chart for nine weeks, while going all the way to No. 3 on the Easy Listening chart. B.J.'s first Scepter compilation album, *Greatest Hits Volume 1,* contained "I'm So Lonesome I Could Cry," "Hooked On A Feeling," "Billy And Sue," "Mama" and "Eyes Of A New York Woman."

At the 42nd Academy Awards presentation on April 2, "Raindrops Keep Fallin' On My Head" earned Bacharach and David an Oscar for best original song, and Bacharach won another Oscar for best original score for *Butch Cassidy and the Sundance Kid.* By then, B.J. had returned from New York to the more laid-back and comfortable surroundings of Tennessee and maintained his chart momentum with a song by heavy-hitter composers Barry Mann and Cynthia Weil. Bobby Vee and Leonard Nimoy previously had taken a crack at "I Just Can't Help Believing," but B.J.'s rendition of the breezy, feel-good love song, produced by Chips Moman in Memphis with a gently rocking musical arrangement by Glen Spreen, hopped onto the pop chart on June 20, 1970. It eventually rose to No. 9, and remained on the chart throughout the summer, for 13 weeks. "I Just Can't Help Believing" was a No. 1 hit on *Billboard's* "Easy Listening" chart. B.J.'s 1970 Scepter album *Everybody's Out Of Town,* which pictured B.J. on a deserted city street in front of an imposing but apparently vacant municipal building, included "I Just Can't Help Believing" along with the title track.

By that time, a studio group under the direction of producer and songwriter Buddy Buie in Doraville, Georgia, near Atlanta, was emerging as a dynamic backing band that eventually would become renowned under the name the Atlanta Rhythm Section (as another chapter in this book describes). Steve Tyrell recognized that Thomas and Buie would work creatively together. "Buddy Buie is a great songwriter, and his studio had a great band. He's one of the greatest guys, and I still talk to him every three or four weeks," B.J. told us in October 2013 [Buie died due to a heart attack in July 2015]. The first successful product of B.J.'s working relationship with the Doraville crew was "Most Of All," which Buie wrote with Atlanta Rhythm Section guitarist J.R. Cobb. Produced by Buie and Tyrell with musical arrangement by Glen Spreen, "Most Of All" premiered on the chart November 28 on the Scepter label, rose to No. 38, and remained on the chart for 10 weeks, into early 1971. On the Easy Listening chart, it shot up to No. 2.

"Most Of All" was the title track of B.J.'s 1971 Scepter album, which also included his next single release. Buie and Tyrell rolled tape at Doraville as Thomas tackled a song by Wayne Carson Thomson and Johnny Christopher beseeching couples with rocky relationships to seek ways to heal their differences and remain together. With musical arrangement by Glen Spreen, the song, "No Love At All," began a 10-week run on the pop singles chart on February 27, 1971, with a peak at No. 16 on the Hot 100 and No. 4 on the Easy Listening chart.

Never one to remain in the same mold for long, B.J. next turned to a gospel-themed composition called "Mighty Clouds Of Joy" that Buddy Buie and Atlanta Rhythm Section drummer Robert Nix wrote. B.J.'s ebullient singing convinced top 40 radio music directors to add the gospel tune to their play lists. It premiered on the *Billboard* pop chart on July 3, rose to No. 34, and stayed on the chart for 10 weeks. On the Easy Listening chart, it hit No. 8.

B.J's follow-up chart entry was "Long Ago Tomorrow," the result of another collaboration with Burt Bacharach and Hal David, who wrote the song and produced the recording session. Bacharach and Pat Williams are credited for musical arrangement on the Scepter single, which slipped onto the chart on November 6 and remained for seven weeks, during which it reached No. 61. Adult contemporary audiences thought much more of it, sending it to No. 13 on the Easy Listening chart. "Long Ago Tomorrow" was included in B.J.'s blockbuster *Greatest Hits Volume 2* album, which also contained "It's Only Love," "Raindrops," "Everybody's Out Of Town," "I Just Can't Help Believing," "Most Of All," "No Love At All," and "Mighty Clouds Of Joy."

All three of B.J.'s 1972 chart singles were produced by his old friend Steve Tyrell and Al Gorgoni, recorded for his album titled *Billy Joe Thomas*, a collection of thoughtfully chosen songs about life's twists and turns, greater understanding of love that evolves with maturity, and living with the consequences of impetuous decisions. "*Billy Joe Thomas* was the first album I did with thought given to sequencing and theories and points behind it," B.J. said. "Back in the old days, no one really cut an album with a reason or theme behind it other than they happened to have a hit single. Back in that day performers might cut three albums a year, whereas now they do an album maybe every few years. When I cut *Billy Joe Thomas* with Al Gorgoni and Steve Tyrell, every song was chosen with a purpose."

The first of three tracks from that album to be released as a single was a Barry Mann and Cynthia Weil composition, "Rock And Roll Lullaby," with strings arranged by Glen Spreen. The song, a sympathetic ballad about a teenage single mom, was distinguished by Duane Eddy on guitar and Barry Mann playing piano, with background vocals by the Blossoms. "Rock And Roll Lullaby" bounced B.J. up to No. 15 after its debut on February 12, 1972, and it stayed on the chart for 11 weeks, into May. It hit No. 1 on the Easy Listening chart. The follow-up was a Paul Williams composition, "That's What Friends Are For" (not the same as the tune by Burt Bacharach and Carole Bayer Sager that Dionne Warwick, Elton John, Gladys Knight and Stevie Wonder recorded in 1985 to benefit AIDS research). B.J.'s recording, with Paul Williams singing background, premiered July 15 and during its six-week stay on the chart rose to No. 74, while hitting No. 38 on the Easy Listening chart. B.J.'s final chart entry of the year, his rendition of Stevie Wonder's composition "Happier Than The Morning Sun," marked the beginning of a drought on the charts for him amid a surprising development. B.J. had been unaware that Scepter Records was in deep financial trouble, badly in debt and no longer able to adequately promote records. After clinging to the No. 100 spot for two weeks in October, "Happier Than The Morning Sun" dropped off the chart as Scepter collapsed in financial ruin and closed its doors.

"As we were finishing the *Billy Joe Thomas* album, which we thought was very good, we learned that Scepter was out of money. They couldn't even make the vinyl pressing of the album, and we were shocked. Scepter had been among the first major independent labels and was very competitive, so its closure was very sad," B.J. said.

B.J. turned disappointment into opportunity by trying his hand at acting. He was cast to play the part of Jocko, a gunslinger in a 1972 western motion picture called *Jory*, filmed in Mexico. Robby Benson played the title role (his feature film credited debut), John Marley starred as a cattle drive trail boss, and Linda Purl as a rancher's daughter. "John Marley is the actor who woke up with the horse's head in his bed [in *The Godfather*]. He was a great guy and we were good buddies," B.J. said. After B.J. returned home from four months of shooting, his wife, Gloria, had an earnest discussion with him. "Gloria sat me down and said, 'Look B.J., you're on the road 300 days a year, so now are you going to make movies, too? Then you'll be gone all the time. Will you just choose one or the other? I love the music you make – will you just be a singer?' I think I could have been an actor, but Gloria was right. So we made a decision right then that I would not pursue acting. The burning desire I have is to make music."

Steve Tyrell (who eventually resumed singing and distinguished himself as an esteemed crooner of jazz and pop standards beginning in the 1990s) negotiated a deal with the Paramount label, which signed Thomas to a contract in early 1973. By then sporting a full beard and mustache, B.J. recorded *Songs*, his first album for the label. Exploring themes of loneliness, separation, and rejection, the pop-country album included three songs by Cynthia Weil and Barry Mann – "Too Many Mondays," "We're Over" and the title track – plus Carole King's "Early Morning Hush" and four songs that Gerry Goffin co-wrote. Even though Tyrell continued as B.J.'s producer of his recording sessions, with arrangement by Glen Spreen, Thomas struggled to regain the momentum he had lost. Paramount's release of "Songs" as a single in June 1973 reached No. 41 on the Easy Listening chart but did not reach the *Billboard* Hot 100 pop chart. Neither did his release later that year of Carole King's "Early Morning Hush," or "Play Something Sweet" by Allen Toussaint in the spring of 1974. Paramount's parent company, Gulf+Western, sold the label in 1974 to ABC, and the artists on the Paramount roster, including B.J. Thomas, found themselves recording

for ABC Records. During that lull period, a Swedish band called Blue
Swede resurrected B.J.'s 1968 hit song "Hooked On A Feeling," gave it a
different twist against a boisterous "hooga-chooga" backing chant, and with
Björn Skifs singing lead, sent it to the top of the U.S. charts. "The hooga-
chooga thing, which was borrowed from Johnny Preston's old record called
'Running Bear,' caught people's attention right away," Thomas observed.
"That was a great production idea in that they didn't try to reproduce that
sitar ride of Reggie Young's. They probably couldn't have duplicated it."

B.J.'s fortunes turned around with breathtaking speed at the beginning
of 1975, as he and Gloria moved from New York to Arlington, Texas.
By then, producer Chips Moman had sold his American Sound Studio
in Memphis, shifted operations to Nashville, and most members of his
first-rate studio band joined him there. Working once again with Chips
in Nashville, B.J. slipped into a country music mode with an album titled
Reunion that included a fine sing-along tune that Moman co-wrote with
Larry Butler. Released as a single, it was a monster hit for B.J. and for ABC
Records. The character in the song was sitting in a bar, trying to drink away
his sorrow about being two-timed by the girl he loved. "(Hey Won't You
Play) Another Somebody Done Somebody Wrong Song," with a foxtrot
tempo and strings arranged by Mike Leech, premiered on the *Billboard* Hot
100 on February 1, and on April 26 knocked Elton John's "Philadelphia
Freedom" from the No. 1 position on the pop chart. It also topped the Easy
Listening and Hot Country Singles charts. Disc jockeys loved saying the
song's title, and listeners loved hearing it.

Thomas was once again at the top of the charts, and RIAA honored
"Done Somebody Wrong Song" with a gold record on May 23. The single
remained on the Hot 100 for 18 weeks, up until early summer. "We cut
'Wrong Song' at a time when the three-hour session did not exist. If you
showed up at the studio 4, 5, or 6 in the afternoon, you might not leave
until 6, 7, 8 o'clock the next morning," B.J. recalled. "We thought at that
time that hanging out and being friends and telling stories was a big part
of what we were going to do in the music. It set the mood. When we got
a song, we learned it on the spot. It wasn't like something we took home
and worked on and learned, and the music was written out and we knew
exactly what they were going to do. We just started doing the music and
what we were going to do with it might come as a surprise. Someone might
play something, and someone else would say, 'Hey, I like that. Let's do that,'
and it became part of the arrangement. When we brought the Memphis
horns in, their parts were not written out. We'd play them the song and they
worked out their parts. So we didn't run by the clock. When we felt like we

were through, that's when we were through."

B.J.'s follow-up to "(Hey Won't You Play) Another Somebody Done Somebody Wrong Song," was a sentimental tune called "Help Me Make It (To My Rockin' Chair)," written by Bobby Emmons. Produced by Chips Moman with musical arrangement by Mike Leach, the song made its debut on September 20, 1975, rose to No. 64, and remained on the pop chart for nine weeks. It was a crossover hit that went to No. 37 on the country chart, and peaked at No. 5 on the Easy Listening chart. That was B.J.'s last chart entry for 1975 and for the ABC label, as he hit another dry spell that lasted nearly two years. That was a dry spell in more ways than one. It coincided with his emergence from longtime struggles with drug and alcohol abuse, which had worsened about the time that he recorded the *Songs* album and reached its depths when he was recording the *Reunion* album.

"I had a spiritual awakening and I woke up to the fact that there are a lot more important things in life than just feeling good – getting high or having a drink," B.J. told us. "I realized that if I had never had a hit record, I would still have a beautiful life, and I got sober when I was 33 years old." But he was not done making hits.

Signed by MCA Records – for which Lynyrd Skynyrd, the Who, Black Oak Arkansas, and Olivia Newton-John also recorded – B.J. went into the studio with producer Chris Christian and executive producer George Lee and, with musical arrangement by Bergen White, cut his interpretation of Brian Wilson and Roger Christian's 1964 Beach Boys hit "Don't Worry, Baby" for an album titled simply *B.J. Thomas*. B.J.'s single hit the chart on July 2, 1977, and began climbing the chart – to No. 17. And it remained on the Hot 100 for 17 weeks, until late October. Adult contemporary radio station listeners love it, sending it to No. 2 on the Easy Listening chart. On November 12, B.J. was back on the pop chart with "Still The Lovin' Is Fun," which Chris Christian wrote and produced. That went no higher than No. 77 and was on the chart for only four weeks, although it was a solid hit at No. 8 on the Easy Listening chart. B.J. returned on January 21, 1978, with what would be his last MCA chart record, "Everybody Loves A Rain Song," which Mark James and Chips Moman wrote, and which Moman produced. That one went up to No. 43 and remained on the chart for eight weeks, while rising to No. 25 on the country chart and No. 2 on the Easy Listening chart. MCA continued releasing B.J. Thomas singles through June 1982, although none of them reached the Hot 100.

B.J. attributes that slide to an unwise shift in musical direction that fans and radio programmers alike misinterpreted. "My demise on the mainstream chart resulted from my decision to make a gospel record in

1977. It was not a very good career move," B.J. told us. "I was doing a concert at Six Flags in Arlington. Texas, and some representatives of Word Records, a major gospel label, came to that show and asked me if I would make a gospel record. I said, 'Yes. Sure,' and that's how that got started." B.J. and his wife, Gloria, think of themselves as spiritual rather than religious people. "We believe in love. That's what Jesus tried to demonstrate with his life. If you can love yourself and be conscious of yourself, you can love other people, and that's what it's all about." Word Records assigned production of B.J.'s inspirational album to Chris Christian,

B.J. Thomas croons a song with feeling in 1981 (photo courtesy of B.J. Thomas).

who had been instrumental in getting top-selling contemporary Christian singer Amy Grant signed to Word Records. Both B.J. and Grant became part of the roster of Word's contemporary Christian subsidary label, Myrrh. B.J. thought he would record a few gospel songs that had personal meaning for him, and that would be that. "It made people think I had become a religious singer, though. Radio stations labeled me a religious singer. I made some other records and we sent them out, but radio stations would reply, 'We don't play gospel music.' I would say, 'This is not gospel.' But that was the beginning of my demise, even on country radio. I regained some ground on country radio, but back then country didn't have the mainstream presence that it does now."

The contemporary Christian market sustained B.J. during that period. "My first gospel record, which was called, *Home Where I Belong,* was just huge. It went multi-platinum, and I became a No. 1 contemporary Christian artist." In 1977, the single release of "Home Where I Belong" peaked at No. 1 on *Billboard's* Spiritual music chart. The album earned B.J. his first Grammy Award for "best inspirational performance" – a category he also captured in 1978 (for his album *Happy Man*), in 1979 for his album *You Gave Me Love (When Nobody Gave Me A Prayer),* and in 1981 for his album *Amazing Grace.* The Gospel Music Association bestowed its Dove Award for *Home Where I Belong* and for *Amazing Grace,* both in the category of "album by a secular artist," and both albums also won Angel Awards from Excellence in Media. Over the span of four years, 10 of B.J.'s singles were top-20 inspirational chart hits. In 1980 B.J. won a Grammy in the "best gospel performance, contemporary or inspirational" category for *The Lord's Prayer,* an album he recorded with fellow artists Andrae Crouch, the Archers, Cynthia Clawson, Dony McGuire, Reba Rambo, and Tramaine and Walter Hawkins. "All of these records were No. 1 on the inspirational music charts for over a year. *Amazing Grace* was No. 1 for 110 consecutive weeks. I'm very proud of that music, but I never intended to be exclusively a 'Christian' singer or religious singer, and I was never able to overcome the reaction to that music. At gospel concerts, fans wanted me to preach and read from the *Bible,* and refrain from performing any of my past music," B.J. said. "I made four or five gospel albums, but it wasn't the music I wanted to make."

B.J. decided to shift from gospel and re-establish himself as a pop singer, returning to his soulful roots. In his concerts, he sought to artfully interweave gospel, blues, pop, and country influences. But he wound up unintentionally alienating three audiences that misunderstood his intentions – the pop stations and fans thought he had gone gospel; the gospel audience objected to his retaining secular music in his repertoire; and the country music programmers thought his attempts to regain standing as a pop singer betrayed country audiences. "I was never able to recapture my career after that huge religious music explosion," B.J. said. "I didn't really mean for that to happen. All of a sudden, I came under a lot of criticism and judgment from Christian people. They would come to my concerts, and would begin booing and yelling at me to stop doing the 'devil's music.' I loved gospel music, and I liked to sing some gospel songs, but I realize I should have made those spiritual comments within my regular records rather than making an out-and-out gospel record."

Still, B.J. returned to the pop chart one more time, on May 21, 1983, with a song called "Whatever Happened To Old Fashioned Love," written by Lewis Anderson. Produced by Pete Drake and released on Columbia's Cleveland International label, it hung up at No. 93 and was on the pop chart for only two weeks. It fared much better on the Easy Listening chart, at No. 13, and on the country chart. The same year he had his last Christian hit, the poignantly titled "Pray For Me." Cleveland International released five more B.J. Thomas singles between then and September 1984, and Columbia released several singles of his in 1985 and '86, but none cracked the Hot 100. He did, however, manage to regain a foothold in country music with a succession of singles, including three top-10 hits in 1983 – "Whatever Happened To Old Fashioned Love" (a No. 1 hit on the country chart), "New Looks From An Old Lover" (another No. 1 country hit, which B.J.'s wife Gloria co-wrote), and "Two Car Garage" (a No. 3 hit). In 1984, B.J. continued to thrive on the country chart with two hit singles: "The Whole World's In Love When You're Lonely" (which peaked at No. 10) and "The Girl Most Likely To" (No. 17). Beginning in 1985, though, none of his singles managed to go any higher than No. 59 on the country chart.

By then, TV had come calling. The producers of the sitcom *Growing Pains,* starring Alan Thicke, Joanna Kerns, Kirk Cameron, and Jeremy Miller, signed B.J. in 1985 to record the show's theme song, "As Long As We Got Each Other." He sang it as a soloist for the show's first season, then for the second season re-recorded it as a duet with Jennifer Warnes. For the fourth season of the show, B.J. recorded an additional version of the theme with Dusty Springfield, which remained on the air for three additional years.

Although radio lost enthusiasm for B.J. amid a flood of younger recording artists, he remained in demand as a concert performer, and so he has continued touring through the years in oldies ensemble shows and in his own headlining gigs in municipal auditoriums, casinos and resort hotel showrooms. He recurrently performed in tandem with his friend Billy Joe Royal on shows they amusingly billed as the "Raindrops and Boondocks Tour." And B.J. appears periodically with his old pals the Triumphs, performing many of the rhythm and blues tunes they enjoyed as youngsters. "We do Bobby Bland's 'Turn On Your Love Light,' and 'St. James Infirmary,' we'll play 'I've Just Got To Forget You,' 'In The Midnight Hour,' and 'I Got A Woman' and other Ray Charles songs. And I sing some of my stuff – 'Raindrops,' 'Hooked On A Feeling,' 'I Just Can't Help Believing.' It's a lot of fun." B.J.'s wife, Gloria, serves as his business manager. "Gloria is a great businesswoman. She coordinates my TV appearances, oversees my record contracts, and all the other details of my career activities," B.J. said. B.J.'s son-in-law, Darrell Moore (married to B.J. and Gloria's daughter, Erin) is the office manager for B.J.'s company, Honeyman Music.

Thomas returned to acting briefly in 2008 when screenwriter and director Jeff Santo (son of former Chicago Cubs third baseman Ron Santo) cast him in the role of "Doc" in a dramatic film called *Jake's Corner,* about the folks who populate the area around a small rest stop on an isolated highway in the Arizona desert. "This group of misfits assume the responsibility of taking care of a young child whose parents have just been killed in a car accident. I played a guy they called Doc, who was a Vietnam veteran," B.J. said.

During the past five decades, 26 singles that B.J. Thomas recorded registered on the *Billboard* Hot 100, along with 16 country music hits, 25 on the Easy Listening chart and 11 singles on the Spiritual Albums chart. He has recorded 54 pop, Christian, and Christmas music albums, and a dozen B.J. Thomas anthology albums have been released. The artistry of B.J. Thomas has been recognized with numerous awards and certifications, including three gold singles and one gold album award from the Recording Industry Association of America; his five Grammy Awards from the Recording Academy; two Gospel Music Association Dove Awards; two Angel Awards from Excellence in Media; and membership in the Grand Ole Opry beginning in August 1981.

B.J. has continued recording music in latter years for various labels, including Reprise, Warner Resound, and Silver City Records. His catalog includes a 2009 album called *Once I Loved – B.J. Thomas In Brazil,* recorded with Brazilian performers, and he built a sufficient following in Brazil to perform there periodically. The album, which consists primarily of B.J.'s takes on Brazilian standards, also includes a bossa nova tempo version of B.J.'s hit "Rock And Roll Lullaby," because it is the theme song of Brazil's most enduring *novela* (soap opera) TV program.

Most recently B.J. recorded *The Living Room Sessions,* an album of warm, intimate duets with numerous singers, reinterpreting B.J. Thomas hits. It came about as the result of recording some other tracks. "Larry Butler, who produced Kenny Rogers' records and was the co-writer with Chips Moman on 'Done Somebody Wrong Song,' called me and said, 'Look, B.J., I'm in Muscle Shoals, Alabama, and I've been writing a lot of music – some of the best songs I've ever written. I want you to sing them.' So I flew in to Alabama and we recorded an album. It was the first album that I had ever done on computer software – not with a band, but piecemeal on the computer. So Larry went to Nashville to pitch the record. At Wrinkled Records, Sandy Knox and Katie Gillon, two longtime songwriters and business people in the music industry, didn't like the album, but they liked me," B.J. said. "So they called me and asked if I would like to cut another record. Their first suggestion was they wanted to re-cut my hits. I had usually resisted that idea, but they said, "We want to do it acoustically and with some duets, so that intrigued me – and that became *The Living Room Sessions.* Wrinkled is the worst name for a label ever, but they were the greatest people to work with." Producer for the album was Kyle Lehning, who had worked with Randy Travis and Ronnie Milsap, among others. Tracks on the 2013 album included B.J. singing "I Just Can't Help

Believing" with Vince Gill, "Raindrops Keep Falling On My Head" with Lyle Lovett, "Most Of All" with Keb' Mo' and "Rock And Roll Lullaby" with his old friend Steve Tyrell.

Although B.J.'s modesty prevents him from taking credit for anything but his own rich catalog of recordings, he made a lasting imprint on the recording business by clearing a path for gospel artists to cross over and gain acceptance among country and pop music fans. B.J.'s late 1970s foray in contemporary Christian music arguably helped pave the way for the Oak Ridge Boys, Amy Grant and Carrie Underwood to reach secular audiences. To B.J., though, it's all just music – songs and styles that he wants to share with his fans.

You see, he just can't help believing in the power and joy of music.

B.J. THOMAS U.S. SINGLES ON THE *BILLBOARD* HOT 100 CHART

Debut	Peak	Gold	Title	Label
2/19/66	8		I'm So Lonesome I Could Cry	Scepter*
5/14/66	22		Mama	Scepter*
6/18/66	34		Billy And Sue	Hickory**
7/30/66	75		Bring Back the Time	Scepter*
9/10/66	80		Tomorrow Never Comes	Scepter*
5/13/67	94		I Can't Help It (If I'm Still In Love With You)	Scepter*
6/22/68	28		The Eyes Of A New York Woman	Scepter
11/16/68	5	▲	Hooked On A Feeling	Scepter
3/22/69	45		It's Only Love	Scepter
7/12/69	97		Pass The Apple, Eve	Scepter
11/1/69	1	▲	Raindrops Keep Fallin' On My Head	Scepter
3/28/70	26		Everybody's Out Of Town	Scepter
6/20/70	9		I Just Can't Help Believing	Scepter
11/28/70	38		Most Of All	Scepter
2/27/71	16		No Love At All	Scepter

B.J. Thomas Hot 100 U.S. Singles (continued)

Debut	Peak	Gold	Title	Label
7/3/71	34		Mighty Clouds Of Joy	Scepter
11/6/71	61		Long Ago Tomorrow	Scepter
2/12/72	15		Rock And Roll Lullaby	Scepter
7/15/72	74		That's What Friends Are For	Scepter
10/7/72	100		Happier Than The Morning Sun	Scepter
2/1/75	1	▲	(Hey Won't You Play) Another Somebody Done Somebody Wrong Song	ABC
9/20/75	64		Help Me Make It (To My Rockin' Chair)	ABC
7/2/77	17		Don't Worry, Baby	MCA
11/12/77	77		Still The Lovin' Is Fun	MCA
1/21/78	43		Everybody Loves A Rain Song	MCA
5/21/83	93		Whatever Happened to Old Fashioned Love	Cleveland International

* previously released on the Pacemaker label

** first released on Bragg, then Warner label in 1964

▲ symbol: RIAA certified gold record (Recording Industry Association of America)

Billboard's pop singles chart data is courtesy of Joel Whitburn's Record Research Inc. (www.recordresearch.com), Menomonee Falls, Wisconsin.

Epilogue: B.J. Thomas

Singer and songwriter

One of the most distinctive voices in American pop music is that of B.J. Thomas, and it's as distinguished today as it was in 1966 – the beginning of his hit-making years. While time has tarnished the vocal resonance of many of the pop stars of the 1960s and '70s, B.J.'s heartfelt timbre continues to enchant his fans. His time-tested voice is not only the work of genetics, or luck; he has consciously worked to retain its quality.

"As I age, I have to treat my voice right. I have to get as much rest as I can, I have to eat healthy, so it takes some effort on my part. I do put some time into trying to keep my vocal ability going," explained B.J. "That's why I like to work, because it keeps me in touch with the music. When you step away from the music and stop working, you kind of lose your feel for it. Right now a big part of my life is keeping that ability to sing going, because I like to do it."

Billy Joe Thomas was born on August 7, 1942 – delivered by his father's mother, a midwife – in rural Hugo, Oklahoma, about nine miles north of the Texas border. While the family moved often as his farther pursued construction work, he and his older brother, Jerry, and younger sister, Judy, grew up in the North Shepherd sector of Houston, Texas, area with their parents, Geneva and Vernon (nicknamed "Bud"). In Houston, Vernon went into the air conditioning business with B.J.'s uncles, as his mom remained

B.J. Thomas in Nashville in 2013 (photo courtesy of B.J. Thomas).

a homemaker. Billy Joe, who loved playing baseball and was a member of the baseball team at John H. Reagan High School, adopted his nickname B.J. because there were too many boys named Billy playing Little League in his area. He earned spending money in the usual ways. "I worked at a service station, my brother and I worked with my dad in the summers, and we threw newspapers some," B.J. said in his soft drawl.

B.J. enjoyed listening to music as a young kid. "I can remember being like a third grader and listening to the Grand Ole Opry on the radio. My dad was a big fan of those great Opry stars back in the day. I was 10 years old when Hank Williams Sr. passed away, and it was a significant moment in my life. My brother and I loved him so much. There was something about him that everybody in pop, country, and blues connected with. He had a huge mainstream following in the States and worldwide. And so I remember the day he died and how I cried about it."

B.J.'s father, who enjoyed music and played the guitar, might have passed on a musical gene or two to his son. "My dad loved to have a good time, and as part of having a good time sometimes he would bust out and start singing," said B.J. "As I look back on my dad and remember those times, I realize that he could have been a musician, though I don't think it had ever crossed his mind. I don't think he ever looked at music as a profession and a career. He loved music so much, and had introduced us kids to the Grand Ole Opry, and all the great singers at that time were like gods to us."

Although B.J. began fooling around with the guitar and strummed it for his own enjoyment, the idea of performing and earning a living never occurred to him – that is, until his family moved 30 miles west of Houston to the twin-town community of Richmond-Rosenberg, where Bud and his brother opened their own air conditioning business. B.J. transferred to Lamar Consolidated High School in Rosenberg. "I was about 15 or 16 years old and got into a little band there with some friends of my brother's and that's how that whole thing got started for me," B.J. said. Formed in the autumn of 1958, the band consisted initially of guitarist Tim Griffith and his bass-playing brother Tom, guitarist Denver "Denny" Zatyka (pronounced za-TEE-ka), drummer Teddy Mensik, and saxophone player Don Drachenberg.

"I was a sophomore, and most of the other guys in the band were juniors in my brother's class. They were looking for a singer." Jerry told his friends about his brother's talent for singing, but B.J. wasn't interested in joining the band. "I was a very introverted, shy guy. The last thing I would ever do was to get up in front of six people and sing. But my brother basically threatened me with bodily harm to get me to one of their practices," B.J. chuckled. "I sang a Buddy Holly song and a Ricky Nelson song, and the next thing I knew I was their singer," B.J. told us. They called the band the Triumphs, because back then, many cool groups were named after cars (recall the Impalas, the Fleetwoods, the Edsels, and Little Anthony and the Imperials).

They rehearsed in the warehouse of Rosenberg's Lone Star beer distributorship, which Denny's father owned. Trumpet player Gary Koeppen subsequently joined the band. While B.J. favored the music of Little Richard, Chuck Berry, Hank Ballard and other rhythm and blues singers, he modeled his early stage presence after a popular pop singer of the day. "When I first started singing with the band, I didn't really know what I was doing, but I knew that if I could act like Ricky Nelson, I'd be okay. He was a TV star at that time, with the *Ozzie and Harriet Show*, and he kinda stood there sleepily singing. He wasn't jumping around. His music was not the music I loved the most, but he as a person had a huge influence on me," B.J. said.

Initially nervous, B.J. quickly warmed to singing in public. "As it turned out, once I began singing with the Triumphs I liked the whole concept of it and how it made me feel. Everything about it just thrilled me, and I wanted to keep doing it. If it were not for my brother's insistence, though, I never would have because of how introverted I was as a kid," B.J. acknowledged. The Triumphs performed publicly for the first time at a dance in January 1959. "Our band began playing the dance halls in the little country towns throughout the area on the weekends." Also playing the same circuit was a band called the Traits, whose singer, Roy Head, went on to record "Treat Her Right," a 1965 smash hit. "Roy was a great performer and the Traits played John Lee Hooker kind of blues, and they set a pattern for us to follow."

B.J. graduated in 1960 from Lamar Consolidated High School and attended Wharton County Junior College, about 25 miles southwest of Rosenberg, for one semester until the music consumed his time. He was drafted for military service, and said he probably would have been sent to Vietnam, had he not sustained a disqualifying musculoskeletal injury while working out. "I've got some regrets about not being involved in Vietnam but, of course, if I had gone over there, I'm not sure I would have come back." The death of a friend in a car wreck persuaded B.J. to seek an existence with a purpose in life, and he contemplated enrolling in seminary school. But the unexpected success of "I'm So Lonesome I Could Cry" set him on a different course. By then, B.J. could no longer deny his burning desire to remain a singer. He said, "I think that's probably one of the main requirements for any profession, but especially for music. If you don't have a burning desire to do it, it can be tough on you. But once I got started in the band, that's all I ever wanted to do."

After scoring three back-to-back hit records during the first six months of 1966, B.J. slid into a slump during which his recordings were mired in the lower quarter of the Hot 100. His personal fortunes changed for the better in 1967, though, in Houston one evening at Van's Ballroom, where he met Gloria Jean Richardson. "I had performed at a nightclub the night before I met her and for some reason I was back at that nightclub the following night with some friends of mine. I was sitting at the table with my friends and across the table was this girl. It was Gloria, and I was just so attracted to her and so beamed into her. Nothing like that had ever happened to me before," recalled B.J. "I leaned across the table and said to her, 'I want to take you home tonight. I'll give you a ride home.' She said, 'Well, I'm with Trent.' Trent was a drummer friend of mine. I said, 'I'll take

BJ Thomas in 1966, during his Scepter Records days (photo courtesy of B.J. Thomas).

care of that.' So I went to Trent and said, 'I'm taking Gloria home.' He said, 'Wait a minute.' I said, 'No. I'm taking her home.' She said, 'I appreciate you taking me home, but when we get outside, if you change your mind, I'll understand.' I had no idea what she was talking about, but when we got outside in the light, I could see her face had all these stitches and scars. She had been in a car wreck and had gone through the windshield, and she had 400 stitches in her face. So she had all these major scars through her eyebrows, her lips, her nose and everything. But we just fell in love right then.

"I would take her to the hospital so they could take the stitches out. Back in that day, it was pretty crude and pretty tough the way they would treat facial scars. They didn't have the plastic surgery technology that they have today. They would sand her face, so when she came out her face would be all red and torn up. It would be smoother, but it was very painful. About the second time I took her, I said, 'If you're doing this for me, forget about it. You don't have to do this. Let's get married.' That was my crude way of asking her, and she said 'yes.'"

In 1967 B.J. moved from Houston to Memphis, and he and Gloria were married on December 9, 1968, in Las Vegas, Nevada. In 1969 Scepter Records wanted B.J. to move to New York to start working with Burt Bacharach. They lived on 86th Street near Second Avenue in Manhattan until 1975.

B.J. recalled, "I had been on the road 300 days a year, and we were tired of New York, so we came back home to Texas, and we were in an apartment for a few months and then we bought this house in Arlington and have lived here since 1975. After we came back to Texas, Gloria and I were separated for about six months. At that time, she came back to Fort Worth. We got back together and that's when we decided to stay here and let the business go for awhile. We always had a great relationship, but because of my addiction sometimes it would be too much to handle."

Their first child, Jeri Paige, was born in New York in 1970. After traveling with a Christian crusade of singers, ministers, and counselors in Taiwan, B.J. and Gloria met Laura Lam Sung, who helped them adopt their second daughter, Nora Jean (who was 8 months old), from a Korean orphanage in 1979. Soon after returning from Korea with Paige and Nora, Gloria discovered she was pregnant with their third daughter, Erin Micah, who was born in 1980.

"People always say, 'God blessed you with this voice.' You know there was a certain technique that I had that I didn't know where it was coming from. I certainly had to put some work into how it sounded and staying on pitch, so it was something that interested me and consumed all of my attention for a long time. It still does. I still work on new stuff and, to me, the most fun and the biggest challenge is to get a song, learn the song, ingest the song personally and really feel what the song is trying to say. I don't like to do anything that I really don't believe in, and when I connect with the song as it pertains to me, there's a thrill that really is a great payoff to do it."

B.J. credits Gloria for all the good things that have happened to him in his life. She supported and guided him the best she could, but his own lack of self-esteem and self-love during his years of addiction to alcohol and drugs was something he had to overcome in order to heal completely.

"I grew up in an alcoholic family. My dad was an alcoholic. He was absolutely the worst alcoholic I've ever come in contact with. He had such a serious problem with it that he never even came close to having any control over it. So I grew up with that, and my dad died young – he was 52, and he was just a guy, but it was so hard to have a relationship with him or any meaningful communication with him because of his problem. So I kind of became like my father. If the right thing was the easiest thing to do, I wouldn't do it, I'd do the other thing," B.J. said as he reflected on that period in his life.

"I was just very lucky that Gloria and I met, and we got married. She could always see me for who I was. I never could see it, but she could see it. She would talk to me and make me think maybe there is another way, because I was getting to a situation where I was OD-ing quite often. We did some self-help things and we put a lot of work into it. It was right after I had 'Wrong Song,' that I got sober, and I told Gloria, 'I can't continue in the business the way I am. I'm so tired of it,' and she was, too. We were living in New York at that time, so we came back to Texas and that's when the change happened, and we devoted our time to raising the family. I would work maybe 20 to 30 nights per year. We just devoted time to the family, and mainly it was because of Gloria."

Following his recovery, B.J. co-wrote two autobiographical books. He wrote the first, titled *Home Where I Belong,* with Jerry B. Jenkins in 1978. It's the true story of B.J.'s rise to fame, drug dependency, and rebirth. He wrote the second book, titled *In Tune: Finding How Good Life Can Be,* with Gloria in 1983. It's the story of their lives together during the ups and downs of B.J.'s career.

"I had been through years of drug addiction and alcoholism, and it had a real major effect on my family, on me personally, and on the people that I loved. I did have a spiritual awakening. Most all I knew about a God or anything like that was what I learned in the church as a kid growing up in the South. I had a real spiritual awakening, and I woke up to the fact that there are a lot more important things in life than just feeling good – getting high or having a drink. Since my dad had been an alcoholic, I was kind of raised in that situation and I probably had it in my genes – in my makeup. I got sober at 33, and we wanted to do a gospel album to make a statement on it – not really thinking there would be any long-term effects other than just selling records."

Many successful country and pop artists recorded an occasional gospel song; for instance, Elvis Presley recorded "Crying In The Chapel," "His Hand In Mine," "How Great Thou Art," and "Amazing Grace," among others. American icon Tennessee Ernie Ford recorded "How Great Thou Art," and "The Lord's Lariat," among his 66 singles in 27 years. But at some point, the Christian music world wanted exclusivity, and rejected the crossover between Christian and pop music, and B.J. was caught in the middle.

"It's such a deep involved thing that if you start trying to straighten it out, it becomes worse. When it relates to the gospel music, I'm not speaking from the mountaintop. I'm not correcting anyone, or criticizing anyone. As long as it doesn't come out like that, I'm fine. I think the most important thing is the public perception and what they feel about me.

We're all God's creatures, everyone on this planet. So we believe in a whole different sphere of spirituality. And a lot of people believe that. We're not totally locked into one religious god better than another religious god. We believe in treating other people the way we want them to treat us.

"You know if I had never had a hit record, I would still have a beautiful life. I never would have made it without Gloria, and we have these beautiful children and these grandchildren [Nora Parker has two daughters, Nadia and Keira; and Erin Moore has two children, Ruby Paige, and Billy Joe Thomas]. I'm really proud of the music, but who I am really is just a person. I'm a man who loves his wife, and cherishes his children and grandchildren, and that's just who I am. I didn't realize that until we had that spiritual awakening."

B.J. and Gloria participate in their community in a variety of ways, including benefit concerts for different causes. When we spoke with him in 2014, he said, "The concert I just did with the Triumphs was for a scholarship program for a junior college in Wharton, Texas. We're involved in a little outdoor theater here in Arlington called the Levitt Theater [one of several across the country] that gives free concerts. Gloria was the first to write a song about child abuse, and this was back in the '80s. It's a beautiful song, and we were heavily involved in the prevention of child abuse for years."

B.J.'s friends include Bobby Goldsboro (about whom we wrote in our book *Where Have All the Pop Stars Gone? – Volume 2*). "Bobby Goldsboro and I were together on that first Dick Clark tour, and we worked together many times," B.J. said. They appeared together in the 2010 PBS special *Marvin Hamlisch Presents: The '70s, The Way We Were.*" Other entertainers on the show included Debby Boone, Three Dog Night, Gloria Gaynor, Guy and Ralna, and Peaches and Herb.

B.J. enjoys playing golf in his leisure time. He has a large collection of golf books and golf clubs, and tries to play a couple of times a week. He and Gloria have a chihuahua dog named Sophia, and a Yorkshire terrier named Humperdinck.

If B.J. hadn't succeeded in music, he said he might have become a minister or a blue-collar worker. He recalled, "If I hadn't had the music, I probably would have been a workin' man just like my dad. He was a blue-collar guy who loved to work, and he instilled that in my brother and me. He would take us to work with him. I probably would have had a fairly non-unusual life. When we'd go through these small towns on the road, I'd look at these people and think just how lucky they were to have their community and their job, and that's a good way of life."

In order for B.J. to keep his rich voice and body in shape, he lives a very disciplined life. "I have to be careful about what I eat, how much rest I'm going to get, and how dedicated I am to my family," he said. "When I perform, people want to hear all the hit records and they're going to wonder if I can still do it. So I keep myself in good shape to fulfill their expectations. Also, I want to be healthy and be here a long time to see these grandkids grow up."

Not surprisingly, several of B.J.'s songs have particularly strong personal meaning for him. "I have a lot of emotions and memories tied to a lot of the music, but every time I do 'I'm So Lonesome...' I get a little film that begins in my head about my dad, so that's a very poignant and special song for me. I love to do 'Hooked On A Feeling' and, of course, I've got all those great memories of 'Raindrops.' To me 'Most Of All' is a song about me talking to Gloria.

"I have a new project I'm working on – a full live band recording of some of the R&B classics. I've always been an R&B singer, and I may even do it with the Triumphs, and that would be great," B.J. mused. "I also want to record a lullaby album for my grandkids. I want to do a Spanish language CD. I always have ideas."

Visit http://bjthomas.com/ for touring, recording, merchandise, and additional information.

Three Dog Night, seen in this early 1970s photo, consisted of lead singers (seated, left to right) Danny Hutton, Cory Wells and Chuck Negron, backed by (standing, L-R), bass guitarist Joe Schermie, drummer Floyd Sneed, guitarist Mike Allsup and keyboard player Jimmy Greenspoon (image licensed from Photofest).

CHAPTER
7

Joy to the World

Three Dog Night

The group Three Dog Night had a remarkable knack of turning other people's underappreciated songs into major hits. During a nine-year run beginning with the band's debut in 1969, Three Dog Night attained a seemingly unstoppable run of success, with 21 consecutive top 40 hits – including 18 successive top-20 hits, of which 11 reached *Billboard's* top 10, and three hit No. 1 on *Billboard* (while four went to No. 1 on competitor *Cashbox,* and seven TDN singles reached No. 1 on the *Record World* chart). Among those were seven million-selling singles, nine RIAA-certified gold studio or live albums, and five albums of hit compilations.

Three Dog Night became an important conduit for writers, giving vast exposure to compositions by Harry Nilsson, Laura Nyro, Randy Newman, Paul Williams, Hoyt Axton, Dave Loggins, Leo Sayer, and others. Songwriters knew that when Three Dog Night recorded one of their songs, there was a good chance it would become a hit. That happened three times for Paul Williams, with "Out In The Country," "An Old Fashioned Love Song," and "The Family Of Man." Three Dog Night turned songs that previously languished into anthems that everyone knew. Harry Nilsson first recorded his song "One" in 1967 and Al Kooper recorded it the following year, but it took the Three Dog Night touch to make it a hit in 1969. Laura Nyro recorded her song "Eli's Comin'" in 1968, but Three Dog Night's arrangement sent it into the top 10 in 1969. The band Argent's 1969 single of member Russ Ballard's song "Liar" failed to reach the charts, but Three

Dog Night's vibrant rearrangement of the song hit No. 7 in 1971. Randy Newman had been writing songs professionally since 1962, and performers who recorded his material included Gene Pitney, Dusty Springfield, Jerry Butler, and Irma Thomas – but not one of Newman's tunes had even cracked the top 50 until Three Dog Night's take on "Mama Told Me Not To Come" in 1970 sent that song straight to No. 1 and earned a Recording Industry Association of America (RIAA) gold record. The March 9, 1974, issue of *Billboard* reported that Randy Newman said, "'Mama Told Me' wouldn't have been a hit if they [Three Dog Night] hadn't recorded it; it's that simple. When I heard it was going to be a single, I thought they'd bomb with it. I'm glad I left them alone; what they did for that song is going to put my son through college." And so it went for Three Dog Night, whose durable body of interpretive work is distinguished by glassy harmonies, dynamic vocal solos, and muscular instrumental arrangements.

Three Dog Night was a major concert draw as well. TDN played and filled big arenas and stadiums, including the Atlanta Braves Stadium on July 9, 1971; Three Rivers Stadium in Pittsburgh (performing the first-ever rock concert there, on November 13, 1971); Tampa Stadium on July 1, 1972; the Cotton Bowl in Dallas on August 19, 1972, and the following night at Atlanta Fulton County Stadium (for which Rod Stewart and Faces were the opening act); and Portland Memorial Coliseum in Oregon on April 8, 1974.

Three Dog Night was a seven-man ensemble consisting of three singers – Danny Hutton, Chuck Negron, and Cory Wells, among whom the lead vocalist role rotated – and four musicians: guitarist Mike Allsup, keyboard player Jimmy Greenspoon, bass guitarist Joe Schermie, and drummer Floyd Sneed. Their varied musical backgrounds and interests influenced the divergent repertoire of Three Dog Night, which encompassed high-energy pop and rock, ballads, and shades of blues and country music.

Danny Hutton was born in Ireland and spent his childhood in Boston and his adolescence in Los Angeles. He broke into the music business by first working on the shipping dock for Disney's Buena Vista record label, where he loaded and unloaded boxes of records. With his sights set more on making records than on lifting them, he began writing songs and singing. Under the name Daring Dan Hutton in 1964 he recorded "Home In Pasadena" for ALMO Records. He landed a record deal in early 1965 with Mercury as Basil Swift and the Seegrams, and recorded a Brian Wilson composition called "Farmer's Daughter." Soon after he was hired at Hanna-Barbera Productions, creators of *Huckleberry Hound, The Yogi Bear Show,* and *The Magilla Gorilla Show.* Hutton was appointed to scout for recording artists for Hanna-Barbera's new HBR label, for which he also began recording. His HBR single "Roses And Rainbows," which he co-wrote with Larry Goldberg and recorded as a demo, hit big in Los Angeles, and broke out in other parts of the country as well. On that recording he overdubbed his voice several times to harmonize with himself. By the spring of '66 he had signed with MGM Records, for which he recorded a single, "Funny How Love Can Be," written by John Carter and Ken Lewis of the British band the Ivy League. Although it earned some radio airplay in Southern California, it never reached the *Billboard* Hot 100. While on a concert tour with Sonny and Cher, Danny met Cory Wells, who at that time was the leader of a band called the Enemys [*sic*]. Cory talked to Danny about forming a band, but nothing immediately came of the conversation.

In the spring of '65, Cory Wells and the Enemys had recorded a gentle rocker called "Say Goodbye To Donna" for the independent Valiant label (for which the group the Association initially began recording). The Enemys had gained important recognition as the house band at L.A.'s premier rock club, the Whisky à Go-Go on the Sunset Strip in West Hollywood. Wells was born in Buffalo, New York, where he became a member of a band called the Vibratos. Seeking better opportunities, the band relocated to L.A. and became the Enemys. Their visibility in the L.A. nightclub scene earned them private-party gigs at the homes of Hollywood stars, television appearances for rock band scenes on *The Beverly Hillbillies* and *Burke's Law,* as well as a role in the motion picture *Riot On Sunset Strip.* Seeking a change, Cory moved to Arizona and formed a new band, the Cory Wells Blues Band and performed at Mr. Lucky's in Phoenix, the Red Dog in Scottsdale, and other clubs. That group lasted for only a few months, however. When Cory returned to L.A. in late 1966 he and Danny resumed their discussion about the two of them starting a singing group – specifically, a trio of lead singers.

They began their search for a third singer. Although Danny and Cory could sing in the tenor range, both primarily were baritones. They wanted to find a tenor to complement their vocal ranges. Danny thought of tenor Chuck Negron, whom he had met a couple of months earlier through serendipitous circumstances. Negron's solo Columbia recording contract as "Chuck Rondell" had come to an end, and he was looking for other opportunities when he was invited to a party for Donovan Leitch. At the party, Chuck met a producer named Tim Alvarado – who in turn connected Danny with Chuck. Danny was so impressed with Chuck's singing voice that he enlisted him to sing background on some of his solo tracks. So when Danny and Cory were searching for a third vocalist, Danny contacted

Chuck and asked him to come to his house to discuss an idea. When Chuck arrived at Danny's house, Cory Wells was there. Chuck had seen Cory and the Enemys perform at the Whisky. They started talking about music and taking turns singing tunes. When Chuck's turn came, he wailed a soulful interpretation of the Holland-Dozier-Holland song "You Keep Me Hangin' On." Cory picked up on it, began playing the piano, and sang along with Chuck.

When the song was done, Hutton and Wells excused themselves and walked into another room to talk. When they returned a few minutes later, they asked Chuck if he would like to become the third member of their trio of lead singers. "Oh, *hell* yeah," Chuck replied. "My Columbia days were over, and I couldn't see anything else in my future. So I joined them, and we began rehearsing our asses off," Chuck told us.

But the group they started was not Three Dog Night. David Anderle, who previously had been Danny Hutton's manager, had become the head of the Beach Boys' new Brother Records label, and Danny and Brian Wilson had become pals. Wilson agreed to produce recordings by the three singers, and he named the group Redwood. On October 14, 1967, Hutton, Wells, and Negron headed into a studio and recorded three tracks that Brian Wilson produced. The songs included the Brian Wilson and Mike Love song "Darlin'" and Brian's composition "Time To Get Alone" (both of which the Beach Boys later recorded). The other Beach Boys objected to the Redwood project because it distracted Brian, so Redwood's tracks were not released.

Not fond of the name Redwood, the trio chose the name Three Dog Night, a reference to the Australian aborigine way of sleeping with dogs to stay warm during cold outback nights. Three Dog Night enlisted a management team, Bill Utley and Burt Jacobs, with the talent management firm of Reb Foster and Associates. Jacobs previously had managed the Standells (about whom this book contains a chapter). An audition in April 1968 with Jay Lasker, the president of ABC Dunhill Records, immediately earned the three singers a recording contract with the label. Dunhill, established in 1965, was young and strong, with a catalog that included the Mamas and the Papas, Steppenwolf, the Grass Roots, and Richard Harris. As the singers began rehearsals in a house they rented on Vine Street in Hollywood, they set about assembling a backing band.

To make a seven-man band financially viable, Three Dog Night adopted a dual-tier wage structure. While the business contract entitled the three singers to split the majority of eventual profits, they also were responsible for covering operating expenses, including studio time, management fees, and travel, equipment, road crew and overnight accommodations costs associated with touring; the band members, meanwhile, would receive a smaller share of compensation apiece, but without liability for expenditures. The trio of singers first hired pianist and Hammond organ player Jimmy Greenspoon, a Laurel Canyon neighbor of Hutton's who was well known among L.A. studio musicians. Former Cory Wells Blues Band bass player Joe Schermie (real surname: Schermetzler) and West Coast Pop Art Experimental Band guitarist Ron Morgan (who along with Jimmy Greenspoon had been in a Denver group called Superband) followed.

The new group found an exceptional drummer who was playing at the Red Velvet Club at 6507 Sunset Boulevard in a band called Heat Wave. When Joe Schermie was strolling past the club, what he heard stopped him in his tracks. "Joe asked the guy at the Red Velvet door who those drummers were, and when the doorman told him it was Floyd Sneed with his band, Joe decided to pay the cover charge and come in and check me out," Floyd said. Captivated by the pulsating beat of the band, Schermie was certain he was hearing two drummers playing in tandem. But when he stepped inside he was amazed to see only one drummer on the stage – Floyd Sneed. An electrifying drummer, Sneed had mastered a technique called "ghost beats," subtle licks played between predominant syncopated beats. He also had developed a hybrid style of playing that he calls "L'African" – a fusion of Latin-American and African rhythm patterns. And he sometimes set his sticks down and beat the skins of his drums with his hands in a furious blur, conga-style, that sounded like a wall of percussion.

"After our set Joe and I talked, and he asked if I would be interested in playing in a new band called Three Dog Night," Floyd told us. "I said I was interested, and a few days later Danny and Chuck came down to talk and see me play, and asked me to join the band." To their surprise, Floyd agreed. "To my mind, Floyd took the biggest leap of faith of anyone joining Three Dog Night, because he already had a steady gig – he was in a band," Chuck observed. Meanwhile, Ron Morgan decided against continuing with the new group (he later became a member of the Electric Prunes), and Three Dog Night needed to replace him.

The rehearsal house was next door to the Vine Lodge Hotel. Two years earlier, Joe Schermie had met guitarist Mike Allsup, who had been in a band called the Nomads playing a gig at a club in Phoenix at about the same time that Cory's blues band was gigging there. Back then, Allsup and Schermie had struck up a friendship, and vowed to remain in contact with each other. But two years passed, and they lost contact with each other – until one day in mid-July 1968 when outside the Vine Lodge Hotel,

Schermie unexpectedly ran into Allsup, who was staying there as a member of a Modesto-based band called the Family Scandal. Cory previously knew of Allsup, and after seeing him perform at a club with the Family Scandal, asked him to join Three Dog Night – to which Allsup agreed. The three singers and the four musicians instantly clicked with one another. Each was exceptional in his own right, but together they created a powerful sound.

As they rehearsed, Chuck, Cory, and Danny each brought song ideas to the group. Chuck brought Harry Nilsson's composition "One" to the attention of the group. Nilsson had written it to the cadence of a telephone busy signal, and recorded it in a melancholy key, but Chuck imagined a rocking version in his head. Danny had amassed a collection of song demo tracks from songwriters. Among them was "It's For You," an obscure Lennon and McCartney composition that Cilla Black had recorded without success. Three Dog Night made it sound spectacular. Cory had favorites from the repertoire of the Enemys and his blues band, including the Randy Newman song "No One Ever Hurt So Bad," which Chuck said was the first track that TDN recorded. Chuck introduced the band to the Tim Hardin tune "Don't Make Promises." Jimmy suggested the Band's "Chest Fever" by Robbie Robertson. Mike, Joe, and Floyd also suggested favorites for consideration. From those listening sessions, Three Dog Night began arranging and rearranging songs, testing keys and chords, harmonizing, and compiling their own set list.

ABC Dunhill Records assigned Gabriel Mekler to produce Three Dog Night's eponymous debut album, which the band took only two weeks to record and mix, and which the label released on October 16, 1968. Mekler already had established a reputation as a dynamic rock producer after overseeing production of Steppenwolf's monster debut album, also on ABC Dunhill. Leading off with the song "One," the TDN debut album included "Heaven Is In Your Mind" (by Steve Winwood, Jim Capaldi, and Chris Wood, then with the band Traffic), "Chest Fever," "Don't Make Promises," and "Try A Little Tenderness" (composed by James Campbell, Reginald Connelly, and Harry Woods). Chuck thought that Dunhill should release "One" as the band's first single, but he was outvoted. Cory sang lead on the album track that instead became the group's first single, "Nobody" (written by Dick Cooper, Ernie Shelby, and Beth Beatty). Released in November 1968, the single did well in L.A. but got little radio airplay elsewhere and consequently "bubbled under" but did not reach the *Billboard* Hot 100.

The band immediately hit the road, beginning with a series of performances in Texas with Vanilla Fudge and B.J. Thomas (about whom this book includes a chapter). Back in Los Angeles, TDN performed

December 13 in a concert sponsored by KRLA (where Reb Foster had been a disc jockey), sharing the bill with Steppenwolf and Black Pearl at the Anaheim Convention Center across the parking lot from Disneyland. Thirteen days later they were part of the lineup in the San Francisco Holiday Rock Festival at the Cow Palace. In the closing week of the year, they performed in Albuquerque, Miami, and on New Year's Eve, in Phoenix.

The group did much better with their second single, "Try A Little Tenderness" (which Otis Redding had recorded as the "B" side of his hit "I've Been Loving You Too Long"). TDN's "Try A Little Tenderness," with Cory on lead vocal, made its debut on the *Billboard* chart February 8, 1969, penetrated the top 30, peaking at No. 29 and remaining on the chart for 12 weeks. It reached No. 22 on the *Cashbox* and *Record World* charts. When "Try A Little Tenderness" first appeared on the chart, Three Dog Night was in the midst of an extensive tour that began the first week in February and kept the band on the road through early March. The septet's concert tour began in Montana and took them from there to the Pacific Northwest, Boston, Chicago, Detroit, Cleveland, New York City, and Philadelphia.

Meanwhile, Chuck phoned label president Jay Lasker and told him he was convinced that the band's version of the Harry Nilsson song "One" was destined to become a hit. Lasker agreed to press and release a single regionally, as a test, in the Pacific Northwest. The record broke big time in that region. After "One" (on which Chuck sang lead) made its first appearance on the Hot 100 on May 3, it quickly shot up the chart. "Jay Lasker sent me a telegram saying that I was right," Chuck said. "One" rose to No. 5 on the *Billboard* chart and hit No. 1 with *Record World*, and remained on the Hot 100 for 16 weeks, through most of the summer of '69. The enthusiastic support of Marv Helfer, Dunhill's head of national promotion and sales, contributed substantially to the rise of TDN. The combination of high-profile touring and two hit singles pushed the *Three Dog Night* album (also referred to as *One*) up to No. 11 on the U.S. album chart and to No. 17 in Canada. Three Dog Night had embarked on a hit-making treadmill, on which they would churn out two albums a year and maintain a ferociously demanding touring schedule that would take them well into the '70s.

TDN was on the road again – this time on a European tour – on June 11 when ABC Dunhill released the group's second album, *Suitable For Framing*. Produced by Gabriel Mekler, the 10-track album included three future hit singles: "Easy To Be Hard," "Eli's Coming," and "Celebrate." It also included a song called "Lady Samantha," written by Elton John and Bernie Taupin. Although Elton had recorded it as a single that the Philips label released in the United States in January 1970, it did not reach the charts. The members of Three Dog Night recognized the talents of John and Taupin, and helped elevate awareness of them by including "Lady Samantha" on the *Suitable For Framing* album. On July 23, the Recording Industry Association of America awarded TDN's first gold record, for the single "One" (recognizing sale of 500,000 copies). While "One" was still on the chart, the group's fourth single, "Easy To Be Hard" made its debut for a 13-week run that began August 9. Chuck had introduced that song to the band, and sang lead on TDN's version. Written by Galt MacDermot, James Rado, and Gerome Ragni for the "rock musical" theatrical production *Hair,* "Easy To Be Hard" hit No. 4 on the *Billboard* chart and No. 1 on *Record World* for TDN.

Only four months after the debut of their first hit single, the group made the leap from nightclubs to arenas and pop festivals. The summer of '69 was a whirlwind for the band, which appeared at the Newport '69 Pop Festival in the Los Angeles community of Northridge on June 22, the Denver Pop Festival on June 27, the Pavilion at Flushing Meadow Park in New York on July 25, the Fillmore East on August 1 and 2, the Atlantic City Pop Festival on August 3, and Memorial Auditorium in Dallas on August 19. Their appearance on two days at the Denver Pop Festival included one set preceding the final appearance of the Jimi Hendrix Experience. "When we played the Miami Pop Festival, Canned Heat was huge. They were headlining the first day, and we were supposed to go on right before them," Negron said. "But Canned Heat decided that they wanted our spot, and we went on last, even though we were a band that had only two records out. That was because the word was out: do not go on after these guys. I'm serious. No one could follow us. That's how hot we were, and how good we were."

Amid that series of pop festivals Three Dog Night was booked for a hometown concert with fellow Dunhill recording artists Steppenwolf at L.A.'s Fabulous Forum in Inglewood. Steppenwolf was billed as the headline act on the strength of their hits "Born to Be Wild," "Magic Carpet Ride," and Rock Me," so Three Dog Night preceded them. As Three Dog Night stepped on stage in front of a packed audience of 18,000 fans, Dunhill recording engineers rolled tape under the direction of producer Richard Podolor (who had come up through the ranks as a talented session guitarist). What happened next affirmed that Three Dog Night had ascended to superstardom. "From backstage we heard the audience chanting 'Three Dog Night, Three Dog Night.' We wondered what the fuck's going on? We went on and we did our show, and we tore that place apart," Negron said. A good part of the exhilarated audience apparently had come primarily to see TDN. "When we were finished, a lot of the people in the audience left. And John Kay and Steppenwolf came out to a house that was half empty. We'd never played in the Forum before, and we stole the evening."

ABC Dunhill packaged nine songs recorded that evening under the title *Captured Live At The Forum,* released on October 16, 1969. Most bands wait until they have at least three or four hit albums under their belts before releasing a concert recording, but Three Dog Night already was so hugely popular that sales drove *Captured Live* to No. 6 on *Billboard's* albums chart and No. 4 in Canada. Meanwhile, on August 15, RIAA awarded a gold record (recognizing sales of 500,000 copies) for the band's 1968 debut album *Three Dog Night.* On October 25, the single release of "Eli's Coming" (with lead vocal by Cory) premiered on the Hot 100 chart, then climbed to number 10, and remained on the chart for 14 weeks. The last month of the year brought another honor to Three Dog Night, as RIAA awarded gold album certification on December 12 for their album *Suitable For Framing,* which had been released six months earlier and had hit No. 16 on the *Billboard* pop albums chart and No. 15 in Canada.

Another turn of the calendar page brought another award: an RIAA gold record on January 16, 1970, for *Captured Live At The Forum.* The timeline from release to gold record was only three months. The band's first hit single of 1970 was "Celebrate," written by Alan Gordon and Garry Bonner (who also composed "Happy Together" and other Turtles hits, and Petula Clark's "The Cat In The Window"). Danny sang lead on the first verse of "Celebrate," Chuck on the second, and Cory on the third. After its February 28 debut, it rose to No. 15 and spent nine weeks on the chart. Three Dog Night spent the first part of 1970 at American Recording Company on Ventura Boulevard at Tujunga Boulevard in Studio City, working with the studio owners – producer Richard Podolor and recording engineer Bill Cooper. There, Three Dog Night created their fourth album, *It Ain't Easy,* as well as a half dozen albums to follow.

In the midst of rehearsing, recording, and touring, the band members also sequestered themselves in the studio for marathon listening sessions, in which they sought new songs to record by listening to hundreds of demo recordings by songwriters or in some cases with composers performing songs live for them. "When we searched for songs, we went for songs by songwriters who were unknown at the time," keyboard player Jimmy Greenspoon said in an interview. The demos typically were spartan, presenting the bare elements of songs with minimal instrumental accompaniment. "If we thought a song had potential, the whole band

307

would arrange everything. The vocalists arranged the vocal parts, and the instrumentalists arranged the instrumental parts. And more often than not they'd say to me, 'now we need some kind of a hook for it. We're going to dinner. Could you stay in the studio and come up with something for it?' Okay, done."

Chuck Negron emphasizes that the band members pictured on the album covers are the musicians who performed on the recordings. "We never used studio musicians. We were the real deal. We had four musicians, three singers, and we did it all. We brought in the material, we arranged the material, we recorded the songs the way we played them live. Our first album is totally live, in the studio. We did it in two weeks," Negron said. "As things went on, and because of time demands and fatigue, we had to delegate times when the band would come in and record, then the singers would come in and sing when the band rested. We wanted the music to be sonically better, and you can't do that recording in the same room together. You have to separate the instruments from the voice so there's no leakage across tracks on the master tape."

Released on March 31, 1970, the 11-track *It Ain't Easy* album included the title track, along with Roger Nichols and Paul Williams' "Out In The Country," in which the group harmonized a beckoning call to escape from polluted cities and take refuge in rural areas. The melodic opening bars of "Out In The Country," which classically trained pianist Jimmy Greenspoon composed, epitomized the instrumental introductions that made many Three Dog Night hits instantaneously recognizable and distinctive. The process of crafting intros was spontaneous, inspired by the body of the song. "Within 10 or 15 minutes, if I didn't have something, it wasn't going to happen," Greenspoon said in an interview. "I would sit down at the piano, and I knew the structure of the song. I would start playing something, and the producer or engineer would go, 'Wow, that was great. *That's* the intro.'" The *It Ain't Easy* album premiered Elton John and Bernie Taupin's "Your Song," six months before Elton's recording was released as a single in the United States.

It Ain't Easy also included Randy Newman's disquieting warning about debauchery, "Mama Told Me (Not To Come)" – on which Cory sang lead. Issued as the band's next single, "Mama Told Me (Not To Come)" became Three Dog Night's first No. 1 *Billboard* hit. After making its *Billboard* chart debut on May 23, it perched at No. 1 on the Hot 100 for two weeks beginning July 11; it also hit No. 1 on the *Cashbox* and *Record World* charts. It remained on the *Billboard* chart 15 weeks, all the way through to the first week of September. "Mama Told Me" was only halfway through its run on the chart when RIAA presented Three Dog Night with double honors on July 14 – gold records not only for the *It Ain't Easy* album (which hit No. 8 on the U.S. album chart and No. 5 in Canada), but also for the single "Mama Told Me (Not To Come)." Released as a single, "Out In The Country" premiered August 29 on the *Billboard* Hot 100 and remained on the chart for 11 weeks, during which time it peaked at No. 15. It also became the first of nine TDN songs to rank on *Billboard's* "Adult Contemporary" (AC) chart, on which it reached No. 11.

ABC Dunhill released the band's fifth album, *Naturally*, in November 1970. Produced by Richard Podolor, the album included Three Dog Night's superbly strident rendition of Argent's song "Liar" (with Danny singing lead), "One Man Band" (with lead verses by Danny and Chuck), and the song for which they became best known: a smash hit that made a household name of a character that singer-songwriter Hoyt Axton had conceived for a children's show. The first single that ABC Dunhill culled from the album was "One Man Band," written by Thomas Kay, January Tyme, and Billy Fox. After its November 21 chart debut, "One Man Band" became TDN's seventh top-20 hit, peaking at No. 19 and remaining on the Hot 100 for 11 weeks. *Naturally* became TDN's fourth consecutive top-20 album, rising to 14 in the United States and No. 19 in Canada.

Hoyt Axton had written a tune he titled "The Happy Song" for a TV special that he conceived. When Chuck heard Hoyt's demo he gave it a "thumbs up," but the other TDN members were divided about whether it was suitable for their ordinarily soulful pop repertoire. "I thought it was wonderful," Chuck said. As the band began recording *Naturally* and improvising arrangements, they turned Axton's children's song into a buoyant, energetic rocker on which Chuck sang lead and captured the imagination of fans, from young children to older adults. With Axton's permission, they retitled the song that introduced the world to the fictional bullfrog, Jeremiah, with an uplifting message: "Joy To The World." After hopping onto the chart on March 13, 1971, the ballad of Jeremiah completed the leap to No. 1 only six weeks later, on April 17 – and there it sat, at the top of the chart, for six consecutive weeks; it duplicated that feat on the *Cashbox* chart, and also was No. 1 on *Record World* for good measure. To put that accomplishment in perspective, consider that Marty Robbins' legendary 1960 smash "El Paso" was No. 1 for only two weeks on the *Billboard* chart; the Rolling Stones' "(I Can't Get No) Satisfaction" was No. 1 for four weeks in 1965; the Doors' "Light My Fire" was at the No. 1 spot for three weeks in 1967; and Simon and Garfunkel's "Mrs. Robinson" held onto No. 1 for three weeks in 1968. "Joy To The World" was in rare company among the few songs that had remained No. 1 for six weeks or longer.

"Joy To The World" turned gold even before it had hit No. 1; RIAA recognized it with a gold record on April 9, and at the same presentation awarded gold for the album *Naturally* for good measure. Three days later, RIAA awarded a gold album for the first Three Dog Night hits compilation, *Golden Bisquits*, which Dunhill had released the previous February. The album included prior single releases "One," "Easy To Be Hard," "Mama Told Me (Not To Come)," "Eli's Coming," "Celebrate," "One Man Band," "Out In The Country," "Nobody," and "Try A Little Tenderness," along with TDN's renditions of Tim Hardin's "Don't Make Promises" and Elton John and Bernie Taupin's "Your Song." Meanwhile, "Joy To The World" remained on the chart for 17 weeks, into mid-July. The Russ Ballard song "Liar," the next TDN single, made its chart debut on July 10, and over the course of its 12-week run on the chart peaked at No. 7.

Three Dog Night delivered pure adrenaline to the throngs of frenzied fans who mobbed their concerts. Floyd Sneed, who once had been accustomed to playing in nightclubs, thrived on massive audiences. "That made me show off more. I had to make a lot of moves for those people in the back to see me. So I accentuated my moves," said Sneed, whose distinctive clear acrylic double bass Zickos drum set trimmed with rhinestones made his appearance all the more striking. In the September 2, 1971, issue of *Rolling Stone* magazine, writer Grover Lewis vividly described the scene at TDN's July '71 Cotton Bowl concert: "From the vast stadium's hotly lit 50-yard line, it's plain to see that all seven of the Dogs take relish in their work. Singer Chuck Negron draws oceanic applause merely by his presence on stage; the day before, he'd broken his nose and wrist in a traffic smashup, but tonight he belts out his golden share of bisquits in a clear, ringing voice, and his foot never stops tapping. Singer Danny Hutton imps about among the massive amps that tower above the bandstand, yowling gleefully and pouring beer on whosever head is closest at hand. The third singer, Cory Wells, executes a wicked bump-and-grind, triggering mass orgasms among the moon-faced teenyboppers who keep crossing and re-crossing their legs in the front rows. Guitarist Mike Allsup and bassist Joe Schermie (the latter being the only Dog with a bleeding ulcer) trade heated acoustic fours, and as a coda, blow dainty kisses at the shrieking girls. Jim Greenspoon further schlocks it to the many mini-ladies on, ahem, organ, and drummer Floyd Sneed (the only black Dog) hurtles into his frantic tom-tom routine, letting his sticks arc and flash off into the audience and continuing to flail savagely at his traps with hands taped like a boxer's."

ABC Dunhill released TDN's second album of 1971, *Harmony,* in September of that year. It spawned three hit singles: TDN's rendition of Paul Williams' "An Old Fashioned Love Song," the Hoyt Axton tune "Never Been To Spain," and "The Family Of Man," written by Paul Williams and Jack Conrad. *Harmony* hit No. 8 on the *Billboard* album chart and No. 11 in Canada, and the Recording Industry Association of America awarded a gold record for it on October 13, 1971. ABC Dunhill issued "An Old Fashioned Love Song" with Chuck singing lead as the band's next single, and it premiered on the chart November 13. It turned into yet another smash that peaked at No. 4 and remained on the chart for 11 weeks. It also became the first of two Three Dog Night songs to hit No. 1 on the AC chart. As the year rolled to a close, all three major record industry trade magazines – *Billboard, Cashbox,* and *Record World* – named "Joy To The World" the single of the year, and all three honored Three Dog Night as vocal group of the year. On December 25, TDN's "Never Been To Spain" made its debut on the chart, with Cory singing lead. That began a 12-week run during which it would rise to the No. 5 position. And RIAA awarded a gold record on December 29 for the single "An Old Fashioned Love Song."

Three Dog Night fans who hadn't partied too hard and late on New Year's Eve 1971 may have awakened in time to see all seven members of the band riding the parade route aboard the FTD floral float. From that nationally televised platform, the band performed its then-new single, "Never Been To Spain." On March 25, 1972, just as "Spain" dropped off the chart, Dunhill's impeccably timed release of "The Family Of Man," on which Danny, Chuck, and Cory sang the successive verses, premiered. It rose to No. 12 and remained on the chart for nine weeks.

The band's penchant for giving exposure to composers was not limited to professional singer-songwriters. TDN's *Seven Separate Fools* album, which the band had begun recording in late 1971, was distinctly packaged with seven elaborately designed, oversized playing cards – one for each member of the band. Released in March 1972, *Seven Separate Fools* included "Black And White," composed by David Arkin and Earl Robinson; "Pieces Of April," which Dave Loggins wrote; and the song "Midnight Runaway," written by Gary Itri, a bass player who worked as a custodian at the studio where the album was recorded. It was yet another hit album for the band, peaking at No. 6 in the U.S. and No. 7 in Canada. RIAA awarded a gold record for *Seven Separate Fools* on July 28, 1972. The single "Black And White," with Danny singing lead, premiered on August 12. Five weeks later, it became the band's third No. 1 hit on the *Billboard* and *Cashbox* charts, its second No. 1 *Billboard* adult contemporary hit, and its fifth No. 1 pop hit in *Record World*. It rested atop the Hot 100 the week of September 16, and remained on the chart for 11 weeks. RIAA recognized "Black And White" with a gold record on October 2.

In the summer of '72 Three Dog Night had embarked on an ambitious 32-city tour. Their equipment included not only instruments, amplifiers, microphones, and mixing boards, but also a large video backdrop on which their live images were projected during their performances – an innovation at the time to enable people in 40,000-seat stadiums to see the band members clearly. To ease logistics, the band chartered a 10-seat private jet aircraft. The group was pictured on the cover of *Rolling Stone* magazine's September 14, 1972, edition, which declared, "More gold than the Stones! Bigger crowds than Creedence! Fatter purses than Elvis! Three Dog Night: See How they Run!"

TDN played a series of gigs in New Zealand, Australia, Japan, and Hong Kong in November and December 1972. With Chuck alone singing, "Pieces Of April," Three Dog Night's 15th chart single, premiered November 18. That song peaked at No. 19 and remained on the chart for 14 weeks, through the end of February 1973. Three Dog Night had helped ring in 1973 by starring in Dick Clark's very first *New Years Rockin' Eve* telecast on NBC. It seemed at the time that Three Dog Night could do nothing wrong. Unfortunately, that was not the case. The first personnel change occurred at the close of 1972, when bass player Joe Schermie left the band, and was replaced by Jack Ryland. "Nine years on the road with 200 one-nighters a year. You get married, buy a house, want to raise a family – and you never get to," Schermie explained during a year 2000 appearance on Tom Riehl's TV program *Food Rules* on which Floyd Sneed demonstrated his cooking technique. Floyd explained to us that another dynamic also was responsible. "Joe and Cory had gotten into a few disagreements because the same woman liked both of them," Floyd explained. "The singers always figure they'll get the girls, but she liked Joe more than she liked Cory. And so that started and it never went away." A seasoned musician, Jack Ryland had worked with Carla Thomas and with Lou Rawls, and was in the band backing Mac Davis and Helen Reddy on tours of theirs.

Three Dog Night, which continued aggressively touring, playing dates nonstop, back-to-back, finally earned some slack in the two-albums-per-year recording regimen they had maintained since 1969. ABC Dunhill released a second live album, *Around The World With Three Dog Night*, in February 1973. The double album's 17 tracks were recorded in Europe and Japan during the band's tours to promote *Seven Separate Fools*. The *Around The World* album, like the prior *Captured Live At The Forum*, was produced by Richard Podolor working with recording engineer Bill Cooper, but *Around The World* duplicated only one song that also appeared on *Captured Live* – "Eli's Coming." It also spotlighted Floyd Sneed in a track called "Drum Solo," and closed with an uncharacteristic 7-minute "Jam" by the band. By March 6, RIAA had awarded a gold record for *Around The World.* TDN's first chart single of 1973 was "Shambala." With Cory singing lead, "Shambala" premiered May 19 and peaked at No. 3 on the *Billboard* chart while hitting No. 1 in *Cashbox* and *Record World,* selling enough during its 16 weeks on the chart to qualify for an RIAA gold record on July 24.

TDN had been maintaining a punishing schedule for five years – rehearsing, recording, touring to promote album releases, appearing on television programs, finding time for interviews with print journalists and disc jockeys, and sifting through piles of song audition tapes. The pressures were unrelenting, not only from their label and concert promoters, but also internal. Drugs served not only as a pressure release valve, but also contributed to further problems, as Chuck Negron explains.

"Drug abuse will decidedly cause tension in marriage, business, anything. And in Three Dog Night, six guys were doing drugs – which

Early 1970s PR photo of Three Dog Night. Front center, Danny Hutton, right Chuck Negron. Behind them, from left, Jimmy Greenspoon, Cory Wells, Mike Allsup, Floyd Sneed, and Joe Schermie.

made the one guy who wasn't using drugs feel awkward and square. So you had that equation," said Negron, who nearly died from the addiction that he finally conquered after a protracted struggle. "Then you had the equation that the movie *Almost Famous* showed about tension forming in a band after the guitar player starts to get a lot of reaction from women in the audience. The lead singer confronts him and says, 'wait a second. You're supposed to be the moody, introspective guitar player, and I was supposed to be the sexual focal point – but you're not playing your role.' That happens in bands. In the beginning members may think, well, 'I'm gonna be this, he'll be that,' and when it doesn't turn out that way, they're not very happy. But you don't know who the audience is going to fall in love with. You do not know. And you can't hate that guy for that happening. And when that happens, it's very stressful for bands. That's why so many people leave bands and make solo records. There are many reasons for trouble in bands. Those are two of them – drugs and the misplaced egos of band members."

Despite increasingly troubling fissures, Three Dog Night continued turning out hits and selling out arenas packed with ardent fans. While retaining Jimmy Greenspoon, the band in the autumn of 1973 added a second keyboard player, former Blues Image member Frank "Skip" Konte. TDN's next studio album, *Cyan,* was not released until October 1973 – a year and a half after *Seven Separate Fools* had been pressed. *Cyan* constituted a departure from prior TDN albums in that it contained three songs by one of the band members: Mike Allsup's compositions "Happy Song," "Storybook Feeling," and "Into My Life." Although *Cyan* contained only two singles, both reached the top 20, and one was an outright smash. First out of the gate the previous May was TDN's rendition of Daniel Moore's "Shambala," one of the band's grittiest, most instrumentally and vocally powerful songs. (Moore co-wrote B.W. Stevenson's "My Maria" and wrote Joe Cocker's "Put Out The Light.")

On October 12, RIAA awarded a gold record for the *Cyan* album, which reached No. 26 on the U.S. album chart, while peaking at No. 8 in Canada. Another track from that album, the band's rendition of "Let Me Serenade You" written by John Finley (of the band Rhinoceros) was released as a single and made its chart debut on October 27. The song rose to No. 17 and remained on the chart for 12 weeks, into mid-January 1974.

For their eighth studio album, titled *Hard Labor,* Three Dog Night switched to a different recording studio, the Record Plant in Sausalito, north of San Francisco, and turned to a new producer, Jimmy Ienner. *Hard Labor* initially hit record stores in March 1974 with a bizarre graphic metaphorical representation of the work involved in creating an album.

The cover depicted a half-human, half reptilian monster giving birth in a maternity ward to a vinyl LP. Like the Beatles' initial release of *Yesterday And Today* (which depicted a mock bloody "butcher" scene with decapitated dolls), TDN's *Hard Labor* provoked controversy and Dunhill relented, using a large band-aid image to cover the album emerging from the birth canal. The 11-song album included three tunes that ultimately would become top-40 hits: John Hiatt's composition "Sure As I'm Sittin' Here"; "Play Something Sweet (Brickyard Blues)" by Allen Toussaint (who wrote "Pain In My Heart" and "Fortune Teller," both of which the Rolling Stones recorded); and Leo Sayer and David Courtney's composition "The Show Must Go On," a song about living with the consequences of poor personal decisions. The closing line was "I won't let the show go on" in the written lyrics, but Negron objected to that conclusion. "When Jimmy Ienner brought that song to me, I said it can't end that way because that's not what Three Dog Night was about," Chuck said. "So instead, I sang that the show must go on."

With Chuck singing lead, "The Show Must Go On," TDN's final top-10 hit, premiered on the *Billboard* Hot 100 on March 16. It peaked at No. 4 on the *Billboard* Hot 100 (pushing all the way to No. 1 on the *Cashbox* and *Record World* charts), and remained on the chart for 19 weeks. With the controversy blunted, *Hard Labor* rose to No. 20 in the United States and No. 16 in Canada. RIAA presented Three Dog Night with a gold record for *Hard Labor* on April 17, as well as another gold disc on May 14 for "The Show Must Go On." The next single culled from *Hard Labor* was "Sure As I'm Sittin' Here," on which Cory sang lead. After its June 29 chart debut, it rose to No. 16 and remained on the chart all summer long, for a total of 13 weeks. "Play Something Sweet (Brickyard Blues)," with Cory singing lead, became TDN's 20th chart single when it premiered September 28. It reached No. 33 and remained on the chart for 12 weeks.

The year 1974 brought more big changes. As much as Mike Allsup admired the musical artistry of Jack Ryland, he missed Joe Schermie's contributions to the sound of the band. He also was aware of a decline in creative collaboration among the band members in working out song arrangements. By his account, all of the band members except Wells and Konte had become involved with cocaine. Wariness had begun eroding mutual trust, and the musicians had been pushing for equity with the singers' share of earnings. Weariness also was taking a toll; the demands of years of continual touring was sapping their enthusiasm. The band had shifted to Caribou Management, working with the team of James Guercio (producer for the band Chicago), Larry Fitzgerald, and Howard Kaufman.

315

Guercio owned Caribou Ranch, 3,000-acre spread in Nederland, Colorado, that included a state-of-the-art recording studio. There in 1974 the band recorded *Coming Down Your Way*, their ninth studio album. Mike Allsup thought a few of the songs on the album were worthwhile, but characterized it as disjointed, the result of the band being unprepared. Produced by Jimmy Ienner with associate producer Bob Monaco, *Coming Down Your Way* ironically opened with Dave Loggins' song "Til The World Ends," on which Chuck sang lead. Also telling was another of the album's 10 tracks – a Jeff Barry song called "When It's Over."

Three Dog Night sustained a double blow in late 1974 with the departure not only of Mike Allsup but also drummer extraordinaire Floyd Sneed. "Joe Schermie and I did the groove together," said Sneed, observing that the bass player and the drummer together set the rhythm of a band. He metaphorically characterized himself as the engine of the band, and Joe as the transmission. "As far as I'm concerned, things started falling apart when Joe left Three Dog Night. He and I had a lock, and when he was replaced, I had lost that thing." Sneed and Allsup reunited with Joe Schermie in 1975 in a new six-man band, S.S. Fools (a reference to the Three Dog Night album *Seven Separate Fools*). The band also included guitarist Stan Seymore, keyboard player Wayne Devillier, and lead singer and keyboard player Bobby Kimball (who later became lead singer of the band Toto). Unfortunately, S.S. Fools didn't stay afloat for long. Despite recording one fine soulful album for Columbia (produced by Richard Podolor) and doing a few live gigs, S.S. Fools broke up.

In November 1974, ABC Dunhill released another Three Dog Night compilation album, *Joy To The World: Their Greatest Hits*. The 14-song album included hit tunes from *Naturally, Harmony, Seven Separate Fools,* and *Cyan*, as well as the band's debut album. *Joy To The World: Their Greatest Hits,* which went to No. 18 on *Billboard's* album chart and to No. 21 in Canada, earned an RIAA gold record on January 14, 1975.

TDN replaced Floyd Sneed with Michael "Mickey" McMeel, and hired James "Smitty" Smith in place of guitarist Mike Allsup. Those changes had occurred before ABC Records released *Coming Down Your Way* in May 1975. *Coming Down Your Way* reached only No. 70 on the American chart and No. 27 in Canada. Released as a single, "Til The World Ends" became the band's last single on the Hot 100. It premiered on July 5, 1975, rose as high as No. 32, and remained on the chart for nine weeks, until the first week of September. Before the year ended, bass player Jack Ryland bowed out (replaced by Dennis Belfield, formerly of the group Rufus), and guitarist Smitty Smith departed (replaced by Al Ciner of Rufus and, previously, the

American Breed).

By the time ABC released the band's next album, *American Pastime*, in March 1976, TDN had become Two Dog Night. The disco-flavored album, produced by Bob Monaco, credited Chuck and Cory, but not Danny, who by then was unable to tour or record. "We had no business making another record at that point. Coming on the heels of replacing a whole band, then losing a lead singer, we were creatively decimated, and we needed time to regroup," Chuck told us. "But we had a contract deal that earned us a bonus each time we completed a record, and management people pressured us because they wanted their cut. But that record didn't have a chance because we didn't have time to do it right." The nine-cut album yielded no chart singles, and the album itself went no higher than No. 123 on the U.S. album chart. Negron and Wells recruited singer-songwriter-producer Jay Gruska to fill in as the third voice for concert touring. When Skip Konte left, keyboard player Ron Stockert joined briefly, but the end was near. The lights went out for Three Dog Night as the group disbanded in the summer of 1976.

Cory decided to go solo, and recorded a couple of albums, including one called *Touch Me*, for A&M Records. Danny focused on talent management and recording production. Gabriel Mekler, TDN's initial producer who helped craft the quintessential biker song, Steppenwolf's "Born To Be Wild," ironically was killed at age 35 in a motorcycle crash in September 1977. In late 1980, Three Dog Night regrouped, with Negron as an unwilling participant because it would have required immediately going on the road – which was inadvisable for Chuck due to his fragile condition. Jay Lasker, who by then was president of Motown, wanted to sign the band. "I was brought back in the band even though I was very sick. I was in the hospital with hepatitis C and had just come out of quarantine and weighed only 135 pounds," Chuck said. "My father took me out of the hospital and drove me to a meeting with Jay and the other band members, who told me that if I was caught with drugs I'd be fired. I didn't want to sign that contact, but I didn't have the courage to tell my father that I was a heroin addict. So I signed it. I was a shell of myself, a very meek, frightened man. Jay Lasker gave me hug, but the band did not want to sign with Motown or with other labels that were interested. The band members didn't want to find themselves in the position of being dependent on me. They wanted to get rid of me. They signed me so I would fail."

The trio of singers regrouped with Greenspoon, Allsup, and Sneed, taking on a new bass player, Mike Seifrit (in place of Joe Schermie). "I got pneumonia, and over a period of months I had to go to ERs on the road, to be hydrated and given antibiotics so I could keep going," Chuck said. In 1982 Three Dog Night resumed recording at American Recording Company with Richard Podolor as producer. They finally signed with an independent label called Passport Records, which in 1983 released a five-song EP (extended-play) record called *It's A Jungle*. By then bass player Richard Grossman had replaced Seifrit in the band. TDN accommodated Mike Allsup's shared child custody arrangement by allowing him to tour for two weeks, then spend the following two weeks home with his son, Jesse. Guitarist Paul Kingery, Richard Grossman's roommate, and sometimes Steve Ezzo, filled in during Mike's furlough weeks. But Mike left at the close of 1984 as a result of a dispute with the group, and Sneed also departed. As Chuck became increasingly ill and weak following round after round of medically supervised detoxification, he checked himself into rehab, at which point the band fired him and went on without him beginning in December 1985. "I left the band to save my life by entering rehab," Chuck said. At that juncture only Hutton, Wells, and Greenspoon remained in TDN, of the original seven. Allsup rejoined Three Dog Night in 1991, which then consisted of Danny, Cory, Jimmy, bass guitarist Richard Campbell, and drummer Mike Keeley. The band underwent numerous personnel changes during the ensuing years. In 2000 Three Dog Night began performing on stage with symphony orchestras. One of those performances was captured on video and released in May 2002 as a DVD titled *Three Dog Night Live In Concert With The Tennessee Symphony Orchestra*. Another release was a CD titled *Three Dog Night With The London Symphony Orchestra*.

Ron Morgan, who had played guitar with the early incarnation of Three Dog Night (before joining the Electric Prunes) died at age 44 in 1989. Depression overcame latter-years TDN bass player Jack Ryland, who died in 1996 at age 45. Original TDN bass player Joe Schermie died of a heart attack at age 56 on March 25, 2002.

Since the 1980s, the MCA, Geffen, and Compendia labels have issued a variety of Three Dog Night compilation albums. Two releases – *The Best Of Three Dog Night* (MCA Records, 1982) and *20th Century Masters – The Millennium Collection: The Best Of Three Dog Night* (Geffen, 1999) – earned RIAA gold album awards. But over the years, the band's recordings have continued selling – sufficiently that on August 5, 2008, sales of the initial *Three Dog Night* album boosted it to RIAA platinum status (for attaining audited sales of 1 million copies). Similarly, Geffen's *20th Century Masters* compilation of Three Dog Night hits went platinum on May 10, 2012.

Keyboard player Jimmy Greenspoon had continued performing with Three Dog Night into the second decade of the new millennium, but after feeling ill in October 2014 he was diagnosed with metastatic melanoma that had spread to his liver, a lung, and his brain. Despite surgical treatment, he succumbed to the disease at age 67 on March 11, 2015, at his home in North Potomac, Maryland.

Singer Cory Wells had gone to a doctor in September 2015 complaining of severe back pain, but he was diagnosed with multiple myeloma. He was undergoing radiation therapy near his home in western New York state when he apparently contracted an infection that he was unable to fight off. Family members told the *Buffalo News* that Wells' death on October 20, 2015, was due to septic shock resulting from the infection. He was 74 years old. He and his wife, Mary, had remained married for 51 years. They had two daughters, Coryann and Dawn, and five grandchildren.

Until September, Wells had been touring with Hutton in Three Dog Night performances. TDN (www.threedognight.com) continues to tour with a lineup consisting of singers Danny Hutton and David Morgan (who replaced Cory Wells), guitarist Mike Allsup, bass player and vocalist Paul Kingery, keyboard player Eddie Reasoner, and drummer Pat Bautz.

Chuck Negron, who in 1991 finally summoned the gritty determination enabling him to break free of the stranglehold of abuse, has been drug-free since then. He now tours with his own group, often joined by original TDN drummer Floyd Sneed.

THREE DOG NIGHT'S U.S. SINGLES ON THE *BILLBOARD* HOT 100 CHART

Debut	Peak	Gold	Title	Label
2/8/69	29		Try A Little Tenderness	ABC Dunhill
5/3/69	5	▲	One	ABC Dunhill
8/9/69	4		Easy To Be Hard	ABC Dunhill
10/25/69	10		Eli's Coming	ABC Dunhill
2/28/70	15		Celebrate	ABC Dunhill
5/23/70	1	▲	Mama Told Me (Not To Come)	ABC Dunhill
8/29/70	15		Out In The Country	ABC Dunhill
11/21/70	19		One Man Band	ABC Dunhill
3/13/71	1	▲	Joy To The World	ABC Dunhill
7/10/71	7		Liar	ABC Dunhill
11/13/71	4	▲	An Old Fashioned Love Song	ABC Dunhill
12/25/71	5		Never Been To Spain	ABC Dunhill
3/25/72	12		The Family Of Man	ABC Dunhill
8/12/72	1	▲	Black And White	ABC Dunhill

Three Dog Night Hot 100 U.S. Singles (continued)

Debut	Peak	Gold	Title	Label
11/18/72	19		Pieces Of April	ABC Dunhill
5/19/73	3	▲	Shambala	ABC Dunhill
10/27/73	17		Let Me Serenade You	ABC Dunhill
3/16/74	4	▲	The Show Must Go On	ABC Dunhill
6/29/74	16		Sure As I'm Sittin' Here	ABC Dunhill
9/28/74	33		Play Something Sweet (Brickyard Blues)	ABC Dunhill
7/5/75	32		Til The World Ends	ABC Records

▲ symbol: RIAA certified gold record (Recording Industry Association of America)

Billboard's pop singles chart data is courtesy of Joel Whitburn's Record Research Inc. (www.recordresearch.com), Menomonee Falls, Wisconsin.

Epilogue: Chuck Negron

Singer

As a college junior in the autumn of 1964, Chuck Rondell was confronted with a life-changing decision. Producers for Columbia Records, with which he was signed as a recording artist, were becoming annoyed that his time availabilities to rehearse and record were influenced by his commitments at college. Columbia execs told him, "We're the biggest record company in the world, people are dying to get a deal with us, and you can't show up sometimes." When Chuck explained "I have basketball games," they incredulously replied, "*What?* You need to do this 100 percent." Meanwhile, Denny Fitzpatrick, Chuck's basketball coach at Hancock College in Santa Maria, California, was perturbed that he was dividing his attention between hoops and singing in nightclubs. "I got benched for doing shows on the weekend. The funny thing was the whole team would come to see me perform music. But the coach didn't want me singing," Chuck said. He figured out that collegiate athletes reach the upper echelon of success by making their sport their job, their singular focus. "I realized that I didn't

The joy of singing for live audiences energizes Chuck these days (photo courtesy of Chuck Negron).

have the commitment I thought I did to basketball. I just loved to play." But he loved singing even more. Forced to decide between the two, he chose music. "At any rate, it all worked out fine."

Chuck Rondell was the stage name that Chuck Negron adopted when he signed with Columbia Records in 1964. His decision to abandon basketball was particularly difficult because only four years earlier, he had viewed basketball as his ticket to a college education by means of an athletic scholarship. He was born Charles William Negron in Manhattan, New York, on June 8, 1942, six months after the United States entered World War II. His father, also named Charles but with a different middle name, was American-born of Puerto Rican descent. His mother, Elizabeth, was British. Chuck and his twin sister, Nancy, and their parents lived at 1051 Sherman Avenue at E. 165th Street in the Bronx, three blocks east of the Grand Concourse. "My father as a very young man went into World War II, and when he came out he worked in the subways giving change, as his mother did. My mother worked at Macy's department store as a colorist, which was very popular back then. People had black and white photos taken of themselves, and then she painted them in color for an extra fee," Chuck explained. Chuck pronounces his surname NEG-ron, as his father did. "But my other Latin relatives pronounced it neh-GROWN," he said, with a trilled "r."

When Chuck was 4 years old, the divorce of his parents radically changed his world. His father moved to the Los Angeles suburb of Montebello, and most of his Latin relatives also moved to Southern California. During the course of the next dozen years, Chuck and Nancy saw their father only two or three times, when they visited him in California during summer vacations. Elizabeth worked very hard to provide for the twins, and then in 1950 consigned Chuck and Nancy to an orphanage when they were 8 years old. "My sister was told that we were going, and that my mother was going to take us back when we got a little older. I was not told anything. So when we left, I really didn't know what was going on," Chuck said. The children who were housed there had previously been neglected or abused; some were war orphans from Europe. "We came to this place and when I saw what was going on, it was devastating, not only because I was there, but because they took my sister to the girls' part, and I was completely alone. And it was terrible. It was terrifying for me. I thought I was being given away and it really changed how I looked at everything for the rest of my life, actually. It made me resolve that I didn't ever want to be in the position where someone could do that to me again, get rid of me," Chuck told us.

The orphanage, on Woodycrest Avenue just west of Yankee Stadium, was less than a mile from Elizabeth's apartment – but it felt to Chuck like it was hundreds of miles from home. "Actually it was a good place, but it wasn't for me because I just didn't want to be there. The woman that took care of us was wonderful, but I used to wet my bed because I was nervous and scared. She was very kind to me. I had to put the sheets in a bucket and then walk downstairs with it – the walk of shame. Everyone knew what was in the bucket. But that didn't bother me so much because the caretaker was so kind to me. Then she got sick and passed away."

Her replacement was cruel. "When I wet my bed, the new person was appalled by it and he put a sign on me that said 'I wet my bed' and he dragged me through the girls' dorm and then actually sent me to school with the sign on me. It was terrible, so I ran away. I didn't know where I was, so finally late at night, in freezing weather, I came back because I was hungry and I was cold." The orphanage had alerted Chuck's mother about his disappearance, and she was there when he returned.

"My mother was really angry at what they had done with me, but she was not willing to take me home. She said, 'no, you need to stay there.' I just couldn't understand it – despite what they had done to me, my mother was going to put me back in there." Young Chuck, who 20 years later would sing about "joy to the world," was living a dreary existence. To his horror, conditions inside the orphanage became even more grim. "The next caretaker they hired was a pedophile. I was a little young for him, but he was getting the kids who were about 10 years old. I was very aware of what was going on, and I turned him in. I don't know where that came from in me, but if I saw someone bullying someone else, I'd tell them to stop, and then they'd want to fight me because I was so skinny and little."

Administrators at the orphanage did not believe what Chuck had told them, and summoned his mother. "She raised her hand to hit me and almost slapped my face, because what I had described was so disgusting to her." Then she left again. Late one night, though, long after "lights out," a worker awakened Chuck and took him to an office downstairs. "My mother was there, and a guy said to me, 'tell me what you've seen.' I don't know if someone else complained about the pedophile, or they reconsidered what I had said earlier. So I told them again what was going on, and in a couple of weeks, the pedophile was gone." Chuck was returned to his ward, but he encountered troubles of a different kind. "They boys he was fooling with threatened me, then beat me, so it was a pretty tough place for me to be." Chuck persevered, though, and survived three years in that hellhole.

Finally, when Chuck and Nancy were 11, their mother withdrew them from the orphanage and brought them back to live in her apartment with her. It wasn't much of an improvement.

"My mom had two or sometimes three jobs and she worked all day and at night also, so my sister and I didn't see much of her. Sometimes she would come home at 6, and we'd have dinner together, but that was rare," Chuck said. "Usually my sister and I had to take care of ourselves, and put ourselves to bed. We didn't have anything. We didn't have a phone 'til I was 11. We didn't have a TV 'til I was 14. I didn't have a radio or a record player." Friends of his did, though, and through them he started becoming interested in music on the radio. One of those friends was Bobby Vittori, a classmate of his at Taft High School at 172nd Street and Sheridan Avenue. "I didn't sing until Bobby started playing his records for me, and he and I would sing along. I didn't think anything about my voice, but he was hearing me, and he thought I was a good singer." So when Bobby put together a doo-wop vocal group he named the Rondells, he persuaded Chuck to join. "We used to go to the YMCA on the Grand Concourse, and then right downstairs from the Y was the 167th Street subway station, where we'd go to sing because of the echo. The tunnel walkway to get to the train is a big echo chamber, and the acoustics are unbelievable. The guys picked me to be the lead singer."

Vittori had visions of becoming a pop music star. "He was very musical, and he took music classes. Many people may have dreams, but because they don't feel they have the voice to do it, they surround themselves with good talent and direct it all. So he did that, although he could sing. I don't know why he didn't make himself the lead singer. I just gather that he didn't think he was good enough." The Rondells practiced and fine-tuned their harmonies, and began earning money and a reputation as they performed at parties; after signing with managers, they began performing in nightclubs, even though they were underage. That led to the group's appearance in 1958 at the Apollo Theater, the legendary soul music shrine on 125th Street in Harlem, where the audience's acceptance demonstrated to Chuck how music crosses cultural divisions.

Although he enjoyed singing with the Rondells, that was not Chuck's ticket out of the Bronx. Basketball was. After returning to his old neighborhood from the orphanage, Chuck had started playing pickup ball with neighborhood kids. It gave him something to do, and it kept him out of trouble. He had talent for the game, and excelled in playground hoops at Jordan L. Mott Junior High. As a 6-foot-1 guard, Chuck did not appear physically imposing. But his determination and speed eclipsed his height.

"I was quick, and I really could shoot. I could jump and I could dunk, and I loved basketball," Chuck said. "I became very well known as a really good basketball player. It was just in me. At the end of the year they had the all-star game, and the players from Taft High School came down. I scored 32 points and really dominated the game, so by the time I went to Taft High everyone was talking about me, and I made the team the first year. I never went to JV; I went right to the varsity. I wanted to play pro ball, and I was so good," Chuck said. "I was an all-city ballplayer in New York and I was all-divisional. I was in the Mecca of sport, and I was shining, so I thought I had a chance. Playing basketball really saved my life."

Chuck's abilities on the court attracted basketball scouts from several colleges, and he received draft offers in his high school senior year from Utah State University in Logan and Alan Hancock College in Santa Maria, California. Officials at Hancock learned about Chuck from a basketball player who had been all-city in New York a year earlier and had enrolled at Hancock. That student became homesick and dropped out to return to New York, but before he left Hancock, coaches asked if he knew of any other good New York high school seniors who excelled in fast-paced basketball. The kid named one player: Chuck Negron. Chuck called his father to tell him about Hancock's offer. His father was excited and said he would make the two-and-a-half-hour drive to watch Chuck play. That sealed the deal for Chuck.

After graduating from high school in June 1961, Chuck took a summer job as a waiter at the Esther Manor, a "Borscht Belt" resort hotel near the Catskill Mountains town of Monticello, New York, to earn money for his relocation to California. "The first night that I was there, Jackie Mason was the headliner. He was outrageous. I loved him," Chuck said. "It was a fun summer, but I worked my ass off. I was taking orders, serving drinks. I worked from about 7 p.m. 'til 2 in the nightclub, and then from 3 to 6 in the morning in the coffee and bagel shop."

Santa Maria is along U.S. 101, in the coastal region about 150 miles northwest of Los Angeles. There, as a freshman at Hancock College, Chuck balanced his basketball practice and games schedule with the classes in his business major, but he also decided to take a couple of music classes. In a chorus class, he became friends with two brothers by the name of Sorensen. It turns out that brothers Alan, Dean, Paul, Eric, and Dick Sorensen had formed their own musical group – the Sorensen Brothers band. One weekend Chuck went to a local dance, where the performers included the Sorensen Brothers. "They invited me up to sing with them, so I sang 'Teenager In Love' and a couple of other songs. After I left the

Chuck as a solo Columbia recording artist in the mid-1960s (photo courtesy of Chuck Negron).

stage, the promoter of the show walked over to me and asked, 'did you see what happened?' I said, 'no, what happened?' He said, 'well, this is a dance. But when you sang, everyone stopped and came to the front of the stage to watch you.' I hadn't noticed." A couple of days later the promoter tracked down Chuck on the Hancock College campus and asked him to do some shows. Chuck, who changed his major to business law and added a minor in music, worked with several bands in addition to the Sorensen Brothers. "One was a Santa Maria group called the Biscaynes, and I did some shows with them, and with a San Luis Obispo group called the Sentinels. Their drummer, John Barbata, became the drummer in the Turtles. But I worked mostly with the Sorensen Brothers, because we had more opportunities to rehearse together and learn new songs. We got a nice big following, and things started moving for us." While Chuck was still a freshman, Marlinda Records signed the Sorensen Brothers and him to a record deal. "The Sorensen Brothers recorded two songs, and then they backed me on two songs, 'When Love Comes My Way' and 'Sharon Lee.' In late 1962, we got signed by another label, Hart-Van [as Chuck Rondell with the Sorensen Brothers] and we released a song called 'I Dream Of An Angel' – which got some radio airplay in central California."

Executives from Columbia Records, for which a record pressing plant was under construction in Santa Maria, heard about Chuck and paid him a visit. "They asked me and the Sorensen Brothers to travel to Hollywood to audition live in the big Studio A there, which we did. Columbia decided to sign me, but not the band. It was very awkward, but the band said, 'Hey, Chuck, you have to do it.' They were very kind to me, and I did sign with Columbia." The August 22, 1964, issue of *Billboard* magazine reported his signing with the label. He chose to record under the name Chuck Rondell.

All the while Chuck continued to excel on the basketball court for Hancock College, which attracted the attention of former Boston Celtics standout Bill Sharman, who was then completing his final season as head basketball coach at California State College at Los Angeles. Recruited as a junior, Chuck had two years of intercollegiate eligibility remaining in the autumn of '64 when he joined the Cal State L.A. Golden Eagles basketball squad, which at that time competed at the Division I level. The Cal State campus is only three miles from Monterey Park, where Chuck's father was living, and that was a big incentive for him to transfer. "My dad had become a very successful insurance salesman for Prudential, and he had a nice life," Chuck said. His father had remarried, and Chuck was able to get acquainted with his stepbrother, Rene, and stepsister, Denise. "My father was a great supporter of my singing because he also had a good singing voice, but he never got to do it professionally. After his military discharge following World War II, he used his GI bill funding to go to music school for singing. But he never got to try earning a living as a singer because he had a family to support. He loved my voice, and said he couldn't believe the range I had."

Relocation to L.A. made Chuck more readily available for rehearsal and recording work at Columbia. Chuck began attending classes at Cal State and practicing under incoming head basketball coach Bob Oldham. But Columbia's rehearsal and recording demands conflicted with his basketball obligations. Forced to choose between them, he left school after attending classes for only a month, in order to devote his full attention to his solo recording career. Paired with producer Edward L. Kleban, Chuck recorded several songs, including "Speak For Yourself, John" and "All's Fair In Love And War," which Columbia released in December 1964. The song got good radio airplay along California's central coast, where Chuck was known, but not much outside that area. "But Columbia at that time was a step or two behind what was happening. Ed Kleban, who had produced [recordings by] Igor Stravinsky, later left Columbia and he wrote [the lyrics for] *A Chorus Line*. That really was his genre. So I was very unfortunate to have a producer who didn't want to do rock or edgy pop. Those records I recorded for Columbia were two sweet, and too lame, too white – really vanilla," Chuck said. "I knew I didn't have a chance, but what was I gonna do? I eventually asked to leave." Chuck and Columbia parted company in the autumn of '65.

Chuck's manager, Burt Jacobs – whose clients also included Ketty Lester, Gloria Jones, and the Standells (see the chapter about them in this book) – shopped around for another label for Chuck. When no deal seemed imminent, Chuck went back to New York to decompress and get his bearings. "In the summer I drove back west across the country with two friends. When we arrived in L.A., they stayed with a friend of theirs, and I was mostly living in my car," Chuck said. "Some nights I stayed at their

friend's place, but he was very unhappy that all of us were in his apartment."
So Chuck had little to lose and everything to gain when his invitation to a
party for Donovan Leitch led to an offer to sing background vocals for some
solo tracks that Danny Hutton was recording.

"Danny and I had started hanging around," Chuck said. "One night
we went to the Whisky, and the band that was playing knew me, and they
said, 'hey, ladies and gentlemen, we have a friend in the audience, Chuck
Rondell.' So I got up and sang some songs, and when I got down Danny
said, 'Jesus Christ, you're great.' So I did some background for Danny," said
Chuck, a tenor who at the time had a four-octave range. "Danny was just
coming off a hit record called 'Roses And Rainbows,' and he was working
on his next record called 'Funny How Love Can Be.' He had Steven Stills
and Neil Young and a bunch of other guys try to sing this one part that had
some pretty high notes, but they couldn't do it. And he said to me, 'you can
sing pretty high. Do you think you can do it?' And I said 'yeah,' and we
went in and I did it."

That was that – or so it seemed. So when Chuck heard that KRLA
disc jockey Dick Biondi was putting together a tour to entertain workers
at Job Corps camps throughout the country, Chuck signed on for the tour
and hit the road. (The Job Corps federal career training program had been
established only one year earlier.) When Chuck returned to L.A. after the
tour concluded, he learned that Danny had been persistently trying to reach
him. "I called Danny and told him I was back, and he said, 'come over here
in a couple of hours.' When I got to Danny's place, Cory Wells was there."
That was the genesis of Three Dog Night. By the summer of '69, Chuck
Negron had gone from sleeping in his car to singing lead on a top-10 hit
single, "One," which went on to earn gold record certification. With dark
shoulder-length hair, the slim, mustachioed Negron was a member of a
group that would become the hottest-selling band in the nation, drawing
sellout crowds to concerts in arenas and stadiums. Three Dog Night
generated frenzied crowds, even as early in their career as December 1968 at
the Miami Pop Festival. At that show, Chuck met a girl named Angie, who
would become a factor in his life three decades later.

Something else important happened when Chuck returned from that
Job Corps tour. He found love. "The night I came home from that Dick
Biondi tour, I couldn't get in the apartment. A guy was in there with my
girlfriend," Chuck said. "A friend of mine lived down the hill. I went and
knocked on his door and said, 'Can I sleep on your couch?' And he said,
'Let me ask my roommate.' Roommate said no. So then he said, 'the girls
downstairs love you. Every time they see you around here they ask me to

introduce you.' So he goes downstairs. Two girls walk out. One is named Paula, and the other is Jessica. And they say 'you can stay with us as long as you want.' So I lived with them. Paula wasn't seeing my friend or any of his roommates." The arrangement led to romance. Chuck and Paula Servetti married in March 1970, and they had a daughter, Shaunti. But the marriage was rocky and short-lived. During his years as a high school and college athlete, Chuck had avoided drugs and booze. Hypnotized by the dazzling, dizzying incense of sudden fame and success as a rock star, with screaming girls tearing at his clothes when he was touring, and money – more money than he had ever seen in his life – he succumbed to the seduction of drugs.

Everyone around Chuck was partying, drugs were readily available, and he could afford them – or people were giving them to him for free. So he dipped, then immersed himself into the drug culture, starting with marijuana and Quaaludes. At a party, a girl slipped him a potent combination of peyote and LSD. He discovered that he loved the ride that Seconals gave him, and then he tried cocaine. He got high daily. As drugs became his mistress, his marriage fell apart. Chuck was on the road much of the time, reveling in a blur of wild, uninhibited sexual orgies with legions of groupies who threw themselves at him, and when he was at home he was wasted on drugs more often than not. Chuck was unconsciously compensating for the denial of fun during his bleak childhood. Whatever Chuck and Paula had seen in each other at the outset was a mirage. They separated in 1972 and divorced the following year. Even while his marriage crumbled, Chuck and the band persevered on the road, performing on a lengthy tour through the South Pacific, including New Zealand, Australia, and Japan.

Chuck said he found recording and concert touring equally rewarding, but in different ways. "Recording, I find, gives you an opportunity to use your brain to the point that you actually are gaining more knowledge. It's almost spiritual in the sense that you can feel yourself growing as a human being. You know you're learning, you know you're getting better, and it's an unbelievable experience. This is the only opportunity you get to hear your voice come back at you, and you go, 'oh, my God, I'm getting better.' So that's very rewarding in a spiritual and in a creative way," Chuck explained. "Live performances are very creative in a more animalistic way, in a more physical way. You're there in front of them, and you're just turning them on, they're loving you, and all your senses are heightened because you're in a situation that isn't normal. You're being adored, you're being respected, and I may be thinking that night, 'oh, I got a lot of range, I'm going to jump a whole octave right now because I just want to. So that's a physically rewarding thing. And seeing people in the audience cry because they care so much is something that is very, very special. So recording and performing are two different things, full of life, and a wonderful gift."

Then nine years after it began, it was all over. Three Dog Night splintered, and its remaining members went their separate ways in 1976. Over that span of time, Chuck had gone from being a clean kid to a heavy cocaine user. Then an acquaintance introduced him to heroin. He had never felt that sick in his life. It made him barf up everything in his system – but he loved the high it gave him. He remained in the paralyzing grip of heavy-duty drugs for 23 years, living from high to high in a self-destructive, nearly fatal downward spiral. Chuck described that and other aspects of his life in harrowing detail in his autobiographical book *Three Dog Nightmare: The Chuck Negron Story*, which he wrote with journalist Chris Blatchford.

He also began a relationship with Julia Densmore, who had been married to Doors drummer John Densmore. While married to John, Julia had an affair with Allman Brothers bass player Berry Oakley, with whom she became pregnant. Oakley died of head injuries he sustained in a motorcycle wreck in November 1972, four months before the baby (Berry Duane Oakley) was born; Julia and John divorced in 1973. Julia was pregnant when she and Chuck developed their friendship. "When Berry was around 2 or so, Julia and I started to see each other, and then one day I went over there and didn't return home." When Chuck and Julia married in May 1976, they spent their honeymoon shooting up heroin. The following year, the couple's son, Charles (known as "Chuckie") was born with a heroin addiction. Chuck drained through his entire fortune buying drugs. His suppliers included members of the notorious Wonderland Gang, whose drug dealing base – a home at 8763 Wonderland Avenue off Laurel Canyon – became infamous as the site of the brutal "four on the floor" murders in July 1981. Chuck frequented the house, but fortunately he was not there at the time of the carnage. He was hospitalized a few times for overdosing on drugs, and in the autumn of 1980 he was diagnosed with hepatitis C, likely from using contaminated needles. He reunited with Three Dog Night late that year, and slogged from one show to the next, drugging himself up enough to perform on stage. He pushed on, in the process contracting pneumonia that was inadequately treated (his right lung is permanently impaired as a result). In between gigs, he was in and out of rehab, only to resume his bad habits back on the road. He was helplessly obsessed with getting and remaining high.

Divorced from Julia in 1985, he sold off all of his possessions to finance his habit. No longer able to perform with Three Dog Night by the end of that year, he became homeless, living in his car or staying for a night or two in the homes or apartments of various friends. Driving in a stupor, he suffered serious injuries when he wrecked his car. For a while former TDN road manager Bob Tommaso let Chuck sleep in an unfinished closet that lacked wallboard. "I had to sleep in there with a mask on, to avoid breathing in the fibers from the bare pink insulation that made my skin itch," Chuck said. Sometimes when friends dropped Chuck off to score drugs in L.A.'s downtown "skid row," he became marooned there for the night and had to sleep in filthy squalor in a cardboard shipping carton outdoors, or on the floor of some abandoned building if he found a way to gain entry. He was an emaciated shell of himself existing from one fix to the next. His 6-foot-1 frame had withered to an emaciated 126 pounds. He also drank heavily, and was arrested numerous times for public intoxication. Realizing the depths to which he had sunk but unable to help himself, he twice tried to commit suicide. He purposely stepped in front of a moving bus, but the driver evaded him. He also tried to hang himself with a belt in the closet of a motel room, but the closet pole snapped. Through run-ins with drug dealers and other addicts, and car wrecks while stoned, his cheekbones have been broken, he's been stabbed, beaten with a baseball bat, and underwent 100 stitches in his face. Chuck was in and out of detoxification therapy and rehab clinics 37 times between 1978 and 1991. Some of the rehab houses gave up on him, because he seemed to be beyond help. While Chuck was still in the grips of heroin, a lawyer named Robin Silna tried to help him manage royalty payments and other finances.

Chuck was unconvinced that anyone could help him, but Robin and her sister, Gail, enlisted the help of a physician who had put Chuck through detox numerous times. Convinced that the only hope was long-term, specialized care, the physician referred Chuck to a North Hollywood drug rehabilitation and recovery facility called Cri-Help. There he was not coddled as a celebrity; he was just another addict who needed behavioral therapy. Cri-Help did not medicate enrollees to ease them off their addiction, but rather took them off drugs cold turkey. Chuck endured the torturous purgatory of sudden withdrawal. Alone with his thoughts on September 17, 1991, he pondered how pathetic his life had become. He knelt down and pleaded with God to relieve him of his suffering – by either taking his life or showing him the path to recovery. As he surrendered to divine intervention, he experienced a revelation.

"I realized that my passion for music and sports and my desire to be the best had turned around on me, and I had been unable to stop because I was a driven person. It brought me to my knees and, more importantly, it broke the hearts of the people who loved me." Cri-Help kept him busy with tasks – endlessly sweeping floors, washing windows, cleaning bathrooms – distractions to divert his attention from his addictive patterns. After Chuck spent nine months in rehab, Cri-Help got him a job in a hospital as a technician, working with drug-addicted and abused adolescents and young adults. Chuck took great pleasure in helping young people, and he planned to make counseling his life's work – that is, until he attended a Cri-Help meeting at which a woman named Nina Feinberg recognized him. She was a producer for the *Golden Girls* television show starring Bea Arthur, Betty White, and Rue McClanahan. She was planning a spin-off called *Golden Palace,* and asked if Chuck would consider recording the theme song – which he did. The series aired for one season on CBS beginning in September 1992.

"An agent for the Sands Hotel and Casino in Atlantic City recognized my voice on the show, saw my name in the credits, and called me up," Chuck said. "He told me, 'I've got a weeklong gig for you, opening for Howie Mandel.' I told him, 'I don't even have a band.' He said, 'We'll put a band together for the show.' So I did it. And it was fantastic. That led to another gig, and others after that. One of the guys in that band was David Morgan, who joined Three Dog Night as a vocalist in October 2015."

In 1993, two years after kicking the habit, Chuck married Robin Silna, and the couple had a daughter, Charlotte. That marriage ended in divorce in 2000. In the late 1990s a young man named Tom, not quite 30 years old, contacted Chuck. He asked Chuck, "Do you remember Angie, from the Miami Pop Festival?" Chuck replied, "Oh, yeah." Tom said, "Well, she's my mother, and she says that I'm your son." Chuck said that Angie had never let him know about Tom. "He's married now, and has a child." Chuck also had a relationship with actress Kate Vernon, and in 2001 they had a daughter, Annabelle. Chuck is not presently married.

Because Danny Hutton and Cory Wells continued to harbor resentment against Chuck over his downfall, he decided to resume recording on his own in 1995 with *Am I Still In Your Heart,* his first solo album, and then he followed that with a Christmas CD called *Joy To The World,* and other CD and DVD releases.

"Making the record was a wonderful experience. My band and I learned almost every tune on that record for live performances, but within two months, we were doing all of the Three Dog Night stuff because no one wanted to hear that record. The audiences wanted to hear the songs that I sang with Three Dog Night. And I was smart enough to know, OK, you know what? Do three Three Dog Night songs, do something from your new album, do three more Three Dog Night songs, do another new one," Chuck said. I knew that I was going to have to rebuild an audience following, and that it would take a while. So I worked House of Blues clubs, and I did packages with other people, and it's taken me all these years to come back." Chuck has been performing in public regularly ever since, touring regularly with his own band, often accompanied by original Three Dog Night drummer Floyd Sneed. Despite his diminished lung capacity, he still sings with exuberance and feeling, and energizes his audiences. He has recorded five solo CDs, four of which are available through iTunes, and his DVD *The Chuck Negron Story: Biography Of An Entertainer* won several awards, including the 2006 PRISM Award, which recognizes accurate depiction of drug, alcohol, and tobacco use and addiction in film, television, and other media.

When Chuck is not performing, he volunteers much of his time to counseling other addicts, being with them to show them that recovery is possible. "I go to Cri-Help on Monday nights when they have meetings, and we all talk and share experiences," Chuck said. "Sometimes I take out a couple of guys for lunch or dinner, to get them back into society in a safe environment." Chuck has now been "clean" longer than he was addicted, but he does not consider himself "cured" and in control of his compulsions. He is still in the recovery process himself, and he has to work hard every day to maintain a focus while avoiding the strong gravitational pull of unwanted distractions. He knows he always will have to keep up his guard to avoid falling back into the abyss.

He also has developed an interest in writing – music as well as short stories and a blog (http://chucknegron.blogspot.com/). He has written articles for music magazines, as well as for *Paradigm* magazine, published by the Illinois Institute for Addiction Recovery.

Chuck has a message to communicate: "It took me a long time – 13 years of going to recovery houses until finally on September 17, 1991, I found recovery by crying 'help,' and I began to turn my life around," Chuck told us. "Junkies and people with addiction have to be in a safe place because we become insane. And when you're insane you have no rational thought. You can't help yourself. You need to be helped. In my time, the medical prognosis on cocaine was that it was medically not addicting. It was considered non-addicting, because it didn't fit the protocol of all the withdrawals and all that stuff, not taking into account mental and emotional damage. Anyway, there was a time where almost every one of us were experimenting. So in Three Dog Night, as kind of a thumbnail look at bands and young people, everybody but one guy took drugs and experimented. Two guys experimented all the way and went to heroin. So out of seven guys, six did hard drugs, and two did heroin. Left and right people were dying, because the information was incorrect. This wasn't mind-expending stuff. And the information that is still not in people's heads today is that pot is a gateway drug. Every one of us in our generation started with pot. We all went on to pills, then a lot went on to cocaine, and some went on to heroin, almost all did LSD, but pot was the gateway drug, the first drug. It's amazing that today some people think that legalizing it is the answer."

Visit www.chucknegron.com for touring, recording, merchandise (including plush toys, tote bags and even "Chuckolate" confections), and additional information.

Chuck's new recordings are available through his chucknegron.com website (photo courtesy of Chuck Negron).

Epilogue: Floyd Sneed

Drummer

The musical repertoire of Three Dog Night drew from a broad spectrum of musical influences, with widely divergent thematic structures. Behind the three lead voices of Three Dog Night was a unit of top-notch musicians playing in cadence to the intricate rhythmic patterns that drummer Floyd Sneed created in unison with bass guitarist Joe Schermie. With perspiration glistening on his muscled body, brawny shoulders bared by a sleeveless shirt, and armbands encircling his bulging biceps, Sneed powered his way through song after song for Three Dog Night like a Kenworth 18-wheeler on a downgrade, blasting through a blizzard. Attacking his clear acrylic double-bass rhinestone-embellished drum kit with force, passion, and blistering speed, clenching sticks or at times playing barehanded, Sneed was the epitome of strength and endurance. Now in the seventh decade of his life, he still is a tornado on a drum stool.

Floyd painting at home in South Pasadena, California, June 2015 (photo by Michael Childress).

He was born Floyd Chester Sneed on November 22, 1942, in Amber Valley, Alberta, Canada, the youngest among three children. His brother, Bernie, had been born three years earlier, and his sister, Maxine, was two years older than Floyd. Amber Valley, 290 miles (475 kilometers) north of Calgary, had been settled in the early 1900s primarily by black immigrant farming families who had fled Oklahoma, where they had been subjected to repressive Jim Crow laws governing labor and all other social interactions. "They ran away from crazy white folks," Floyd told us. Amber Valley was a small community of no more than 300 people. When Floyd was 3 years old, he and his siblings moved with their parents, Napoleon and Willa Sneed, to Calgary (which Floyd pronounces cal-GARY). Napoleon, who was born in Texas, spent 20 years of his life as a porter for the Canadian Pacific railway before establishing a trucking business hauling gravel. He contracted with the government agency building the Trans-Canada Highway. "My mom was the first black child born in the province of Alberta – that was in 1912. She did domestic work," Floyd said.

Both Napoleon and Willa played piano and guitar, and sang at church. "I sang the best I could in church. My mother had the loudest voice. In my memories, I hear her singing right now in church as you mention this," Floyd told us. The Sneed home was filled with the music of Mahalia Jackson, the Five Blind Boys of Alabama, and other gospel performers. "That's all we grew up with," Floyd said. "Our folks were Christian people, and I was raised in a Christian home. My dad said, 'believe in Jesus, do what you want to do in life, go at it, stay out of trouble, and work hard.' That was his basic philosophy." Floyd took that advice to heart. By the time Floyd turned 4 years old, he had become fascinated by drums. Even though his parents bought a piano when he was about 5, he refused to take piano lessons. His resolve to learn to play the drums grew after his father won the family's first television set in a "name that tune" contest that a local radio station sponsored. "I began watching drummers whenever I could on TV, and also whoever performed around Calgary," Floyd said. Eventually, his parents gave in and let him take basic drum lessons, but he taught himself from then on.

At school, Floyd took an interest in drawing and painting, and enjoyed playing soccer, ice hockey, baseball, and volleyball. "We played hockey outdoors, even when the temperature got down to 30 below. I played left wing." Floyd was less enthusiastic about school or sports than he was about playing drums, though, and by age 13 he was playing bongos with his keyboard-playing brother, Bernie, in a mixed-race band called the Calgary

Shades, consisting of singers Tommie "Little Daddy" Melton and Dick Byrd, guitarist Tommy Chong (who later teamed in a comedy duo with Richard "Cheech" Marin), and his brother Stan Chong on bass guitar. "It was an integrated band – Chinese, white, black, and Indian. That's why they were called the Shades," Floyd explained.

The Shades performed rhythm and blues and rock and roll at dances, most frequently at the alcohol-free Royal Canadian Legion Hall. The Shades were really good at stirring audiences into a frenzy; public intoxication among groups of rowdy underage kids who caused damage in the surrounding neighborhood during and after Shades performances became so recurrent that public officials told the band to leave town. Tommy and Bernie and a couple of the other guys thought that was a good idea, and went on the road playing gigs in towns throughout Alberta and British Columbia, and took up residence as the house band in a club in Vancouver for about a year. Floyd was too young to go on the road, though, and hadn't finished high school, although his attendance had become sporadic. For example, on a whim when he was 16, he answered a newspaper job opening advertisement for a short-order cook at the Banff Springs Hotel, a resort in Banff National Park 80 miles west of Calgary. "I told them I can cook, and they said come on up for an interview. I jumped on a Greyhound bus and went to Banff. I got this job in that magnificent hotel. I was there for only about a week, but that was quite ambitious for a 16-year-old," Floyd said.

In 1959 the Shades disbanded, and Bernie Sneed and Tommy Chong returned to Calgary, where Chong took a job as a truck driver for Canadian Freightways. Floyd dropped out of school for good at age 18 to concentrate on practicing and improving his drumming. Tommy Chong eventually became Floyd's brother-in-law, after Bernie introduced Chong to Maxine. In 1961, Tommy and Maxine embarked on a 10-year marriage. They are the parents of two children: Rae Dawn and Robbi Lynn, both of whom have had successful careers in acting. "I got my first set of drums on my 19th birthday," Floyd said. "And I practiced like crazy." He studied and played along with various kinds of music, including country, which was the predominant club scene in Calgary.

"My first professional job ever was with Conway Twitty's band," Floyd said. "His drummer became sick in Vancouver the night before a show in Calgary, and the promoter called and told me that Conway is coming into town and needs a drummer, and asked if I could do it. I said, 'But I'm just learning to play drums.' I did it, though, and Conway was so gracious. I got through the night OK, and I've stayed friends with him and his family over the years."

Floyd was in his late teens in Calgary when he met and fell in love with Sandra (Sandy) Hoiland. They married in 1962, by which time Tommy Chong and Tommie Melton had formed a new band in Vancouver with keyboard player Bernie Sneed and bassist Wes Henderson. They called the group Little Daddy and the Bachelors. Floyd and Sandy drove 600 miles west. "Calgary was basically just country [music] at that time and nothing else. All kinds of stuff musically was going on in Vancouver, though. I got a daytime job as a garbage man, and worked at night with Tommy Chong and the band," Floyd told us.

Hatching an idea, Chong and Melton scraped together what little money they had, rented the Alma Theatre at West Broadway at Alma Street, and staged it as a nightclub they called the Blues Palace. They began booking other established performers there, for which Little Daddy and the Bachelors served as the opening act and backup band. Complaints from neighboring businesses about the messes their patrons left on the sidewalks prompted Chong and Melton to buy an actual nightclub that they called T's Cabaret, at which time Bernie Sneed left to form his own group. T's Cabaret was small, so they unloaded that and in late 1964 bought a club called the Elegant Parlour, in a basement below the Embassy Ballroom at 1024 Davie Street. That year, Floyd and Sandy welcomed the birth of their first daughter, Shannon. All the while, Floyd was refining his drumming techniques and strengthening his shoulders, arms, and wrists, developing the clenched-fist grip and staccato conga-style rhythms that would come to full force with Three Dog Night. "Do you remember the [1950] movie *King Solomon's Mines* with Stewart Granger? The natives were doing some kind of beat in that movie. I remembered it and practiced and learned some beats around that particular rhythm and developed it further," Floyd said.

Little Daddy and the Bachelors established a reputation as a solid R&B group, and attracted enough attention to sign a recording deal with RCA Records. The band recorded a version of Chuck Berry's "Too Much Monkey Business" with "Junior's Jerk," a soulful instrumental that Chong and Henderson wrote, on the flip side. The single on the RCA Victor Canada International label (which spelled the band's name "Little Daddie and the Bachelors") sold a little bit regionally, but not enough to result in a second single. When singer Bobby Taylor joined the group and it became Bobby Taylor and the Vancouvers, Floyd decided he was ready to go in a new direction.

With musicians Floyd had met in Vancouver, he formed an R&B quintet called Heat Wave in 1965. The band members included singer

Jimmy Milton, guitarist Freddie Ardiel, keyboard player Clyde Harvey, and bass player Donny Gerrard. "We performed in Vancouver for a while, and then we decided to go to Los Angeles." By that time, the L.A. music scene was in full bloom, and opportunities abounded. Heat Wave landed gigs in several small clubs in Hollywood and nearby areas, and also in Hawaii. But with no big breaks on the horizon, the band was on the verge of splitting up in the late spring of 1968. That's when bass player Joe Schermie – newly signed to the recently formed Three Dog Night – became captivated by Floyd's drumming in the Red Velvet Club in West Hollywood. Now that Floyd and Sandy had a second daughter, Tracy (born in 1967), a stable source of income was imperative. Since Three Dog Night already had signed a recording contract with Dunhill, Floyd didn't hesitate when he was invited to join. "I was different from any other drummer in rock music at the time, and I just knew inside that this is what Three Dog Night needed. I knew that I would be part of the key to success. And I needed them, too," Floyd said.

The wide-ranging repertoire of Three Dog Night encouraged Floyd to broaden his explorations of complex polyrhythm drum patterns. Although he was playing a black-and-white Rogers drum set when he first began using twin bass drums, he soon switched to the strikingly distinctive colorless, transparent Zickos set on which he fully developed his "L'African" fusion style in which he blended Latin-American and African rhythm patterns.

Sneed emphasizes that the Three Dog Night members, rather than studio musicians, performed on the recording sessions. "We did everything. I'm on the first 14 albums," Floyd said. "That's why our sound was the same on stage – our live performance was part of the key to our popularity and success." Floyd said he has "a small percentage of Three Dog Night," and also received a salary for performances while touring. "I enjoy both recording and touring," Floyd told us. "I have been around the world twice with Three Dog Night, and I loved all of that, and I loved recording. I had a great time with Three Dog Night. I remember more good than bad. It was like a marriage for a while."

Among all of Floyd's days on the road with Three Dog Night, several stand out – notably July 9, 1972. "In the pop festival days, we played at the Pocono Raceway in Pennsylvania with Emerson, Lake & Palmer, Humble Pie, the Faces with Rod Stewart, and the J. Geils Band. We were supposed to go on stage at 4 o'clock that afternoon, but we didn't get on until 7:30 the following morning. *7:30.* More than 400,000 kids were there with campfires as far as your eyes could see, all night long. Everybody was just partying. There was a 75-mile traffic jam of people trying to get into this concert area. It was raining, but they all stayed," Floyd said. *Billboard* magazine reported that the $175,000 in earnings that Three Dog Night took with them that day was the largest payout for a single performance in pop music history as of that date, eclipsing the prior one-show record of $100,000 that both Elvis Presley and Jimi Hendrix had set.

Floyd was both hopeful and remorseful when he helped form the band S.S. Fools with bass guitarist Joe Schermie and guitarist Michael Allsup after the trio left Three Dog Night. "Bobby Kimball was a really good singer, and one of the best keyboard players in the business. We saw ourselves becoming the new Three Dog Night," Floyd said. "But we didn't go on the road. We just did a couple of little gigs here and there, and the band didn't last for too long anyway. I basically named that band Seven Separate Fools, because we were all fools for breaking up Three Dog Night in the first place." After S.S. Fools fell apart, Floyd worked as a session musician in L.A. and for a while became a member of the Ohio Players' touring band. In 1978, Floyd began a long-term romantic relationship with a woman named Rita Husak, with whom he had a third child: son Zoli Sneed.

When Three Dog Night regrouped in early 1981, Sneed signed back on with them, and remained for three years. July 4, 1984, was an especially memorable day for Floyd. "We played at the July 4 celebration in Washington, D.C., with Julio Iglesias, the Beach Boys, America, Ringo Starr, the O'Jays, Justin Hayward and John Lodge of the Moody Blues, La Toya Jackson and Roy Clark. There were nearly 600,000 people in the Mall by the Washington Monument. And when we performed 'Joy To The World,' it was absolutely breathtaking. About 400,000 people were singing along with us. Then we jumped on a plane and flew to Miami that same day, and played on the beach with the Beach Boys and most of the same bands. There were 300,000 people on the beach. We played in front of a million people that day," Floyd recalled. That was his last year with Three Dog Night, although he remained in contact with Michael Allsup and Jimmy Greenspoon. And after Chuck Negron emerged from rehab and resumed performing in 1992, Floyd reunited with him. He often plays drums for him to this day on tours, and has backed up Chuck on his solo albums. Floyd keeps busy with other activities as well.

For a while he became a collector of antique cars. "I went to Rosario, Argentina, and brought back four cars from there in the early '70s. Argentina has car lots full of antique automobiles, for example Packards from the 1930s and '40s, '29 Willys-Knight touring cars, '32 LaSalles, '29 Mercedes. I'm a Packard man. I had 11 antique automobiles at one time or another. But the restoration and upkeep got too expensive, so I don't have them anymore," Floyd said.

In the late 1980s, he opened and operated a restaurant, Floyd's Rock 'n' Riginal Chicken and Ribs, in the L.A.-area beach city of Santa Monica. He initially did all the work himself, including cooking, using his own recipes. "I'm a good cook, and I like pork ribs. I don't like sauce on the beef ribs; I just like them plain — mainly salt, pepper, and garlic. For the pork I use molasses, honey, and a few other things. Running the restaurant was a lot of work. I hired a couple of employees, but after I had the restaurant for a year I sold it," Floyd said. He quite naturally played the part of a drummer in the 1990 motion picture *Far Out Man*, starring his ex-brother-in-law Tommy Chong, his niece Rae Dawn Chong, C. Thomas Howell, and Martin Mull. In the early 2000s he hooked up with a Texas band called Dog and Katt, in which Katt "Kitty" Kleiber was the lead singer. "We recorded an album, but that didn't go anywhere," he said. Floyd, who lives in South Pasadena, California, also performs with friends for enjoyment. "I get together with some local guys and we jam at a couple of clubs here in the area."

In the early 2000s he also resumed his interest in creating visual art, which has become his passion. "I paint in oil pastels and acrylics, and also do works in pen and ink," Floyd said. He has exhibited and sold his artworks in galleries, and makes them available for sale through his website. He also has become interested in helping organizations that work with disadvantaged kids, and does so by donating paintings for such groups to auction off.

Floyd learned in 2012 that his older daughter, Shannon Rozak, a kindergarten teacher, had developed cancer. Her husband, Darryl, had died of a heart attack in 2009, and Shannon was raising their son Riley (born in 1998) and daughter Payton (born in 2000). As Shannon began treatment, Floyd himself confronted serious illness in late 2013, when he saw a doctor about a lump under the left side of his jaw and was diagnosed with non-Hodgkin's lymphoma. "The doctors were concerned that it might have gone into my bone marrow, but it hadn't," Floyd said. "I had 19 treatments of radiation, and the tumor disappeared. So I consider myself healed."

Unfortunately, Shannon's illness was more resistant, and she died at age 50 on June 18, 2014, in Valencia, California. The year 2015 brought additional heartbreak to Floyd. His ex-wife Sandy, who had spent much of her life in staff positions with the American Cancer Society, died from cancer-related complications. Floyd and Sandy had been married for 29 years, and although the couple divorced in 1991, they had remained in contact with each other. The couple's other daughter, Tracy May, has a daughter named Kaitlyn (born in 1989). Floyd remains unmarried. His faith has helped him cope with his emotionally wrenching losses, and he takes comfort in his firm beliefs. "I know that Jesus loves me, and that I'm going to heaven when I die, to be with all of my family members. And that's true," Floyd declared.

In January 2016, *Classic Drummer* magazine selected Floyd Sneed among the 2016 inductees in its Hall of Fame, which honors drummers for their talent, innovation, and influence in music. Floyd was in distinguished company – the 2016 inductees also include Jim Bonfanti of

Floyd Sneed hanging out with fellow drummer Steven "Styxxx" Marshall (photo by Michael Childress).

the Raspberries; Terry Bozzio of Missing Persons; Bun E. Carlos of Cheap Trick; Dave Clark of the Dave Clark 5; Dino Danelli of the Rascals; Dave Grohl of Nirvana and the Foo Fighters; Elvin Jones of John Coltrane's quartet and the Elvin Jones Jazz Machine; ubiquitous session drummer Russ Kunkel; Simon Phillips of Toto; Cozy Powell of the Jeff Beck Group and Black Sabbath; and Alan White of the band Yes.

Floyd keeps his 6-foot-1 frame fit through consistent exercise. He swims regularly, and he rides horseback. "I'm a good rider. I'm basically a cowboy," Floyd said. "Even during my days with Three Dog Night, I didn't get crazy with the drugs. I stayed fairly clean and healthy." Drumming, of course, also helps keep him in shape. "I really enjoy drums. Drumming is so therapeutic for me. I play drums in church every Sunday. You've got to enjoy what you're doing in life, and I never wanted to be anything else but be a drummer. It's such a pleasure to see people moving to your music, and dancing and enjoying themselves."

Floyd has written an autobiography titled *Floyd Sneed: In Black and White*, scheduled for late 2016 publication by LeRue Press. Visit www. floydsneedart.com and http://www.facebook.com/OfficialFloydSneedPage for touring, recording, merchandise, and additional information. Floyd is represented by MAC Creative Management.

Index

Index

About the Authors

Marti Smiley Childs and **Jeff March** are business partners in EditPros LLC, an editorial services firm in Davis, California. Their first book, *Echoes of the Sixties* (1999), consisted of 12 chapters about hit-making singers and bands, including the Fireballs, Gary "U.S." Bonds, the Tokens, the Angels, Peter and Gordon, Mike Pinder of the Moody Blues, the Beau Brummels, Sam the Sham and the Pharaohs, the Lovin' Spoonful, Gary Puckett and the Union Gap, Country Joe and the Fish, and Iron Butterfly. *Echoes of the Sixties* is available only in e-book format (ISBN 978-1-937317-02-7) through Amazon, Barnes and Noble, Apple, and other online book sellers. The authors' website – **www.editpros.com** – offers more information about Childs and March and their works. We invite you to "like" our Facebook page at **www. facebook.com/WHATPSG** for updates and conversation about these performers.

Where Have All the Pop Stars Gone? – Volume 3, is the third in a series of books of the same title that feature "then and now" portraits of bands and artists whose music helped define the popular culture of their time.

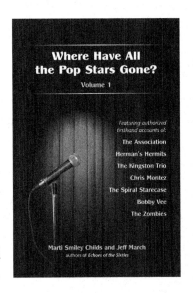

Where Have All the Pop Stars Gone? – Volume 1 (2011) contains authorized firsthand accounts of the adult lives of 26 singers and musicians who recorded top hit songs in the late 1950s and '60s.

This 320-page book, published by EditPros LLC, consists of chapters on the Association, Herman's Hermits, the Kingston Trio, Chris Montez, the Spiral Starecase, Bobby Vee, and the Zombies.

Volume 1 is available in print (ISBN 978-1-937317-00-3) and e-book formats (ISBN 978-1-937317-01-0) through Amazon, Barnes and Noble, Apple, and other online book sellers.

Where Have All the Pop Stars Gone? – Volume 2 (2012) includes authorized biographies of the Buckinghams, members of the Moody Blues, Sam and Dave, Ray Stevens, Bobby Goldsboro, Donnie Brooks, and the Grass Roots.

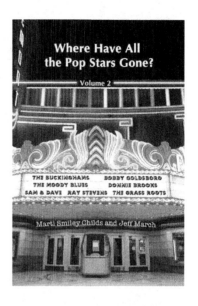

Volume 2 is available in print (ISBN 978-1-937317-05-8) and e-book formats (ISBN 978-1-937317-06-5) through Amazon, Barnes and Noble, Apple, and other online book sellers.

Childs and March additionally served as coauthors for two autobiographical books by other authors:

- Mike Penketh's *Within My Grasp: A Double Amputee's True Story* (2013; paperback ISBN 978-1-937317-09-6, and ebook ISBN-13: 978-1-937317-10-2)

- Max J. Young's *Reckoning at Sea: Eye to Eye With a Gray Whale — A 12-Year Circumnavigation* (2013; paperback ISBN 978-1-937317-11-9, and ebook ISBN-13: 978-1-937317-12-6)

CPSIA information can be obtained
at www.ICGtesting.com
Printed in the USA
FSOW03n0642200616
21705FS

9 781937 317256